Fragile Oath

THE LOCHLANN DECEPTION

BOOK TWO

ROBIN D MAHLE

ELLE MADISON

Author's Note

Please be aware that there are sensitive topics and situations in this book dealing with domestic violence. For a complete list of content warnings, visit the FAQ section of our website at mahleandmadison.com

SNOWWALL
MOSSFALL
BAKKE
MOUNTAIN PASS
RAM
BEAR
WOLF
CRANE
KINGDOM OF
SOCAIR
ISON
LYNX
TUNNEL
VIPER
EAGLE
ELK
GONDIE R.
DORCHA FOREST
HAGAIL
FALAMH R
BALA DAM
THE WESTERN SEA
WHITMIRE
OTHACH VILLAGE
UTHLINGLAU ESTATE
CONDRIS
CAILLTE
DEADROCK

THE LOCHLANN REALM
OAKENWELL
ROSS
NGDOM OF
CHLANN
CHRIDHE
NIRUS
GONAND
KINGDOM OF
RIONN
NN
THE
EASTERN
SEA
THE
ISLES
ECH
TISAS
HASLA
VILLAGE
RIVERWELL
DRY ROCK
MIDSIDE
BAY
AND

SOCAIR
BEAR
MOUNTAIN PASS
RAM
CRANE
WOLF
OBSIDIAN PALACE
BISON
THE SUMMIT
LYNX
VIPER
TUNNELS
EAGLE
ELK

Chapter One

GALINA

HALF AN HOUR.

Once again, that's all it had taken to turn my world upside-down. An appallingly short time for me to be wrenched away from the castle that had started to feel like home.

From the person who already *was* my home.

To add insult to injury, the carriage still smelled like the Autumn festival, a cruel reminder of how happy Davin and I had been only the night before. I breathed in the faint scent of spiced pumpkin, remembering the pastries, the games, the hippocras. And the faint scent of evergreen that had blown in...

Had he been there? Watching us? Waiting for his moment to take me?

A band of soldiers galloped by our carriage, interrupting my thoughts, and Alexei's hand tensed on my arm.

"Remember what's at stake, *Radnaya*."

His reminder was unnecessary. I was hardly likely to forget his flawless plan to ensure my parents would die if I didn't obediently accompany him. He alleged he had a series of check-ins and meeting points that led all the way back to Socair, ensuring his safety and my compliance.

There hadn't been time to think my way into a different solution with his hand around my neck and his breath in my ear. But honestly, even hours later, I wasn't sure there was another way.

Davin will come after me, I had said. So confidently. Brashly. The Lochlannians were rubbing off on me. But Alexei had only tightened his hold.

Then I trust you will make sure he doesn't. Your parents aren't the only lives at stake.

So I knew the soldiers weren't a threat to Alexei, knew that I had probably done my job of convincing Davin to stay away a little too well. But whether it was Davin's men or the residual traitors in the ranks, they were unlikely to look twice at a nondescript merchant's carriage in a sea of other plain carriages cluttering the road home from the festival.

Alexei knew those things, too, but it didn't stop his fingers from digging into my bruised skin in a warning I didn't need. I froze like the terrified rabbit he turned me into, an ingrained reflex I would have given anything to burn out of my soul.

"I will allow you to sulk for now, *Radnaya*, because these Lochlannians have poisoned you, but I expect you to remember your place by the time you are my wife."

I know my place, and it is not here. It is not with you.

If you wanted a willing wife, perhaps you shouldn't have kidnapped your bride.

But I couldn't say any of those things, not when I had agreed to be obedient. Not when I had agreed to be *his*.

"I'm sure the journey home will give me ample time to come to my senses." In my head, the words were dripping with sarcasm, but I managed to deliver them evenly.

Or at least, I thought I had.

Then, something sparked in Alexei's almond-colored eyes, a warning that had my heartbeat pounding wildly in my ears. He leaned in, his voice a quiet murmur that belied the anger radiating off him in waves, made more ominous by the icy wind howling outside the carriage.

"You can't think I would wait to claim you this time." *After last time*, he meant, though he never entirely acknowledged that I had run away from him. "We will wed here. In Lochlann."

If I had been standing, my knees would have given out. Alexei nodded, like he knew exactly what his declaration was doing to me, in spite of my best efforts to hide it. Like my terror satisfied him on some primal level.

Was this why he had let me live? Not only for the sake of his pride, as I had assumed, but so he could make sure I suffered every day for the rest of my life, all for the sin of leaving him?

Yours, I had told Davin. *Only yours. Always yours.*

It was like the universe had heard me, like the stars themselves had been determined to make a mockery of the promise I had finally brought myself to make.

"Will that make you happy, Galina?" Alexei said my name the way he always did, with the condescending exasperation of a parent chastising an obstinate child.

I forced myself to look into the eyes so devoid of the warmth and wit and laughter that Davin always held in his piercing blue gaze. And slowly, I nodded.

"Of course, My Lord."

Did he know I was lying? Did it matter? There was power in forcing me to appease him. It was a game he never tired of.

Despair crashed over me in waves before I forced myself to breathe, to remember why I had come willingly rather than raise an alarm that would have killed my parents. *Storms*, that might have killed Davin, if Alexei's threats about the rebels were genuine.

I was not strong in combat like Gwyn. I did not command armies like Rowan. I could play Alexei's games, though. I could lie, for the sake of my parents. For Davin.

Even if he would never forgive me.

Chapter Two

DAVIN

THE LETTER FELT HEAVIER than it should.

For what felt like the hundredth time today, I scanned Galina's words, trying and failing not to crease the parchment as my fist clenched the paper.

I supposed it wouldn't matter if I ruined it now—if I crumpled the note into a ball and tossed it into the hearth's dying embers—not when I had already memorized each painstaking letter of every single word on the page.

This was never supposed to be more than a means to an end.

Had she written it this morning? Last night, before she came to my rooms? Did it matter?

The same questions chased each other through my mind in a never-ending loop. Such small, unimportant details, all things considered. After hours of questioning the guards, the servants, my own parents... No one had anything new to offer.

There was nothing outside of what her ring and letter had said for her.

I have an obligation I allowed myself to forget.

Even then, with her ring in my hand, and my gaze fixated

on the inked words, I could still only barely bring myself to terms with the reality so stark before me.

She was gone. She had left me.

Again.

I clenched my fists once more, letting out a slow breath through my nose.

"There doesn't appear to be any sign of a struggle." Uncle Finn interrupted my thoughts.

His statement was equal parts reassuring and a reminder that if Galina left by choice, there was nothing we could do. Whereas there was another, more glaring issue waiting to be dealt with.

It could wait a while longer, for all I cared.

"I see that," I replied quietly. Bitterly.

As twisted as I knew it was, I hadn't been able to deny the small part of me that hoped I had misinterpreted the letter, like there was any other way to read her, *we let things get out of hand.*

It was better this way, though. Better that she hadn't been taken. That she wasn't in danger.

That she left by choice.

"And the letter...?" Gallagher began, his tone questioning.

"In her hand," I said evenly, noting the familiar artful penmanship.

There were no jagged lines or blots in the ink, nothing to indicate she had even been the slightest bit upset as she was writing. Had she sat down with the same icy calm she had when writing a simple thank-you note while she decimated whatever semblance of a relationship we had?

We both know you'll never be happy with just one woman.

Her words were like a carefully poised scalpel slicing into all the right wounds. All this time when I thought we were moving forward, had our mistakes been haunting us both – haunting each other?

I ran a hand over my face, exhaustion beginning to edge in past the adrenaline. With it came memories from last night, rushing back with a crushing intensity.

The smell of rosemary and lavender. The way her skin tasted of honey and the sweet tang of her sweat.

Perfect.

Mine.

Her voice, barely more than a whisper in my mouth as I tried to swallow each word, breathing her in, savoring her.

Yours. Always yours.

Had she meant it when she said it? Or was she already having second thoughts? Was that her way of giving me a last reassurance before she said goodbye?

"Dav." Gallagher's voice caught my attention.

I followed his concerned hazel gaze to the floor, where crimson drops were falling from my clenched fist to splash against the pale wood floor.

I opened my hand, but averted my eyes before I glimpsed Galina's ring covered in my blood. The ring I had walked by countless times in the family vaults, picturing it on her elegant hand in spite of myself.

The ring I had told myself she would never wear by choice. And she hadn't, when it came down to it.

"We need to question the castle," I said, letting the ring clatter onto her vanity. I tried to infuse a nonchalance into my tone but heard myself fall short.

"Absolutely," Gal said as he reached out to grab my injured hand. "Just might not want to add more bloodstains to your mother's pristine floors before we do."

I barely felt the skin stitch itself back together as Gallagher used his fae *woo-woo powers* to heal the tiny wound in only a few seconds. Generally, he refused to lend his ability to injuries this small, so he must have been feeling spectacularly sorry for me.

"Isn't her uncle on his way to Chridhe?" he asked when he was finished. "Would she try to meet him there? Or head back to the tunnels?"

"That's a fair point," my uncle acknowledged. "Either way, we can't let anyone know she's missing. Not when she's already been a target."

A sharp exhale escaped my lips, something close to a laugh – one entirely bereft of humor. Had Galina considered that when she left? That she was putting herself in danger? Or had her visceral need to run as far from me as possible outweighed any fear of rebels?

"Of course," I agreed. "We'll need to be subtle, gear the questioning toward Tavish and see what else we can glean."

"Did you hear that, Gwyn?" Gal arched an eyebrow at his twin. "That means you can't help."

For a rare change, Gwyn didn't laugh at her brother's teasing. She only glowered, shaking back her auburn waves like an irritable lion.

"I wouldn't have helped anyway," she spat.

"Gwynnie—" Gallagher cut in, his eyes moving to me.

"No," she cut him off. "You're all acting like this is some great mystery, like she didn't up and leave her last fiancé on exactly no notice, disappearing from a well-guarded castle in the middle of the night with a plan she concocted. This isn't exactly new behavior for her, is it?"

Silence fell, a charged hush thicker than the blood pooling on the polished floor. A thought dawned on me, one that had me questioning everything about Galina and my role in her departure from Socair.

Alexei might have been an utter arseworm, but had he loved her, in his stodgy Socairan way?

Had he felt like this when he discovered her gone? Like

someone had kicked him in the stomach and all of the air had been sucked from his lungs?

"We don't know the circumstances of her departure from Socair," Gallagher finally responded, a flat note to his tone that made me snap my eyes to him.

He looked away, and Gwyn cut in before I could question him on it.

"No, we don't," she agreed. "And we never will, because she wouldn't bloody well tell us."

"What about the missing guards?" I couldn't help but add.

"The ones she probably paid off to help her?" She scoffed. "I'm sorry, Dav, I really am, because I wanted her to be someone different for your sake, and there was a moment..." She trailed off, and I saw something underneath her anger. Betrayal, the barest echo of my own. Her voice softened when she continued. "But she keeps showing her colors and you keep ignoring them, both of you."

I cleared my throat, the truth in her words a serrated blade that sliced through me. That might have been the worst part of her denunciation, that I couldn't reasonably argue with a single thing she said.

So I didn't try.

"Be that as it may," I responded quietly, "we can't risk the rebels getting a hold of her."

My eyes went reflexively to the last line of Galina's letter.

You promised me that I had a choice. If you meant that at all, don't come after me.

Gwyn made a sound of protest, but I held up my hand.

"If not for her sake, then for the rest of ours," I said in a louder tone.

Galina might not have wanted us to come after her, but she had apparently forgotten everything that was at stake. She could go to the stars-damned border for all I cared, once she was in a position to get there without getting herself killed and endangering both of our kingdoms.

"He's right," Uncle Finn spoke up before Gwyn could argue again. "But first, you've delayed long enough. You need to deal with the magistrate."

Of course I did. It wasn't enough that Galina had left me. I also had to go face an accusation of murder.

At least, I assumed that's where my conversation with Ward would go since Tavish had been inconsiderate enough to be murdered in my home, right after I threatened to do said murdering.

If only.

Sighing, I cleaned the rest of the blood from my hand before moving toward the door. The sooner I spoke with Ward, the sooner I could find her. Then, I could finally put this entire mess behind me.

For good this time.

Chapter Three

GALINA

DREAD POOLED in my stomach as I turned Alexei's words over and over in my mind.

Some small, naïve part of me had thought there would be time to get away once my parents were safe. That he would want to wait until Socair for the wedding, to make it legal and binding.

I hadn't consciously relied on the hope of being able to explain things to Davin one day, to escape, to work out another plan, but now that the option had been taken from me... I squeezed my eyes shut, trying to search for a fragment of the determination I had felt only hours ago.

It was gone, though, along with the last shred of hope I had been unknowingly clinging to.

My fingers danced along the charms on my bracelet as I tried to use it to ground me, but there was no escape. Even if the rebels attacked us now, Alexei's death would mean the death of my parents.

Not that he would ever allow my escape to happen, nor his death.

My gaze flickered over Alexei's massive frame and the

sword strapped to his back. He had a vicious reputation on the battlefield, both for brute strength and strategy, and he wouldn't have come all this way without a plan to keep me safe.

He had certainly accounted for everything else, from getting me out of Lithlinglau to providing me with a trunk full of traveling clothes. Surely, he had considered our security in an enemy kingdom.

After all, he was the only one allowed to hurt what was his. That's why my uncle had given him the power to *punish* me.

My thoughts drifted back to the last letter I had received from Socair. Was there something in there I had missed? Uncle Mikhail said he was coming to fetch me, but he had to have left Socair well after Alexei did.

"Does my uncle know you're here?" I found myself asking, though I should have known better.

I didn't have time to lie or expound on my question in a way that didn't sound impertinent before Alexei responded. He wrapped his hand around my wrist in a warning, digging the charms on my bracelet into my already bruised skin.

"You think me so weak? I do not answer to other clan leaders."

It was an effort not to flinch, even as the wolf's head charm bit into my skin and every part of me begged to shrink away from his touch.

"Of course not, My Lord," I said, dipping my chin demurely.

Alexei dropped my wrist; his mouth twisted. "These people have made you impudent."

He narrowed his gaze on me, searching my face for any sign of reaction, only looking away when I failed to give him one.

It was an even more tense ride after that. By the time we stopped for the night, it felt like years had passed rather than the roughly twenty-four hours since I had agreed to marry Davin.

Just thinking his name sent a pang through me. I pushed it away, taking Alexei's proffered arm as he led me from the carriage around to the back of an inn. His two Socairan guards trailed behind us, while the Lochlannian driver checked the horses into the stables.

Inside the inn, the serving girl and cook both pointedly peered in the other direction after being handed a few coins.

Had Alexei planned this? Had he known which inns were full of traitors to the crown? Had he threatened these people into compliance, or were they doing it out of some misguided sense of justice?

As though he read my mind, Alexei chuckled under his breath.

"Lochlannians have no loyalty to their own." He spoke in Socairan as we ascended a narrow staircase. "Here, it is too easy to find those willing to work against their own monarchs."

His words dripped with disgust, and for once, I could find no argument. Most clan members would die before turning on their duke, but this kingdom seemed to be teeming with those who were willing to betray their own king.

Then I thought about what Jocelyn said. Love versus loyalty. Before Rowan came along with her Unclanned army, the Socairans had served out of fear. The Lochlannians were loyal out of love. It was earning that love to begin with that was the problem.

Something Davin and I were accomplishing together, before...

Those thoughts cut off abruptly when Alexei stopped outside of a door, motioning for his guards to take up position on either side.

My heart dropped into my stomach, icy dread pooling through my veins. Somehow, it hadn't occurred to me that we would be sharing a room. We never had before. Alexei followed his own demented brand of propriety.

But of course, I should have known he wouldn't let me out of his sight.

Alexei walked into the room first, doing a quick check around to ensure that it was empty. But I was frozen in the darkened hallway, my limbs like lead as my eyes landed on the single, tiny bed in the corner of the room.

He turned when he realized I wasn't following him. His narrowed eyes flickered to the soldiers on either side of the door, then back to me. He wouldn't hurt me in front of them. He was too smart for that, but his other threats still hung in the air between us. After taking a breath, I forced myself inside the room, shutting the door behind me with a trembling hand.

The lock clicking into place echoed through the small space and rattled my bones. I barely turned around before Alexei was crossing the floor to get to me. He moved with the silence and grace of a predator, and I was reminded, once again, of the stories that followed him from the battlefront of his prowess. His bloodlust.

"Is there a problem, *Radnaya*? Do you not expect me to see to your safety, here in this land where you have so many enemies?"

There was no note of falsehood in his words, only a cold insistence.

"I'm only concerned about the propriety, My Lord." Immediately, I knew that had been the wrong thing to say, even before he raised an enormous hand to my neck.

Rather than close around my throat, his thumb slid downward, dipping just below the neckline of my dress before looping back up.

"Propriety?" Though his voice was pitched not to carry, there was a deadly undertone.

His thumb traced the same arc. I suppressed a shudder, bile rising in my throat. My skin crawled everywhere he touched it, and I was so focused on fighting back that feeling that it took me entirely too long to realize what he was tracing.

Then he dug his thumb into the gently bruised skin and the blood drained from my face. Abruptly, a memory hit me of Davin's lips on my skin. Then his tongue. Then his teeth, just there, below my collarbone.

Rage sparked in Alexei's gaze as he pressed harder along the mark, this time ensuring he would leave his own bruise to cover the one that was there.

"Were you concerned about propriety when you let that *svolach* disrespect us both by taking you to his bed?"

Deny, deny, deny. The words repeated like an alarm bell in my head.

"It was just a mistake, My Lord, but I didn't let him take me to his bed. I would never do that to you," I lied.

"Is that so?"

Alexei's other hand came to my waist, his fingers digging into my ribcage, demolishing the memory of Davin's patient hands with the sickening sensation of his possessive grip. He loomed over me, lowering his face to mine, and I squeezed my eyes shut, bracing for the forceful collision of his lips on mine.

But what followed was so much worse. His mouth pressed against mine slowly, like he was savoring the taste of me. He kissed first my top lip, then my bottom, while I stood frozen against the door.

His tongue darted out, pushing at the seam of my lips. When I still didn't respond, he moved his thumb from Davin's mark up to my neck, squeezing lightly until my lips parted. Then he was invading my mouth, suffocating me from the inside out.

Finally, he backed away, and the disgust flooding my veins turned inward. Shame prickled through me, stabbing at the backs of my eyes and pooling in my gut. The kiss had lasted less than a minute, but that was enough to stake his claim.

Enough to make me feel like I had betrayed Davin even more thoroughly than when I had penned a letter designed to break him.

"Don't worry, *Radnaya*," he said. "I am not one of these Lochlannian beasts. I can be patient until our wedding, as long as you remember who you belong to."

It took everything I had not to wipe away the taste of him, nodding submissively instead. He was giving me a small stay of execution. There was no sense in provoking him to change his mind.

But that wasn't enough.

"Say it, Galina," he demanded, squeezing his fingers around my neck once more.

I blinked, long enough to imagine a different room, a different set of hands on my skin, a different future than the one I had damned myself to.

Yours. Always yours. Only yours.

Then I opened my eyes, resigning myself to my fate all over again. After all, what was one more lie in a sea of them at this point?

"I belong to you, My Lord."

The worst part was, it didn't feel like a lie at all.

Chapter Four

DAVIN

"FORGIVE ME, my laird, but you say you were not in Laird Tavish's rooms at any point after your threats at the festival?" The Magistrate's obsequious tone grated on what was left of my patience. "Which was at the festival?"

I already didn't want to think about last night. About the way that Tavish had threatened Galina or what had happened after we returned to my rooms, and whether all of this mess was part of what pushed her out the door, the politics and the prejudice and the constant threats.

As pleasant as it should have been that my least favorite cousin was no longer breathing, I didn't want to think about his death, either. Though I couldn't dredge up any real sorrow at his passing, a man had still been murdered under my roof on a day that was supposed to be a celebration for our people.

"Correct." I answered the Magistrate's question for at least the twelfth time since my uncle and I came to the study. "I was not in his room, not before or after threatening him."

The casual setting was a flimsy façade for what was quickly turning into an outright interrogation, one Master Ward was enjoying every minute of. The Magistrate had been in Tavish's pocket before, but the death of my cousin, his benefactor, didn't seem to evoke any strong emotion in him. At least, nothing like the joy I was apparently bringing him by appearing guilty of murder.

Every time my temper flared, Uncle Finn would shoot me a warning look, a reminder that my cooperation was necessary to appease the masses. It was the same reason that only the three of us were in this small, tucked-away room. The last thing we needed was the assembly claiming that my family intimidated the man from doing his job.

But I was quickly approaching the end of my rope.

Instead of being cowed, the Magistrate leaned forward with thinly veiled satisfaction.

"Then why was this found near his body?" Reaching into his pocket, he pulled out a small linen bag, turning it upside down over the antique birch wood desk.

The quiet clink of the silver against wood echoed through the room. I looked from Ward's smarmy smile to the blood-stains crusted in the groove of the intricately engraved D on the familiar cufflink.

That is rather unfortunate.

My uncle cursed under his breath, his golden eyes darting from me to the cufflink in question. Not accusation, but rather a giant *what-the-actual-hell* was practically imprinted on his face.

If there had been a single doubt in my mind that someone wanted to frame me for what happened to my cousin, it was gone now. Really, though, I shouldn't have been too surprised that Tavish would manage to make me suffer, even in death.

Keeping my expression as neutral as I could, I forced my gaze away from the damning evidence. I weighed my options. I could lie, but it wouldn't be hard to disprove, so I settled on the truth.

"I wasn't wearing that last night," I said, thinking back to the last time I had worn the cufflink. "I haven't seen them since I was last at Chridhe."

Ward arched a graying eyebrow. "Did they go missing?"

I drummed my fingers on the chair as I contemplated the question, my eyes going distant as I tried to recall exactly how I'd lost them. I vaguely remembered Blaine mourning their loss, but they weren't my favorites to begin with, so I hadn't been overly concerned with my manservant's fretting. Truthfully, I had suspected they had wound up in someone else's bed.

I shifted uncomfortably. It hadn't been...the proudest time in my life.

"I'm not sure, but they didn't make it back here." Only now did I think to wonder if they had been taken from my rooms after I left Chridhe.

Was this all part of a nefarious plan? To wait nearly a year to pin my cousin's murder on me? Or was it merely a contingency plan from an enemy?

"Apologies, My Laird." The words rang out as falsely as they had every other time he started a question that way. "But if that's true, why did you never attempt to track them down?"

The corner of my mouth ticked upward in a humorless smirk. I was tired of this game. Exhausted. And impatient. "My manservant tried. You can feel free to ask him about it."

A condescending chuckle escaped the Magistrate's lips. "A man who is paid to keep your secrets is not the most reliable source of information. If, perhaps, someone could corroborate your whereabouts last night..."

Uncle Finn looked sharply my way again, and I forced myself to take a deep breath.

"Regrettably, my fiancée has already left to visit her uncle in Chridhe, as I've told you." *Several times now.*

It wasn't quite a lie, given that Mikhail was on his way

there and Galina was, apparently, desperate to get back to her life in Socair. It made sense that she would meet him at Chridhe or on the road, unless she was planning on getting all the way through the tunnels with whatever escort she had wrangled for herself.

"A visit which was, for reasons unknown, being kept secret?"

It wasn't *reasons unknown*. I had told him several times now that Galina had been a target for the rebels, a truth that was slowly gnawing at my insides with every moment I delayed taking off. I reminded myself that she had rather graciously left me in a precarious position that would lead to a demolished reputation and an apparent lack of alibi, but it didn't matter.

I still needed to make sure she was safe. Because it was my obligation, obviously.

"My family does not make it common practice to announce our comings and goings, and Lady Galina is free to go where she pleases. You can question her when she returns." *Which will be never.* "But in the meantime, please do go about finding the actual culprit."

I smoothly got to my feet, keeping my emotions tucked squarely away.

"And I trust you'll keep the contents of this conversation private, as is your duty," I said pointedly, not bothering to hide the threat in my tone.

Ward merely bowed his head, which was as dubious an answer as any.

Uncle Finn nodded behind me, and we made our way into the hall. Neither of us spoke on the way to my parents' private study, but he clapped a hand on my shoulder in a gesture of comfort.

We took the back halls, since most of the guests were headed down for dinner. I had less than no desire to run into any of them after my encounter with Ward, nor did I want to hear any of their gossip about what happened.

All I could do now was hope that my family had made some progress while we had been tied up with the magistrate — a hope that was quashed as soon as I saw their frustrated expressions.

"Any updates?" I asked, walking directly toward the drink cart and pouring myself a dram of whiskey. I already knew the answer, but it was still disappointing when my father confirmed it.

"Nothing," he said with a subtle shake of his head.

While his expression hovered somewhere between confused and concerned, my mother's features were hardened and impassive. I studied her, not for the first time since Galina disappeared. When she glanced up at me, she rolled her eyes.

"For the last time, Davin. No, I did not help Galina leave," she said irritably. "Of course, I would have helped her to the border, had she asked." She paused, bringing her whiskey glass to her lips and taking a long sip. "But not like this."

Gallagher nodded in agreement, disappointment evident in the slumped set of his shoulders.

I clenched my jaw. Did Galina realize I wasn't the only person she hurt when she disappeared in the middle of the night? Did she care?

"Well," I sighed, "I'll have to go after her."

My proclamation didn't come as a surprise to anyone in the room if their resigned expressions were anything to go by, though the frustration in my uncle's tone was very clear when he spoke.

"Do you have any idea how that will look?" He was using his Captain of the Guard voice. "You running away during a murder inquiry?"

I took a dreg from my glass before shrugging with all the indifference I didn't feel.

"Probably about as bad as it will look if my fiancée turns up dead trying to escape Lithlinglau."

A stilted silence filled the room. There was nothing he could say to argue that, not when we all knew just how true the statement was.

"She may be willing to risk her life, but I'm not willing to risk what it will do to Lochlann and Socair if something happens to her here." I swallowed hard, wondering if they knew that was only half the reason I needed her safe. No one called me on it, though the sympathy in my father's eyes almost made me wish he would.

"Besides," I added a moment later. "I have my own spies, and they won't talk to anyone else. This is the fastest way to ensure her safety."

Uncle Finn groaned, running a hand over his face. "Fine," he relented after a moment. "You have until the end of next week, but then I expect you back here. This Tavish situation isn't just going to go away, but we can deal with it then if we must."

IT WAS QUICKLY DECIDED that my cousins would come with me, which was a mixed bag considering Gwyn's feelings about Galina. At least between her strength and speed, and Gal's ability to heal, I had a veritable army at my side.

There was no one else I would want next to me in a battle — or whatever this was. It didn't hurt that we were taking six trusted soldiers with us, giving us a bit of strength in numbers, should we need them.

Though every hour we delayed pricked at the edges of my

nerves, we left the estate well after dark to avoid the prying eyes of the remaining guests.

Or so I thought.

"Laird Davin," a familiar voice purred from the garden, stopping me in my tracks.

When I had entered the aviary, the grounds had been empty, but now I found myself face to face with Fiona Shaw. She wore a heavy cloak draped over her nightdress, and though her hood was pulled low, I would recognize the sharp lines of her face and the pitch of her voice anywhere.

I glanced around to see if anyone else was waiting in the shadows. Knowing Fiona, she wasn't likely to be alone. Not for long, anyway. But when I saw no sign of anyone, my gaze flicked back to her, wondering just how calculated this meeting was.

Her head tilted toward the sky as the sound of wings flapped above us. Seven birds were headed to my spies in the north, asking them to keep an eye out for someone of Galina's description. An eighth bird was on its way to my uncle in Chridhe.

Fiona's lips pursed in question, her gaze flitting from the birds back to my face. She twirled her loose raven locks around a long, delicate finger, studying my face for a long moment.

"Wherever could you be going at this hour?" she asked coyly, stretching her free hand out to run along my chest.

"Dealing with a personal matter." I smiled tightly, stepping away from her touch and toward the stables.

Fiona glanced behind me, her gaze settling on the cloaked figures already waiting for me on their own horses.

"Might this have anything to do with your supposed role in your cousin's murder?" she asked with all the innocence of a ravenous panther.

She shouldn't know that. No one should know that the magistrate wanted to blame me for his death… But of course,

Fiona had always had a way of getting the information she wanted.

I suppressed a gag as the unwanted image of her and the man three times her age came to mind.

"I had nothing to do with his murder," I finally said. I wouldn't confirm what she thought she knew, but I could at the very least try to clear my name. "Now, if you don't mind, Lady Galina is waiting for me to catch up."

May as well let Fiona use her gossip network to spread the excuse for our absence.

She arched a perfectly sculpted eyebrow, mischief lining her features as she closed the distance between us. The heady scent of her amber perfume filled my lungs, and it took everything in me not to shove her away.

"I think you and I both know that Galina is not on a social visit to Chridhe." She whispered the words into my ear before stepping back again. "Nor waiting for you to catch up to her."

Damn her. That confirmed at least part of where she got her information. I hadn't told anyone besides Ward that Galina was on her way to Chridhe.

She knew more than that, though. If she knew Galina had fled, was it because she been responsible? Had she said something to scare Galina off? Was history doomed to repeat itself? First the maid in Socair, now Fiona.

"Did you say something to her?" I practically growled, my breaths billowing out in the frosty air like clouds of smoke.

There was an arsenal of personal history between us. Sordid and damning, and exactly the sort of fuel Fiona could use to set fire to my relationship with Galina if she had truly wanted to.

She tsked, shaking her head as if my accusation disappointed her.

"Honestly, Davin, if she left you, that is entirely on you," she said coolly. “Besides, it would be terribly gauche for me to kiss and tell, don’t you think?”

I considered her words, wondering whether or not she was telling the truth. Fiona rarely missed an opportunity to gloat, and this would have been a prime opportunity for her to do so.

Sighing, I clenched my fists, torn somewhere between relief and anger. Would it have been better to have Fiona to blame? Was it worse knowing that I couldn’t?

My heart pounded with uncertainty as I stepped into the waiting carriage, leaving Fiona and all the information she shouldn't have behind in the shadows. The last thing I needed was another enigma in this already maddening puzzle.

Chapter Five

GALINA

TRUE TO HIS WORD, Alexei didn't touch me again. At least, not intimately.

He was still quick to stop my hands if I fidgeted, or roughly grip my chin to force my attention back to his if I dared let it wander. But every night, he turned his back while I bathed and changed and left me to my silence while I ate the food he ordered me.

I had never been more grateful for the Lochlannian gowns that allowed me to undo my corset with ease, an impossible feat in a Socairan one.

None of it was a true relief, though, not with our wedding day looming closer with each turn of the carriage wheels, each mile that carried me farther from Lithlinglau Estate.

It didn't help that we hadn't rested for long. Not that I could have slept well, regardless, but there were nights where we didn't stop except to swap out the horses and occasionally our carriage.

Gone were the smells of the festival. In their place, the scent of Alexei's aftershave became more potent and cloying, especially when he insisted on pulling me closer to rest against him whenever I nodded off in the carriage. He would pull me against his arm or shift to the side of his carriage so my head lay on his leg. Never improper, always cushioned by one of the furs while he covered me with another.

I might never understand his warped sense of honor. Though I supposed I had a lifetime now to figure it out.

Whenever we stopped at inns for a few precious hours of sleep, I would lay awake, waiting for the steady sound of his breathing while debating the relative merits of murdering him in his sleep.

Could I do it? Even if his death wouldn't result in my parents' deaths, could I bring myself to slide a knife between a sleeping man's ribs, the same man who hurt me and shielded me in equal turn? My parents would be safe once we were married and back in Socair. Could I wait to poison him then, as I suspected Jocelyn had done to her first husband?

Or would he have broken me so thoroughly by then that I wouldn't even have the nerve to try?

I could only distract myself with those thoughts for so long before thoughts of Davin crept in, as I knew they would. It was easier to keep them at bay in the carriage, but at night, with Alexei's breaths too harsh and too loud, his body too large and too heavy, the wrongness of it seeped through to my bones.

All I could see was what Davin's face must have looked like when he walked into my empty room. The way his eyes would have scanned his surroundings, his brilliant brain working to put the pieces together. His deft fingers running through his hair.

Was he worried? Furious? Resigned?

Hurt, definitely. Even if I hadn't just promised to marry him, my leaving had put him at risk of losing his home, not to mention the reputation he had worked so hard to salvage. He must hate me now.

I swallowed a lump in my throat, reminding myself what this was all for.

He was alive. So were my parents. And that would have to be enough. Someday, he would move on and marry another, have a relationship with someone who could love him in an uncomplicated way, like Gracie MacBay.

And I would be...with Alexei.

Something dark unfurled inside of me, clawing at my insides and threatening to burst through my skin. Perhaps I was capable of murder, after all.

Perhaps it wouldn't take very much at all to push me over that edge.

TENDRILS OF EXHAUSTION wrapped themselves around me. Every step felt heavier than the last and the lack of sleep was catching up to me.

Maybe that's why I didn't hear my name at first or sense the immediate danger it put the man in that recognized me.

We had just stepped outside of the inn, when a stranger in a straw riding hat approached us.

"Lady Galina?" His deep, accented voice stopped me in my tracks.

Judging by the insistence in his tone and the anger radiating off of Alexei, it had likely not been the first time the man had said my name.

When I turned slightly to look at him, he removed his straw hat and beamed at me in recognition. "Ach, I thought it was you."

It only took me a moment to recognize that he had been in charge of the Skittles booth at the festival. He was the one who handed me my award for winning, four days and a lifetime ago.

I was suddenly more awake than I had been before, and painfully aware of everything around me all at once.

The cold morning air that bit into my skin. The low sounds of the stirring town waking up. The savory scents wafting over from the food carts on the street. The creak and groan of the wooden sign above the Red Lion Inn's door, and the stomping of impatient horses ready to get on the road.

He was carrying two freshly-baked, still-steaming meat pies from one of the food vendors, and he was headed toward the inn we'd just come from. I carefully darted a glance around, relieved that no one else was paying us any attention, or waiting just behind him.

"Master MacDoyle," I greeted, my voice higher than I wanted it to be.

The man in question slid his gaze from me to Alexei, who was stiffening at my side, and I waited for the betrayal to dawn on his features. Instead, fear flitted through his gaze. Not of me, I realized, but *for* me.

It was an unwanted reminder that somewhere along the way, these people had started to become mine, as well. And I was betraying them as surely as I was their marquess.

The man's smile slipped. "Is everything alright, milady?"

Alexei's guards were at the carriage, but a small contingent of soldiers wasn't far off. It would be so easy, I realized. Easy to give the man the smallest sign that I was in trouble, let the soldiers come dispose of Alexei. I wouldn't have to marry a monster.

I could go home...to Davin.

For a fraction of a moment, I let myself consider the possibility that Alexei was bluffing. Perhaps there was no system at all, no check-in, no one waiting to murder my parents in cold blood.

As much as I wanted that to be true, the overwhelming likelihood was that he had thought this through as meticulously as he had his battles during the war. So I lifted my chin, giving the warmest, most disarming smile I could muster.

"Of course. My guard is only accompanying me home to fetch my family before the wedding. I left a little early, because I'm hoping..." I lowered my voice, looking around conspiratorially. "I'm hoping to have time to make a detour, to convince the queen to come back with me, as a surprise for the marquess, but I have no idea if she'll be able to get away. Please don't mention you saw me. He'll suspect something if he knows what excellent time I'm making when I'm such a slow traveler ordinarily."

Something fractured inside of me, imagining the words were true, that I was merely fetching a surprise for the betrothed I loved in time to come back to marry him. Swallowing back that emotion, I widened my smile, forcing a blush to my cheeks.

The man visibly relaxed. "Aye, my lips are sealed. Though, if you'll take some advice from an old man, that'll make him happy, milady, but nothing so much as marrying ye. Just be sure yer back on time."

He chuckled before taking a bite of one of the steaming hand pies, raising the other almost in a salute to me.

"I will." The lie chafed against my lips like sandpaper. "Thank you, sir."

With that, he winked before turning to continue inside.

Alexei eased ever so slightly at my side, leading me into the carriage. He was never particularly talkative, but his silence here felt pointed somehow. Heavy.

After securing a blanket over our laps, he knocked on the window separating us from the driver before finally turning his attention back to me. His gaze flitted over my face like he was seeing me for the first time, and what he saw was disappointing.

"You were always lying," he finally said, his breath heavy with the scent of coffee.

There was no note of bitterness in his voice. There was a small hint of surprise, however, like he was replaying every time I had leaned into him or whispered soothing words in his ears, now seeing them in a different light. I looked away, guilt and defiance warring in my gut.

"I didn't have a choice." No choice but to marry him. No choice but to keep him calm.

Instead of reacting with fury, the way I expected him to, he only scoffed. "And you think that I did?"

I opened my mouth to respond, then closed it. It had never occurred to me to wonder if he had wanted to marry me. Our uncles had arranged our betrothal on behalf of us both.

But he certainly had a choice in hurting me. Was it worse if he felt like he didn't? Like it was a necessary form of discipline for the fiancée who couldn't seem to behave?

I chanced a look at him. "And now?" The words were barely a whisper.

I wasn't even sure what I was asking. If he had a choice? If he would consider giving me one? If he realized that all this would accomplish was to make us both miserable for the rest of our lives?

The angular lines of his face hardened, whatever moment of humanity he had let slip disappearing as quickly as it had come.

"Now, I will do my duty for the sake of both of our clans, since you could not be bothered to do yours."

Whether he meant punishing me for my disobedience or dragging me back to marry him, his resolve was absolute, so I didn't respond.

For once, I was silenced by choice as much as by circumstance.

Chapter Six

DAVIN

THE CACOPHONY INSIDE THE BROTHEL – excuse me, gambling hall – did more to exacerbate my racing thoughts than it did to quell them.

Gwyn let out a whoop of victory, sliding her coins across the velvet table while one of the soldiers lit her long cigar. Gallagher sipped more quietly at his whiskey, gently declining the eager offers of the ladies who worked here.

We had all been here before, even Gwyn playing the part she needed to play for the sake of information or sheltering against a storm Rowan sensed.

It was almost too familiar, the discordant symphony of coins and music in the main hall, laughter and whispered pleasures emanating from the back rooms, but tonight it only served to remind me of my failure.

All my contacts and carefully laid-out system of spies, the endless hours I had put into a façade for the sole purpose of gathering information, and I couldn't find a single missing Socairan woman in my own kingdom.

We had been searching for three days without a trace of

her, despite my resources. This wasn't even the first route we had traveled, or, hell, the fifth. It had been an endless venture of backtracking and sidetracking, combing through the overcrowded roads and inns as well as the lesser used ones.

Every family and merchant who had been at Lithlinglau for the festival was now headed back to their homes, but she shouldn't have been able to blend in with them quite so easily.

I was missing something.

Had she really planned things meticulously enough to avoid being spotted by my most capable spies, or did something happen after she left? Were all of my contacts working for the rebellion? I refused to consider the alternative, the other reason no one would have seen or heard from her.

Subconsciously, I traced the outline of the folded parchment in my pocket, the wrinkled letter I had read over and over again.

No. I shook my head, my fingers pressing into my temples to ground me.

Galina couldn't be dead. The rebels would have made a spectacle of it, wanting to hurt either me or Lochlann. It was just a matter of finding her.

Finally, my contact emerged from one of the private rooms, her dark eyes scanning the room until they landed on me.

She kissed her client on the cheek — a local laird who smiled as she whispered something into his ear. He nodded, placing a hefty bag of coins in her hand before turning to leave while she made her way toward our table.

"My Laird," she hummed, taking a seat in my lap.

The heavy scent of her perfume filled my senses.

"Isobel," I said, trying to keep my tone inviting as I ran my hand down her back.

The simple touch made my skin crawl.

I used to be good at this, pretending with courtesans and

playing this game of seduction and secrets. But despite the clear evidence that Galina wanted nothing to do with me anymore, I couldn't turn off the part of me that felt loyal to her.

I didn't want to look at another woman, let alone pretend to take them to bed.

"I apologize for keeping you waiting," Isobel purred as she leaned closer, her finger tracing the line of my jaw. "But I'm yours for the rest of the night, if you wish."

I did not wish, but this was the opening I needed.

"If you think that's enough time." I gestured for her to stand as I followed suit. "Shall we move this to our usual room?"

A small, knowing smile tilted the corner of her full lips as she took my hand in hers, leading me to the most secure room at the back of the brothel.

"We might be a while," she called over her shoulder to my cousins.

Gwyn audibly groaned in response, only half for the sake of the onlookers.

A few snickers sounded throughout the room, along with some drunken cheering. It was all for the show. A performance. If there were any rebels or gossipmongers present, all they would see was the womanizing nephew of the king with his favorite whore, settling in for a night of fun. It would make sense, once word got out that I had been jilted.

Ignoring the pang of guilt that twisted my stomach, I told myself that reputation was what I wanted right now — needed, in fact.

As soon as the door closed behind us, the smile fell from Isobel's lips. After securing the lock, she tucked one of her long, silk scarves under the gap in the door — an added measure to ensure our words wouldn't carry.

"What is it?" I asked, noting the tight set of her shoulders and the concern filling her deep brown eyes.

She didn't answer right away. Instead, she blew out the candles in the room until we were shrouded in darkness. Her shadowy figure moved to the window, slowly pulling back the curtains before gingerly opening the glass panes and poking her head out to look around before closing them again.

The silver glow of the moonlight filtered in, illuminating her tense features.

"Isobel," I said more firmly, my hand instinctively going to the hilt of my sword to fend off whatever threat she was so concerned about.

Still, she was silent. When she was satisfied with whatever she did or did not see outside, she turned back to face me.

"There are eyes everywhere," she said in a low tone.

Isobel was always careful, but this was another level. Only one group inspired that kind of fear. The Viper's rebels.

"The Uprising?" I asked quietly.

She gave the barest dip of her chin. "They know you're looking for her."

My insides went cold, and I pitched my voice even lower. "Have you seen her?"

"No," she whispered, with a shake of her head. "But I know there was a body at the Red Lion today."

Panic seized my lungs, my stomach dropping as the worst possible scenario came to mind. Was it–

"It was a man," she clarified before I could voice the unspoken question aloud. Her expression softened, her large black eyes turning thoughtful as she studied me.

Gradually, my lungs filled with air once more.

"Lots of bodies turn up there," I said, willing my heartbeat to calm.

"Yes," she agreed. "But this one was killed by the Viper's men."

I didn't ask how she knew. Half the court might have been pointedly ignoring the threat of the Uprising, but the rumors had spread fast amongst the people. Everyone knew what it meant when a body was mutilated with deep purple veins.

That poison was unique to the Viper.

It shouldn't have been connected to Galina, not when bodies had been turning up all throughout the kingdom. But it felt too close, and I had no other possible leads to follow.

PULLED by some combination of instinct and desperation, I snuck out the back door of the brothel and made my way over to the Red Lion Inn.

The dusty street and chilly night air were honestly preferable to the seedy inn. As soon as I opened the door, the scent of Perpetual Stew filled the air. There was something extremely off-putting in whatever ingredients were added to the pot.

The inn had once been an impressive establishment. No expense had been spared when the inn was first constructed. Between the large stone columns and the carved creatures that sat atop them, the quality of the floorboards, as well as the bedframes, it was clear that the building had been grand in its day.

The perfect blend of time and mismanagement had gracefully led to its current state, those charmingly rotting wooden planks and beams coated with the finest layers of dust, a masterpiece of disrepair.

My first stop was the body, which was still waiting in the back to be transported to the local mortuary. After slipping the man on guard a few coins, I looked under the tarp to confirm what I already knew. Purple veins contrasting against pale skin. Black foam at the corners of his lips.

It was the Viper's poison.

Once I was inside, I similarly bribed the crotchety innkeeper to reluctantly show me the room where the man's widow was staying. Not that it was entirely necessary. I could hear her sobbing from the hall. She answered on the second knock, the surprise of my presence stemming her flow of tears.

"My Laird." Something about her was familiar — with her graying hair, kind brown eyes, and matronly way of speaking. It took me a moment to place her past her features that were swollen from grief.

She had been at the festival. Her husband ran the Skittles booth. Just a few days ago, he had smiled while he handed a victorious Galina her prize. And now he was dead.

"May I come in?" I asked quietly, darting a glance around to ensure no one was watching from the hall.

She nodded quickly, ushering me through the door and closing it behind me with a soft click.

"I wasn't expecting to see you here of all places, My Laird," she sniffled, pouring two glasses of water from the pitcher on the table. She offered one to me with a shaking hand.

"I happened to be passing through and heard the unfortunate news about your husband," I said, skirting around the reason for my visit to the town. "I am sorry for your loss."

Her eyes glistened with more unshed tears, her brow furrowing as if in an effort to hold them back. Finally, she dipped her head in a nod, taking a seat on one of the small chairs and gesturing for me to do the same.

"It doesn't make sense, My Laird. No one wanted to hurt my Roger. He was kind to everyone he saw. I told him the inn was dangerous, but he said I was too worried about it."

My fists clenched before I could stop them. The village of Othach wasn't under Lithlinglau's purview, but it was still my family's kingdom, and we couldn't even keep the people safe from the rebels determined to terrorize them.

Assuming, of course, that her husband wasn't working with them. It was impossible to tell these days. Taking a deep breath in through my nose, I addressed the woman calmly.

"I know you spoke with the local magistrate, but would you mind walking me through what you remember? Who he saw that day or spoke to? Anything that might have thrown him into the path of...an enemy?" I stopped short of saying *The Viper*, unsure what the woman knew or had heard.

"He spoke to everyone as we went. As I said, he was kind that way," she said, her eyes pooling up with tears.

"Is there anyone specific? Perhaps in the last couple of days, or since you arrived at this inn?"

She shook her head, then stopped. "Just the young lady."

My breath seized in my lungs. "What young lady?"

She took a sip from her glass, her gaze turning toward the window for a long moment before answering.

"He didn't say her name. Said she had asked him to keep her being here a secret and that I'm too loose-lipped, but that I'd know when it was too late for me to go blabbing." The edges of her mouth curled up before twisting in a pained grimace again, like it had been a joke they shared.

I hated to push her on this, to make her grief worse, but my heart was pounding in my chest, every instinct I had told me this was important. If Galina had been here...

"What did she look like?" I pressed.

"I only saw her from behind, out the window." She gestured toward the small pane of glass. "She was with a large man, who looked to be her guard."

One of our missing guards?

"But you said she was a lady? A noble lady?"

"Well, her cloak was very fine, and she had a poised way of standing," she added quickly, almost defensively.

I considered her description, though impatience was growing inside me. A woman in a fine cloak with a guard could have easily been one of the courtesans next door, come to visit a client they were unsure of.

There had to be something else to go on.

Meeting the woman's eyes, I let her see a small bit of the desperation that I had been keeping at bay. "Please, I'm so sorry to push, but this could be important. Is there anything else at all that you can remember?"

She considered the questions for a moment before shaking her head. Her hands trembled as she sat her glass down on the table, an apology tumbling from her lips.

"I'm sorry, My Laird. All I could tell you was that she was tall. I could hardly see my Roger's face over her head. He smiled at something she said, and then, that same day, he was dead."

She burst into tears then, and I ran a hand through my hair. It could have been Galina, or it could have been a brothel woman turning on the charm.

I got to my feet, thanking her for the few details she had been able to share. Once I made sure she had someone coming to help her take care of things, I set a small stack of coins on the table, despite her protests. If she was on her own now, with funeral expenses to cover and a future to sort out, she would need this and more.

The woman's gaze followed the motion of my hand as I set down the silver, lingering on my signet ring, and something sparked in her eyes.

"She was wearing jewelry," she said, her face scrunched up like she was trying to remember. "A bracelet."

I froze. "Do you remember what it looked like?"

"I just remember the way the morning sun caught it when she moved her hand. It was silver, with tiny little baubles hanging from it. I'd never seen anything like it."

My heartbeat thundered in my ears.

Baubles. Or *charms*.

Of course the woman had never seen anything like it. They weren't common here, but all of the ladies in Socair wore them.

And Galina never took hers off.

Chapter Seven

GALINA

Galina

Somewhere in the back of my mind, I had held on to an unreasonable belief, a small shred of hope that Alexei might change his mind, that I might find a way out of this.

But there was no one to rescue me this time, and certainly no way for me to rescue myself from three Socairan warriors. It wasn't an option anyway, not with Alexei's leverage.

So I walked with my head held high from the carriage to the tiny, tucked-away building where I would forever bind my life to Alexei's. He trailed behind me, his hand protectively on his sword.

The driver walked in front of us, stopping at the door to deliver a sharp rap. A man's face appeared in a small opening in the door. He raised an eyebrow, and the driver sighed, yanking at the collar of his shirt.

Just above his heart was a brand, a mark carved into his skin of a snake coiled around a broken crown. I hadn't seen anything like it before, but I had seen Davin sketch it out when he and Gwyn told the story of the assassin who wanted to kill me when I first came to Lochlann.

It was the mark of the Uprising.

The man on the other side of the door grunted some form of approval before closing the small square and opening the door for us to enter. No one in our party seemed surprised or bothered by this interaction or the brand on the driver's chest.

Almost as if they'd grown used to it. Expected it.

A shiver ran up my spine, dread pooling in my stomach as the realizations dawned on me. Why it was so easy to get me out of Lithlinglau. Why Alexei wasn't worried about our safety. How there were so many people willing to betray their own kingdom – not for a random Socairan and a bag of gold, but for their precious Viper.

Alexei was working with the Viper.

Just being here, in the room with men who sanctioned the murder of innocent Lochlannians, felt like another betrayal to Davin, even if I had no control over this one. Even if it paled in comparison to the vow I was about to make.

"Yer the magistrate?" the driver asked once the door shut.

The man nodded, gesturing to the small podium on the other side of the open room. My chest was hollow, and stars lined my vision. This was it. Where I would forever bind my life to Alexei's.

Everything I had risked and done and worked for the last few months had culminated in this, my wedding to the very man I had tried to escape. It almost felt fitting that it was here, in a room that smelled like mildew, dusty curtains blocking out any trace of sunlight while surrounded by traitors and murderers.

Alexei grabbed my arm when I hesitated too long, dragging me down a makeshift aisle. I blinked and imagined a starlit sky and candles on a lake. Then I was standing across from Alexei, my knees barely supporting my weight.

Another blink and I saw Davin's face, his smile beaming at me. The flower in his lapel matched the same ruby shade of my gown. Then I was back in the dingy room, reality crashing in on me in a whole new way.

Though Alexei and I were both dressed to blend in, his clothes were finely made in the gray tones of Clan Wolf. His dark hair was cropped short, like all men in Socair, no threat of obscuring their vision in battle.

He was handsome, in a distant way. And for all that he had dragged me to this altar, he didn't look particularly happy to be here now, either, though there was a note of triumph. Satisfaction at a task accomplished, another enemy subdued.

I wondered if that was the look he would wear tonight, when he could finally claim me in truth. My heart pounded, and I blinked away the threat of tears that I refused to let him see.

"You are beautiful." Alexei said the words regretfully, like it was a fact he wished he could dispute or a consolation prize for my other undesirable qualities.

I wondered if that was true, even sleep-starved and worn out as I was. I hadn't looked in the mirror, but I was sure I didn't look like anyone's bride. My dress was plain, and my hair was braided back neatly, but listlessly, my shoulders wrapped in the gray scarf he had brought for this very occasion.

"Do you, Alexei Pajari, promise to love and cherish, to protect and shelter, to forsake all others, as long as you walk in this world together?" The magistrate sounded bored, a contrast to my own racing thoughts.

My insides twisted. This couldn't be happening. Not after everything.

"I do," Alexei said, his almond-colored eyes never leaving mine.

I studied his features for signs of the lie he had just told. He might be faithful and he might even be protective, but he wasn't capable of that kind of love, let alone of cherishing another person. His expression was like stone, though, unyielding and expectant.

"And do you, Galina Zhakarov, promise to love and cherish, to obey and serve, to forsake all others, as long as you walk in this world together?"

I gritted my teeth. Though I had prepared my entire life to say a version of those vows, somehow I doubted that Davin would have demanded I promise to obey, let alone to serve. Was it common in Lochlannian vows?

It hardly mattered, though, since I'd be promising it all over again in front of our own people in a couple weeks' time. At least, that's what I told myself when I opened my mouth to lie even harder than my new husband had.

"I do." It was an effort not to choke on the words.

Alexei leaned forward, and his aftershave overpowered me, overwhelming my senses until I was suffocating in a haze of wintergreen and regret. Then his mouth was on mine, not half as gentle as he had been last time.

Perhaps he had been given no choice outside of marrying me, but he was clearly here to savor his victory all the same.

Chapter Eight

DAVIN

IT ONLY TOOK us two more inns to come across another body.

This one was a maid, spotted less than a day after we left Othach. The same inky veins spider-webbed across her plump face and chest, and her hands still clutched her white apron. The inn wasn't dilapidated like the Red Lion, but there was a general feeling of...something. Malcontent? Rebellion?

Whatever it was, the staff was less than forthcoming. Short of taking the time to extensively question everyone there, we were forced to make due with even fewer results than before.

Of course, the maid had spoken to new people. She worked at an incredibly busy inn. No, no one stood out. They hadn't seen a Socairan woman.

Only when I asked if there had been any guests they *weren't* supposed to tend to did I stumble across the truth. It was what I needed to know, that Galina had been there.

"It could be a coincidence," Gallagher said once we were on the road again.

Gwyn nodded. "There are more people on the main roads

in general, and so many heading on this exact path back to Chridhe, so more rebel activity makes sense."

They weren't wrong, and I couldn't find a clear reason behind a connection to Galina. Why would the Viper want to kill someone she had spoken with? To keep me from finding her...so they could find her first?

Or had they already?

The questions haunted me as we rode through the night. Whenever I blinked, I was haunted by images of her perfect face marred by spider-webbed veins and black foam bubbling at the seam of her lips.

Forcing myself to breathe, I banished the thoughts from my mind, focusing instead on what I did know. All of these questions would be easier to answer if I had even a clue to the Viper's identity.

Until the festival, I had been convinced it was Tavish. There were signs he was working with rebels, and stars knew he would have stopped at nothing to secure his seat at Lithlinglau. Then he had looked terrified when he mentioned the Viper, glancing...into the crowd.

Was the Viper there that day? Or was it a general paranoia, more along the lines of Isobel's caution and the traitorous soldiers who insisted that *the Viper was everywhere.*

Now Tavish was dead, and the Viper clearly wasn't, putting me back at square one.

"Do we think the Viper could be a group?" I asked when we slowed our horses, although I already harbored a suspicion about the answer.

Gal looked thoughtful, but his sister shook her head.

"I don't," Gwyn said. "The prisoners were terrified of the Viper. If it was about a movement, about accountability to one another, it would be a general fear of the Uprising."

"True," Gal chimed in. "Besides, not one of them gave any outward signs of lying when they mentioned him."

"Or her," Gwyn chimed in, biting into one of the meat pies she had procured in the last village.

Gal inclined his head. "Of course. Gender equality comes first when we're dealing with mass murderers."

Gwyn shrugged like that was fair. Despite the noose hanging over us and the unrelenting sense of danger and dread that followed us everywhere these days, I couldn't help but offer a small half-grin in return. Not for the first time, I was grateful my cousins had come along.

"It's probably old Lady Fenella, poisoning the tips of the copious amounts of feathers she uses in her clothing," I managed to infuse more lightness into my tone than I felt. "She certainly seems capable of such atrocities."

Gwyn heaved a sigh.

"First of all, that fashion is an atrocity all on its own," she said around her next bite. "And I'm only saying, I'm just as likely to murder someone as you and Gal are. Station and gender have nothing to do with it. Maybe Lady Fenella wouldn't murder someone, but I bet Fiona would."

Gallagher shook his head, the moonlight highlighting the exasperation in his features. "I know you don't like her, but I doubt she spends her spare time torturing people...unless it's by sleeping with their husbands or taunting them about their inadequacies."

Was he right? I tried to picture the gorgeous courtier handing out poison capsules like candy and weaving a tenuous web of fear and revolution. She liked to push buttons, to be sure, but that was a whole different level of insane.

Gwyn wiped the crumbs from her cloak. "Our options are hardly narrowed down to those two. Man or woman, we have to consider half the lairds and their wives. MacBay, MacArthur, Jameson, just to name a few. Anyone who has the resources is a suspect."

"Not just anyone," Gal said. "They just have to have a

special kind of ruthlessness, and the ability to inspire mass amounts of fear in their followers."

"Or worse, loyalty." I shook my head grimly, thinking of the soldiers we had executed. Some of them were afraid, but others, like Scottie, had just been zealots. It was a different level of commitment.

That realization effectively soured the mood. It was an unwelcome reminder that the Viper was cruel and capable and manipulative, a lethal combination in a revolutionary.

And they wanted Galina dead.

Our next stop was the most productive yet. After hours of visiting the brothels just outside of Whitmire, I finally heard word from one of my contacts. For the first time since we set out on this journey, I had a name, an actual lead instead of just the feeling in my gut propelling me down back roads on a wild goose chase.

Horas Atcheson, owner of the Fair Maiden tavern, was, at present, the only person standing between me and the information I needed.

"Do you know who I am, Horas?" I asked once Gallagher and I had cornered the man in his office.

Gwyn stood guard just outside the door while our men were positioned at the front and back of the tavern, each of them on alert for anything suspicious. The man blanched, looking between my cousin and me as if I had asked a trick question.

"It's an easy enough question," Gal said when Horas hesitated too long. He leaned casually against the door. "I recommend that you answer it."

A wave of gratitude washed over me for his ability to stay calm in situations like these. As much as I loved Gwyn, it had been all too easy to decide who would stand guard and who would join me for questioning. The duchess wasn't known for her subtleties.

Horas dipped his head once, the knob in his throat bobbing nervously. "Yes, of course, mi'laird. You're the king's nephew. Both of you."

"We are indeed."

"Pleasure to meet you in person, Horas," Gal chimed in. "Apologies for checking your mouth before we gave a proper greeting, but one can never be too careful these days, what with the rebels poisoning themselves left and right."

He paled. "I'm no rebel—"

"Of course you aren't, Horas," I cut him off with a wave of my hand. "But more to the point, we are currently in a bit of a pickle, and you seem to be just the man who can help us out of it."

His mouth clamped shut, his gaze hardening.

"Don't make us do this the hard way, not when we were just becoming friends. I would hate to use our power and rank to get what we need, but I suppose if we must..."

"What were you thinking, Cousin?" Gal asked, his expression the picture of nonchalance.

"Well, we could always arrest him for conspiracy of collaborating with the rebels," I suggested. "Or, we could simply leave and spread the word about how helpful and cooperative he's been."

"The Viper wouldn't be too pleased with that," Gal offered, and Horas blanched, his head shaking back and forth.

"Quite right, Cousin. Quite right," I said with a nod. "And that would take any potential blood guilt off of our shoulders, since the Viper's men would be doing all of the actual dirty work."

Gallagher made a mock thoughtful expression, tilting his head back and forth as though weighing the pros and cons of that scenario.

Horas swallowed hard, his eyes darting between my cousin and me like he was searching for a tell that would clear up this entire situation — proof that we weren't willing to throw him to the wolves.

Gallagher nodded confidently. "I like this plan. Where do we think the news would spread fastest? Here, in the inn? Or perhaps down the road at the brothel? We could always go straight to the magist—"

"I don't want any trouble, My Lairds," Horas said quickly, panic widening his eyes.

"And I really don't want to be responsible for the deaths of you or your family," I responded with a shrug. "So help us both out, will you?"

He nodded emphatically. A bead of sweat dripped from his wrinkled brow, and he wiped it away before placing his hands on the desk in front of him.

"All I know is there was a girl. A Socairan lass."

I feigned a sigh, though inside, my heart was pounding at the confirmation. "That's old news, Horas."

"She came in a carriage," he added quickly.

"Obviously," said Gal, his tone bored.

We hadn't actually known that, but it was our going assumption.

The man looked frantically between us. "There were guards with her."

My eyebrows climbed, prompting him to go on. It was the first anyone had mentioned of more than one man accompanying her. Horas caught my reaction and nodded.

"They were wearing cloaks, all of them, but I heard them talking...in Socairan, just like her."

FURTHER QUESTIONING PROVED that Horas had little more to offer, aside from a basic description of a carriage that could have belonged to any merchant in the kingdom. We left with a scribbled note to the local magistrate, telling him where to find the rebel sympathizer. Then I sent another bird to the guard station at Hagail, asking for the names of every Socairan trade envoy or emissary who had come through the tunnels.

The pass was closed, so whoever was with Galina should be on that list. After what felt like far too long, we headed back to the stable.

"Still think she wasn't planning this?" Gwyn asked, her thoughts a bitter echo of my own.

Gallagher looked away. "I think that not everything is as simple as you want to make it, Gwynnie."

"Well, *I* think that she left Davin's room of her own accord," Gwyn shot back. "She had guards outside her room in Lithlinglau that she didn't bother to call for. She left a note, for stars' sake, and we've had nothing but confirmation that she's traveling of her own accord."

One by one, she ticked each point off on her fingers, waggling her thumb for emphasis on the final blow.

"Now we find out she's with her own people – people she would have had to collaborate with well in advance – and you're still trying to pretend like this was all an unfortunate accident."

Gallagher opened his mouth, probably to offer another vague, overly optimistic defense, and I cut him off.

"It doesn't matter." The words came out sharper than I meant them to.

It doesn't matter if she left. It doesn't matter how either of us feels about this. It doesn't matter if she has no regard for her own safety.

The twins looked at each other, then me, analytical glances that only contributed to the temper I was trying to quell. I took a deep breath, continuing in a calmer tone.

"Nothing has changed. What's important now is that we know where she's headed, and we aren't far behind."

As if the final word was a cue he had been waiting for, Ewan and the other soldiers rounded the corner with our horses in tow. Once we were all mounted and ready, we took off toward the main road, keeping the same punishing pace from the past few days.

It still wasn't enough to quiet the storm that raged relentlessly in my mind, the ongoing battle of my instincts clashing against every ounce of logic at my disposal.

Maybe Gwyn was right, and Galina had designed all of this. Maybe she had planned it all, right under my nose while lying in my bed while I imagined our future together.

But I couldn't shake the small voice in the back of my mind telling me that there was something else at play.

Chapter Nine

GALINA

It should have been a relief that we couldn't consummate our marriage right away, since we had to wait to stop at an inn that was deemed safe, which I determined to mean, *controlled by the Uprising*. Instead, each hour in the carriage ride only served to add to my dread.

Was this how soldiers felt in the tension-filled moments before a battle broke out? Wanting to run, when their only option was to stay? Wondering if they would survive the carnage ahead?

Alexei had been almost civil since our forced union, but his reinforced ownership over me was in everything he did. He sat even closer to me on the carriage bench, his hand territorially resting on my thigh, sending spiders crawling along my skin for the entirety of the ride.

I wasn't sure how I made it out of the carriage on my weak knees when we finally stopped at the inn for the evening. One step, then the other, all the way up the stairs. By the time Alexei closed the door behind us, I had stopped breathing.

He turned to me expectantly, his gaze heavy with a mix of resignation and determination. Was it me he wasn't sure he wanted, or just an unwilling bride? Still, there was a small trace of the victory I had been expecting, the satisfaction of accomplishing what he had set out to do.

For all that the carriage ride had felt interminable, being in this room with him was markedly worse. Every part of my mind rebelled, but this is what I had agreed to when I left. This was the life I had knowingly come back to. There was no escaping it now.

Even if I could find a way to delay, it would only make things worse down the line. And *that* was the best-case scenario. He had made it clear my parents' lives were tied to my willing obedience, not merely my reluctant compliance. So I stood firmly when he crossed the room to me, reaching for the gray scarf he had made me wear.

In slow, deliberate movements, he unwound it from my neck. Then his hand was on my jaw, his thumb skimming gently down to my neck. It was a jarring contrast to the pressure that had left bruises only days ago.

He leaned forward, brushing his lips against mine, and I squeezed my eyes shut. I didn't pull away, but I couldn't respond.

Wouldn't. Couldn't. The distinction felt important, but it wasn't one I could make when I was frozen like the roses in my father's garden after an ice storm, somehow both fragile and unyielding.

Alexei stopped, pulling back to examine my expression. Whatever hint of hesitation had been in his eyes before was entirely gone now, replaced with an implacable sort of pride.

"Are you not enjoying yourself, *Radnaya*?" he demanded.

There was only one answer I could give. "Of course I am, My Lord."

I could see it, then, a frozen bloom falling to the stone path, the jagged shards of ice shattering in every direction. And the flower inside was dead.

He sighed bitterly. "Such a good little liar. But it is not your honesty I require. Merely your obedience."

There it was again, resignation in his tone because I was always, always falling short in his eyes, and I always would. I wasn't what he wanted, what he was promised, what he thought he deserved.

No matter how hard I tried to keep him satisfied, it would always come back to this. His hand on my throat. His growl in my ear. His endlessly condescending *Radnaya*.

This was my life now, keeping him calm at the cost of myself.

So I took a deep breath, forcing myself to lean closer to him while I gave myself a thousand reassurances that didn't make this moment any easier.

At least this wasn't the first time. That first night, it had been Davin's patient, skillful hands and his gentle words. At least Alexei was still calm tonight. At least his duties would take him away from me most of the time.

At least...

I squeezed my eyes shut, tucking every emotion I had far away in the back of my mind and bracing myself for the creeping sensation of his hands on my skin.

Instead, a knock at the door sounded out. Alexei froze, a frustrated growl sounding from the back of his throat.

"What is it?" he barked through the door.

"You told me to tell you if anyone asked after your...your guest." It was the innkeeper, stuttering through every other word of his response.

Had I been recognized again?

Alexei's features went flat with rage and an undercurrent of concern, but I felt nothing at all. Not relief. Not fear, even if I was beginning to wonder how sure Alexei was of whatever deal he made with the rebels, for him to look that worried.

He wrenched the door open, addressing his next words to his guard. "Stay here and let no one enter."

The soldier gave him a sharp nod, pointedly avoiding my gaze. When he was gone, my trembling knees gave way, and I sank down to the floor. With my head between my knees and my arms shrouding me in darkness, I took slow, even breaths, shutting myself further away with each one. It felt like only seconds passed before I heard a scuffling outside the door, then a hand on the doorknob.

I shot to my feet, feeling even less ready than I had before, despite my best efforts to keep myself under control. How was he already back? Had I lost track of time trying to get myself under control?

There was no time to wonder about it further before the door swung open. I was still hastily adjusting my features to reflect something calmer when my expression froze, shock numbing me from the inside out.

Devastatingly familiar blue eyes stared back at me from underneath artfully disheveled black locks. There was a shadow of a beard on his defined jaw and a foreign expression on his perfect features, but I would have known his face anywhere.

My lips parted, his name escaping on an exhale. All the things I hadn't been able to feel before flooded in now, panic and terror and fury and the smallest, shameful hint of storms-damned selfish relief.

Davin was here. He had come for me.

But he was going to get my parents killed.

Chapter Ten

DAVIN

As much as I wanted to hold on to my anger, the first thing I felt when I saw Galina was a crushing, overpowering relief, so potent my knees nearly gave out. I had found her. She was alive, standing in a simple traveling dress, her hair braided to the side, saying my name in the same breathy tone she had used only a few nights ago.

For a moment, I was convinced that it had all been a lie. Her letter. Her leaving. That she was here against her will, but miraculously unharmed. Then she straightened, her features turning to ice.

"I told you not to come."

I reared back as though she had slapped me. It would have been less painful if she had, rather than her cold indignation after I had spent days stewing in the panic that the Viper's men would find Galina before we did, the horror I felt when I learned one of these guards was sharing a room with her, wondering if–

"You told me a lot of things." The words were out before I could stop them, each one dripping with the bitterness I had sworn I would keep to myself.

She just barely winced before shaking her head and shoring up her *resting Socairan face*. "I've already explained that, but –"

I narrowed my eyes. "I would hardly call that letter an explanation."

The low light of the hearth flickered in her pale-blue gaze. She lifted her chin, clasping her hands in front of her.

"Is that why you came, then?" she asked, arching an imperious eyebrow.

Still, there was something in her tone I couldn't read. Trepidation? Hope?

"I came to make sure you didn't get yourself killed, or have you forgotten about the merry band of rebels we went to great lengths to keep you safe from?" I shifted on my feet, the creaking of the floorboard echoing out through the frosty silence. "Because they sure as stars haven't forgotten about you, if the string of corpses in your wake is any indication."

Her eyes widened in what might have been fear. "All the more reason for me to be on my way, then."

"Is that why you left?" I asked, trying to make sense of the motives that felt even less clear with her standing before me. "Because of the rebels?"

She squeezed her eyes shut, and I pressed, wondering if I had finally landed on something close to the truth.

"Galina, if anyone is threatening—"

"No," she interrupted sharply, taking a deep breath before meeting my gaze. "You're so mired in conspiracies that you're building them where there aren't any. It isn't as complicated as you're making it out to be. I left for all the reasons I put in my letter, Davin."

She shook her head like a disappointed teacher explaining a simple concept to a willfully obtuse child.

"Your people hate me, and my clan needs me..." she hesitated, looking away. "And we both know you aren't really capable of settling down. Why do you think I didn't accept your proposal the first time around? We were only ever going to make each other miserable."

I blinked once, trying to recover whatever scraps of pride I had left. "That didn't seem to be a concern the other night," I said flatly.

She let out a small sound, something between a scoff and a whimper. "That was only ever supposed to be a goodbye."

For the first time since I entered her rooms, her eyes glossed over with a sheen of tears.

Despite myself. Despite every word she had just hurled at me, my inclination was to step forward — to comfort her. Before I could take a single step, she spoke up once more, saving me from humiliating myself further.

"But I was caught up in a moment, and for that, I do apologize."

For that? For making that promise, but not for leaving in the middle of the night. Not for whatever the hell this was.

I stared at her, some foolish part of me still looking for a sign that she was lying, but there was none. Perhaps the only lie was the person she had pretended to be.

Finally, I straightened to my full height, averting my gaze from the woman I had thought I would spend the rest of my life with.

"Regardless of how very horrified you are at the prospect of a future with me, you had your reasons for leaving the first time, enough that you were willing to set your precious pride aside for five seconds to call in a life debt and risk both of our kingdoms," I said more quietly. "I wouldn't have gone back on my end of our deal just because you turned down my proposal. You don't have to go back to Socair."

"Yes, I do." Her words rang with conviction. "You may not give a damn about duty, but I've run from mine for far too long. I have to do this, and you have to let me."

She certainly wasn't pulling any punches today. Did she honestly think, after everything, that I didn't care about duty, or my people? That I was just a womanizing arseling who would never settle down or take any responsibility?

And what did she mean, *let her?* As if I would stop her from leaving if she wanted to. Hadn't I offered that more than once?

"I've never had nor desired any control over your actions, Galina," I said flatly. "I had no plans to forcibly drag an unwilling fiancée back to my home."

Her expression flickered, but it was back to stone with a single blink. "Yet here you are."

Just when I thought the knife couldn't get any deeper. How the hell had we gotten from being allies, from joking on a rooftop, to hurling accusations across an icy chasm?

"Yes, here I am," I fired back. "To see you safely to the border, as I would have done if you had bothered to let me — or anyone know you were planning on leaving. For all your talk of duty, surely you can understand that I have one as well, to my people and my cousin."

The blood drained from her face. "That's not necessary. I have guards."

A low, dark chuckle rumbled through me. "Worry not, I have no intentions of escorting you myself. I have —" *A murder investigation that will be made worse by your absence.* "— business to attend to back home, but Ewan and Hamish are here."

Something like guilt glimmered in her eyes. At least she was capable of the emotion. Just not where I was concerned. Still, she opened her mouth to argue, but the door banged open, cutting her off.

I spun around, then promptly wished I hadn't. Two figures stood in the doorway. My cousin, who was wearing a warning expression, and another, larger man, one whose existence had mocked me since the day I realized Galina was still wearing her Wolf's head charm. I wasn't sure if the puzzle pieces were clicking into place or if they were just catching fire on the ground around me, but belatedly, I realized I should have been prepared for this.

If she was going back to Socair, she was going back to *him*. Except that it appeared he had saved her a step. Alexei had come for her, and she had left with him the moment he did. Even knowing that, I was still wildly unprepared for his next statement.

"Laird Davin, would you care to explain what you are doing alone in a room with my wife?"

Chapter Eleven

GALINA

NOTHING in my life could have prepared me for this moment.

If it was possible for a hole to open up in the ground and swallow me and this entire storms-damned situation, I would have welcomed it. Hell, I would have welcomed literally anything that kept me from the shattered, shocked expression on Davin's face when Alexei called me his wife.

My new *husband* may have sounded nonchalant, but I had, by necessity, learned to decipher the emotions that just barely churned in his gaze. Fury that Davin was here. Betrayal that I might have welcomed his presence, called for him, even.

And triumph, so similar to the kind he had displayed when he had pressed his lips against mine to seal the promise he knew I had no desire to make.

But there was no sinkhole. No salvation. I had less than a handful of seconds to realize I would actually have preferred to spend a wedding night with Alexei than to be the cause of Davin's pain this way, and even less time than that to figure out how to keep Alexei from punishing my family for what he perceived as my disloyalty.

So I crossed the room to him in three quick strides, pointedly avoiding Davin's accusatory gaze and Gallagher's hurt one. My booted footsteps echoed against the old wooden floor like the poignant beat of a drum, each step a stark reminder of the irreversible choices I had made.

"He only came because he heard rumors of rebels after us," I said in a placating voice, resting my hand on Alexei's taut arm. He was practically vibrating with rage, but he softened incrementally under my touch.

"Is that why he killed my men?" Alexei demanded, staring daggers at Davin.

"They aren't dead," Davin said, his tone implying that Alexei was being overly dramatic.

"At least, not unless Gwynnie got carried away," Gallagher added with a shrug.

In the brief time I had known him, Davin's cousin had never looked more than lightly irritated, but there was something darker behind his eyes when he looked at Alexei.

"Can't blame us for being too careful, since we had no way of knowing you were here, Lord Alexei." Davin said his name like a curse. "Had you sent word, Lithlinglau could have welcomed you properly. Or did I miss your letter?"

Alexei narrowed his eyes at the reminder that he was here illegally, and Davin was one of the few men in the kingdom with the power to punish him for it. Gallagher moved to his cousin's side in a show of support.

"Surely you are not here to speak to me of propriety when you ran away with my bride in the night like a coward." Alexei's voice was deadly calm. "Perhaps I missed your letter announcing that."

Davin's nostrils flared, and even Gallagher's hand twitched toward his sword.

"Lady Galina is her own person," Davin said in a voice like ice. I couldn't tell if he was defending himself or me.

Alexei raised a challenging eyebrow. "No, she is not. As of this morning, she is officially mine."

Davin shook his head, more in disbelief than any real denial. He looked from my unwanted husband to me, his cobalt eyes scrutinizing me in a way that was achingly familiar.

"This is what you want?" His tone was so even, I couldn't be sure if the question was an accusation or if he was giving me one last opportunity to tell him this had all been one giant misunderstanding.

Storms, how I wanted to do just that.

I had to remind myself of how hard I had worked to make him believe my deception, how hard I still needed to work.

"As I said," I lied smoothly.

Alexei donned a satisfied smirk, and Davin clenched his jaw. There was a long, stifling silence before he apparently came to some conclusion. Crossing his arms in front of him, he leaned back against the wall, putting up his casual façade like a shield between us.

"Well, as *I* said, you need an escort to the border, for your safety."

"She already has an escort to see to her safety." Alexei was quick with his reply. "Your people have targeted her since she arrived, or I would not have been forced to come as I have and with so few men to keep us both unharmed."

Guilt flickered behind Davin's ocean eyes before it disappeared behind his mask of nonchalance.

"I am unconvinced of your adequacy in any department, let alone where the peace of our kingdoms is concerned," he said dismissively. "Besides, you can only skulk around for so long since you didn't announce your presence here, unless, of course, you'd like me to do that for you."

Alexei's face turned purple, but he didn't respond. He couldn't when Davin had so neatly boxed him into a corner. He was outnumbered here, in Davin's kingdom, with the

Lochlannian army at Davin's disposal and Alexei on the wrong side of the law. It hadn't been part of his plan to get caught, obviously.

Alexei may have been a brute, but he wasn't an idiot, and he hadn't come back alive from war by starting fights he couldn't win.

That didn't mean he wouldn't find a way to retaliate.

"Very well," he relented. "We will take your men."

The corner of Davin's mouth tugged upward, the expression almost cruel in its perfection. He looked between Alexei and me, something glinting in his gaze I knew I wouldn't like.

"What kind of a former fiancé would I be if I didn't escort you myself? After all, it is the peace of two kingdoms at stake here."

A wave of heat washed over me, anger beginning to edge out the panic and guilt that had been suffocating me only moments ago.

When Davin had first walked into this room, it had taken everything I had not to confess the truth and throw myself into his arms, but now it was a fight not to strangle him.

I had told him not to follow me, had asked him to leave, and whatever reasons he had for staying anyway were going to make an already impossible situation downright unbearable.

How was I supposed to sit across from him for days in a carriage, to go back to the inn at night knowing he was only a room away while Alexei was hurting me? I couldn't even feel relief over my interrupted wedding night, knowing it would be so much worse now that Alexei was furious and had something to prove.

And that was the best-case scenario. That was if he didn't decide to punish one of my parents for what he presumed to be my disobedience. If his newfound friendship with the Viper didn't get Davin killed.

I shot Davin a look, somewhere between angry and pleading, opening my mouth to protest before I remembered that Alexei would not welcome my direct interference. He was furious enough as it was.

Forcibly, I clamped my lips shut, putting an unbothered expression on my face just in time for Alexei to turn to me, his eyes boring into mine. I tried to convey that I had done my best, that I hadn't asked Davin to come, that I would keep this ruse up for as long as it took. But perhaps I conveyed that a little too well.

Or more likely, Davin had just done *his* job a little too well. Alexei was entirely up against a wall, something he must have known.

Finally, he nodded, turning back to Davin.

"If you wish to escort my new bride and me to our home kingdom, I see no problem with that," Alexei said.

If Davin was bothered by Alexei's words, he didn't show it. He only nodded once, his lips tilting up in a bare imitation of his usual smirk.

"Excellent. We leave tonight."

Chapter Twelve

DAVIN

I STAYED BEHIND after the happy new couple stormed out – well, he stormed out, pulling her along with him. Gallagher followed, but I couldn't quite move my feet from the room – *their* room, where I stood staring at the bed I might have found them in had I arrived only moments later.

The flickering firelight cast long, menacing shadows on the shabby furniture and threadbare curtains of the dingy bedroom. Other than their shared trunk of clothes, there was only a delicate gray scarf left in the room.

I swallowed down my revulsion at the significance of it. Gray. For Clan Wolf. Likely a wedding gift from Galina's new *husband*. It still didn't make sense. She had said she was tired of running in circles, and that she would stay. Instead, she had left to marry someone else.

Out of desire? Duty? Part of a deal she had struck to return home?

The heady scent of lavender and rosemary wafted off of the fabric when I picked it up. Had she removed it herself? Or had she whispered that she was his as he unwound it from her perfect skin?

Another scent clung to the scarf, fainter and more masculine than hers.

Bile rose in my throat, and I hurled the entire length of fabric into the fireplace. It did nothing for the gaping void that was expanding in my chest, a pain I hadn't felt since Mac died.

Feather-light footsteps sounded behind me, and I knew who it was without turning around.

"Gal catch you up?" My voice was almost even.

"He did." Gwyn stepped closer, watching the fabric turn to ash.

"I had to destroy the evidence that we were here," I explained, not bothering to make it sound truthful.

"Of course," she said flatly. "We wouldn't want the rebels who told us *exactly* where to find them to know they were, *in fact*, at this inn."

I nodded like she was being serious, soaking in the momentary reprieve her presence offered. "I'm glad you understand."

"I don't understand any of this," she muttered darkly.

That makes two of us.

I switched back to the matter at hand, rather than focus on the crushing feeling that was returning with Gwyn's admission.

"Did we take care of the guards and the driver?" I asked her.

While Gallagher had been tasked with distracting who we thought was a guard, after we...convinced the innkeeper to lure him out of Galina's room, Gwyn and Ewan had come with me to take care of any remaining men.

She sighed. "The guards, yes. The one I took out just woke up, and the other was sleeping next door until his shift. They're both awake now, downstairs with our men. No sign of the driver, though. He must have left before we locked things down."

"Of course he did," I bit out.

By all accounts, the driver had been Lochlannian. He would have recognized us, and it wouldn't have been hard for him to blend in with the party who was leaving when we arrived. I rotated my neck until it popped, trying to relieve some of the tension that had taken root in my soul.

"Ewan can take his place," I decided.

Gwyn snapped her gaze to mine, turning with the lightning speed she usually kept at bay, and I braced myself for her fury.

"You're not seriously going to escort them to the border." Sure enough, her hazel eyes burned like twin flames of indignation.

"I thought you said Gal caught you up," I said evenly, rather than respond outright.

"I hoped he was joking." She let out a disbelieving exhale. "You need to get back to Lithlinglau."

I sighed, running a hand over my face. "There are other things at play here."

"Are there?" she demanded. "Or are you only seeing what you want to see? She's married. To someone else. If she was in trouble, Davin, she could have told you when you were alone in the room with her. She has to know we outnumber them, but she's still just clinging to him like you're the enemy here."

She gestured through the window where Galina was, in fact, hanging on to Alexei's arm while she waited for a soldier to open the carriage door.

I wanted to bite back at my cousin, but instead, I forced myself to consider her words. Was this niggling feeling in the back of my mind only an unwillingness to come to terms with Galina's choice?

Maybe Gwyn was right, and Galina, too. Maybe I was only seeing conspiracies where there weren't any. One by one, I weighed the things I knew, trying like hell to be objective about them.

Past my hurt, past Galina's resting Socairan face and even her hateful letter, there was a smattering of facts that didn't quite add up.

It was true that she hesitated every time I asked if she was sure about leaving her family, and went visibly pale when she received letters from her uncle. She also still wore Alexei's charm on her bracelet, but there were no letters exchanged between them the entire time she'd been at Lithlinglau. He hadn't been reason enough for her to stay in Socair, and she had vehemently denied any romantic involvement with him. She had left, forcing herself to ask for help, leaving the parents she loved, risking Unclanning.

Then she had thrown it all away and married him anyway, all for the sake of the obligations and duties she had willingly abandoned months ago. Or rather, had run away from.

I thought of her fingers caressing his arm, the way she leaned into him just as she had the night before we left Socair. Maybe she *did* want to marry him, for whatever reason. She had certainly made it clear she *didn't* want to marry me.

But there was a missing piece here, somewhere between the rebels and Alexei, our missing guards and Galina's impromptu flight.

"No." I responded to Gwyn at last. "There's something here."

She shook her head, her voice barely above a whisper. "How many times are you going to risk yourself for her, Davin?"

Frustration oozed from every word, laced with a heavy dose of exasperation.

"This isn't just about her." It was almost true.

"Then let me escort her, and you go back home," she said, her eyes wide and her tone challenging.

Right, because that wouldn't end in mass bloodshed...

"That would be an excellent plan," I replied diplomatically. "Except that we need information, and you aren't exactly a shining example in the art of subtlety."

She arched an eyebrow. "What could you possibly need to know more than you need to get back?"

I ran a hand through my hair and shifted on my feet. This conversation was nearly as enjoyable as the one where I had discovered Galina was married to Alexei, except that no one was ripping my heart out of my chest and setting it on fire.

"Whatever else happened, how the hell did Alexei get here without us knowing?" I sighed. "Don't you think that's worth looking into?"

A muscle tensed in her jaw. "Maybe, but I don't think it's worth what it's going to cost you. You and I both know that leaving like we did, being gone this long... It's not going to be pretty when we go back."

I rolled my eyes, forcing a nonchalance into my tone. "If you're so worried about it, you can go back and stall for time."

She narrowed her eyes. Gwyn may not have been subtle, but she wasn't stupid.

"You were always getting to that, weren't you?"

I shrugged, giving her a smirk I didn't quite feel. "In fairness, I also need you to look into the missing driver and whoever married the happy new couple."

She let out a slow breath, shaking her head once more.

"I don't like leaving you with this," my cousin said softly. "With them. I don't trust either of them."

"I don't either, Gwynnie," I said honestly. "But we need to know what's going on. You know what's at stake for our people right now."

She looked away. Neither of us liked being reminded that we were closer than we had been in decades to an outright rebellion. And all of these things, our relationship with

Socair, our reputation as royals, were feeding directly into their fire.

"It's important, and I know that," she acknowledged. "But you're important too, Dav, and all of these things that keep happening...you're right at the center of them. Don't you see that someone is trying to hurt you by any means necessary?"

I couldn't deny her words, not after the last few months. Still...

"They might be starting with me, but they'll be moving on to all of us. If we have a chance to head that off, to deliver them a blow, or hell, to at least stop them from delivering one to us, we need to find out all we can. I know you don't trust them, but can you trust me? Please? Or at least trust that I wouldn't be volunteering to spend the week across from my almost-fiancée and her new husband."

Gwyn hesitated for a long moment, her arms dropping to her side, before she finally relented. Whether it was because she was done arguing, or because she finally understood, I couldn't be sure.

"Fine," she said. "I'll trust you, Dav. But I sure as stars hope you know what you're doing."

I didn't respond. I wouldn't repay her trust with a lie, and we both knew I *didn't* know what I was doing.

All I could do now was hope that this time around, my instincts were leading me in the right direction. But that was a flimsy hope where Galina was concerned.

THAT HOPE WAS, indeed, in vain.

Each hour spent facing the newlyweds was like subjecting myself to a never-ending torture chamber. Slowly carving away at my skin with an apple peeler would have been preferable to watching Alexei and Galina practically cuddle under their shared blanket.

He made sure it was tucked around her completely before taking her hand in his possessively, and it took everything I had to keep my features casual.

Gallagher was also tense at my side. Whether that was because he was thinking about all the crow he would have to eat with Gwyn when we returned or merely stewing in his own sense of betrayal, I wasn't sure.

Galina pulled the blanket tighter around her, and Alexei tracked the motion in the low light of the carriage lantern. He produced a flask from his coat, uncorking the top and holding it out to her.

"Drink some vodka." It was as much an order as it was an offer.

"Or would you prefer whiskey?" I asked lightly, fingers drumming on my own flask.

Truthfully, I knew she would prefer neither, since the whiskey I brought was woodsy and strong, nothing at all like the one I had offered her in my rooms. But where she didn't love whiskey, she despised vodka.

Mostly, I just wanted to know how she would react.

"No, thank you, Laird Pendragon." She shuffled closer to her precious new husband, resting one hand lightly on his thigh while she reached for the flask with the other.

He smirked in satisfaction, and I shot him a cold smile. Did he honestly not know that she was lying, or did he just not care? Was it all the same to him?

With a single fluid motion, she took a delicate sip of what she had once sworn to me tasted like the astringent Gallagher used to clean wounds. Then she smiled, peering up at Alexei through her lashes.

"Thank you, My Lord."

He nodded, holding out his arm for her to lean against him. She did without hesitation, and he pulled her closer.

"You need rest, *Radnaya*."

And I needed a hearty serving from my own flask. Or possibly a bowl to hurl in.

Gallagher nudged me when I was finished with my swig, clearly desirous of some fortification of his own. I couldn't help but remember Galina the night before we left Socair, when she took Alexei's proffered vodka and lied through her teeth about it.

She had simpered then, too, leaning into him and trailing her hand along his arm while she whispered in his ear. Then she had shown up hours later desperate to leave Socair. To leave him.

And now, it was like nothing had changed. Between them. Between us. The last few months may as well never have happened at all.

Alexei tilted his head back and closed his eyes, though I knew he wasn't sleeping so much as taking a soldier's version of rest. Galina didn't close her eyes, but she avoided my gaze enough that it gave me a chance to study her.

She did look like she needed rest. The circles under her eyes were more pronounced when her face wasn't quite as guarded. It would have been one hell of a journey to have made the time she had by carriage.

And again, I wondered why. Why go to that trouble, staying in dangerous inns and hiding and traveling nonstop when she had to know we would have escorted her, perhaps not happily, but at least willingly.

Maybe she had been lying the entire time she was with me,

and she was sure as hell lying now that she was with him, but there was something more here, too.

The not knowing was going to drive me insane as surely as Alexei's proprietary hand on Galina's waist. I needed answers. As soon as I had them, I could return to Lithlinglau.

And let Galina return to her life without me.

Chapter Thirteen

GALINA

IT WAS a small consolation that Davin wasn't forcing me back to Lithlinglau. Instead, he was only forcing me to endure the world's most agonizing carriage ride under his casually scrutinizing gaze.

Another lurch of the carriage had my muscles straining and aching under the effort to stay perfectly still. I took a slow breath in through my nose, trying to ignore the bruises on my ribcage and spine.

I had to be even more careful than usual not to wince whenever the carriage jolted, unwilling to let Davin or Gallagher see just how weak I was with Alexei—to see the proof of injuries women in their family would have never endured to begin with. The smallest reaction would be a sure-fire sign that I was lying.

My fingers twisted the rosemary charm on my bracelet. Another bump and I bit the inside of my cheek.

Despite the thrumming pain, this carriage ride was still preferable to when we would eventually stop to sleep. The only thing worse than being forced to endure a wedding night with Alexei was having it occur under the same roof as Davin.

I wasn't sure I could bear that, wasn't sure I could keep up the show the next day even if I did.

I twisted the charm with the jeweled egg next, fiddling with the clasp as I replayed my fate over and over again.

But I didn't have a choice.

So I would find a way to endure.

After all, what was one more boulder in my veritable mountain of humiliation?

"Galina." Alexei's voice was sharp as his hand came to cover mine. My fingers stilled just over the smooth rubies hidden inside the egg-shaped charm.

I was too tired, too distracted by Davin's presence and all of these thoughts.

"Apologies, My Lord," I said automatically, clasping the egg shut once more.

Davin's narrowed stare burned into me, and I was grateful for the lantern's low lighting to hide the flush rising in my cheeks.

"It will take time to remedy the damage done by your time here, Radnaya." Alexei said it like he was being gracious, rather than insulting everyone in this carriage.

"Indeed," Davin said, a lethal edge to his airy tone. "Perhaps if you're fortunate, you'll forget how to speak entirely and save you both the trouble."

I opened my mouth to respond, but Alexei's hand tightened on my wrist, so subtly, his thumb exerting just enough pressure into the inflamed skin to make me bite back a gasp. Trying to make it look as casual as possible, I closed my mouth, looking toward the window, though the velvet curtains obscured any view I might have had of the outside world.

Perhaps Davin was right. Perhaps I would forget how to speak. Or would it just become so unnecessary that I would stop bothering? Alexei didn't respond, either, and a weighty silence filled the carriage once more.

When we stopped for our first break, Alexei went to talk to his soldiers, probably to inform them of our new plans, or perhaps about the rebels we were no longer working with.

I watched him anxiously. There hadn't been time to speak to him alone, to ask if our change in travel arrangements had affected his plans, or if he had been able to get word to whoever he needed to in order to keep my parents safe.

As it was, the only real comfort I had was in knowing that Davin had enough men with him and in the surrounding areas that he wasn't under any direct threat from Alexei or the Viper. Though I hadn't seen her, Gwyn had been at the inn, and she wouldn't have left if she hadn't thought Davin was safe.

I hovered near the carriage where Alexei had told me to stay, well within his line of sight. Gallagher and Davin went to talk to their own men briefly before the latter returned. He stopped short when he saw me standing between him and the door.

The air between us crackled with tension and anger and something worse, something I couldn't put a name to. Shame, maybe, at least for me. Even the stars seemed to be judging me, reminding me of all the times we had stood underneath them with an altogether different sort of tension between us.

My pulse raced as I took a step to the side that put me closer to him, hating the way I could smell the subtle hint of clove and spiced bergamot of his cologne.

"It's not too late for you to turn around." My voice was low, but I still worried it would carry through the still night air.

"And why would I do that?" He looked toward Alexei as he responded, each word forming a frosty cloud in front of him.

I took a breath, bracing myself to speak again.

"Because your presence is only making this harder on both of us." Did he hear the plea in my words?

He tilted his head to fix his cerulean gaze on me. "Is this hard for you, Galina?"

I should have thought about Alexei's hands on my skin, his lips intruding on mine, the vows we made just this morning. Instead, all I could see was Davin sitting two feet and a world away from me for endless hours in a carriage filled with animosity and lies.

The wall between us fractured just a hair, and bitterness rushed in to fill the cracks. He had to know it hadn't been easy to walk away, even if he couldn't understand why.

"Don't be a *laskipaa*," I bit out in a harsh whisper, careful not to let my voice carry. "You know that it is."

Davin scoffed. "I don't know, actually. What I know is that you said you would stay and you were gone by the next morning. You said you were leaving for duty, and I found you fawning over your former fiancé, so no, I'm not really sure that I know anything about you at all."

Part of me knew everything he said was fair, but it still stung, when he knew me better than anyone ever had. I told myself this was for the better. He would be angry, then he would move on.

"Then why won't you go back?" I hissed.

He ran a hand through his already disheveled locks, sighing bitterly. "Because people are trying to kill you, Galina, and I can't seem to smother the part of me that cares as easily as you do."

I was so wrapped up in my conversation with him, I didn't notice Alexei's return until the smell of wintergreen was accosting me.

"Did you get things taken care of with your men?" I asked quickly, forcing a lightness to my tone that I didn't feel.

It was as close as I could come to asking if my family was safe.

Alexei's eyes narrowed on mine, wrapping an arm around my waist to pull me closer to him and further from Davin.

"For now." His words were low, dangerous. A clear threat that if I didn't do what he wanted, he could destroy everything I loved. "What were you discussing, Galina?" His free hand wrapped around my upper arm, the part that was closest to him and out of view of the others.

He spoke in Socairan, so I answered in the same.

"Just plans for where we're stopping." My lie must have fallen flat, because he tightened his hold around the contusions that were already in the shape of his hand.

"Radn—"

"Lady Galina." Another voice interrupted the threat Alexei had undoubtedly been about to make.

Gallagher had crept on silent footfalls to stand between me and the carriage.

"Allow me the honor of escorting you, since I've hardly had a chance to greet you." His tone was odd, as was the request. Even more so that instead of waiting for me to respond, he reached out to grasp the hand that was closest to him.

Alexei practically growled, his hand on my hip tensing. "I don't know how things are in Lochlann, but in Socair, we do not touch another man's wife so casually."

"Apologies," Gallagher said, but he held on a second longer before pulling away.

His hazel eyes were silver in the moonlight, but there was no mistaking the way he looked me up and down before he finally removed his hand. It wasn't lewd, but rather...assessing. The scrutiny was uncomfortable, which must have been why I imagined his concerned stare lingering just a bit longer on my wrists, my arms, my ribs.

Each place where I was injured.

That was impossible, though. Surely. What I wasn't imagining, however, was the flash of rage on his features before he turned to climb back into the carriage, or the consternation on Davin's face as he watched the charged exchange.

Tendrils of dread crept along my spine like a warning. Whatever had just happened, I couldn't help but think it had changed things.

Chapter Fourteen

DAVIN

IF I THOUGHT the first part of the carriage ride was torture, then I didn't have a word for the latter half. Galina spent most of the journey glued to the window, as if hoping the thick curtains would miraculously turn transparent and give her a glimpse of the stars to lose herself in.

Her utter arseworm of a husband sat dispassionately at her side, his ever-watchful gaze on her.

Those things weren't unusual, in and of themselves. But for all I thought I wanted answers, as the pieces started to come together in my mind, it wasn't bringing me any sort of peace.

As the night wore on, Galina's façade slowly cracked at the edges, beginning with our conversation outside the carriage. From there, I started to notice other things. The lines under her eyes might have spoken to the hours we spent on the road, if it wasn't for the wariness that crept into her expression.

Similarly, the hesitation when Lord Arseface touched her could be explained by her general indifference to him. Except that she didn't just hesitate. She *froze*. A minuscule, almost imperceptible moment, a fraction of a second that could easily be dismissed if I hadn't been watching so closely.

Once I saw it, it was impossible not to notice the trace of fear hidden behind her delayed smile, or the almost frantic way that her hand rested on his arm.

Just when I thought I might be imagining things, there was Gallagher. He had refused to meet my gaze since his odd behavior on the break. Well, behavior that would have been odd, had I not known exactly what he was capable of.

The mystery wasn't what he was doing when he gracelessly stepped in to escort her to the carriage. It was why he felt the need.

We finally arrived at my chosen inn, putting a temporary pause on the endless questions. Though not the contention, of course, especially once I told Ewan how many rooms we needed, and it was one more than Alexei was expecting.

"My wife will stay with me." He bit out the words as we waited inside the carriage.

For a long, stilted silence, he challenged me with his glare, his beady brown eyes alight with fury.

A muscle clenched in my jaw, and I reminded myself of all the reasons I had decided not to set him on fire and be done with it.

"In your kingdom, you're free to do what you want," I began, sitting forward, not bothering to hide the threat behind each word. "But in mine, the woman I announced as my betrothed only a few months ago will not be staying in a room with another man."

It was a blunter approach than I might normally have taken, but it was late. We were all exhausted, and there was no way in hell I was letting him stay in the room with Galina when I still wasn't sure what was going on.

I had the power here, and he knew it.

Galina shot me a warning look he couldn't see, but I

ignored her. I didn't particularly trust anything she was trying to convey right now, not until I had more of the facts she refused to divulge for reasons only she knew.

Alexei's eyes burned with fury, and I met his gaze head-on. His anger was palpable when he turned to her, wearing an expression that was a curious mix of ownership and a challenge. There it was again. The barest widening of her eyes before she placed a soothing hand on his arm, leaning in to plant a chaste kiss on his cheek.

"It's only another couple of days, My Lord."

Nausea churned in my gut, and Gallagher's fists clenched at his side. Alexei pulled away, his shoulders not quite as tense and his lips tilted up in victory.

"Very well, *Radnaya*," he conceded. "For your sake, I will agree to these ridiculous terms. Of course, there will be a guard outside your door."

To keep her safe? Or to keep her in?

"Of course." She nodded, shooting me a nearly imperceptible sideways glance as Ewan approached the carriage door.

I nodded sharply in response to Alexei's demand, not trusting myself to speak. Our guards would be stationed in the hallway as well, so I took the not-quite-win without further commentary, desperate to get out of the carriage.

Once I was sure they were both in their respective rooms and Hamish was standing guard in the hall, I made my way to the room I would share with Gallagher. He trailed behind me like a man marching to the gallows.

As soon as I heard the door click shut behind him, I spun around to confront my cousin.

"Would you like to tell me whatever it is you're hiding?" I demanded.

He hesitated for a moment, clearly contemplating a lie. I could practically see the falsehood forming on his lips. At a warning glance from me, he snapped his mouth shut.

There went any lingering uncertainty I was harboring.

All he had to do was touch someone to see everywhere they were hurt. I had tried and failed to come up with another plausible explanation for him to step in the way he did. Even if he wanted to take the ire off Galina, it didn't make sense to incense Alexei by insisting on taking her hand.

Unless he had a damned good reason.

He took a deep breath, letting it out as he took a step further into the room. "It's not my place to—"

"Don't you dare." I bit out the words, cutting him off completely. He stopped moving, his auburn brows rising to his hairline as he clamped his mouth shut once again. "If you were so concerned with boundaries, you wouldn't have touched her to begin with, so tell me why you felt the sudden and overwhelming need to check her for injuries."

It wasn't something he did out of habit. He specifically tried to avoid being intrusive unless he had to.

He looked away, his jaw working. "Don't pretend you didn't see the way he was with her."

"Beyond typical Socairan arsehattery?" I wasn't sure why I was asking when the answer was written all over his face. But I was still hoping I was wrong, that he would deny it, that he would tell me he found nothing.

That hope died with the cautious look he flashed at me. "Dav—"

I shook my head, my body vibrating with rage. "No, you don't get to *Dav* me right now. You had no problem invading her privacy for your *own* knowledge."

Gallagher raised his hands in surrender as he took a seat on one of the narrow beds.

"In fairness," he sighed, sinking down into the old mattress, "it was an accident the first time."

"The first–" I started to ask, but then cut myself off when the answer dawned on me.

The first time, when he must have had to help her on and off of her horse on their way here, inadvertently touching her skin in the process. That was the reason she had been so desperate to leave, and still she had stood there with her stars-damned pride and risked the chance that I would tell her no.

Then what would she have done? Gone back to him, rather than tell me the truth?

Isn't that what she's doing now?

"How bad?" I barely got the words out. "At least tell me that, since you've apparently known for months that my fiancée was escaping a man who laid his hands on her and didn't damned well bother to tell me."

Gal exhaled slowly, empathy softening his expression. "They're minor contusions this time."

"But last time?" I pressed.

Had she been seriously injured when she sat in my rooms at Rowan's castle, her perfect features revealing none of the desperation she must have felt? When she slept on the freezing ground in the tunnels and rode for days on end to reach Lithlinglau?

When she insisted on taking every ounce of the blame for her departure from Socair, knowing the man who hurt her would surely find out?

"Last time, she was already safe in Lochlann," he said evenly. "This time, we were both biding our time for more information. Don't act like you're refraining from arresting him — or murdering him — out of mercy. You know as well as I do that something is off about this entire situation. It would have changed nothing for you, and she obviously didn't want anyone to know."

I shook my head, pulling the flask from my cloak and taking a long swig.

"Since when has someone wanting something to be kept secret stopped anyone in this family?"

Gallagher swiped a hand over his face, sinking into a solid wooden chair.

"She needed someone on her side." His tone was close to pleading, and something inside of me deflated.

Galina came to Lochlann entirely alone. She had no friends, no family. Gwyn didn't trust her or take to her, and she and I shared a tense, complicated history. I thought of her sleepless nights and her haunted eyes and her distant expression as she stared out at the endless night sky.

Though, it hadn't mattered in the end. She hadn't confided in Gallagher either.

"She may have needed someone on her side, but she sure as hell doesn't seem to want it," I muttered, taking a seat on the other bed. "Or at least, not from any of us."

"Not from anyone, I think."

I couldn't disagree, but I wasn't sure that was a consolation. Instead of focusing on that, I thought back to his earlier words. *You know as well as I do that something is off about this entire situation.*

"That's why you've been fighting so hard for her," I said as realization dawned on me. "You knew when she decided to go back that she was returning to someone who hurt her."

"I didn't know if it was him or her uncle or her father."

"Not her father," I said automatically.

The few times she had spoken to me about him, a peaceful smile had played at her lips. Her favorite charm was the rosemary one he had given her, and her interest in the herbs was entirely from him.

Gallagher nodded, like he had put that much together also. "But honestly, even then, I wasn't sure what it meant about her leaving. I'm still not. It isn't unusual for women to return to men who have hurt them, and she's had duty ingrained in her since she was born. Do I think he came to convince her? Sure. Could there be more to the story? I honestly don't know." He took a deep breath and shook his head. "Maybe I only want there to be more."

I ran a weary hand through my hair, picturing roughly seventeen thousand ways to eviscerate Alexei to slow my furiously beating heart. One way or another, I was going to see him dead, but first I had to figure out if there was a reason she hadn't let our guards take care of him back at Lithlinglau.

"There's only one way to find out," I said, taking another long swig from my flask. The whiskey burned my throat but refused to quell the anger brimming inside me. "In the meantime, we need to make sure he doesn't have access to her rooms."

"Already taken care of," Gal said.

Of course it is.

"Is there anything else you haven't bothered to inform me of?" My tone was heavy with sarcasm.

"No," he said, refusing to rise to my bait. "But I do have a subtle way to incapacitate the guards if we can wait until tomorrow to speak to her."

He glanced at the bag where he kept his herbs.

Grunting some form of assent, I walked out of the room before I could lose hold of my temper entirely. I might not be able to talk to Galina tonight, but there was someone else I needed to reach.

I HAD to write the letter three times before I could send it. I was so furious the first time that my quill kept poking holes in the parchment. The second time, I heard the fury in my words, and I couldn't bring myself to take my irritation out on the cousin who had put her life and happiness on the line for mine.

Finally, I managed something workable.

Dear Favorite Cousin,

Remember that time something disappeared from your kingdom and it had nothing at all to do with me, and I subsequently and unrelatedly got engaged? As it turns out, my (now previous) fiancée's previous fiancé (now current husband) made a trek to our dear homeland, and I am, at present, escorting them back to the tunnels.

If, perchance, there were a reason for their renewed relations outside of overwhelming desire for his sunny Socairan personality, might you be able to inquire as to what that could be?

We'll be taking the long way round, so you'll have to send word discreetly to our favorite inns.

All my love,

Dav

P.S. Speaking of sunny Socairan personalities, please accept my sincerest apologies for the roughly seven hundred and sixty-four irritable sighs you'll have to hear as your husband reads this letter over your shoulder.

. . .

As satisfied as I was likely to be, I rolled up the letter and marched out of the inn. In the past couple of days alone, the season had taken a sharp turn into winter. The ground was frozen beneath my feet, a thin coating of ice covering the walkway to the aviary.

Heavy snowfall sputtered from the sky, nearly concealing the figure rushing out of the building. It took me less than a second to place him — the smaller of the two Socairan guards. He had his hood drawn low, but he couldn't hide his warrior's stride or the Socairan sheath that peeked out from under his cloak.

I turned my face to the side, easing out of his field of vision. Once I had sent my own bird, I inquired after his, sliding a single copper coin across the counter.

"Socair?" I asked.

"Nay, mi'laird," the man responded. "There's only one bird trained to go through the tunnels, the one we're sending for ye."

Avani had managed to find a breed of falcon that could go through the tunnels, so at least I could get word to Rowan nearly as quickly as I could to my uncle now.

"Then where did his go?" I asked with a note of frustration.

He hesitated for a long moment until I withdrew two more coins from my purse.

"Bala village, mi'laird," he said, pocketing the coins.

I nodded, filing that away and adding it to the growing list of things that didn't make sense. A hazy picture was starting to form in my mind, one that might have made me furious if Alexei's death warrant hadn't already been signed.

Now I just added it to the growing list of reasons he had to die.

Chapter Fifteen

GALINA

DAVIN WAS FURIOUS.

Angrier than he had been yesterday. Perhaps angrier than I had ever seen him.

The signs were so discreet. His eyes were usually warm and amused and surprisingly patient, but today they were like twin shards of ice. His mouth was turned up at one corner like it always was, but the smirk was endlessly cold.

Where I had come to recognize Alexei's rage as a burning, palpable thing, Davin's anger was calm and icy and, I suspected, all the more lethal for it.

But what had happened between yesterday and today to put him in this state?

Or perhaps I was simply more observant, having finally enjoyed more than two scattered hours of sleep without Alexei in my bed.

I didn't think so, though. Gallagher was on edge as well, and neither was shy in their assessment when I climbed into the carriage. Their intense scrutiny made me feel nearly as uneasy as Alexei's growing displeasure with our current situation. He had fumed all the way from the inn.

"Did you sleep well, *Radnaya*?" The question was outwardly polite, but I knew better.

He had to see that some of the bruising under my eyes was fainter, the bags less pronounced. If I admitted I slept better without him, though, it would be a direct attack to his pride.

"Not as well as I would have with my lord in the room," I lied, willing my cheeks not to burn.

It was bad enough cowing to him, let alone in front of two people who knew me well enough to know that I was lying. I felt rather than saw the probing gazes from the other side of the carriage.

At least Alexei looked satisfied. Of course he did. Obedience over honesty, every time with him.

By the time I snuck a glance at Davin and Gallagher, they were both looking pointedly elsewhere, though a muscle ticked in Davin's jaw. Black stubble peppered the skin on the lower half of his face, thicker than I had ever seen it. His traveling clothes were simpler than what he wore at Lithlinglau, but they were still finely made and tailored to perfection, accentuating his broad shoulders and the muscles in his biceps.

He sat with his hands casually resting on his thighs, one of them holding the flask he occasionally pulled from.

"Galina." Alexei's sharp tone dragged me from my unwitting inspection.

Storms.

"Yes, My Lord?" I asked.

"I asked if you were ready to eat."

His eyes were already narrowed in ire, and I didn't have the right answer. Was he hungry? Had he asked the first time to be solicitous, or in a pointed manner? I tried to think back, but I had missed his words entirely.

When I took too long to answer, he reached for my wrist. I braced myself for the warning squeeze, but Davin was suddenly there, putting far more of his body between us than was necessary to knock on the panel behind us.

"Apologies," he said, not bothering to strive for sincerity. "I need to speak with Ewan."

If I were being charitable, I would allow that he had a pressing need to know when the next stop was, but somehow I doubted it.

"I, for one, am famished," Gallagher said as soon as Davin returned to his seat.

He pulled out a satchel with breakfast from the inn and all but shoved the contents in Alexei's lap. Alexei glowered, and I placed a hand on his arm. My permanent position for this ride, it would seem.

"I could eat," I said softly.

He grunted agreement, handing me my portion of the food, my punishment forgotten. For now.

The day went on in that fashion. The next time Alexei shifted near me, Gallagher had an immediate need to stop the carriage.

"Too much coffee, I'm afraid," he said, his tone only marginally more convincing than Davin's had been.

And so went a series of stops and interruptions that made increasingly little sense. By the time we stopped at the inn for the night, Alexei was livid, and my stomach was churning with an altogether different sort of dread than I had grown accustomed to at Alexei's hands.

Growing up, my mother had taught me how to knit, as all proper Socairan ladies could do. I hated the signs of my errors so much that I was given to unraveling the entire thing at the first missed loop.

That's what I felt like now, like I was one of those scarves, coming apart entirely as the result of a single mistake.

So when my door swung open on silent hinges that night, I wasn't half as surprised as I should have been. Still I froze, unwilling to turn around and face whoever had come into my room. Whether it was Davin's frigid ire or Alexei's blind rage or Gallagher's quiet disappointment, I wanted no part of what came next.

The door clicked shut, and I squeezed my eyes shut in a long, fortifying blink.

"What is he holding over you?" Of course, it was Davin. Had I ever really doubted it would be?

Each of his words fell like the first flakes of snow in a blizzard, heavy and portentous.

"What's who holding over me?" I shot back, forcing my features into an icy neutrality before I turned to face him.

As lies went, it wasn't my best work, but I hadn't expected him to hit the ground running that way.

He ran a hand through his hair, causing a single strand to tumble onto his brow. Then he let out a frustrated huff of air. "Aren't you tired of playing games, Galina?"

"This is not a game to me," I bit out.

Far from it.

Davin's expression hardened, his chest rising and falling too quickly. He crossed the room in three long strides, and my heartbeat picked up in my chest. This was nothing at all like the fear that overtook me when Alexei was close. Davin's nearness was dangerous in its own way, sending every one of my nerves on alert.

Perhaps that's why I was too distracted to notice when his hand stretched out to mine. I wanted to pull away, should have pulled away, but I was rendered immobile by the intensity of his gaze as it bored into mine.

Slowly, and so, so gently, he peeled back the sleeve to my nightgown, revealing the charm bracelet I never took off. And the purpling bruise underneath it.

So many things crossed his features, I could hardly read them all. Anguish and fury and resignation. His hand moved from my sleeve down to the mark, barely trailing over the discolored skin like he could heal it just with his touch.

"So you're just going back with him by choice, then?" he growled, his voice a sharp contrast to the gentle fingers still tracing the marks that Alexei had left.

I tugged my hand back to my side, and he released it without protest.

"I told you that I had a duty," I said.

His eyes snapped back to mine. "And this is part of it?"

I took a fortifying breath, reminding myself all over again why I needed to keep up this ruse. "It's nothing I can't handle."

Murder flashed through his features before he covered it with something calmer.

"I don't believe that you had a sudden, burning desire to return to a man who hurt you without a single bit of coercion," he said. "Not even for your precious sense of duty. Last chance, Galina. Tell me, or I'll walk into his rooms and extract that information from him myself like I wanted to do from the start."

Davin's tone was low, deadly in a way I had never heard it. Though it should have been the furthest thing from my mind, all I could think about was how *this* was the thing that pushed him over the edge. That he would torture and likely kill a man, not for stealing his fiancée or invading his kingdom, but for hurting someone he cared about. For hurting *me*.

I hesitated, though I wasn't sure why. There was no real choice here. Davin was filled with nothing but resolve, and if he made good on his threat, then all of this would have been for nothing.

Frustrated at my lack of options, I threw my hands at my side.

"You can't intervene. This is why I told you not to come." Did he hear the way my voice cracked slightly at the end?

"So Alexei could use you as his punching bag without interference?" His indignantly raised eyebrow only ignited my own anger.

"So I could do what needed to be done without having to worry about you putting the people I love in danger," I hissed, careful not to allow my voice to carry through the walls. "If you had respected my wishes–"

He shook his head, his ocean eyes hardening to ice. "Do not talk to me about respect right now."

I wasn't sure if he was referring to Alexei, or to the multiple and varied lies I had been telling.

"Just tell me what he's threatening you with."

There was a long silence where I held his stubborn *lask-ipaa* gaze. I hated him. I hated myself, and Alexei, and this entire *storms-damned* situation we were drowning in right now. Most of all, I hated that I couldn't even accomplish what I had hurt us both to do.

I was out of options, though.

"My parents." My whisper was hoarse. I hesitated only a second before adding, "And you."

Davin nodded, spinning to go without another word. My heart raced in my chest, my mind running through a thousand scenarios where one of the people I was trying to hard to protect wound up dead.

Because of me.

"You can't kill him," I called after him. "He can't know that you know. It's bad enough he'll know you were in here —"

"He won't," Davin replied without turning around. "The guard has been otherwise occupied for a few minutes. And I'm not going to kill him yet."

The *yet* hung in the air between us, filled with a promise. But Davin didn't realize all that was at stake, the reason Alexei had been able to so neatly corner me.

"You don't understand, he—"

"Is working with the Viper?" Davin cut me off. "Yes, I know."

He was still facing the door, so I couldn't be sure if the timbre in his voice was accusation or only frustration that I hadn't believed in his ability to unearth Alexei's secrets.

"What are you going to do?" I forced the question out through trembling lips.

Davin sighed, his fist clenching at his side.

"I'm going to take care of this." He said the words like they were obvious, or rather, like they should have been obvious to me.

The barest trace of bitterness laced his tone, a tacit disappointment in me for not trusting him with that very thing to begin with. I wasn't sure if that was fair. None of my choices felt clear anymore, let alone their consequences, and the people I loved were still very much in danger.

"Just...be careful, Davin," I whispered. "Be safe."

A single huff of air escaped him. "What, like you were?"

He didn't give me a chance to respond before he walked away, leaving me wondering what the hell I had just set into motion.

Chapter Sixteen

DAVIN

SLEEP DIDN'T COME EASILY that night, or the night after.

As soon as I had left Galina's rooms, I penned eleven letters for my contacts in Socair. I also sent one to Gwyn regarding the magistrate who had officiated their farce of a wedding.

Once she responded with his location, I sent a guard to take care of things.

His instructions were crystal clear: retrieve the marriage certificate and wrap up any loose ends. Given the magistrate's direct ties to the Viper, I felt no remorse in condemning him to death.

After that, there was nothing to do but wait.

The atmosphere inside the carriage was fraught with icy silence, further intensified by intermittent wintry weather outside. The wind howled and lashed against the carriage, compelling Galina to huddle even closer to Alexei for warmth.

I struggled to maintain my composure, resisting the urge to slit his throat as he wrapped his arm around her or tucked a blanket over her lap in some perverse display of affection. He truly did believe that she belonged to him, that she was his to hurt and protect as he saw fit.

Meanwhile, I could do nothing but sit quietly and count down the hours until I could end his life.

At the end of the second day, the innkeeper was certain to tell me that I would enjoy room number five, insisting that Gallagher and I would appreciate the view. Given my frequent stays at this particular inn, I knew this to be untrue, as the window overlooked the war-ravaged ruins. Still, my cousin and I accepted the key, drawing our swords as we entered the room – a move that left the waiting maid visibly shaken.

Gal shut the door, and we kept our weapons drawn as we made a rapid search of the room for any other guests who might have decided to visit. Once we were certain we were alone, I gestured for the maid to speak.

She timidly presented me with a small scroll, sealed and tied with a red ribbon. "This is for you, mi'laird," she said.

Her hand was trembling, even as I handed over a few coins as payment for her discretion. Gal apologized for the misunderstanding, seeing her out of the room while I focused on the scroll.

The ribbon dropped to the floor, and I used my dagger to cut the black wax from the scroll, slicing through the familiar image of a rowan tree to unfurl the letter.

Dearest Favorite Cousin,

It has come to my attention that the family of the person in question just so happens to be visiting their new in-laws. Supposedly, on purpose, despite being in such close proximity to the rather odious personality of someone I would just as soon have executed.

According to my husband, there is nothing we can do to step in, since, by all appearances, they are visiting of their own volition.

If your ladyfriend would like to speak on this matter when she returns home, we would be happy to greet her at the tunnels once she arrives.

MY ARSE AM I sending her all the way through the tunnels with Alexei.

Please write back soon and let me know how I should proceed.

All my love,
Row

P.S. Interestingly enough, Socairan law dictates that you are no longer considered married if your spouse dies.

P.P.S. I'm told that the elbow is one of the most painful places to be stabbed.

So that was how Alexei was doing it. Holding the Zhakarovs hostage in Wolf until he could force her to return. I considered what I knew of the intricacies of Socairan politics. The clans still retained a degree of autonomy from the throne, creating a substantial gray area when it came to inter-clan politics.

If the Zhakarovs were in Wolf willingly, or at least appeared to be, there wasn't much Rowan could do. Galina's word would pale in comparison to the influence of the Duke of Wolf and potentially the Duke of Ram.

Frustrated, I sat down to pen another stack of letters with clear instructions and significant bribes. It was good that I had built up a solid reputation for paying my debts, if nothing else, since I couldn't very well send a stack of coins with a tiny falcon.

If working above board wasn't an option, I would need to try more discreet methods. That was fine. My parents hadn't trained me to be the spymaster for nothing.

It was another two days of trying not to eviscerate Alexei before I heard back from my contacts. At least he wasn't an idiot, just an arseling. He caught on quickly that Gallagher and I would intervene if he tried to hurt Galina, so his attempts got less frequent.

He was probably comforting himself with thoughts of how he could discipline her once he got to the tunnels. My vision went crimson with rage at the thought, the words of my letter blurring.

"Bad news?" Gallagher asked.

"Actually, no, for a rare change. Just thinking about..." I didn't elaborate, and he didn't ask.

He knew exactly what would garner that level of ire from me.

"But it's done. Now we just need to figure things out on our end."

For the next several hours, Gallagher and I exhaustively explored every potential scenario, carefully weighing the pros and cons of each. We were down a couple of soldiers, plus Gwyn, and I wasn't willing to take chances where Galina's safety was concerned.

But there weren't many men we could trust.

"We need to involve the family," I finally told him.

"You want to ask Uncle Logan to come?" he raised an eyebrow, his tone dripping with skepticism.

We both knew of the political quagmire that would ensue if we asked the king to intervene in Socairan politics, and it would render it nearly impossible to deny Alexei had ever been here. But that wasn't who I was referring to.

"No." I shook my head, looking through the window to the snow-covered trees. "Our other family."

A small smile crept onto his lips while he followed my gaze. So I sat down to write one final letter.

I had a response before morning even came, written in familiar elegant script.

You know we do love a good time.

A savage grin crept onto my lips. Just one more day, then.

THE NEXT MORNING, we were silent as we entered the carriage. Even Alexei's shoulders seemed more tense, as if he knew there had been a shift in the air. He ordered his men to be on the lookout as we went deeper into the forest, though it was nearly impossible to see anything.

The sun barely reached through the canopy, and the snow-covered ground had blanketed us in silence.

Galina fidgeted nervously, and a pang of guilt gnawed at me. There hadn't been time to tell her our plan. Even if there had been, I didn't want to risk it. Not when Alexei was watching her so carefully, and not when I knew exactly how he would vent that anger.

I inhaled deeply through my nose, exhaling a frosty cloud in an attempt to steady myself. It was an impossible task, especially when I couldn't tear my gaze away from the way Alexei's hand remained tightly connected to Galina's, his thumb resting against the pulse point on her wrist.

As for her part, Galina kept up her show admirably. It might have been impressive how well she played the role of an adoring bride, if I wasn't so furious for her. At her. At everything.

But I supposed that wouldn't matter for too much longer.

Whether or not she trusted me to handle this, I had no intention of leaving her to this monster. Once he was out of the picture, she would finally be free to...make her own choices.

I hadn't allowed my thoughts to wander much beyond that point—didn't want to, not when everything was still so murky and uncertain.

Alexei shifted closer to Galina, and I tensed, ready to intervene. I might not be ready to think about what happened when this was over, but this...this, I could take care of.

I was so focused on the bastard's demented brand of affection toward her that I didn't hear it, at first, the commotion in the surrounding trees. Then Gallagher went rigid at my side, and Alexei's hand tensed toward his sword.

Ewan slowed the carriage, and Alexei shouted at him to keep going.

"The road is blocked!" he called back.

Adrenaline coursed through my veins, my heartbeat racing as the sounds drew closer. I pulled back the small curtain in front of the window, risking a glance outside. At the edge of the tree line were shadows, the few sparse rays of light that had managed to peek through the canopy glinted off of silver swords and the tips of arrows.

Galina's sharp intake of breath pulled my attention back inside the carriage. Her eyes were wide with alarm, and I felt guiltier than I should have when I made eye contact with her. I didn't want to care this much anymore, but my stomach churned at the fear behind her crystal-blue gaze, even more so when I opened my mouth to make it worse.

"It's the rebels," I said evenly. "At least ten of them. Stay in the carriage. I'll check it out."

"No, you can't," she shot back. Her cheeks blushed a deep shade of pink, panic creeping into her expression.

Alexei turned to glare at her. For speaking? For daring to argue with a man? For caring what happened to me?

It hardly mattered, though. Because just like I knew he would, the prideful bastard spoke up next.

"I will see to these rebels myself," he announced.

His shoulders were set in determination, but there was an undertone of concern lining his words. In his sick way, he did seem to care what happened to Galina, when he wasn't the one inflicting the damage.

He darted a glance between me and his unwilling bride before finally opening the door to the carriage and climbing down the small steps.

I exchanged a quick look with Gallagher, and he nodded grimly, turning to follow suit.

A sharp intake of breath passed through Galina's lips, her blue eyes shot with panic. I couldn't risk saying anything, so instead, I pulled out the tiny scroll that I had received from my man just yesterday, silently setting it down next to her.

Then I turned and left the carriage, drawing my sword with more anticipation than I ever had before.

Because honestly, after everything, I was going to enjoy this.

Chapter Seventeen

GALINA

I COULD BARELY HEAR my own thoughts over the drumming of my pulse in my temples. My chest was tight, my palms sweating as I lifted the parchment and carefully unfurled it.

The script was tiny, three squashed lines written in sharp, hurried Socairan.

It is taken care of.

They left once they knew their daughter was safe.

Out of enemy territory now.

HOPE WARRED WITH DISBELIEF, and I held my breath as I reread the lines two more times.

It had to be about my parents. They were safe?

The paper shook in my trembling hand, causing the lines to blur. This wasn't possible. It couldn't be.

Questions swirled in my mind like a tornado. My breaths came fast and shallow as my gaze traveled to the open door of the carriage. Gallagher was standing guard, his hand on the hilt of his sword and his attention fixed on the scene in front of him.

Suddenly, I heard everything, all of the sounds my racing thoughts had drowned out before. The clang of steel, the grunts of pain. Each clash of swords reverberated through the forest like thunderclaps, leaving a lingering tremor in the air.

I pushed the carriage door open further, to risk a glance at the rest of the scene. One of the Wolf soldiers lay dead at Alexei's feet, while the other had only just fallen to his knees, Davin's sword stained red as he wrenched it back from the man's body.

His blood sprayed out over the pristine white snow, while his lifeless eyes drifted closed.

Judging by their positions, they had died defending Alexei, who was still going strong in the center of whatever makeshift battlefield they had created.

He was completely surrounded by Davin and his soldiers, and these newcomers, who clearly weren't the Viper's men.

"Is it true?" I finally found my voice, holding the parchment out for Gal to see.

His gaze darted from the note up to my face just as a cry rang out across the road.

We turned just in time to see one of the rebels go down. Her dark ringlets fell into her face as she gripped her stomach, blood pooling from the wound out onto the ground. Davin called out for his cousin, succeeding in gaining the attention of Alexei as well.

Gal darted past me, dipping into the carriage to grab his medical kit.

"Yes," he said, before turning away once again. "It's true."

I hadn't realized I'd been holding my breath until he confirmed it. My parents were safe... My knees trembled and vision swam.

I didn't have long to feel relief, though, not when Alexei's sword was dripping with blood and he was circling Davin like a predator.

Davin gave a quick nod of his head, gesturing for the rest of the rebels and soldiers to fall back. Alexei let out a low laugh, a sound wholly unfamiliar in the rough cadence of his voice.

"You actually think you can best me in combat?" he asked, adjusting his grip on the hilt of his sword.

Davin arched a midnight brow, his eyes narrowing as he took up a defensive position. A ghost of a smirk crossed his lips, but fury blazed behind his eyes.

"I guess we'll find out," he said coolly.

Alexei glanced from me back to Davin, a flash of betrayal evident on his features before he lunged at Davin without warning.

Then there was a blur of motion, an endless clash of steel. I waited for the inevitable moment. Surely, if it came down to it, Gallagher would intervene. He wouldn't let his cousin die for honor. That's not who the Lochlannians were, certainly not the royal family.

But my fears, as it turned out, were unnecessary. Davin was grace in motion. He blocked each of Alexei's attacks with movements that bordered on lazy.

I had somehow forgotten that when I got out of the carriage, his sword was stained red with blood — that he had been fighting the Wolf soldiers and hadn't even appeared to break a sweat.

Another flash of steel, another thunderous crash of sword against sword. Davin ducked and weaved, dodging Alexei's attacks with the grace of a dancer. And he took advantage of his battlefield, pushing Alexei toward the uneven ground, using it to off-foot him until he stumbled.

The moment he did, Davin kicked up some snow and dirt from the road into Alexei's eyes, using the distraction to go on the offensive.

His sword sliced through the air with an intensity I had never come to expect from him. His expression was carved in stone, unyielding and unreadable as he brought his weapon down again and again like one of the relentless storms in Socair.

Gallagher came to stand next to me. In my periphery, I noticed the blood on his hands and the girl he'd helped, standing next to her friends — only barely nursing the wound that should have killed her.

Still, I couldn't focus on those things for too long, not when I could barely tear my eyes away from Davin and Alexei.

"Davin might be the least competitive of our family. He doesn't try when it comes to casual sparring," Gal said after a moment. "I think he likes to make people forget that he's trained with the best swordsmen in the kingdom since he was old enough to hold a blade."

Of course he did. Because Davin always had a plan, and half of that plan was in making people underestimate him. He didn't carry his power around on his shoulders, wielding it like a battering ram the way Alexei did. He carried it like a poisoned dagger, tucked out of sight and twice as deadly for it.

Alexei was not the only one who had underestimated him, and damn if I didn't hate being part of that short list.

It was over faster than I would have believed possible, with Davin's sword back at Alexei's throat. With a sweep of his leg, Davin forced Alexei to his knees, kicking his sword away in one swift motion.

Just as I thought he was going for the finishing blow, he

hesitated. His gaze found mine without hesitation, like he knew exactly where I was standing by instinct alone, like he was pulled to me by the same force that constantly tugged at my own soul.

"Your choice," he said quietly, speaking to me like we were the only two people in this clearing, in the world. "The sword or the cell."

I looked at Alexei, a giant felled by a man he had done nothing but mock. His face was impassive, every inch of him defiantly clinging to whatever pride he had left in the end. Being put in a cell — a Lochlannian cell, no less — would effectively rid him of that dignity.

Perhaps I should want that. Perhaps some part of me did want him to feel as small, as helpless, as insignificant as he had made me feel.

Wanted him to know what it was to be crushed under the heel of someone you would *never* be able to defeat.

But hadn't he ruled over my life for long enough? I didn't want the threat of his return looming in my existence. I didn't want to know he was alive out there, waiting for a chance to reclaim what he believed was his.

And more than any of those things, I didn't want to turn into the kind of monster who would hurt someone just because they could.

Not knowing whether it was mercy for a man who scarcely deserved it, or preservation for whatever was left of my sanity, I took a deep breath and looked Alexei straight in the eye.

"The sword."

Davin nodded once, though I barely caught the movement. With a flick of Davin's wrist, it was over. His blade was dripping with blood as Alexei's body slumped to the ground, his empty brown eyes still locked on mine.

Chapter Eighteen

DAVIN

I WIPED my blade off on Alexei's coat before sheathing it once again. It had been too quick. Too easy. Not nearly as painful as he deserved and not as satisfying as it should have been when I pictured the way he had loomed over Galina, trying to force her into submission.

Galina observed my actions with the same unflinching expression she had worn when I ran him through with my sword. The silence in the clearing grew intrusive, punctuated only by the steady drip of blood from Alexei's wound pooling on the frozen ground below.

I wasn't sure where to go from here, how to talk to my former fiancée when she was standing only inches from the encroaching puddle of her dead husband's blood.

A pointed throat cleared, bringing my attention back to the thieves. Well, former thieves, if they could be believed. They were family, though, and they had been the only people I could think to trust who were close enough to lend aid.

"Exquisite timing as always," I said with a lightness I didn't feel.

My not-quite uncles — and Fia — nodded in response.

The fae thief had aged scarcely five years in the more than twenty I'd known her, but her eyes held a weighty sort of discernment that belied her years. I looked away from the probing gaze, not wanting to know what she made of this whole mess I'd called her into.

"O' course, lad," Cray said, removing his well-worn hat and dipping into a bow. The years had aged him, hunching his shoulders so that his already-short stature only barely reached my torso. "We weren't never going ter let something happen to ye or yer wee lassie."

Galina blinked, and I bit my tongue before I could tell him she wasn't my anything anymore.

"Yes, gorgeous girl would be having our heads if we did," Sai added in his deep, accented tone. He was the complete physical opposite of Cray in every way. Tall with smooth, dark-brown skin, and a full head of hair. "I will never win her love that way."

"Yer an eegit, Sai. The queen was no' to be having ye before, and certainly no' when she's been marrit for over two decades now to a man a right lot prettier than ye are."

Rather than comment on Sai's longstanding, one-sided adoration of Aunt Charlie, I cleared my throat.

"Appreciation, all the same. We need to...take care of things here, then we should get going." Though, I wasn't sure where to go from here.

I had to get back to Lithlinglau, but I didn't know if Galina wanted to continue to the tunnels or make her way to Chridhe. It was one of many topics I would just as soon set myself on fire as broach with her right now. In any event, we had to take care of the bodies first.

One thing at a time.

Sai and Cray exchanged a look.

"Ach, no. What ye be needin' is some rest and a good

meal." He looked at Gallagher and Galina in turn, and a hint of concern showed behind his eyes. "All of ye."

"Aengus has the stew already cookin'," Sai added quickly. "Enough for everyone and then some. You wouldn't be wanting it to go to waste now, would you?"

I wondered what they had heard about the situation, or what they had gleaned from my short letter. The offer was more than a little alluring. Their home in Thieves Forest was safe and familiar, a smattering of tents and cabins always punctuated by the smell of whatever was cooking in the giant shared hearth.

Then there was Galina, still examining Alexei's rapidly cooling corpse like it held answers to the questions that relentlessly tormented us both.

But we had to get back.

"As tempting as that is, we need to be on our way."

Fia sighed in disappointment. "Just when I call you the least useless of the bunch, you go and prove me wrong."

Gallagher made a sound of offense, but she ignored him. Snow fell into her pale blonde hair and down onto her dark lashes as she fixed me with a glare.

"You look like hell. No one in your party has slept, and you'll move slower and be less safe if you take off in this state. You'll make up the time this way instead of falling prey to rebels. If you won't do it for yourself..." she trailed off, looking pointedly at Galina. "Do it so you don't undo all of our hard work in rescuing you."

"Besides, we might need Gallagher to check up on Ruby's injuries back at camp," Sai's son chimed in, looking anxiously at the woman with dark, curly hair and skin nearly as fair as the snow around us.

Fia smirked at that, and I rolled my eyes. None of them were wrong, though. We did need rest, and food. And I wouldn't forgive myself if Ruby died after coming to our aid.

My gaze drifted to the bodies. "All right, but we still need to—"

"The boys will be taking care of that." Sai gestured to the rest of their party.

Of course, they were used to disposing of bodies. More than one rebel had tried to find them before, but they didn't take kindly to those who tried to invade upon their haven. I nodded, finally forcing myself to address *her*.

"Galina," I said quietly. "We need to go."

She looked up at me, then back at Alexei's despicable body, her expression indecipherable.

"We burn our dead." She spoke for the first time since she ordered his death.

Was it a mistake, putting that decision on her conscience? I wanted her to have a choice, not a mountain of guilt to carry around. Though, it was impossible to tell what emotion she was hiding behind her icicle eyes.

"I know," I assured her.

All the more reason to bury Alexei, may he rest fitfully in whatever eternal slumber awaited him. Sadly, we were too close to the forest, and frost had already settled into the ground.

"The lads will build a pyre," Cray confirmed, and she nodded.

Another uncertain beat of silence passed before Fia gestured for us to follow on foot into the depths of the forest.

"We may as well take the fast way home."

THE SAVORY SMELL of stew and the sweetness of freshly baked bread greeted us as soon as we made it to the home of the thieves. Aengus, who served as somewhat of a leader, came out to meet us. He was old enough to be my grandfather, but he moved with all the spryness of a much younger man.

Unsurprisingly, he didn't comment on the unusual circumstances of our arrival or on Galina's presence.

That was what I loved most about being here. We could show up in any state, after any event, and be welcomed with good food, a stiff drink, and a pat on the shoulder.

Gallagher led Galina to the fire at the center of camp, sitting down next to her on one of the logs that served as benches while I hung back to talk with Fia and Aengus. It was just as well. I needed a moment to breathe.

"How've you been, Davin?" Aengus asked evenly.

"Or as I like to call him, Mini-Oli," Fia amended.

"Let the lad alone, Fia," Cray said. "He's a lot better than his father was back then."

The man shivered dramatically, and Sai slapped him upside his balding head.

"That's not saying much," Fia responded with a shrug, but I didn't miss the way her eyes roved over me with genuine concern, somehow twice as discerning with their different colors — one nearly golden and the other a bright blue.

I tried to shore up my expression while Cray and Sai argued over who wanted to strangle my father more the first time they met him.

"We be liking him now, and that is all that matters," Sai assured me before they both took off in the direction of food, where Galina had gone.

Aengus, Fia, and I followed, settling across the fire.

I tried to take solace in the familiarity of Cray and Sai's banter, Aengus' steady presence, and Fia's lethal protection, but my gaze returned endlessly to the figure on the other side of the campfire. Gallagher sat next to her, and they were talking in low tones.

Part of me wanted to go to her, to say something to help chase the shadows out of her eyes, but that wasn't who we were to each other right now. Hell, I wasn't sure that was who we had ever been to one another.

We didn't have a history of comfort, of anything resembling a real relationship. Just fleeting moments on a rooftop in the dark.

Forcibly wrenching my attention away, I turned to Fia and Aengus, broaching the subject I would have been happy to never think about again.

"Have either of you heard anything?" I asked.

I didn't need to clarify. They were just as plagued by the Viper's reach as we were, though they were a little more protected by their hidden camp and the safety of the forest.

Fia raised an eyebrow, and it tugged at the scar that sliced through her blue eye. "Not since last time you wrote."

I looked at Aengus, who shook his head. "I'd tell ye if we had, lad."

"And the poison?" I asked.

Fia let out a low whistle. "It's like nothing I have ever seen, which is saying something."

I opened my mouth to ask another question, but she shook her head, nudging me with her shoulder. "There's nothing else. Take the night to rest."

I ran a hand through my hair, thinking how unlikely that felt when there was so much left to take care of.

"I will, after I get Galina settled and figure out what the hell we're doing tomorrow." We had left the carriage in the clearing, but it was a slow way back, anyway.

Gal and I had brought our horses, and there were the extras from the Socairan guards for whatever Galina decided to do...

"And I need to write Row," I added as an afterthought, running a hand through my hair.

Fia studied me before exchanging a look with Aengus that I was too tired to read. She got to her feet with the lethal grace of a predator, disappearing before returning with a quill, parchment, and a cup of warm mead.

"I'll take care of the girl," she said. "We can figure out the rest tomorrow."

"Galina–"

"Will be fine tonight," she said, all but shoving the cup and the left-handed quill into my hand. "We'll get her wherever she needs to go tomorrow."

"All right," I agreed reluctantly, taking the parchment and focusing on what I would say to my cousin rather than all the conversations I wasn't ready to have with Galina.

Fatigue weighed heavy on my bones, but Rowan deserved to know what had happened. I couldn't very well go announcing all the details in the event the bird was intercepted, so I settled on something short.

Dear Favorite Cousin,

I was moved to take your advice on the matter of Socairan law, and it has thusly become a nonissue. Unrelated, I took a trip to see our uncles. We built a bonfire - a cleansing ritual, if you will – purging ourselves of all the demons of our past.

I, for one, feel much invigorated, though I wish you had been here to enjoy it.

Stars, but I did. With a bottle of vodka and a plate of pastries and a ridiculous story about the last time she stuck her foot in her mouth in the stuffy Socairan Court.

In other news, apparently visiting one's new in-laws isn't all the fun it's cracked up to be, since the family in question is, at present, on their way home. They may stop in to say hello.

All my love,

Dav

P.S. I'll be sending a case of whiskey as soon as I get home. You know, as a thank you for whatever headache this may or may not cause you, or your husband, or likely, both.

P.P.S. Please assure him of my deepest devotion. I feel like it's been a while, and he's probably worried my affections have waned.

That was another thing I needed to follow up on. It had taken a great deal of gold and not a few threats to get Galina's parents out of Nils' estate in a way that wouldn't give the bastard cause for retaliation. At least, not by law.

He was hardly going to miss the fact that his hostages had left just as his nephew stopped checking in. By all accounts, Galina's father was smart. Once he knew she was safe, he would likely be taking measures to keep himself and his wife safe.

It wasn't something I wanted to leave to chance, though, so I sat down to pen a few more letters, just to be cautious.

And if it kept me from the campfire where Galina sat with her unfathomable expression and her thinly veiled scrutiny, that was just an unfortunate coincidence.

Chapter Nineteen

GALINA

THE ATMOSPHERE in the forest had gone from quiet and tense to loud and bustling as soon as we entered the makeshift village.

Rows of cabins, some new and some older, stretched out over a small clearing. Music filled the air as a few of the villagers played instruments by the fire, and laughter rang out along with the rumble of conversation.

The snow didn't fall as heavily here, and more sunlight streamed through the canopy than had on the road. It was warm in a way that had little to do with the roaring fire.

It took me a while to name what was so different about this place, the concept so foreign to me these past couple of weeks.

Safe. It felt safe.

Or maybe I was just becoming numb.

The woman named Ruby approached, introducing herself with a bow and a flourish that made her wince, before focusing her attention on Gallagher. She sat next to him while he inspected her wound, her green eyes bright as she spoke excitedly about things that had transpired since they last saw each other.

Every now and then, she twirled her bouncy brown curls around her finger while she watched him work. I was content to sit on the outside of the conversation, absorbing the sights and smells around me.

I still didn't know what to make of the people who had apparently come to our rescue. They weren't soldiers, obviously. Were they friends? It would seem so, by the way Davin and Gallagher both eased in their presence even when some of their men had stayed behind to take care of...things, but I couldn't quite feel the same amount of calm.

Couldn't feel anything, really.

"Here, lass." The small man from earlier pushed a steaming bowl of soup into my hands with a fresh roll on top.

Nodding in thanks, I perched on the edge of the log, allowing the heat from the small wooden bowl to warm my hands.

"We didna get to properly introduce ourselves earlier. Name's Cray, and–" he began, but a tall, dark-skinned man cut him off.

"We are the crooks of the cozy copse, the heisters of the hazy holt, the raiders of the –"

Cray reached up to smack the other man on the arm. "Shut it, Sai. We're just humble t'ieves, milady."

I blinked. In Socair, thieves were punished with losing a hand, but here, they were friends with royalty. I couldn't muster the energy to wrap my head around that, so I only nodded again.

"And when yer ready, we've made up a few tents just o'er there." He gestured toward three tents, open to reveal makeshift mattresses made of furs that looked surprisingly cozy.

"Thank you." I said the words aloud this time, finding

that I meant them sincerely. Doing things the Socairan way hadn't gotten me very far lately, anyway.

Cray smiled widely, revealing several golden teeth before tugging on Sai's arm and turning to walk away.

I forced myself to take a bite, not wanting to appear rude. The flavors reminded me of home — seasoned beef and vegetables in a thick broth. I took another bite with far less reluctance, my gaze flicking up to catch Davin's on the other side of the fire.

He quickly looked away, returning to his conversation with the man at his side — the one named Aengus — who I took to be the leader of the whole establishment. The ethereally gorgeous woman joined them, shoving a mug and quill into Davin's expectant hands. It gave me a chance to finally study her.

Her hair was silvery blonde, a common color in Socair, contrasting with olive-toned skin that was barely a shade lighter than mine. A suspicion formed in my mind. She met my eyes like she knew what I was thinking and was daring me to voice it aloud.

"I would say she's not as scary as she seems, but that would be a lie." Gallagher sat next to me holding a similar roughly hewn bowl.

"I gathered that," I said shortly.

"You don't have to worry about her, though. She's family to us."

I wasn't sure if he meant that I didn't have to worry about her murdering me or didn't have to worry about her with Davin, but I chose to believe the former, even if his knowing look said otherwise.

"I wasn't," I lied. "Do you know where she's from?"

"No. No one asks questions here. You share your story if and when you're ready to." Gallagher looked at me, and I looked away.

It was an odd sort of comfort, knowing that perhaps I wasn't the only one who had left behind a life in Socair they would just as soon never think about again.

"I'm sorry," he said quietly.

"For what?" I asked, bafflement plain in my tone.

For staring? For coming after me?

He shook his head like he wasn't sure of the answer either. "For not coming to you sooner. For not being someone you could trust. I was your friend, and I can't help but feel like I failed you somewhere along the way."

"It wasn't that simple," I told him, looking away. "And I'm certainly not the only one who kept secrets."

He didn't respond right away, and my stomach sank. It shouldn't have mattered. One more casualty in the wake of Alexei's destruction. One more divide I didn't know how to bridge.

Then Gallagher sucked in a breath, nodding as though he had come to a decision.

"Well, if you aren't ready to share your story, then I could start by sharing mine."

My lips parted. "Why would you offer that to me, after everything?"

He gave me a small smile. "Because I care about you. Because you're family, whether you like it or not. And honestly...because you're going to need someone on your side. Especially once we catch up to Gwynnie."

I swallowed hard, not only at the reminder of the person who most certainly hated me by now, but because I couldn't truly consider Gallagher's offer when I could never return it. At least not now, not when the words felt stuck in my throat, burdened by the weight of things I might never be able to say to anyone.

"You don't have to live in the shadow of everything that's happened," he said in a voice so quiet it was nearly a whisper.

It didn't feel true. My eyes wandered back to Davin as he accepted a bowl of stew from Sai, tipping his head in thanks. He felt further away than the small clearing accounted for.

"Some things can't be undone," I said darkly.

Gallagher tentatively stretched a hand out toward my wrist, which I belatedly realized had become uncovered when I lifted my spoon to my lips.

"And some things can," he whispered.

My brow furrowed, my mind racing through the tiny, irrational suspicions I had considered these past few days. He met my gaze evenly, just the smallest raising of his brows indicating the challenge he was putting forth.

Would I let him take this first step toward trust?

I took a deep breath, considering. Wherever things stood between me and Davin, Gallagher had been nothing but a friend to me. So I placed my wrist in his waiting hand. I had no idea what to expect, but I knew that he would never intentionally cause me pain.

He nodded, looking around at the empty seats around us before he gently closed his fingers around the contusion. Heat covered my skin, and I gasped. It wasn't uncomfortable, precisely. More like the soothing warmth of a sauna.

"What?" I asked.

The edges of his lips curled into an uncertain smile, and he pulled his hand away. I looked down at my wrist, shaking my head in disbelief.

The bruise was gone, and so was the pain.

"How?" I choked out. "It's like something from a *vila* story."

He furrowed his brow, and I searched my mind for a translation before shaking my head.

"Children's tales about magic, like your faerie stories," I finally landed on.

"You're not too far off." He chuckled. "Though this is more science than magic."

I pieced that together in my mind.

Though it should have been impossible, somehow the knowledge that Gallagher could heal felt right, less jarring than the rest of the events of the day. It fit with what I knew of the girl who had miraculously recovered from her head wounds after the rebel attack, the way Gallagher could diagnose without so much as spotting an injury. Even today.

I glanced up at Ruby who was yawning and leaning her head on her friend's shoulder while they laughed about something Cray was saying. Alexei had stabbed her. She was badly bleeding out on the road less than an hour ago.

Still, the idea was...unfathomable.

"I'm not sure I understand," I admitted.

"Well," he said, pitching his voice low, "the logistics are easy. I can coax your body to heal itself, within reason. Though, it does take energy from us both. Some wounds or illnesses are beyond my reach. The *how* is a longer story, one that involves more secrets than are mine to tell."

"Davin?" I couldn't help but ask.

"Has no secret abilities hiding anywhere. But for whatever it's worth, he didn't need them to put things together. He figured it out nearly as fast as I did, and I had an obvious advantage."

I filed that away, not ready to face the implications of it yet, the exposed feeling of being constantly laid bare before Davin.

"Did you always know, then?" I asked, averting my gaze.

He must have. He had helped me onto my horse when I first arrived. For some reason, the realization made my cheeks burn to consider. All the work I had put into hiding the state I was in, and he had always known.

"That you had been hurt?" His tone was gentler than his

blunt words. "Yes. I can tell by touching someone where their injuries are."

"So that's why you were so nice to me," I mused aloud.

"No," he said firmly. "I was nice to you because I liked you, and because I, not being half as blind as either of my cousins, could tell that you loved Davin." He raised an eyebrow. "Now, are you done looking for reasons to chase everyone away?"

I hardly had to look for reasons, but the truth of his words sank in anyway.

"Likely not," I said, returning the honesty he had just given me in spades.

"Look," he remarked, all false airiness. "We're trusting each other already."

I shook my head again. I shouldn't have felt even the slightest bit lighter. The smoke from Alexei's corpse seemed to follow us into the forest, mingling with Davin's ire and the weight of my mistakes.

Maybe it was Gallagher's friendship, or maybe it was the unblemished skin on my wrist, the revelation that I would never have to wear Alexei's brand again, but somewhere sitting on a log in the middle of a band of outlaws, I almost started to feel like I could breathe again.

Chapter Twenty

DAVIN

I SHOULD HAVE KNOWN that something was off the day before – would have, if I hadn't been so distracted. It was in the look exchanged between Sai and Cray, the way even Fia insisted we rest at their camp for the night, the mead she had brought me herself.

Even now, the camp was oddly quiet for a typical bustling morning with this many people present.

But I didn't put those things together until I heard the sound of thundering footsteps right outside of my tent. I didn't have time to react, or even sneak out the other side of my tent before two massive hands ripped apart the sides of the opening, letting an obscenely bright burst of light shine through, followed abruptly by a massive shadow.

"Fancy finding you here," a familiar voice boomed.

It was my luck, really, enduring everything that had happened with Galina and the Viper and stars-blasted-damned Tavish only to wind up here, facing down the most feared man in our entire kingdom when I was less than half awake.

"Good morning, Uncle Logan." I sat up, wincing.

Stars, I hadn't had that much to drink last night. Though

more than I should have, since the thieves had apparently been luring us into a false sense of security until my uncle showed up.

"Ach. It's a good morning when I don't have to drag my men to Thieves Forest to track down both of my eejit nephews," he bellowed, stepping further into the tent. "Dinna fash, though. You were easy enough to find, once I followed the trail of smoke from the corpses ye left behind."

That last part was clearly for dramatic effect since my uncle knew perfectly well where the Thieves Forest was.

My gaze moved behind him of its own accord, pulled in the direction of Galina's tent.

He sighed. "The lass is safe. She's drinking her coffee with Gal and Ruby."

"Is everyone awake, then?" Another suspicion formed in the back of my mind about why I was so groggy, and I cursed. "I should have known not to trust them."

"Ye really did need rest, lad," Cray said, edging in next to my uncle.

"We only be looking out for you both and the girl." Sai crept in as well, looking thoroughly repentant.

"Don't lie to the kid," Fia chimed in. Her features held none of Sai's remorse. "We just like him less than the king."

"Oh good, you're here, too," I muttered. "I'm glad we could all be here together this morning in my very small tent."

"Did you sleep well?" she asked innocently.

I narrowed my eyes. "You would know."

She shrugged, unbothered by being found out.

"Did you drug the others, too?" My tone was all false lightness. "Or was that honor reserved for my drink?"

Fia smirked. "No, they went to sleep when I told them to. You were the only one insisting on guarding your lover's tent instead of getting some stars-damned rest."

I threw my pillow in her general direction but only succeeded in hitting Cray when she ducked behind him.

"All right, ye numpties," my uncle said, catching the pillow before it came sailing back toward me. "I need a moment alone with the lad."

With a few grumbles and threats to withhold my breakfast, the three filed out, allowing me some breathing room with the king of Lochlann.

"How bad is it?" I asked, fumbling around for my clothes. It wasn't hard to guess the answer if he had come himself.

"How bad is it that ye ran away when the whole blasted court suspects ye of murdering your own family, or how bad is it that ye aren't there to defend yourself?" His brogue thickened with each word, a sure sign that he was upset.

"In my defense, I didn't actually kill him," I said, lacing my trousers.

Uncle Logan sighed, running a hand over his face and cropped beard.

"I know that, lad," he said. "If ye'd have done it, ye never would have gotten caught."

I grunted in acknowledgement, pulling my shirt over my head.

"But ye need to be there, finding out who did."

"I'm not sure being there will make a difference," I muttered, lacing up my shirt and running a hand through my hair. "I'm no closer to figuring out who the Viper was than we were a few months ago, unless you count the fact that we've effectively ruled out Tavish."

He cursed under his breath.

"One thing at a time. At the very least, we need to get back to get the blame away from you." Now that he had gotten his ire out of his system, he had already started to calm down, evidenced by his lightening brogue.

The trick with him, much like Avani, was to keep them

talking until they no longer had the desire to yell. It was a coveted artform, passed down from my father to me.

"If you were in such a rush, why did you insist on making sure we stayed here until you caught up?" I asked, only being a little sarcastic.

"Because I dinna trust the lairds if I'm not there to intervene on your eejit behalf right now," he said darkly.

On that auspicious note, we emerged from the tent to join the others for coffee. At least, that was my intention, until Uncle Logan called for the men to be prepared to leave.

Galina looked up, surprised either at the sheer volume of his booming voice or his proclamation. Gallagher, on the other hand, blew out a breath, not even bothering to hide his relief at escaping my uncle's wrath. Which, of course, did not escape the king's notice.

"We'll be having words later," he said, causing the corners of Gallagher's mouth to pull down. "But for now, we need to get moving."

I tried to decipher Galina's features, but aside from the initial widening of her eyes, they revealed nothing.

"You're free to do as you wish," I told her, stepping closer and pitching my voice lower.

She blinked, and I tried not to think about the reality of what I was offering. About the fact that she might take me up on it, and I might never see her again.

Or that she might stay, which felt...complicated, in its own right.

"I already spoke with the thieves about escorting you," I explained in as neutral a tone as I could manage. "Rowan says she'll meet you on the other side of the tunnels, or you can go to your uncle in Chridhe, or–"

"No," my uncle interrupted me. "Her uncle is already on his way to Lithlinglau, and we have things to take care of there. All of us."

He shot me a pointed look, and I surmised that someone in my family had let slip to him that Galina was my only alibi. The last thing I wanted was to force her into one more thing on the grounds of duty or obligation, especially when the lairds weren't likely to believe what my former Socairan fiancée said anyway, but my uncle had no such compunctions.

"She's free to do as she will after, but for now, the lass needs to come with us." Though his emerald eyes weren't unkind, he spoke in his king voice, as Rowan and I had dubbed it.

And there was no arguing with that tone. Not for any of us.

Chapter Twenty-One

GALINA

We were switching to horseback for the return journey to Lithlinglau. One of the thieves had retrieved my trunk from the carriage, but I wanted nothing to do with any of the items in it.

The night before, Fia had offered me a nightdress that I took gratefully, ripping off the dress I was wearing and all the memories that came with it. After a moment's hesitation, I had taken my bracelet off, too.

This morning, she had brought a fresh gown for the day shortly before the trunk arrived. The hem was a bit short, but otherwise the fit was workable.

My bracelet weighed heavy in the deep pocket of the dress. Part of me wanted to leave it behind with the dress where I would never again have to feel the edges of a charm biting into my wrist and see Alexei's ghost bastardizing yet another thing my people had held dear.

But I couldn't quite force myself to part with it. Neither could I put it back on, though my wrist felt as empty as the rest of me. So instead, I tried to forget about its existence entirely.

Reluctantly, I crossed over to the trunk to pick dresses for the road while Davin and Gallagher were readying their horses. The idea of changing back into one of the dresses that Alexei had chosen for me made me feel like centipedes were crawling on my skin, burrowing straight through to my insides.

I wasn't sure if Fia could tell by my expression, or if she liked the idea of trading, but before I could be forced to open the trunk, Fia appeared once more.

"Here," she said, holding out a pair of riding boots along with a satchel. Inside were two more wool gowns. "These will likely be more suited for the weather than that thin gown you were wearing yesterday."

When I didn't respond right away, she added, "If you're really attached, I can always send the trunk—"

"No," I said quickly. I wish I had asked them to burn it yesterday, along with Alexei's body.

She met my gaze, tilting her head as if she could hear the unspoken thoughts in mine.

"Noted," she said with a dip of her chin. Then she ordered the man to take the trunk to her cabin before offering a small salute as a goodbye.

We rode hard through the day, stopping well after dark. My body ached and my lungs burned from the cold, but all of it was preferable to another stint in that storms-forsaken carriage.

Still, whatever respite I had managed to find in the forest dissipated like the hazy puffs of steam from our breaths by the time we finally stopped for the night at the inn.

Perhaps that was only the looming threat of seeing my uncle, or the way that the smoke from the pyres had still been burning when we rode out this morning. Or perhaps it was the secrets in the glances between Gallagher and Davin and the king, questions I couldn't ask without answering some of my own.

So I didn't try, instead losing myself in my own complicated feelings about heading back to Lithlinglau when I had no idea where things stood with Davin and me.

Even now, he was framed by the black smoke that plumed high into the sky, the remnants of everything that towered between us. I had married someone else, and he had ignored my request not to interfere, then all but told me to go home. Where the hell were we supposed to go from here?

Would I have taken him up on it? I had been so shocked when he suggested it, the idea that I was finally free from Alexei's reign of terror. My uncle would likely forgive me to save face. My parents missed me. I could go home.

The problem was that home no longer felt like a colorful castle nestled in a snowy mountaintop village. But somewhere in Davin's distant gaze and his icy *free to do whatever you wish*, I wasn't sure what my other options were.

Even if I could have forced myself to ask, I hadn't spoken to him all day. Our breaks were short and seldom, the pace grueling under the watch of Lochlann's former Captain-of-the-Guard-turned-King. I was exhausted and sore by the time we finally made it to the inn, and no closer to any answers.

After a short conference with Davin in which there appeared to be some sort of disagreement, Gallagher escorted me upstairs to my room. Someone must have sent word ahead, because there was a steaming bath waiting for me.

Then I was alone, taking my first pain-free bath in over a week.

Last night, between the steady, soothing noises of the camp and the fatigue from Gallagher healing the rest of my bruises, I had passed out almost immediately. There hadn't been time to think. To feel. To do anything but sleep before Gallagher woke me for coffee, followed by a long day on the road.

It should have felt freeing, the silence. All my life, I had relished the opportunity to be alone to think, to process, but my thoughts were too loud, and the solitude, even more so.

Even the swish of the water and pad of my bare feet on the wooden floor sounded obtrusive in the empty space. I could still feel Alexei's gaze on my bare skin, the odd way he regarded me with protectiveness and resentment and disdain and the slightest bit of curiosity. His death had put an end to his questions, but certainly not to mine.

Had his uncle forced him to come? If I had been a better fiancée to begin with, one who wasn't already in love with another man, if he hadn't sensed that distance from me, would our lives have gone differently?

It shouldn't have mattered after everything he did, but the thoughts haunted me all the same.

Was this the way Davin had felt when he had sentenced the traitors to death? Like you were judging the difference in a stolen life weighed against your own soul, however justified?

Over and over again, I could see the flicker of acceptance when Alexei knew he was going to die, the fleeting moment of gratitude when I granted him a strange form of mercy in the form of death.

It contrasted with the memory of his fingers digging into my skin, the endearment I despised nearly as much as the sharp, clipped way he would utter my name in three distinct syllables of disappointment. The pieces of him were jagged and mismatched like a broken blacksmith's puzzle, each one bearing down on my soul with a suffocating weight.

I didn't regret my decision, and I didn't regret being the one to make it. That didn't stop me from picturing his dead eyes staring from a burnt corpse as I slipped my nightgown over my head, from wondering if his family would mourn him or only regret the loss of the future of their clan.

My heartbeat thundered in my ears, so loudly that it took me a moment to realize the rhythmic thud wasn't only coming from me. Instead, there were two solid raps against the solid wood door.

It was too insistent for Gallagher, but altogether different from Davin's impatient tapping. I crossed the floor, easing the door open. When I caught sight of who was on the other side, my eyes widened in shock.

"Davin," I breathed. "Your knock was wrong."

He only blinked at that, uncharacteristically quiet. There was no banter, no emotion at all coming from his perfect façade. He, too, had bathed, and shaved, apparently. The shadow on his defined jaw was gone. His hair was still disheveled, but it was more intentional now.

He looked pointedly behind me, and I stepped aside, scarcely daring to breathe.

"Ewan and Hamish are exhausted," he said once the door was shut.

"All right." My tone lilted at the end with the barest indication of a question.

He took a deep breath like he was frustrated I wasn't putting something together. Was he looking for an apology? A solution?

"There are other guards, of course," he explained slowly. "But given the situation with the rebels and...recent events, I don't plan to leave you at the mercy of strangers."

Oh. He was here to stay.

Why did that fill me with a mix of relief and terror, an overwhelming cocktail of safety and grief I couldn't quite choke down?

"I—" I stopped, not sure what to say from there, and he ran a hand through his hair, tousling the damp locks even more.

"There's no need for us to talk, certainly not tonight." His tone was carefully detached. "Just get some rest, Galina."

Relief and terror. Safety and grief.

I would have argued if I had been capable, or if I hadn't sensed that he was saying the words as much for his own benefit as for mine. Instead, I only nodded, mutely watching Davin fall onto the small sofa before I climbed into my bed with all the pretense of going to sleep.

But sleep never came for me.

Chapter Twenty-Two

DAVIN

THOUGH I WOULD SOONER DIE than admit it to her face, I wished Gwyn had stayed.

Now that we were out of the safety of the forest, she could have been in here with Galina without rousing the suspicion of the entire squadron, and she loved me enough to keep Galina safe no matter her personal feelings on the matter. Besides, Gwyn stirred at the first sign of intrusion. She had proven that more than once.

Maybe then I could have gotten some sleep.

Or maybe it would have always been a lost cause when I could hear Galina's ragged breaths from the bed, when I homed in on every noise outside the door, wondering if yet another person had come to try to hurt her, to take her against her will.

Which then led me to wondering if Lochlann had been just another place she existed against her will, no more than the lesser of two evils. All of that was to say nothing of the dread for what awaited me back home.

So instead of resting, I chased shadows across the ceiling and watched as the flames in the hearth dwindled to ash.

By the time morning came, I was more than anxious to get back on the road. I left while Galina was still feigning sleep. Of course, it was a short-lived reprieve since her horse was next to mine.

She didn't try to speak, though. Not then. Not on our short breaks throughout the day. Not during another endless night in her room.

Though Hamish and Ewan were back to taking shifts standing guard outside of her room each night, I still slept on her sofa for reasons I refused to put into words. She didn't question it, either, opening the door each night and padding soundlessly to her bed.

Instead of getting closer to speaking, we seemed to be drifting further from it, the air between us taut with lies and secrets and broken promises and burnt corpses.

Five days passed that way, in icy mutual stoicism and unspoken questions. The night before we made it to Lithlinglau started out like the others. I reluctantly knocked, and she answered with her expression perfectly guarded, though her narrow shoulders were more rigid than usual.

The faint scent of lavender wafted off of her and I tried not to think or breathe or remember the way that scent tasted on my lips in the early hours of the morning. I walked around her, more desperate than I should have been to reach the relative safety of the room's sofa.

Except that there was no sofa. Which explained her tension.

"I'll sleep on the floor," I said shortly.

"That isn't necessary," she responded in the same brisk tone.

"It is, actually." Another beat of silence fell, this one even weightier than the last.

Then I pulled the additional blanket I had ordered from

the bedside table and threw it on the floor between the door and the bed. She sucked in a breath like she might argue again, but I grabbed the extra pillow and laid down before she could get the words out.

Slowly, she exhaled, the sound somehow both gentle and disruptive. The silence between us stretched on, filled only by the soft shuffle of Galina settling into the bed and the occasional distant footsteps from beyond the room.

Though every night had been tense and sleepless, this one felt different. Perhaps it was the way she seemed poised just on the edge of speaking, of broaching the impossible divide between us, and I couldn't decide if I was ready to hear what she had to say – if I would be able to believe it, anyway.

Or perhaps it was just that somewhere on this very hard floor, it was getting more difficult to ignore just how far we had come from rooftops and murmured affirmations in the dark, and I still didn't understand where the hell everything had gone wrong.

The questions assaulted me like a barrage of hailstones, unyielding and unforgiving, leaving me battered and bruised before I finally forced myself to voice aloud the one that plagued me the most.

"Were you ever going to tell me the truth?"

I hadn't realized I could hear her breathing until she stopped. One heartbeat passed, then another.

"No." One word, delivered without an ounce of uncertainty.

I wasn't sure what I had been expecting. For her to lie? Again? Was it better that she had told me the truth?

Some part of me believed she would take it back or elaborate, but the minutes stretched on in another unending silence. I let out a slow breath, something finally clicking into place inside of me.

However I felt about Galina, I couldn't keep holding out for whatever scraps of truth or affection she chose to dole out. Besides, if everything my uncle warned me about was true, I had more than enough to concern myself with right now.

At least, that's what I kept telling myself.

Chapter Twenty-Three

GALINA

MY *NO* RESOUNDED in the space between Davin and me, following us through the night and well into the next day.

A thousand times, I opened my mouth to take it back, but I couldn't lie to him again, after everything. And the truth was, *no*.

Given the choice, I never would have told him, or anyone, what had happened with Alexei. I would have closed the door on that part of my life and never looked back, never let Davin see that small, defenseless part of me. I couldn't explain that to someone who had known nothing but strength in his own life and in the women around him.

So I said nothing, and Davin said nothing, even as the silence ate away at us both.

Which is why I was surprised to see him trotting his horse closer to mine shortly after our midday break. Though we technically rode next to one another, Davin maintained a distance between us. He had always been watchful, but he was visibly on alert since we left, his posture wary throughout the entire journey.

He looked like that now, too, only his expression became markedly more closed off as he drew nearer to me.

"We need to talk before we get back." His tone was impartial, absent of any ire or accusation or feeling at all.

It was worse, somehow.

Though I knew he was right, just thinking about discussing what had happened made me feel like a hand was closing around my windpipe. Alexei's hand on my throat. My back against the door.

I gritted my teeth, looking down at my lap and adjusting my gloves, using literally any excuse to buy myself time before needing to broach that subject.

"Not about...," Davin began, his voice pulling me back to the present. "It's not about you," he finished.

I turned back to him, trying to appear far less affected than I felt.

"What is it, then?"

He sighed, a muscle tensing in the sharp contours of his jaw.

"The night you le–" he cut off, correcting course. "The night of the festival, Tavish was found dead."

My brow furrowed, the part of me that was lost in my mind scrambling to catch up.

"Where?" I asked.

"In his rooms at Lithlinglau."

Several things dawned on me at once. His pressing need to get home. His uncle's ire at Davin's departure. The night of the festival, Davin had drawn his sword on Tavish. For me.

"They suspect you, because you threatened him," I surmised.

And now he was accused of murder because of something he had done to protect me, only hours before I left. Shame ate at my gut, the choices I had been so sure of at the time growing murkier by the minute.

"I'm sure nothing will come of it," he said dismissively, his gaze fixed on the snowy road ahead.

"That's why your uncle wanted me to come back, because otherwise, you have no one to vouch for your whereabouts." It was another guess, but he dipped his chin in affirmation.

Distantly, I wondered what else the lairds might ask.

I had already given Gallagher the details of my departure while we were on the road. Though I couldn't bring myself to talk about Alexei coming into my rooms or his threats, I did manage to describe the guard who helped him take me from my balcony to the window below, then sneak out a side door. I hadn't wanted to chance that there was anyone they had overlooked, but Gallagher assured me they were already searching for the two missing guards.

Surely that wasn't common knowledge, though.

"In terms of...everything else," Davin interrupted my thoughts. "I've received word that the magistrate you dealt with on your journey has met with an untimely demise by fire. Sadly, his official records all burned up with him, so one way or another, you'll be free to do as you wish."

He didn't look at me, didn't put any inflection in his voice at all. Still, I got the feeling he was waiting for something.

Did he want me to leave, but felt guilty forcing me out? Did he want me to stay? Would I never stop owing him for things?

Before I could find the words to ask, he cleared his throat.

"Anyway, I didn't want you to walk in blind."

Like I had done to him. Unsure if the subtle accusation was intentional or not, I only nodded.

Another long pause stretched between us as I watched the snowflakes fall onto his dark lashes. The wind howled and lashed at us, but I welcomed the piercing cold, anything to escape the overwhelming void that was growing inside me.

"Speaking of which..." He reached into the pocket of his

fur-lined cloak, pulling out a tiny furled-up scroll and handing it over.

I unrolled it, looking at a hurried scrawl that was far messier than one would expect from royalty. But then, Rowan had never been one for meeting expectations.

Dear favorite (albeit, most-vexatious) cousin,

Nils has written, concerned that he hasn't heard from his nephew in some time. So naturally, we are searching Socair high and low, as there is no reason to think he went anywhere else.

We did, in fact, have a visit from a couple from Ram today.

I SUCKED IN A BREATH. My parents had made it safely to the palace.

It's been eventless so far, which is more than I can apparently say for home. I wanted to come, but Avani insists my presence would cause more harm than good.

IT ABSOLUTELY WOULD, if I knew the lairds here at all, but it was telling that she was concerned. I scanned to the end of her letter where she poked fun at her new life and told him she missed him in her Rowan way. When I was finished, a strange combination of relief and worry mingled in my gut.

My parents were safe. But between the King's presence and Rowan's concern and Gallagher's cautious glances, I wasn't convinced that the same could be said for Davin.

Chapter Twenty-Four

DAVIN

THE GATES of Lithlinglau hadn't even shut behind us before a soldier came forward to meet our party. He had been sent by my parents to direct Uncle Logan and me to the Assembly chamber that hadn't been used since before the war two decades past.

That already boded well. My confidence in this entire situation grew dimmer with each new revelation that unfolded.

He handed us each a hot towel to wash our face and hands, under my mother's guidance no doubt. It was all the freshening up we were going to be allowed to do before facing down a room full of accusatory lairds.

Once clean, my uncle withdrew a simple golden circlet from his satchel — his travel crown, as we liked to refer to it — carefully placing it over his brow. Though neither of us was expecting to be dragged into an Assembly meeting the moment we passed through the castle gates, we did know how important appearances were right now.

After he was confident it was situated perfectly, he turned and gestured for me to follow him, but I held back.

"I'll make sure everything is taken care of with Galina's rooms," Gal said, correctly interpreting my hesitation.

She had been taken from that room once before. I wasn't anxious to just throw her back into potential danger without knowing who was on guard.

I gave him a sharp nod of appreciation before releasing my reins to the stable hand, resisting the urge to look back at Galina. I wasn't sure I wanted to see her reaction to being back here.

I followed my uncle in through a back door of the castle, winding down servant's halls and corridors until we found ourselves in front of two massive iron doors. I had been in this room many times while growing up at Lithlinglau, but I had never seen it used, let alone with this many people.

The Assembly chamber was already full, semicircular rows stuffed to the brim with lairds and the only two ladies who currently sat on the Assembly. Some of those in attendance were even forced to stand along the edges of the room, as there were no seats left.

Somehow, even the outlying title holders from as far as the outreaches of Oakenwell to Dead Rock had managed to make an appearance, for what was clearly the Assembly of the century.

I wasn't sure if I should be flattered or offended that so many of them had shown up so quickly. Then again, I suppose they had been headed this way for the vote already.

Mamá and Uncle Finn sat among the Assembly instead of at the seats up front, my father noticeably missing. We were going for subtlety, then.

If the lines of exhaustion rimming their features were anything to go by, they had been having as much fun here with the lairds as we had on the road. My mother's gaze raked over me in concern, assessing me for injuries. When she found none, she nodded, giving me a small warning look that wasn't hard to interpret.

Whatever had happened, she didn't feel confident in these proceedings. We needed to be careful.

My uncle and I sat on the bench behind the table at the front of the room next to Lairds MacArthur and Jameson.

"Hear ye. Let us take our start." MacArthur called for the proceedings to begin in his nasally voice, and I suppressed an eye roll at the unnecessary excess of pomp.

Though the docket master was an arseworm of epic proportions, one who had most assuredly been taking bribes from Tavish, at least Jameson was known to be fair. He spoke up in a strong, even tone.

"We are here to discuss the murder of Laird Tavish Anderson—"

"No, we are here to discuss his *murderer*," Laird Wilson called out, pointing his crooked old finger at me.

A cacophony of voices sounded at once, like a gaggle of enraged chickens, some in clear agreement, several more to argue. I scanned the crowd, noting the scattered few neutral expressions. MacBay looked chronically disappointed, while Lady Fenella's expression was almost pitying behind her judgment.

Even Fiona's calculating stare was less vengeful than I might have expected. I could only hope that at least half of the other two hundred thirty-seven lairds felt the same way.

"We do not convict men without clear evidence in this kingdom," Uncle Logan's voice rang out louder than the rest. "Unless there's been a change to the Lochlannian law since last I was at Council."

A beat of silence fell while the members of the Assembly looked at one another, trying to decide who was brave enough to challenge their king. One of them eventually found their courage.

"The evidence speaks for itself—" Laird Stewart began, but Laird Buchanan cut him off.

"Are we really going to try the marquess with murder?" he asked, indignation lining his wrinkled brow. "An esteemed member of our royal family convicted and tried for murder like some commoner?"

"We are when his cufflink was found at the scene of the crime," Wilson fired back.

Right. The cufflink. Something I still had no way to account for outside of the obvious, that someone was clearly framing me for this murder.

"And when he fled the moment he was questioned," Buchanan added.

Camdyn MacBay stepped forward. His family was one of the oldest in the kingdom, and he was, by all accounts, a genuinely decent laird. His people adored him. The Assembly viewed him as the epitome of what a Lochlannian should be, stable and loyal and strong.

He had been a longtime friend of our family, specifically my Aunt Charlie and Uncle Finn, but he hadn't been happy since we decided against retaliation to Socair for taking us. He also wasn't particularly fond of me these days, since someone had let slip to him my...history with his daughter.

Still, he was known to be fair, so I wasn't worried when he cleared his throat, gathering the attention of the room...until he turned to me, something like an apology written across his features.

"I think we would all like to hear a plausible explanation for those things."

The demand wasn't unreasonable, nor was the tone in which it was being delivered. But for all his reputation of fairness, I could have sworn I caught a hint of something... pointed.

Uncle Logan stiffened, but my mother made a subtle

gesture with her hand. I gave a broad look around the Assembly chamber, being sure to meet several eyes.

"I haven't seen those cufflinks in months, as I already told Master Ward," I said evenly. "And as for why I left, it was because my betrothed had been kidnapped. So I went to ensure her safe return."

My words echoed in the silent chamber while I hastily scanned the expressions around me, looking for a sign of anyone who didn't look as surprised as they should. I met Fiona's cobalt gaze, and she raised a challenging eyebrow.

Because she had known? Or because she detected the hint of a lie behind the reason for my initial departure?

There was a smattering of other faces that didn't look as surprised as I may have expected. MacBay merely grimaced in disapproval.

"If that's true, why did you not call the guard?" Laird Stewart asked, his tone grating against my already frayed nerves.

I bit back a long-suffering sigh. "I'm sure you'll understand the need for discretion, under the circumstances."

Wilson scoffed. "So you expect us to believe your betrothed was stolen the same night your cousin was murdered in some bizarre coincidence?"

"I don't think it was a coincidence at all, actually," I countered. "I think it's clear the rebels are responsible for both."

"Was it also the rebels who were responsible for threatening Laird Tavish at the festival that same night, or will you at least be taking responsibility for that?" Laird Wilson sneered.

I was beginning to get whiplash from the constant barking of questions on either side of me. There was no point in explaining that the threat had been in retaliation, not now that Tavish wasn't here to defend himself. Before I could formulate another response, Laird MacArthur chimed in.

"Of course he wanted Tavish dead. I have it on good authority that he was going to lose the vote."

This time, I didn't bother to suppress my sigh, my fingers coming up to massage my temples. That was a bald-faced lie. If anything, Galina and I had been swaying things in our – in my favor.

"MacArthur, how could you possibly have authority on a vote which had not yet taken place?" Laird Jameson asked with a trace of exasperation.

"Perhaps with the same divine knowledge that led him to moving up the vote, against all precedent," Mamá suggested drily.

Titters sounded from all around, and MacArthur's cheeks reddened.

"The man was killed with his own sword — a vindictive and cowardly act, if I have ever heard of one," he sputtered. "That he was poisoned and defenseless, is only further indication that someone close to him did this. Someone with a vendetta who also had direct access to his rooms and his food."

Poisoned… Well, that was news to me, though not altogether surprising. Still, I couldn't help but wonder why both?

"Or," I offered, my voice echoing off the domed ceiling and spacious room, "perhaps it was two people who tried to murder him on the same evening. He had certainly amassed plenty of enemies, outside of myself."

"This is not a joke—" old MacArthur began before I cut him off.

"No," I said flatly, forcing him to meet my eye. "Me being stupid enough to kill my cousin with his own sword in my own castle is a joke, and a tired one at that."

Several Assembly members argued back and forth about the logistics and likelihood of my guilt, far too many of them falling back on the fact that I had seemingly fled the scene of the crime, shutting down the magistrate's questions when he was investigating the murder.

I exchanged a look with Mamà. This was going nowhere.

"As I said, there were extenuating circumstances," I began, but MacBay's voice cut me off.

"There always are with your family," he said evenly. The room quieted at the sound of his voice, allowing him a much more obvious stage to speak from. "Isn't that what caused such animosity with your cousin to begin with? The extenuating circumstances by which you acquired an estate that should have been his birthright?"

I glared at him, careful not to allow a single emotion to slip past my features. That was a gross oversimplification, one that ignored all of the reasons I had a legitimate right to Lithlinglau, including the will written by my mother's bastard of a first husband, himself.

"Were there also extenuating circumstances when you and Princess Rowan were caught breaking our own king's laws like common thieves?" Laird Wilson added before I could voice any of that.

"Not to mention how the family rose to power to begin with," Laird Stewart said.

"Perhaps we would not have such trouble with rebels if the royal family could instill its people with any sort of confidence. Even the heir to the throne flouted law and tradition both when she married a commoner."

Uncle Logan cut in sharply. "*That* was a law that was in need of change."

I fought to keep my own features under control. Mac had been a singularly decent person, outside of being my best friend and the love of Avani's life. He was not a stars-damned weapon to be wielded in a political argument against our family, least of all her.

"But you cannot argue that the timing was self-serving," MacBay countered quietly.

"I will remind you that we are not here to try the entire royal family for our perceived sins," Uncle Finn said, his tone far calmer than Uncle Logan's had been.

MacBay met his eyes solidly before looking at the rest of the Assembly, squaring his shoulders like he was bracing himself for something.

"Perhaps we should be." His words sliced through the air like a freshly sharpened blade.

My lips parted. Belatedly, I realized we should have been prepared for this. On some level, we had been.

Just not from MacBay.

"The monarchy cannot refuse to abide by the very laws they enforce," he said, almost like he was reasoning with us to understand.

"And what of loyalty, Camdyn?" Uncle Finn asked. "Is anyone abiding by that?"

Laird MacBay's eyes tightened, and he shook his head. "My first loyalty is to our people, where yours should have been."

The air shifted with the change of allegiances, the weight of MacBay's accusations suspended in the air above us. The world was tilting on its axis, and the future of my family hung precariously in the balance.

"The real question is whether or not the monarchy is loyal to us in turn. If the royal family cannot be bothered to hold itself accountable, then I question whether there are stronger changes that need to be made." His statement fell like the executioner's ax.

Though there was an uproar in argument, there were too many nods of assent, too many eager expressions. Betrayal and anger filled the air like a combustible gas. One wrong move, one more spark, and everything would explode.

The king was practically vibrating with fury, his body tense, his lips parting to voice an objection. I knew I had seconds to act before all of this went up in flames.

"You're absolutely right," I announced, much to the general shock of the room. "We should — and do — hold ourselves to the same laws. Avani did not break the law when she married Mac. She changed it. Rowan and I both paid for our misdeeds, as you well know," I couldn't help but growl.

MacBay was one of the few Lochlannians who had seen my cousin's scars, the deep gashes in her skin that had nearly killed her.

"And," I said in a louder tone, "I am not trying to escape any responsibility now. I was merely expecting the same benefit of the doubt we extend to each of our citizens."

"We also expect them to plead their case," Laird MacArthur said. "To submit to an interrogation, to provide us with some sort of evidence of their innocence, none of which you have done."

"None of which I have had a chance to do in my absence, but naturally..." I ignored the king's warning look. "I will now."

Uncle Logan swore under his breath. We both knew providing evidence of my innocence wasn't as simple as they made it out to be, not when someone was working to make me look guilty and the real culprit was a phantom who had eluded us for months.

But there was no other way.

A few grumblings sounded throughout the room, some about the inanity of the general proceedings, some about my apparent guilt, but I kept my attention fixed on MacBay. After a moment, he nodded, something that seemed to mollify those on his side.

Within moments, a vote was put forth, with over half of the Assembly voting to move this to a formal trial. I took careful note of where each person placed their loyalties, including Fenella's vote against me and, more surprisingly, Fiona's in my favor.

More contention ensued on the appropriate amount of time to go to trial. Some of the lairds were willing to give me months. Others insisted a whole day should be sufficient to collect myself and evidence.

"Very well," MacArthur stated after a general consensus was reached. "We will reconvene in three weeks. Until such time, you will remain under armed guard within the castle walls from a neutral third party."

Even he couldn't keep a straight face on that last part. Neutral, my arse. MacBay was the one who had volunteered guards, and he had made his stance more than clear.

Now, I had three weeks to gather witnesses and evidence. Three weeks to find the Viper.

I swallowed hard, schooling my features into a semblance of confidence while the lairds stood to leave. MacBay caught my eye on the way out. Something churned in his gaze. Pity? Remorse? Disappointment?

Did he think about the children he had been an uncle to, the way he had grieved with Avani and defended Rowan and supported the rest of us until he decided we didn't deserve that anymore?

His expression shuttered, and he looked away before I could decide if his abandonment was justified. Or if he was just another pawn in the Viper's games – unwittingly or not.

Chapter Twenty-Five

GALINA

GALLAGHER LED me inside a different door than the one Davin had entered, though no less tucked away.

"The last thing we need is more attention," he said under his breath.

"I don't disagree, though that ship has rather sailed," a smooth voice cut in.

Prince Oliver waited at the bottom of the stairs. It struck me all over again how like his son he looked. They had the same build, tall and broad without being bulky, the same cobalt eyes and obsidian locks, though the prince's were shot through with gray at the temples.

I gave him a Lochlannian curtsy, and he shook his head.

"None of that now." He turned to Gallagher. "I can escort her from here."

"Her rooms–" Gal began.

The prince made a face of grim understanding. "We've increased the guard all around, but you'll have time to check in on it since we aren't headed straight there, if you need to for... *your* peace of mind."

Gallagher gave him a small smirk. “I see you understand entirely.”

Davin’s father shrugged. “I know my son.”

It wasn’t surprising, exactly, since I had seen his hesitation before he left. Storms, I had seen his every protective instinct for the past two weeks, and before that. Still, it filled me with a feeling I couldn’t name, something between gratitude and guilt.

Prince Oliver cleared his throat. “For now, you should go find Gwyn before she, too, faces accusations of murder.”

“She wants to be in the Assembly room?” he guessed.

“Indeed, she does,” the prince confirmed, “which I think we can all agree is a spectacularly terrible idea.”

I privately agreed but held my tongue. Gallagher shot me a questioning look, and I dipped my head in assent. Only then did he leave to find his twin.

“Sadly, we have even less pleasant interactions to face,” the prince told me.

My eyebrows climbed upward without my consent.

“Your uncle is waiting.” He said the words casually, though concern was etched into his dark blue eyes.

“He’s here?” I wasn’t sure why I asked when Oliver had no reason to lie, but my mind seemed to have gone blank with dread.

Dread for Davin, and whatever was transpiring in the Assembly chamber. Dread for facing my uncle after everything that had happened, the way my secrets and lies and mistakes all seemed to be catching up to me in one paralyzing blow.

The prince dipped his head once. “He just arrived, along with an escort from Chridhe.”

Was it more of Davin’s family? It would make sense that they had come to support him, which belatedly occurred to me was where Oliver would ordinarily be also, were he not stuck babysitting me.

"I'm sure a guard could escort me so you could be with Davin," I said.

Oliver pursed his lips thoughtfully before taking a step forward.

"As much as I would like to be in that room, we decided it might be better not to show up like a battering ram when that's already the Assembly's primary complaint. And you might have noticed my brother is rather a battering ram all on his own..." He trailed off with a small smile that was far more forced than usual, and my stomach churned.

Both of Davin's parents were exceptionally good at putting up appearances, much like their son. The fact that his worry was showing meant there was legitimate cause for concern. I wanted to press him on it, but I couldn't bring myself to add to his burden.

"Still, I'm sure there are things you could be doing," I protested.

"There's always something to be done," he allowed, proffering his arm for me to take. "But I thought, perhaps, you might want an ally in that room. If you would prefer your privacy instead, I will leave you at the door."

I opened my mouth to tell him not to worry about it, that of course he could attend to whatever else needed attending. Then I thought about my uncle's last threatening letter, about what it felt like to be coerced from the castle against my will, and I couldn't quite bring myself to ask Oliver not to accompany me.

Nor could I force myself to ask for his help when there were a million other things he could be doing to help Davin. *Storms*, I was a mess.

Finally, after taking his arm, I settled on a short, "Thank you," which he took with far more grace than I deserved.

Walking down the familiar hallways of Lithlinglau was bittersweet. A part of me felt like I was coming home, while a small voice in the back of my mind whispered that it would never really be my home again. It was never mine to grow attached to in the first place, let alone now.

Oliver silently led me up the marble stairs to the living quarters, turning left toward the guest suites, instead of right toward those reserved for family. We were halfway down the hall before we stopped outside an impressive set of double doors, my heartbeat thundering ominously in my chest.

"Ready?" he asked.

I nodded, unable to speak when my throat was suddenly so very dry. He nodded for the guards to open the doors, and I stepped in to find the duke of Clan Ram sitting imperiously in a wing-backed chair.

For a stilted moment, I couldn't look at him, couldn't move, couldn't breathe.

"Sir Mikhail," Oliver greeted, gently putting pressure on my arm to pull me out of my head.

Finally, I sucked in a breath, forcing myself to meet the eyes of the man I had been taught to revere above all others, back when he had looked at me with nothing but pride. He didn't have children of his own, so he had tutored me in Clan politics himself, treating me more like a daughter than he would a niece.

You are the pride of Clan Ram, Galina.

Then he had sold me into marriage for the sake of a war he didn't even believe in, and I had betrayed him as thoroughly as any one Socairan could betray another – not only him, but the crux of everything he taught me.

I wanted to fall to my knees and beg forgiveness nearly as much as I wanted to scream at his failure to protect me, his refusal to even try.

Instead, I squared my shoulders, greeting him with a deep nod in the Socairan fashion.

"Uncle," I said respectfully.

He looked me up and down, disapproval evident in his dark gaze.

"Galina," he responded.

Not niece. Not *my dear*. Just Galina, cold and distant as the mountain town we hailed from.

He turned to the prince. "Thank you for escorting her, but I will speak with her privately now. This is a family matter."

"Of course it is," Oliver said congenially. "And in her time here, she has become family to us. So I'm sure you'll understand why I wish to stay."

Did he even realize that he was lying, that I wasn't anything close to his family anymore? That Davin and I hadn't spoken more than a handful of words since Alexei's corpse hit the ground?

My uncle bristled, and I felt both disloyal and foolish for hesitating to assure Oliver that I was fine in this room, safe with the man who had half-raised me. But I couldn't bring myself to argue.

"Very well," Uncle Mikhail gritted out.

I settled onto the long cream-colored sofa across from him, bracing myself for whatever came next. Prince Oliver crossed the room to the liquor cart near the large bay window to pour us each a dram of whiskey. As soon as his back was turned, my uncle finally addressed me, speaking in our native Socairan dialect as a clear dismissal of the third party in the room.

"Do you even begin to understand the repercussions of your actions?"

Was he talking about my parents, his pride, Nils' wrath? Either way, ever since Alexei's threat, I had suspected the answer was no. I hadn't fully comprehended the fallout, and I still wasn't sure if I did.

"I don't know," I said, responding in the same language.

Though I meant no disrespect to Oliver, it would only

incense my uncle more to deny him that. Besides, I had a suspicion that the prince could understand us just fine, if he was anything at all like his son.

Mikhail deflated a small amount at my honesty.

"You put your family in danger." Was he concerned about that, when he had willingly handed them over? Had he been given no choice?

"They're safe now," I said before I could consider the implication.

He narrowed his eyes. My uncle was many things, but he was not stupid.

"How could you possibly know that?" he demanded.

I was spared from immediately answering by the prince's return. He held out a glass of whiskey to Mikhail and pressed another into my hand. Though I didn't care for most whiskeys, I sipped at it gratefully, using the burn in my throat to center my scattered emotions.

When I looked up, Mikhail was still studying me for the answer I was unwilling to provide. A muscle clenched in his jaw.

"I see," he said. And the worst part was, I believed that he did see, that he had put together exactly where I had been and why I had returned with Davin.

He knew that Alexei had come for me. He must have suspected it had been a possibility to have come to the conclusion so quickly. My heartbeat raced in my chest.

"I suppose that answers the question of why you willingly left the place you were so desperate to escape to," he said before raising his glass to his lips.

"I would not say willingly," I bit out before I could stop myself.

His eyes flashed with an emotion I couldn't read. The crackling of flames in the hearth punctuated the yawning silence for several heartbeats until he decided to speak again.

"Nonetheless, it is time for you to come home."

"Home," I echoed, the word as dissonant out loud as it had been in my head.

"To Wolf Estate, to await your betrothed," he corrected.

I blinked. He wanted me to return to Socair, to go to the same estate where my parents had been held hostage, to stay with a man who hated me while I awaited the return of the husband we both knew was dead.

He continued in the same commanding tone. "You will apologize for any hardship you caused him and his nephew, who you care deeply for, and explain that you were coerced into leaving Socair and all ensuing communication."

The irony of that was not lost on me. I had been coerced into leaving somewhere, but it wasn't Socair.

"And in return..." He paused, his gaze boring into mine. "I will graciously overlook your disloyalty to your family, your clan, and your kingdom. In the event that your betrothed does not return from wherever in Socair he journeyed to, I will arrange another suitable marriage for you."

It was an offer I would have killed for only months ago. Forgiveness. A marriage to anyone who wasn't Alexei. The ability to return to my parents.

But it wasn't one I could accept now.

"The king has demanded my presence for Davin's Assembly proceedings," I said, my fingers absently tracing the grooves of my whiskey glass.

My uncle sucked in an irritable breath at the subtle refusal.

"After which time you will return," he said in a low, controlled tone.

"And if I don't, will my parents be in danger again?" It was as close as I would come to asking if he was behind the threats.

There was a flash of anger in his eyes, and his hand clenched around his glass.

"They were never in danger from me," he said plainly.

"But it would be a shame if Laird Davin was accused of yet another murder."

So he wouldn't threaten my parents because they were *his* family, just the man he knew I cared about. He couldn't have known beyond a doubt what had happened, but it wasn't hard for him to surmise when I had left with Alexei and returned with Davin. He had to know Alexei was dead, and if he did, it wasn't a secret who had killed him.

"I agree, it would indeed be a shame," I said, fire building up from a place I scarcely recognized. I chose my words carefully. "To say nothing of the dishonor it would bring Sir Nils to believe my chosen betrothed deprived him of his remaining heir. I only hope that it wouldn't reflect badly on Ram, all things considered."

Or that Nils wouldn't exact retribution from my uncle.

Any doubts I had that Davin's father was fluent in Socairan disappeared in the tilt of his lips at my thinly veiled threat.

Anger and disappointment warred in my uncle's features as he held my gaze for several heartbeats. Finally, he sighed, like he was exasperated by this conversation and me.

"You need rest. We will discuss this again after you have slept."

For the first time, I noticed that I wasn't the only one who was tired. The lines in my uncle's face had never been so pronounced, and guilt pricked at me in spite of myself. The stay of execution was as good as anything else I was going to get tonight, so I nodded, setting my glass down on the side table before getting to my feet.

"As you say."

Oliver moved to join me, and together we turned to leave. Just before he opened the door, my uncle's voice sounded out.

"There are debts to be paid, Galina, whether either of us would wish to do so. Whatever you may believe, I have no desire to punish the man who kept you safe, but our obligation is to our clan."

I left without responding.

Maybe his obligation was to our clan, but I wasn't so sure where mine rested these days.

Chapter Twenty-Six

DAVIN

After our delightful meeting in the Assembly room, the members finally filed out, leaving us in a somewhat stunned silence.

Uncle Finn walked a quick round to ensure the doors were shut and no one was lurking, nodding when his perusal was complete.

"Well," I spoke first, breaking the uneasy hush. "Now would be a phenomenal time to tell me all about how you caught the Viper whilst I was off chasing my beloved."

I couldn't help the way my voice turned bitter at the end. My mother frowned, but graciously refrained from comment.

"Not for lack of trying," Uncle Finn responded, running a hand over his short black curls. "Though we've all agreed it has to be someone in the nobility. No one else would have the resources to fund something like this. Unless they're working with our neighbors, which seems unlikely."

I agreed. Rionn had closed borders and everything with Socair was monitored closely.

"So probably someone who just left this room." I searched

the empty chairs like they held the secrets to the sins of the men and women who had occupied them.

"Someone like the very bastard who just turned on our entire family?" Uncle Logan grumbled, setting his crown on the table with a forceful clatter.

Finn made a sound of disagreement, crossing his arms and leaning against the column closest to us. "Camdyn has always been fair. I don't like what he just did any more than you do, but I don't think he's working from malice so much as a misplaced sense of righteousness."

"That would be fairly obvious of him," Mamá commented. "And I agree that he doesn't exactly seem the type, but we can't argue he has the most to gain by destabilizing the monarchy. We both know who the lairds would put on that throne if our family wasn't in the running."

She wasn't wrong. Even in the room today, the Assembly had deferred to him.

"If not him, the question is, who else would gain from our family's fall?" I said.

"And there's where we fall short." Uncle Finn's tone was dark. It was, technically speaking, his job as Captain of the Guard to root out this problem, and it was clear the failure was grating on him. "It could be, in theory, everyone in that room or no one."

"This is why I didn't want you to promise them evidence you didn't have," Uncle Logan growled, his fists clenching. "What's going to stop them from exiling you when they decide not to believe the lass or your manservant or anyone else?"

"He hardly had a choice when they were putting the entire monarchy on the line," Mamá said. "We'd be lucky if all they did was dethrone us. No one leaves a former royal family around to spearhead pesky rebellions."

She cast a concerned glance in my direction.

"Do they honestly have that kind of power?" Uncle Finn asked.

Castle Alech was far more involved in the judiciary side of Lochlann than the political one, so it wasn't surprising he didn't know the answer. My mother exchanged a dark look with Uncle Logan, but it was the latter who replied.

"We didna want another rebellion like the one that started the war. We thought that by giving the Assembly more say, we could avoid that." He scoffed, either at himself or at the Assembly leading us to the very rebellion he hoped to avoid.

Of course, according to them, that was our fault. And stars, maybe it was. It felt like everything else was these days.

"So we don't have a choice but to go along with this charade," Uncle Finn surmised.

Uncle Logan shook his head. "For now, maybe, but I'll not let my nephew pay for a crime he didna commit, whether we find the Viper or no."

My mother met his eyes, her own like ice. "I have no intention of letting it come to that."

Something passed between them. Not for the first time, I wondered about the rumors of what had happened to the man whose estate I had inherited, my mother's first husband. And not for the first time, I wondered if MacBay had a point when he spoke of unchecked power, because in that moment, I knew with certainty that my family would do whatever they needed to protect me.

And I would do the same for them.

I COULDN'T TELL if I was relieved or disappointed when Anna answered Galina's door.

"She's in the bath, mi'laird, but if ye want to wait–"

"No," I said quickly. "That's not necessary. Can you kindly let her know that the proceedings are over, and that..."

I trailed off, not sure exactly what to say. But I still saw the concern she couldn't hide when I mentioned it. Whatever else had happened, we had been allies once, and it didn't feel right not to give her something.

"Just tell her that there's no cause for immediate concern," I finished up, backing away.

Anna nodded, closing the door with an uncertain nod. Perhaps my tone had been a bit more formal than usual. *Stars.*

I spun around, grateful to leave my new armed guards outside my room. There were soldiers from Chridhe already guarding the entrance to my suites, and I suppressed an eye roll.

"Surely this is overkill," I muttered, pushing open my doors.

But they weren't here for me.

A familiar head of crimson curls peeked out from over an armchair near the fire. The small sofa was occupied by Gwyn and Gallagher, but truthfully I was far more relieved to see the only politically inclined cousin I had.

Avani stood at the sound of the door, crossing the distance to me and enveloping me in a hug that I returned with a spin, squeezing her a little tighter than I normally would have. She hadn't left Chridhe since she lost Mac, but she was here, now, for me.

"When did you arrive?" I asked, suspecting it was recent if the faint smell of horses that clung to her hair was any indication.

"Just this afternoon, along with the world's most odious Duke."

"Ah, so dear Mikhail has arrived." I had to remind myself

that it wasn't him Galina had been afraid of, only his choice of husband for her.

But he was still an utter arseworm.

He was probably thrilled at this turn of events, given his feelings about our entire family, and Lochlannians in general. Did Galina go to him, arranging for her way home as soon as she gave her statement? She had definitely hesitated when I told her she could do what she wished. Did she have any idea what she wanted? Was it only the rest of us she kept in the dark?

"Unfortunately," Avani broke into my thoughts. "I do hope his niece doesn't take after him, though the twins seem to have conflicting opinions on that."

I glanced at the siblings in question. Gwyn was taking advantage of the excessive spread Blaine must have brought up. He always went overboard when I was gone. She shrugged unapologetically at me before shoving one of the white-chocolate-covered cranberry-and-orange pastries into her mouth.

Gallagher shot her a look before turning to me. "Don't let her act like she doesn't care. She checked Galina's rooms with me herself, and set up the guards."

"Only so Dav didn't spiral again," she said, wiping the granules of sugar crust from her gown.

A muscle clenched in my jaw, though I couldn't deny feeling better knowing they had taken care of those things.

"They're both heavily biased," I said to Avani, sinking into my only remaining chair and helping myself to some of my favorite pastries – or I would have, if Gwyn hadn't already eaten them all.

"Obviously. Which of course, is not a problem you would share." Avani reclaimed her chair, lifting up a furry little gray-and-white sphere in the process.

"New friend?" I asked, pointedly ignoring her remark and

forestalling any further conversation about Galina. I didn't want to talk about her when I finally had some space.

Avani took my cue with ease.

"He was injured," she said, tracing the dark stripes behind the creature's ears.

"Was he injured, or was he just too portly to walk?" I asked in a mild tone.

Truthfully, I wondered if Avani had just needed a companion more than the animal needed her help.

She made a face of mock offense.

"Albert doesn't appreciate your insinuations." She cradled the creature to her chest and, in spite of my day, in spite of everything, I felt a small smile creep onto my lips.

This was familiar, Avani with a rescued animal. After Mac had died, it was almost like she had stopped existing. She had barely left her rooms and stopped talking to everyone, animals included.

But now she was here, with little...*Albert*, apparently.

"What exactly is Albert?" Gwyn asked, tilting her head to examine the creature, who was nibbling obliviously on a fig Avani had given him.

Avani paused, squaring her shoulders defensively and refusing to meet any of our eyes.

"A flying squirrel," she finally answered.

There was a pointed silence, thick with the skepticism she had clearly anticipated. It was Gallagher who valiantly cleared his throat to ask aloud what we had all been wondering.

"But...*can* he fly? Physically, I mean," he clarified.

Avani sat up straighter in her chair, shielding the world's most ridiculous rodent from our scrutiny. "As your future queen, I am not obligated to entertain this inquisition. I decline, on Albert's behalf."

"Well, oh great omnipotent future ruler," Gwyn began, giving a flourish and a half bow from where she was seated. "If we aren't talking about that, are we at least going to talk about what we all really want to know?"

They all looked at me, and I sighed. I didn't blame them for needing to know about the Assembly, but stars if I wouldn't just as soon avoid the topic forever.

"We could," I allowed. "Alternatively, I could throw myself into this very fireplace."

"Why not both?" Avani asked sardonically, arching a crimson eyebrow.

"Yes," Gallagher chimed in, unhelpfully. "Put those legendary multitasking skills to work."

I rolled my eyes, snatching his glass of wine from his hand and downing it. He narrowed his eyes, but instead of complaining, he grabbed the bottle for himself.

"Where shall I start?" My tone was sardonic. "At the murder accusations hurled my way or the heavy implication that there would be a coup if I didn't comply with an investigation?"

Another beat of silence fell before Avani sighed.

"Well, I feel like we could start with the coup and work our way down."

So we did. Blaine brought more whiskey while we talked semantics to death and rehashed everything we knew. Avani listened, interjecting occasionally until we were done.

"So," she summed up. "We need to find out who the Viper is, but we also need to work on winning back the favor we've lost. Otherwise, it will just be something else after this."

I nodded, unsurprised by her quick grasp of the situation.

"Let's start with who voted against us," she suggested before going down the list of names I had given her. From there, we considered potential avenues of reconciliation.

"And Fenella," I added.

Gwyn and Avani made twin faces of irritation.

"That old bat is just mad none of us will marry her son,"

Avani seethed, and her small, furry companion gave a squeak of support.

"Well, Gwynnie, here's your big chance to help," Gal said, nudging his sister with his shoulder.

She shot him a look of pure murder. "I'd actually rather we were all beheaded than marry into Fenella's family."

"But you could have a feathered wedding dress," I offered.

"Well in that case," she deadpanned, her expression going flat.

Avani raised an eyebrow. "At the very least, be nice to him."

Gwyn shrugged a single shoulder. "I'm always nice."

We all looked pointedly elsewhere, and she glared at no one in particular.

"If it's so important to marry into their family, why doesn't Gallagher court Lady Fenella herself?"

Gallagher gagged audibly. "On that note, I'm ready to sleep for roughly forever and purge my mind of the very disturbing mental image you have just painted."

The twins bantered back and forth for a few more minutes before the sound of the grandfather clock alerted us to the hour. Then Gal did leave. Gwyn followed to go to her own rooms, leaving me with Avani. And Albert, of course.

Once they were gone, my cousin took the opportunity to scrutinize me.

"This wasn't your fault," she said after a long moment.

Whether she was referring to the general unrest or Tavish or Galina's kidnapping, she was wrong on all counts. I had had a hand in each of those things, from pissing off the Assembly to publicly threatening my cousin to letting traitors amongst my guard.

"It wasn't *not* my fault," I protested, going for a sip of my drink only to find it empty.

"Well, if it's your fault, it's all of our fault."

"Not yours," I argued.

"Here." Avani sat her surprisingly light squirrel on my lap and I found myself reluctantly petting it while she got up to pour us both another drink. "Don't think I don't know what they say about . . . Mac." Her voice softened on his name, like it always did.

"Yes," I shot her a look of mock-disappointment. "Damn you for falling in love."

"Isn't that what you're beating yourself up over?" she asked, setting the drink next to me. She made no move to take Albert back, and I, in spite of myself, made no move to hand him over.

"Yes, well." I took a hearty sip. "Mac loved you back. You weren't just an idiot."

She snorted.

"I was plenty of an idiot. But yes, he did," she acknowledged, a sad smile pulling her lips downward. She blinked, and her expression cleared. "You think Lady Galina doesn't love you?"

It was a sincere question, so I considered it as such, weighing all of the things I knew against each other without Gallagher's championing or Gwyn's ire to interfere.

"I don't know what to think anymore," I told her with more honesty than I had even given myself so far. "But I'm glad you're here."

Her smile was less sad this time, though it was tired. "Remember that when I force you to sleep on your own couch."

"Is that why your trunks are in here?" I asked, nodding in the direction of her things positioned against the far wall.

She nodded. "They prepared the wrong room."

The room she used to share with Mac, she meant.

"And I didn't want to tell them, and I'd like to actually sleep tonight, which rules out Gwyn and her snoring."

Of their own accord, my eyes drifted back to the balcony that led to the rooftop I shared with Galina. Then my mind took that further, crossing the familiar distance to her balcony, where someone had taken her against her will.

"I see," Avani said thoughtfully. "You're not going to sleep anyway, are you?"

I didn't do her the disservice of lying.

She sighed, staring into the fire for several moments before turning her attention back to me. "If I stay with her and promise to be extra on my guard, will you promise to sleep?"

I tilted my head, raising both of my eyebrows in challenge.

"Will you promise not to interrogate her?"

Her emerald eyes widened in a picture of innocence. "I can't help that people like to talk to me."

"Avani," I pushed.

"Ugh. Fine." She got up and scooped Albert out of my lap, turning to the door. "Send my trunk in a moment."

"Thank you," I called after her.

She waved me off, and I slumped further into my chair, alone for the first time in I couldn't recall how many days.

There was no clarity in that solitude, though. No magic answers waiting to be uncovered. Just the same weary thoughts running through my mind in an endless race against themselves and reason.

Chapter Twenty-Seven

GALINA

ANNA WAS WAITING in my room when I arrived after my conversation with my uncle. She eagerly greeted me as soon as the doors opened, her endless stream of words cutting off Oliver's goodbye.

Her large brown eyes welled with tears as she looked me over, fretting and fussing until I had assured her more than once that I was all right.

It wasn't true, of course. Not when memories haunted me in every corner of the room. Near the merrily crackling fireplace rested the plush, cream-colored chairs where Davin had asked me to marry him, not for games or politics or necessity, but simply because he wanted *me*.

Then, in the center of the polished floors, just beneath the delicate golden chandelier, was the spot where Alexei had laid waste to that dream with a hand over my mouth and a whispered threat in my ear.

It was a cacophony of memories, like standing on a ballroom floor with a different musician at every corner, each playing a different song. The clamor rose until even my favorite melodies were tainted by the discordant screech of the others, scraping against my mind like a silver fork on a dinner plate.

Anna's gentle hand touched my shoulder to usher me toward my bath, and the music in my head quieted to a bearable din.

She took special care tonight, choosing the finest oils and soaps to scrub me clean. All the while, my thoughts raced toward the Assembly chamber, wondering what was happening with Davin. The hot water had a soothing effect, making it easier for me to sort through my thoughts, but it didn't allay any of my worry for him.

Would he lose Lithlinglau? After all the work we had done to secure his vote, to keep his home, would he lose it now anyway? Or would he face imprisonment? Exile?

Surely not more than that, not with his uncle on the throne.

Like my thoughts had summoned him, there was a familiar double tap on the door. It was still more subdued than the one I had become accustomed to, instilled with a reluctance borne of my flight and our subsequent...whatever was happening with us.

Anna answered, and his voice floated toward me through the cracked lavatory door. I was torn between wanting to throw myself from the tub to see that he was all right for myself and being grateful I had a reason to hide when I was already feeling so raw tonight.

Then she closed the door, rendering the consideration moot.

"He's right as rain, his lairdship," she insisted, holding out a towel for me to wrap myself in.

I got to my feet, stepping out of the tub and into her towel while I contemplated the slightly false note in her words.

"There was nothing amiss?" I asked.

"He has a couple of extra guards, but nothin' to be worrit about, milady."

Sure, it wasn't. I swallowed back another wave of concern, giving myself over to Anna's ministrations.

Anna must have been grappling with her own kind of anxiety, or else she just sensed mine. Either way, she seemed to drag out the act of readying me for bed, finding an array of excuses not to leave me alone in my room. Once I had eaten most of the meal she ordered up for me, she gently placed a mug of hot tea in my hands. Judging by the strong scent, it was heavily spiked with whiskey.

I eagerly sipped at it, grateful for the way the alcohol warmed my body and helped slow my rapidly beating heart.

Just as I was nearing a place calm enough to consider sleep, a knock sounded from the hallway. I went still. It wasn't Davin's, not even the more subdued version he had adopted on the road, and it wasn't Gallagher's. Gwyn didn't bother knocking at all.

The door opened before either Anna or I could answer it, though, revealing a face that was entirely foreign to me.

Or nearly so.

"Your Highness," Anna dipped into a curtsy to address the woman.

"Hello, Anna. It's lovely to see you again." The newcomer's voice was smooth, her tone even and confident.

"Of course. I was just leaving." She sent me a look, ensuring I was comfortable, and I nodded, rapidly putting together the identity of the newcomer.

Anna curtsied again before bustling out, and I was left with the not-quite-stranger.

She had crimson curls that were the same shade as Rowan's, but not nearly as riotous. Her eyes were the exact shade of green as the king's, but held all the discernment I had come to expect from Gallagher. And while she was on the taller side, like Gwyn, her curves were more pronounced.

Where Rowan was cute, and Gwyn was striking, this woman was downright gorgeous. Gorgeous and powerful, if the short sword at her waist and the resolute set of her shoulders were any indication.

Thoug,h her elegance was somewhat at odds with the round, fuzzy animal in her hand.

"Princess Avani?" I guessed.

Excepting her clear resemblance to her family, there were also only so many *highnesses* in the kingdom, and only one that would be close to our age. Davin's cousin, and the widow of his best friend.

Add to that the wall of portraits in the family hall depicting the princess with a variety of creatures, and it wasn't hard to put together.

What I didn't know was why she was here.

She nodded while she openly examined me, her expression reserved but not unkind. When she was finished with her assessment, the corner of her mouth tilted upward in an expression so reminiscent of her cousin's, only hers didn't quite reach her serious eyes.

"Lady Galina. Well, it all makes sense now." Her accent was refined, like Davin's, with the barest hint of her father's brogue.

"Does it?" I asked.

"I suppose you're wondering what I'm doing here," she said, skirting around my question as she stepped further into the room.

"Did you come to discuss Davin?" I asked, though it wouldn't explain why she had come instead of one of the others.

She took a moment to read my expression before answering, her tone grim. "I'm afraid there's not much more in the way of news. They're conducting a formal investigation, and we have roughly three weeks to find the real murderer. That's all we know for now."

"Thank you for telling me," I said neutrally. Not that I didn't appreciate the information, but it was certainly something that could have waited until breakfast.

A beat of silence fell, but it wasn't precisely awkward. I got the feeling the princess knew how to wield silence to her advantage, a laughable contrast to both Rowan and Gwyn.

But I was Socairan, and her silence didn't faze me.

Much.

Until a knock sounded on the door, the same single, heavy beat that had always heralded Alexei's return from the privy or seeing to his men or whatever other small errand would pull him away from our rooms for far too short a time.

My blood ran cold, and I froze, trying and failing to force a breath into my lungs.

"It's only a guard with my trunk," Avani said in a voice gentler than the one she had used so far.

She turned to open the door, but rather than let the soldier enter, she shooed him away, dragging the trunk in herself.

"You don't have to–" I began, shocked out of my stupor. Though I shouldn't have been, knowing what I did of Lochlannian royals.

"Please," she grunted. "I'm training with Gwyn first thing in the morning. This is nothing."

"I meant any of it." I gestured vaguely to her trunk, the fact that she was clearly planning to stay here for reasons I wasn't sure I wanted to understand.

Because they didn't trust me alone? Because I was too weak to manage even with guards outside my door? It was worse because it was fair. All of it.

She closed the door, then sat on her trunks, more casual than she had been since she walked in.

"Well, Davin is..." she only hesitated briefly, but it was long enough to let me know whatever she was about to say next was a stretch on the truth, if not entirely a lie. "Confined to his suites at night." She gestured across the hall. "And Gallagher staying here would be wildly inappropriate, even by our standards. Gwyn could have come, but we wanted you to be more safe, not less."

Her mouth quirked up like she might have been joking but probably wasn't.

I had a feeling she knew precisely how much I had been wanting to know why the others hadn't come, that she had been holding on to that information intentionally until she gauged whether I was deserving of the knowledge.

It wasn't surprising that either Davin or Gwyn chose to avoid me, but it still bothered me more than it had a right to.

And now this stranger – the heir to the throne – was staying in my rooms to protect me...for political reasons? As a favor to her cousin?

I didn't know. But between worry for Davin and seeing my uncle and the unexpected knock at the door, I was too exhausted to ponder it further. All I wanted was to sleep, which I could reluctantly admit might be easier with another person who didn't seem inclined to kill me in the room.

"All right," I finally said, any remaining fight or curiosity leaving me in a single breath.

She furrowed her brow in a small show of concern I found I couldn't tolerate right now.

Though I knew it was unconscionably rude, I turned without another word and climbed into bed, ready to be done with everything about today.

If I had thought the world would look better on a full night's sleep, I couldn't have been more wrong. Though perhaps that was because the next morning brought with it a summons from the Assembly.

"Posturing old bastards," Avani muttered when she saw the scroll Gallagher had delivered.

"There was, indeed, a posturing old bastard involved, but in this case, it wasn't one of ours," Gwyn said darkly.

She hadn't looked at me beyond an initial cursory once-over, but neither did she seem inclined to leave.

"My uncle must have pushed for me to give my statement sooner, so..." I trailed off, and Gwyn let out a bitter huff of air.

"So you can leave again," she finished my sentence, her tone caustic.

"Gwyn," Gal cautioned.

"No, no," she fired back. "The sooner she can be off, the better. At least then she can stop toying with him."

"I had no choice," I reminded her sharply.

Finally, she met my eyes long enough for me to see the fury burning golden in her own. Fury, and something closer to betrayal.

"You had plenty of choices leading up to that one. You just never could seem to make any of them with Davin in mind." She shook her head, blowing out another breath. "Stars, you don't even see what you do to him."

I wanted to argue, but I thought of Davin's silence, of his strained question in the night, of all the lies between us. I swallowed thickly.

"That's enough, Gwynnie." Avani was firm. "We don't have all of the facts."

"And we never will, where she's concerned," Gwyn bit back in the exasperated tone of someone who has made an argument so often that it's become rote.

Gallagher's voice was quiet when he spoke, casting an apologetic glance in my direction. "She doesn't owe us an explanation."

His twin raised a challenging eyebrow. "Maybe not us," she countered, her implication clear.

It was Davin who was owed an explanation.

There was a tense beat while Avani and Gallagher exchanged a look that said they agreed with Gwyn but wanted to forestall this conversation all the same. Whatever wordless communication they were having must have reached some sort of consensus, because Gal who cleared his throat.

"Regardless," he said in a slightly louder voice, "now is hardly the time for this conversation. We came to get our story straight for the Assembly. They've already been questioning Davin all morning," he added to Avani and me.

Gwyn nodded, once again refusing to look at me. At least that explained her clearly reluctant presence here.

"Speaking of," Avani trailed off, standing up and walking into my closet.

It was painfully reminiscent of when Davin had gone to find me a scarf, and even when Gwyn had come to help me pick a dress for the festival, when I was hesitating for reasons that felt so stupid in comparison to these. At this point, Gallagher might be the only member of this family who hadn't helped himself to my closet.

"Rumors have already started that your relationship with Davin was fake to begin with." Gwyn's tone was all begrudging business now. "So be ready to defend that first."

Avani emerged holding a red dress, but Gwyn shook her head before I could respond.

"Too bold. She needs to look subtle, and...honest." She said it like the word itself was a lie, and I bit back a sigh.

I didn't bother telling them I could dress myself, not when they knew their people and Assembly better than I did and... not when Davin's future was on the line.

Gallagher eyed the exchange but didn't comment, instead picking up where Gwyn had left off. "Davin's told them the rebels coerced you into leaving, which is close enough to the truth. As long as you stick with that, don't mention Alexei, obviously, and just say that Davin caught up with you to take care of things as quickly as he could."

"And when they ask where things stand now?" I finally forced myself to address the one question I had been avoiding, one I realized I should have discussed with Davin while I still had the chance. I had thought there would be time, after we were back at the castle for a while, after we had space to think.

A beat of silence fell before Avani emerged again, a deep blue dress in her arms this time. Gwyn nodded sharply, and Avani turned to me.

"Blame your uncle," she suggested with a small shrug. "Socairan law. Whatever you need to. His presence here gives us something convenient to work with, and he's been clear enough on his feelings about this arrangement for it to be believable."

It was a good plan, a workable plan. It wouldn't even be a lie, but it didn't feel like enough. From the looks the others were exchanging, they felt the same way. Anxiety clawed at my chest, and I fought to focus on the small tips they were giving me.

"You want a subtle look today," Avani went on. "The ones doing the questioning are all powerful men, so better that you remind them of their children than–"

"Us." Gallagher supplied with a small, bitter twist of his lips.

"Exactly," Avani agreed, ducking back into my closet, presumably for accessories.

Shame pooled through me when I realized I had been just as bad as these lairds before, blaming Davin and Rowan for not upholding the perfect standards of royalty when they had just been young and grieving.

Gallagher walked the perimeter of the room, checking the locks on the doors and windows before leaving for me to get dressed.

"I'll be just outside the door, and I'll escort you once it's time to leave."

I thanked him and he left. Gwyn was on his heels, but she paused on her way out.

"I am glad that you're safe," she said, the cadence of her words implying heavily that there was a *but*.

"You just wish I was gone," I filled in.

She let loose a slow exhale. "What I wish is that you would make up your stars-damned mind about what you want and bloody well commit to that decision. Davin only knows how to love one way, with everything he has, and he deserves someone who can give him that in return. So if you can't be all in, then put him out of his misery and leave for good this time."

Then she was gone, leaving me to wonder if she saw more than anyone gave her credit for. If perhaps she was the only one who did.

GALLAGHER ESCORTED me through the castle to an enormous set of double doors where Princess Jocelyn was waiting for me. He nodded to us both before turning to go, leaving Ewan as my guard.

Jocelyn stepped closer to me, her head barely reaching my shoulder. Her navy eyes swept over me in a single assessing glance, like she was assuring herself both of my wellbeing and of my preparedness. Her hands hovered, poised to tuck in a stray hair or pull out a dangling thread. She brought them back to her side after a moment, apparently finding no fault with my braided updo or the placement of my understated jewels.

"I should know by now I don't have to worry about you," she said.

Though she was ostensibly referring to my outward appearance, there was a determination in her features that hinted at more, a confidence I didn't deserve. She didn't give me a chance to argue, or respond at all, before she moved on to what was in store.

"They're sure to run in circles, so just answer as best you can." *Lead them astray when you have to*, she meant. "If they ask you anything you aren't comfortable with, you do not have to answer. Look to me, and I will interject for you."

I nodded, appreciation washing over me in waves. Though I caught the double meaning here, that she would find an excuse for me not to answer if I couldn't come up with a suitable lie, I also knew that her promise was genuine. If I actually was uncomfortable, she damned sure wouldn't let that stand.

"I understand," I told her.

She looked at me like she heard the echo of the words from my room all those weeks ago when she had told me I could choose my loyalty. When she had told me that no one would take me from here by force.

Was she disappointed now, knowing I had let that happen anyway? Knowing I hadn't trusted in her family's protection after they so freely offered it?

A gentle hand came under my chin, lifting it higher. "None of that now. We all do what we must."

Whether she meant to express understanding for the past or bolster me for the room ahead, it worked. I nodded, donning what Davin liked to call my Resting Socairan Face.

It was a familiar shield, one I had worn for years, and again since Alexei came for me. It would be more than enough to get me through the next few hours.

Though, it wasn't entirely the Assembly I was worried about as much as it was Davin. Rather, it was his reaction to the decision I had come to somewhere on the long walk here. It didn't matter, though, because Princess Jocelyn was right.

We all do what we must.

Chapter Twenty-Eight

DAVIN

Despite only giving me three weeks to find my evidence, the lairds had decided to rob me of the very first day by requesting my presence back in the Assembly room to answer their unending slew of inane questions. It was all the more frustrating because I wanted a chance to talk to MacBay outside of all of these proceedings, but there was hardly time now.

I wondered if that was intentional on his part.

If it was, though, MacBay gave no sign. He only sat across the same table I was at yesterday, flanked by Jameson and Wilson. The three of them made up the chosen leads for the investigation, while a scribe sat at the end of the table as a neutral third party to record the meeting.

My father and I sat opposite the men with two empty chairs at my left. For hours, I answered the same questions, all posed slightly different from the last. It was a true exercise in patience to respond with even a modicum of respect, especially when it felt like a way to stall for time.

My fists clenched beneath the table as I gave yes or no

answers, only able to expound briefly before Wilson interrupted or picked apart the few words I uttered.

"Yes, I was in my rooms all evening," I repeated with dwindling patience.

"And you didn't leave until morning?" he asked for roughly the thousandth time.

I took a deep, calming breath, in through my nose, out through my lips. "As I said."

"I'm sure you appreciate that we have to be thorough," Wilson remarked disdainfully.

"And I'm sure you can appreciate that I am not eager to repeat myself." I said flatly.

Wilson opened his mouth to argue but Jameson smoothly cut him off.

"The laird is being more than cooperative, even though you have taken hours away from his own investigation. So, if we could move forward more expediently, it would be most appreciated."

A look was exchanged between him and MacBay before the latter gestured for the questioning to continue.

Before Jameson could speak, though, the doors to the room swung open, revealing Galina's slender form in the frame, followed slightly by my much more diminutive mother. Galina's eyes immediately darted to mine, holding my gaze for several heartbeats before she finally looked away.

I sat up a little straighter in my chair, watching her in my periphery as she floated across the floor in an elegant gown that seamlessly blended Socairan modesty and Lochlannian fashion in a way that honored both. It was a perfect outfit to sway an Assembly who couldn't quite decide if they wanted to hate either of us.

Her hair was braided up in its usual fashion, tucked around a small, jeweled circlet. She hadn't been precisely disheveled in our days on the road, but neither had she looked like herself, the way she did now. Pristine and composed and preternaturally gorgeous.

It was hard to look at her, even harder not to.

Then, of course, she took the empty seat just next to me, sliding just a hair closer than I expected her to, bringing with her a slight earthy aroma of lavender and rosemary. Trying to take shallow breaths before I was accosted by an unwanted wave of memories, I inclined my head in a greeting. She returned it with a sideways glance, her neutral court expression never shifting.

"Lady Galina, what perfect timing," Jameson greeted her.

"Yes, I believe we met at the ball, just a few weeks ago," Galina said to him and Wilson before carefully turning her attention to the final man at the table. "Laird MacBay, it's lovely to see you as well. I do hope that we aren't taking too much of your time away from your wife. Laird Gallagher informed me this morning that she is ill."

MacBay's expression was impartial when he responded. "She is. And I'll return as soon as my duties here allow it."

"Please let me know if there is anything I can do to help in the meantime," she said, folding her hands neatly on the table. "I do have some small knowledge in herbs, so I'd be happy to send a salve or a tea."

She had worded it so carefully, *in the meantime,* making it clear that she wasn't trying to offer a bribe or coerce him into treating the proceedings differently.

MacBay blinked, appearing genuinely taken aback that she would grant assistance under the circumstances. "I will, Lady Galina. Thank you for such a kind offer."

"Of course," she dipped her head demurely.

I was once again reminded that, unlike nearly every other member of my family, Galina was uniquely skilled at politics, and she had not come unprepared.

Once the greetings were out of the way, the questions

shifted to her. She wielded her manners like a weapon, carefully responding to each inquiry in a way that was both polite, but somehow questioned the intelligence of the interrogators.

The lairds started with the details of our relationship, where she skirted admirably around the truth.

"You hadn't seen him when he visited Socair, but you were willing to risk an Unclanning, something I understand to be an extreme punishment for your people, to come back here with him?" MacBay asked, his tone markedly softer than it had been with me.

"I was," she said simply.

"Why would you do that?" Wilson phrased the question like an accusation.

She needed to get away from Alexei.

She gave him a bland smile, though I could have sworn I saw a shadow of remorse pass through her eyes. "People do a great many foolish things when they love someone."

Ah, yes. That must have been the emotion burning furiously from her eyes when she glared at me on our entire journey back from Socair. At least no one could fault her lying skills.

"Like lie to help them avoid a murder conviction?" Wilson pressed.

"I have no need to lie," she said mildly, turning to face the sniveling laird. "He was with me."

"Doing what, exactly?" he demanded.

Her cheeks colored, and a white-hot bolt of rage shot through me. Her gaze slid toward my mother, but I was already sitting forward, fighting to keep my fists unclenched.

"She doesn't have to answer that," I bit out coldly. "Unless, of course, you'd like to speak about the specifics of what you do behind closed doors with your wife. Or at the brothel, in your case."

I met Wilson's gaze, refusing to back down even as his face

flushed with anger. It was an intentional reminder of the secrets I held, and it did its job admirably. He sputtered some half-arsed denial.

But he refrained from asking any more unnecessarily invasive questions.

The questions continued mostly in that vein, covering things I had more or less put together by now. It was impossible to say how much of it was true since she seamlessly blended facts with a few scattered lies.

No, I had never seen the man before. I went with him because he threatened Davin and his family. I didn't have a choice.

Then they got to the letter, which only hours ago, I claimed to have burnt rather than pass over to them.

"You say you only left because of the threats?" MacBay asked Galina.

"That's right." She fiddled her hands nervously, pushing back her sleeves to expose her hand along with her empty wrist where her bracelet used to sit.

"Yet you purportedly wrote a very convincing letter to the contrary," Wilson huffed.

Nice to know the soldiers in the hallway had been feeling talkative.

If I hadn't been watching her for it, I wouldn't have noticed the way one blond eyebrow raised the smallest fraction of a millimeter. It was as close to a challenge as she had come.

She looked him straight in the eye. "Not convincing enough, apparently."

I bit back a scoff. *Don't sell yourself short, Love. It was plenty stars-damned convincing.*

"So you didn't want your betrothed to come after you?" MacBay challenged.

She met his eyes, her expression carefully vulnerable. "I never want Davin to do anything that puts him in danger."

"Because you love him?" Wilson didn't bother to keep the sarcasm from his tone.

I would almost imagine he knew that each clarification he insisted on was like slicing open a raw wound and pouring an entire shaker of salt into it, except that Galina was too convincing for them to guess at the truth.

Even now, she nodded. "As I've said."

Her features were earnest, and her tone was utterly devoid of falsehood. Not that it meant anything. It had been impossible to tell that she was lying this entire time, so why would this be any different?

Even if she was telling the truth, the problem with us had never been feelings. If I was being honest, I could admit that I had been drawn to Galina from the moment I saw her, perfectly poised and put together. Standing demurely and silently at her uncle's side, she still had a presence that drew every eye in the room.

Even then, I had wanted to know what it would be like to watch her unravel. And for all her protests, the endless nights she spent on a rooftop with me in a castle full of men who wanted her told me she felt that pull as well.

But attraction wasn't love, and it was everything else that seemed to get in the way with us.

Laird Wilson's eyes lit up, like he had led her exactly where he wanted to, but it was MacBay who spoke.

"Forgive me, Lady Galina. But I can't help but wonder, if everything you say is true, why are the two of you not betrothed at present?" He glanced pointedly at her empty hand, the finger where only weeks ago had rested the most sought-after ring in all of Lochlann.

I bit back a curse. I thought back to Gracie telling me she believed our relationship was a ruse, my mother constantly enforcing how important it was that we make this believable. The lairds were already struggling to buy my alibi, and now this matter of our fake engagement, when my entire defense of this crime hinged on Galina's honesty.

We should have prepared for these questions, should have forced ourselves to talk to one another, should have known that the Assembly would try to blindside us both. But of course, I hadn't realized we wouldn't have a single moment to breathe.

Instead of looking taken off guard, though, Galina looked almost...triumphant. I thought back to the way she had fidgeted openly, moving her sleeve out of the way. She had known they would ask this, and for some reason, she wasn't bothered by it.

She squared her shoulders, solidly meeting MacBay's eyes. Something churned in my gut, a foreboding at the defiant way she refused to look in my direction, like she knew I wasn't going to like what she said next.

Still, it took everything I had to keep my expression even when she spoke next. Like she had lit the fuse on a thousand kegs of black powder, her words hit with a blinding impact.

"I can assure you that Laird Davin and I are still very much betrothed." With that, she slid her gaze to me. "After all, you don't risk death and Unclanning for someone just to walk away and leave it all behind."

Chapter Twenty-Nine

GALINA

I FORCED myself to look at Davin while I sold what I wasn't entirely sure was a lie. It was an effort not to lose myself in the way he was back to being every inch the marquess of Lithlinglau, perfect and devastating.

We hadn't talked about the future, but considering we weren't speaking and he could barely look at me and he had told me more than once that I was free to go back to Socair, I could hazard a guess that he wouldn't be thrilled with this plan.

I sure as storms wasn't going to walk away and leave him to this mess after everything. He could hate me for it later, but he would be alive and out of exile, which was more than I could say if they thought our entire relationship had been a ploy.

At least he was every bit the liar I was.

When the lairds looked to him for confirmation, he gave a sharp nod, edged with just the smallest bit of condescension. As if to say, obviously, they should have known we were still engaged, not like he was just as surprised by that proclamation as they were.

"And on that note, my *fiancée* has been through an ordeal already," he gritted out, likely as an excuse for the mounting tension in his shoulders. "You've asked her everything you need to know."

Laird MacBay softened a bit at that, a trace of guilt clouding his features.

"Just about," he added, before glancing at my left hand once again. "May I inquire as to the ring?"

I blinked up at him to buy myself a moment.

The last time I saw my ring was when Alexei tore it from my finger and tossed it carelessly on the letter he had forced me to write.

"It was taken from me," I finally said, not bothering to hide the emotion in my voice. "I'm not sure what the man did with it after he removed it from my hand, but it was hardly a priority when we came back to this insanity."

A truth and a lie, one that should cover Davin adequately. Before anyone could respond, Davin stood up.

"Yes, we're looking into it. Thank you for your time, gentlemen."

I nodded demurely, standing and taking the arm Davin held out to me while I pretended not to be affected by his unexpected proximity.

The taut muscles in his bicep belied all the strain he wouldn't let show on his features. I took a deep breath. This was what I signed up for.

"Please let me know if I can be of any more assistance in your inquiry. I'm sure everyone is anxious to ensure that the other lairds are safe from whoever actually did this." My words were far more casual than the situation warranted, a bleak reminder that there had been a murderer in this castle only a few short weeks ago.

Then we walked out of the chamber like the united front we most definitely were not.

I PACED THE ROOFTOP, fighting for some semblance of my usual calm. Rather than follow me into my rooms, Davin had only flickered his eyes upward for a fraction of a second before disappearing into his own suites.

There had been no conversation after we left the Assembly chamber, not with two guards flanking Davin like he was a criminal. His own soldiers followed more closely, so he wasn't at the mercy of men he didn't trust. That was a small consolation, I supposed.

Now I was here, waiting for him in the bitter cold like he had done for me so many times before. Hamish was stationed up here tonight with another guard, but they had both backed away to give me distance when I arrived.

By the time Davin showed up a solid quarter of an hour later, his hair was markedly more disheveled, indicating he had run his hand through it more than once. If anything, he appeared to have worked himself into a state of aggravation rather than out of one.

He opened his mouth to speak, then closed it without uttering a single word. Once, twice, a third time. Finally, I couldn't stand it any longer.

"It was the only way," I said shortly.

He scoffed, his breath forming a wispy cloud. "You seem to think that a lot."

That might have been true, but I certainly wasn't the only one with tenuous boundaries. He, of all people, should understand.

"Don't pretend you aren't willing to cross lines the same as the one I crossed today," I said.

A muscle ticked in his jaw, and he looked away, not

pretending to misunderstand the comparison between him coming after me for my safety and me faking an engagement for his.

"That was...different," he hedged.

I arched a single eyebrow. "Was it?"

"It was my job to protect you in my kingdom." His tone was sure, but his averted gaze told a different story.

Annoyance prickled at my skin, and I lifted my chin in a challenge.

"While my job is, what, exactly?" I fired back, suddenly much less aware of the cold than I had been before. "To be a constant burden on everyone around me? To stand back while the people I care about are threatened and do precisely nothing about it?"

"Care about?" he echoed, his voice tilting up in both a question and an objection.

I didn't know if he was arguing that I cared or daring me to use the word I had thrown around to the Assembly. The air between us was charged, each measured breath crackling like lightning.

"You know I didn't leave by choice." My hands clenched on the railing. "Certainly not because I didn't care."

A bitter huff of air escaped his lips. I hated the sound of it nearly as much as I hated the distance between us.

"I don't honestly know what you've done by choice or by obligation or by necessity at this point, Galina," he said, running his hand through his hair for what was probably the twentieth time this hour.

"Is that why you're so upset? Because you think I'm doing it out of obligation?" *Or because the idea of being engaged to me is so abhorrent at this point?*

His sapphire gaze bored into mine. "I wouldn't have asked you to pretend with me, after..."

The blood drained from my face. After he had watched

me play a similar game with Alexei. He couldn't possibly think this was the same thing.

"You're nothing like him." It might have been the truest thing I had said all day.

Davin looked up at the overcast sky for several stilted heartbeats, as if it held the answers he was searching for.

"I told you that you were free to go, and I meant it," he said after a moment, not quite responding.

"Am I also free to stay, then?" It was as close as I could come to asking if he wanted me to leave.

He heaved a long sigh. "You're free to do whatever you want, in the unlikely event that you can figure out what that is, let alone admit it."

"I knew what I wanted."

"Did you?" He would have sounded genuinely curious, if it weren't for the backdrop of an altogether darker emotion. "Or did you just know what you needed and manage to convince yourself of the rest?"

I froze, more stung by his words than I had a right to be. Why would he believe me now after I had done nothing but lie to him for weeks? Weariness crept into my limbs, settling deep in my soul. I couldn't convince him of the truth, and we were running in circles, just like we always did.

"Would it matter if I did?" I countered.

He didn't respond, only clutched the icy banister tighter. Suddenly, it was hard to breathe in a way that had nothing to do with the blustery winter air.

"I can leave as soon as this ridiculous farce of a trial is up," I offered as soon as I could force words out past the lump in my throat. "But don't throw your life away for the sake of a handful of weeks."

Davin blew out a breath. "Like you almost threw yours away for the sake of your secrets and your pride?"

Anger flared up within me, and I latched on to the

reprieve. "If you think I had an ounce of pride left after a week with Alexei, you can think again."

He visibly winced, and I shut down, realizing that was a road I had no desire to travel. A long silence fell, punctuated only by the occasional gust of wind.

"I didn't think," he finally said in apology. "I don't know what to think about anything anymore. I would ask you what happened, but you'd say it was nothing. I would ask you how you were doing, but you'd tell me you were fine. I'd ask why you're really doing this, and you'd give me some half-arsed reasoning that only scratched the surface of the truth."

He sighed, more tired than I had ever heard him.

"*Stars*, Galina, you can't even bring yourself to tell me what kind of soup you hate." He pushed back from the railing, putting his hands in his pocket. "But if you're willing to do this, then I'm hardly in a position to argue with you. I suppose if we got through the last three weeks, the next three will be nothing."

It didn't escape my notice that he included the festival in that timeframe, and the night he asked me to marry him. I supposed that was fair, even if it killed something inside me to admit it.

"Right," I whispered.

With one final nod, he turned to go, but he stopped just before he reached the winding staircase that led to his rooms. "Thank you, for doing this for me."

I stood up straighter, remembering Jocelyn's bolstering from earlier. "Thank you for coming after me."

It was gratitude long past due, but he nodded his acceptance all the same. Then he continued down the stairs, leaving me alone on the rooftop with all the words I couldn't bring myself to say.

Chapter Thirty

DAVIN

THOUGH IT WAS dark outside and felt impossibly late, I still had dinner to look forward to. With my newly fake fiancée and her bastard of an uncle, who would no doubt be even more pleasant than usual now that Galina and I were so happily engaged.

I would have given anything for my best friend and a village tavern right now, a perfect evening away from politics and murder charges and almost-fiancées.

No matter. Dinner with Mikhail was almost the same.

"You can't honestly be upset with her for doing the same thing that you did," Gallagher chimed in, helpfully assisting in my unpacking of all the things Galina said while we had a pre-dinner whiskey in my room.

A muscle worked in my jaw. "Yes, well...no one asked you."

Truthfully, I hadn't finished parsing through how I felt about any of it. I couldn't very well be upset with her for not discussing it with me when I had intentionally avoided her the night before she was questioned. And she was right, it was the only real option.

Gallagher raised his eyebrows in an especially irritating, *that's what I thought* way, and I glared at him.

Whether either of them was right or not, it didn't make me look forward to the prospect of spending the next three weeks watching her pretend to want to spend the rest of our lives together. I couldn't be sure if any of it was real, if she was going to want to stay when it was over.

If I even wanted her to.

"Are you going to give her the ring back, then?" Gwyn asked, pulling me from my thoughts.

She had been quieter since learning what Galina had done today, not nearly as vitriolic in her commentary.

My gaze drifted toward the desk in the corner of my room — specifically to the drawer where the ring was safely tucked away and had been since the day I found it with her letter.

"I'll make sure she has a ring," I said. "But she's already told the lairds that one was lost."

Gal looked at me like he knew exactly how flimsy that excuse was but didn't push.

"I'll escort her to dinner, if you like," he offered casually.

Something ugly reared up inside of me, in spite of everything, and I opened my mouth to tell him *no* when I saw the smarmy grin on his face.

"Next time you wonder why Row is my favorite cousin, picture this moment," I told him, moving the whiskey bottle out of his reach just as he went to refill his glass.

He shrugged, pulling a flask out of his coat instead. "I just thought you might want some help sorting through your feelings."

"Yes, I'm lucky to have you," I deadpanned. "In any event, that would hardly look good to MacBay's guards, who are no doubt reporting on my every move."

"Admirable attempt at recovering your dignity," Gwyn offered.

"Wow." I stared at her unblinking, but she only grinned back.

"Please report all hurt feelings to your favorite cousin, who is no one in this room," Avani said from where she was warming her tiny squirrel by the fire. "For what it's worth, I agree with Gal. I'm happy she took the initiative. Even dear Gwynnie is, though she'll never say it out loud."

Gwyn grunted something that might have been an argument or an agreement.

"Where is she, anyway?" I asked, glancing at the large clock against the wall. If my cousins were all in my rooms, then Galina would be alone, save perhaps, for Anna.

Avani turned her attention toward me, her long fingers still stroking the rodent's head.

"I thought she might appreciate a few minutes alone," she said, piercing me with that emerald gaze of hers that was far too knowing. "Well, alone with Anna."

I nodded once, my conversation with Galina playing out in my head over and over again, the reminder of how much she felt like a burden, how dependent she had to be on everyone else, and how vulnerable she truly was.

Avani's squirrel gave a small squeak, its chubby head tilting toward the sound of footsteps outside the door as it locked eyes with my cousin. She followed his gaze, explaining to him that it was only the soldiers before scratching his head.

She had tried to explain how her ability worked, though it was still a little murky. She got vague impressions from the animals that she could interpret more clearly if she knew them better.

But they could understand her just fine.

An idea formed in the back of my mind. It wasn't perfect and it wouldn't solve everything, but at least it would be a start.

SINCE I HAD ASKED Avani to hang back, we were running a few minutes behind. Galina was ready and waiting by the time we made it to her rooms.

Wordlessly, she answered her door, her eyes flitting between Avani and me. Once again, a wave of rosemary and lavender washed over me as she took my arm, bringing with it an unwanted barrage of memories I tried in vain to keep at bay.

She was dressed in a gown made of pale purple silk with delicate silver embroidery, her hair half braided up and pinned with diamond and amethyst hair combs. Black kohl lined her pale eyes, and her lips were stained soft pink.

Anna had worked hard to hide the signs of fatigue, but they were there, hidden under her carefully applied cosmetics. It cemented in my mind the plan from earlier.

"Good evening, Lady Galina." The greeting was stiffer than I meant for it to be when MacBay's guards were watching, but of course, she took it in stride.

"Laird Davin, Princess Avani," she greeted back demurely.

She was already playing her part better than I was, though she made no move to close the distance between us. That was easily explained away by Socairan propriety, though. It wasn't any different from the way we had acted before, back when we were lying to ourselves far more than we were the court.

My cousin addressed her politely in return as both Galina's guards and my incessant escort fell in line behind us. Avani kept up a steady stream of mostly one-sided conversation on the way to the hall to cover for the tension flooding the air between Galina and me. She talked about how she had left Albert by the fire and asked Galina a few pointed questions about her feelings on animals while I occasionally hummed noncommittally.

I was struggling more than usual with this show, Galina's proximity...all of it. How many times had we walked these halls under the same pretense we were engaged in now? *Stars*, if the weight of it all didn't feel heavier tonight.

We eventually reached the dining hall, the crowded room quieting as we strode to the head table. The duke of Ram eyed us with irritation from his position at the end of the table with Uncle Logan. It was a seat of honor, but he was also boxed neatly away from his niece.

There were only a few seats left, and none of them were next to Mikhail. Two were to the left of Fiona Shaw, and one was further down next to Laird and Lady Jameson. For a very brief moment, I considered how terribly it would look if I sought refuge at that end of the table, leaving Galina to sit with Avani near Fiona.

At least the Jamesons were on our side. Lady Andra had always been kind, a reprieve from the rest of the court with the quiet wit and general warmth that she offered nearly everyone she knew. Even now, she smiled graciously at us over a steaming cup of cider, an expression that held none of the duplicitousness shown by the rest of the court.

As soon as Avani saw my predicament, she cleared her throat of the laugh I was certain was lodged there. I glared at her.

"Not all is lost, cousin," she whispered, releasing my arm to join the Jamesons. "You wanted to know what she knows."

That was true enough. Whether Fiona knew about the Viper, or hell, *was* the Viper, she had access to enough pillow talk to bring a kingdom to its knees. Either way, with just under three weeks left to find evidence, I didn't have the luxury of ignoring her.

So, I seated Galina next to Laird Gray, taking the spot

between her and the woman who had spent more than her share of nights in my bed.

She practically purred as I sat down next to her. When I reached for my wine glass, she subtly reached for something else. I swallowed hard, taking a sip before setting the glass back down on the table and removing her hand from my thigh.

Galina was at least distracted by conversation with the younger Laird Gray, who was seated next to his father.

Attractive and witty, she had called him once. Was she finding him so tonight?

"You know that I'm engaged," I said quietly to Fiona, keeping my hand in my lap, lest she be bold enough to try again.

Fiona grinned, as if the rejection had never happened. She tasted her wine, the deep red matching the shade of her painted lips.

"Are you?" she whispered behind the rim, her kohl-lined eyes dancing between me and my fiancée in question. "That's not how I heard it."

"Your sources are wrong," I said, continuing the conversation under my breath while the servants brought out the first course.

It was a small cup of potato soup that looked a lot like the crab bisque Galina pretended not to hate so much. My eyes sought her out, but she was barely looking at it, intent on her conversation with the Grays.

"My sources are never wrong," Fiona's coy tone pulled my focus back to her, and dread pooled in my stomach.

Of course they weren't, though it wasn't exactly privileged information at this point. The entire Assembly had insinuated that Galina and I had ended things, the contents of the letter having somehow become semi-public knowledge. So, she was likely fishing.

Surely.

My thoughts drifted back to every conversation my cousins and I had on the road, about motives and secrets and the identity of the Viper. I suddenly wondered what other information Fiona had access to.

Laird Rollings interrupted our conversation momentarily, asking some benign questions about the Lithlinglau stables and the horses we bred.

Fiona appeared wildly amused at the interruption, turning her attention to the MacBays while I placated Rollings. Gracie was standing in as the Lady of Gadleigh, as she often did when her mother was too ill to leave the estate. Camdyn seemed only moderately uncomfortable by whatever Fiona was saying, so she had probably made some vaguely inappropriate insinuation.

Unless it was something else entirely, like the fact that he was leading a murder investigation against me while eating dinner at my table.

Under the pretense of returning to my soup, I continued my conversation with Fiona, ignoring MacBay entirely.

"Then feel free to find out who actually killed my dear cousin," I said lightly. "Unless, of course, you already know."

"And rob you of all the fun you're having?" Fiona asked, tucking a strand of midnight hair behind her ear. "I wouldn't dream of it."

Whatever the vixen read in my expression caused her to let out a small, seductive laugh. The sound drew the attention of a few of the nearby lairds. She had a way of doing that, capturing the attention of the room, whether or not it was her intention.

Unfortunately, it also drew their attention to me. A few narrowed gazes looked between us, some of them with obvious disdain, and some more inscrutable. And of stars-damned course, MacBay was one of those.

He watched us carefully, hiding his expression behind his

glass of wine, and I bit back a curse. Did he think I was colluding with her? Or was it something more?

Was he judging whatever he thought he saw between us against everything Galina had said in the Assembly room?

Either way, I worked hard to distance myself from Fiona's attention for the rest of the evening, focusing instead on the other conversations surrounding us. Everyone from the Assembly was accounted for, along with their families. The odds were high that the Viper was someone in this room.

And they only needed to slip up once.

Chapter Thirty-One

GALINA

DINNER HAD BEEN PREDICTABLY TERRIBLE, between Davin's distant presence, Fiona's blatant flirting, my uncle's subtle glowering, and the smug satisfaction of the court members who were far too happy to see the lofty house of Lithlinglau under fire.

I hated all of them.

Though if I was being honest, I hated one of them a little more than the rest. Picturing her chiming laugh and her wandering hands made bile rise in my throat, but I stuffed it down before Anna could ask what was wrong.

Instead, I directed her attention to the herbs on one of the small dressers. Despite her best intentions in caring for my plants while I was gone, Anna had both overwatered them and exposed them to too much light, her overly nurturing nature getting the better of her.

And my poor herbs.

Dead leaves littered the pots like sad, wilted corpses, though the plants themselves were still technically alive. It felt like an unfortunate metaphor for my own wellbeing, one I had no desire to examine.

I smiled and thanked Anna for being so thoughtful and attentive to them while I was gone. Then I spent my morning sipping tea, gathering the dead leaves to store while Avani's maid readied her at the vanity. Her plump rodent leapt from her shoulder to her lap and back again, letting out squeaks that sounded more like a language than should have been possible.

And Avani seemed to understand each squeak.

I wondered briefly if it was just her nature to talk to the creature, or if, like Gallagher, she had some tie to the *vila* as well.

They left shortly after she was dressed, though Anna remained. She chattered about court gossip as she braided up my hair and applied my cosmetics in her usual maternal way, patting my shoulder and brushing hair back from my forehead in gentle gestures as she worked.

As usual, she took her time tidying up my room when she was finished. Before...everything, she would have waited until I left to come back, and it would have been with the help of a few other maids. Now, no one else was trusted in my rooms, and either Anna knew I couldn't tolerate being alone or she had been ordered not to leave me.

"I can ask Hamish to escort me to tea early," I offered, thinking about my plans for the day.

I only had three weeks, but I knew enough about the court here to know how the lairds were swayed by the opinions of their wives. Whether they accepted Davin's evidence could come down to sentiment in the end, so I had work to do on my part.

"Ach, no milady," Anna said with an apologetic shake of her head. "Her Highness asked me to wait for her this morning."

I supposed that made sense, since she would likely be at tea as well. I assumed, at least, though that was dangerous where the Lochlannians were concerned. She could just as soon be out questioning the lairds alongside Davin.

I still didn't know much more about the princess than I had gleaned that first night, other than she seemed to inherently understand my need for space. Or she just had a need of her own if the haunted, faraway look in her eyes sometimes was any indication.

I couldn't help but wonder if it was her husband she was thinking of, if being here was a constant reminder of everything she had lost, since she wasn't staying in the rooms I knew they shared here.

Either way, she never forced conversation on me. Not that it stopped me from feeling scrutinized when her perceptive gaze reminded me a bit too much of Davin's.

It was an effort not to pace restlessly around the room, but I didn't want to make Anna feel uncomfortable. Fortunately, it was only another few minutes before the princess returned.

And she wasn't alone.

With her was one of the most beautiful animals I had ever seen. Not her ridiculous squirrel, obviously, though Albert was there, too, wobbling precariously on her shoulder. She had brought a dog...or perhaps a wolf, though not quite like any version I had seen of either before.

It was nearly as big as my uncle's hunting dogs, and somehow fiercer, too. Though it was meekly trotting at the princess's side, there was a lethality to its every step. I wasn't afraid, but I would have been foolish to not be wary.

Avani was closely watching my reaction to the creature, so I tried to make my features a bit more even. She smirked, shaking her head.

"You do play your cards close to your chest," she commented.

"Is that a bad thing?" I inquired.

"Not always." She shrugged. "But I imagine it gets exhausting."

Did she mean for me? Or for the people around me, like Davin. I thought about his frustration that I couldn't tell him the soup I liked, Gallagher's casual observation that I didn't trust anyone, even Gwyn's accusations, and I couldn't quite bring myself to argue with her either way.

"It does," I said instead.

She nodded, like my response satisfied her.

"Is this the newest resident of this room, then?" I asked, stopping just short of saying *my room*. Though I thought of it that way, it felt presumptuous to say out loud.

Avani shrugged. "I suppose that depends on whether or not you like her."

I furrowed my brow. She certainly hadn't asked whether I liked her furry little squirrel before plopping him on the pillow next to mine. Again, she raised her eyebrows like she knew exactly what I was thinking.

"You're going to make me ask, aren't you?" I decided on a blunter route than I normally would have taken, remembering that this was Rowan's sister and Gwyn's cousin.

That caused her to laugh outright, a wide grin splitting her beautiful face. She wasn't quick to smile like Rowan, but the expression looked like it belonged on her features all the same.

"Well, court games are all good and well, but you'll never survive in this family if you can't be just a bit demanding sometimes."

I couldn't quite bring myself to tell her that surviving in this family was likely a non-issue for me, not when she must have known that, so I only nodded. "Very well. Why does it matter if I like her?"

I glanced at the creature again, and her fluffy tail subtly wagged at the attention.

"Because she's more than just a pretty face," Avani said,

patting the dog's head. "She's a guard dog. Or rather, a guard puppy right now, but she'll get there. That way, you wouldn't have to share a room with me and Albert anymore."

My mind worked on overdrive to piece together the implications of that, how every single thing that had happened since Alexei came could have been avoided if I had known about his presence before I walked unwittingly into my rooms.

How maybe I could find a way to sleep on my own without being terrified of every stray gust of wind on my balcony. Already, I had spent yesterday morning moving my outdoor collection of herbs and plants further toward the balcony so they didn't brush up against the window when a breeze blew through, something Avani hadn't commented on.

"You got me a guard dog?" I finally breathed.

Avani raised a single eyebrow, and it didn't take me long to amend my assumption. The dog was already tall enough for her head to come to my hips. Long, sleek black hair covered most of her body, but her face was white, along with her chest and the underside of her belly and tail. She was exquisite, chosen by someone with exacting taste. Someone I had told just last night that I was tired of being a burden to everyone around me.

And of course, he had listened. He had taken care of it, like he always did.

"Davin got me a guard dog," I corrected myself.

She inclined her head. "He did. Or rather, the option of a guard dog. This one can be used by the palace guards if you don't want her."

Already, part of me rebelled at that for reasons I couldn't define.

"But yes," she went on. "She was chosen to meet your specific needs."

I furrowed my brow curiously. "Which are?"

Avani straightened her shoulders, a small grin tugging at the corner of her mouth.

"She doesn't shed, and she scares the hell out of people. Besides, she was top of her class." She patted the dog's head proudly, and it basked in her praise. "And obviously, she'll go where you go."

Like to tea? Or back to Socair? Something in Avani's pointed expression made me think she meant both.

I looked at the dog — or puppy, as she insisted, though I couldn't imagine how massive the thing would get if that was the case. Piercing blue eyes studied me curiously in return.

"You don't have to decide right now," Avani said. "Why don't you let her stay with you for the day, and we can see how things go?"

I let out a slow, relieved breath. "That sounds perfect."

As soon as the words left my mouth, the dog trotted over to stand at my left side, sitting down at my feet and leaning ever so slightly against my leg. The weight and warmth was gentle and comforting.

I had a suspicion I had already made up my mind.

"WHAT IN ALL of the stars is that?" Gwyn exclaimed by way of greeting outside the tearoom.

She had been...not exactly warm since she heard I was staying for the trial, but at least less angry.

"The dog?" I clarified, my brow furrowed. It wasn't like Davin's family kept secrets, so I assumed she knew about it already.

Avani had spent several minutes teaching me commands

for my potential new guard until I was comfortable enough bringing her along for tea.

"No." Gwyn shuddered. "That thing on your finger."

Oh. That.

Davin's first gift of the day may have been a success, if you could call a guard dog a gift, but his second one was decidedly less so. Though it wasn't really a gift, either, so much as a loan, delivered by his manservant, who I was beginning to suspect of hiding a wicked sense of humor under his dour expression.

I hadn't yet dredged up the nerve to ask Davin what had actually become of my ring, the elegant ruby set into a delicately woven gold band that had felt at home on my hand from the moment he placed it there. This was not that ring.

"Blaine dropped it off," I said, trying to ignore the substantial weight of the ring currently on my finger.

"Does Blaine hate you?" Gallagher asked. He had arrived with Gwyn, though he would be leaving to spend the afternoon with the lairds soon.

"It's not outside the realm of possibility," I said, inspecting the atrocity all over again.

Davin and I might not be precisely getting along, but he wouldn't have wished this ring on his worst enemy, let alone someone he publicly associated with.

Every lantern in the hall, along with whatever rays of sunlight reached this part of the hallway, caught on each of the gemstones. The colors were reflected on the walls like an abstract painting done by a small child, all oversaturation and clashing hues.

There was, to be fair, a rather large ruby in the center, accented with every other gem in existence, including but not limited to a massive iridescent pearl on either side.

Gallagher cleared his throat. "Well, perhaps you could accompany me to my sparring match tomorrow and assist me in blinding Gwyn so that I might actually best her this time."

Avani choked on a laugh, and Gwyn snorted.

"I'd still win," she said casually.

Jocelyn walked toward us then, looking slightly more harassed than I generally saw her. She stopped short when she saw me, looking first at my furry companion with approval, then at my hand with rather the opposite emotion.

Her eyes widened with shock or horror, I couldn't quite tell. She blinked several times as if to clear her vision of the unfortunate appearance of my finger.

"Is that Granny Siobhan's ring?" she asked, her tone managing more neutrality than her features.

"It is," Avani answered gravely.

Jocelyn's nose wrinkled before she quickly smoothed it out. "She always did have...extravagant taste."

That was one way of putting it. The ring was probably worth as much as one of my uncle's priceless jeweled eggs.

"Blaine chose it," Gallagher supplied.

Jocelyn's eyes shot over to him, then back to the ring before she looked up at me again. "I suppose he thought he was being helpful."

That was a charitable assessment, but I didn't argue.

"In any event, it has already been spotted." Jocelyn tilted her head subtly toward Lady Wilson, then squared her shoulders with all the outward appearance of a woman resigned to march into battle. "No matter. In Lithlinglau, we set the trends. So..." She trailed off, seeming to be at a rare loss for words that only this particular piece of jewelry could have garnered.

Gal sighed dramatically, placing a comforting hand on his aunt's shoulder. "Steady on."

She dipped her head in a nod, stepping through the door to the tearoom.

"Indeed, Lady Galina. We shall face this new challenge

together, with bravery," Avani said in an undertone. "For Lochlann."

"For Lochlann," Gwyn and Gal echoed.

The brief moment of levity ended the moment I set foot in the tearoom and remembered why I was here. I had a job today, one that involved spending quality time with at least two of Davin's former bedmates.

Gracie MacBay tilted her head toward me before her soft brown eyes drifted to the dog at my side. Her eyes widened briefly before she let out a delicate sneeze, casting me an apologetic glance. Fiona Shaw, on the other hand, only arched a perfectly sculpted brow, her dark gaze taking my measure as she scanned me from head to toe.

She paused her assessment of me to look at the giant ring on my finger. I wasn't sure if it was jealousy or something else that forced her eyes to narrow.

Every other eye in the room also turned to us, conversation coming to a near halt. I could hardly blame them. Here I was, the recently kidnapped Socairan, with a hideous, sparkling ring the size of a chandelier, a wolf-dog at my side, and a fiancé accused of murder.

There were a few who were kind, like Lady Andra. I had spoken with her only briefly the night before, but it was enough to convince me that she was a rare welcome addition to the court. She smiled at me from behind a purple fan, her blue eyes widening with curiosity at the sight of the dog.

Then there was Lady Fenella, who was judgmental under her feathered headpiece, but not outrightly gleeful. Beyond them, most of the ladies wore expressions closer to Fiona's. I could see in their faces the same thing I had sensed at dinner last night. Whether Davin was guilty or not, they wanted him to pay for this.

They wanted Lithlinglau to fall.

Chapter Thirty-Two

DAVIN

THE SMOKING PARLOR was full today, which was unsurprising since Lithlinglau itself was nearing capacity. Plumes of sweet-smelling cigar smoke filled the air, cut only by the woodsy scent of the whiskey the lairds were drinking.

I spent the afternoon cutting cigars, filling glasses, and making shallow small talk, because no one can pretend the world isn't on fire quite like nobility can.

Even Uncle Logan forced himself to laugh and reminisce, though he declined the cigars the way he always did. He had always been more the people's king, disdainful of the politics in the inner circle, but that's where my father came in. While they told war stories with Uncle Finn, the lairds visibly softened at the reminder of the way their king had fought for them. Bled for them.

Not that it meant they wouldn't play both sides of this until the bitter end.

Of course, it wasn't my uncle's generation the lairds so vehemently objected to. It was who he was handing the leadership to down the line. So I joked and visited, asking after families and letting slip small initiatives I had in place for the commoners and nobility alike, eventually managing to coax smiles out of even the most surly lairds.

Except for Laird MacArthur, naturally, but I was fairly certain he didn't know how to smile.

As my luck would have it, the one laird I really needed to speak with the most was noticeably absent. MacBay hardly needed to curry favor, what with his spotless reputation, but his absence was interesting, all the same. So when the afternoon in the parlor came to an end and the ladies were finished with tea, I approached Avani.

"Fancy a visit to our favorite semi-traitorous laird with me?"

She pursed her lips. "I was just thinking how I hadn't used my widowdom to emotionally manipulate anyone in weeks."

I didn't bother pretending that wasn't half of why I sought her out. Camdyn MacBay wasn't a monster – at least, I didn't think he was, and Avani was his favorite.

Or had been at one time, anyway.

"And here I come with a golden opportunity." I held a hand to my chest. "You really should be thanking me."

She let out a dry chuckle, and her small rodent popped its head out of her pocket at the sound. Albert glanced between the two of us before stretching his pudgy little paws for her to pick him up.

She nestled him on her shoulder, shooting me a flat look. "Would you like that gratitude expressed during our meeting with the man trying to take my throne from me, or after?"

"Dealer's choice," I offered with a shrug.

She rolled her eyes but followed me to the second floor of the guest wing, all the way down the hall to MacBay's suites. They had used the same ones for years, long before Gracie's belated arrival in court, back when MacBay's wife was healthy enough to travel and they came with their sons for social visits rather than to incite a coup.

It felt odd now, knowing his sons and his wife were all back up north, that it was only him and Gracie in the vast suites. She was the one who opened the door, her eyebrows climbing into her hairline.

"Davin. And Your Highness," she added with a quick curtsy for Avani. "Come in."

Gracie was pretty, with round, pink cheeks, wide brown eyes, and a kind smile. Though Avani had often speculated her late arrival at court was a pointed bid to wait until I was ready to settle down, she had never indicated anything of the sort, and she was one of the few ladies who had made an effort to reach out to Galina.

I hated that she would be present for this less than pleasant conversation, but there was nothing to be done about it now.

"I'll get Da'," she said, correctly sussing out our reason for coming.

I nodded my thanks, and she left, returning moments later with MacBay. Was it my imagination, or did he look more tired than he had the day before?

His sandy blonde hair was shot through with gray, his brown eyes harder than they had been when we were growing up. Still, they softened when he looked at Avani, even as he let out an exasperated breath.

"One might think you weren't happy to see me, Uncle Camdyn," she said lightly.

"Not your usual level of subtlety," he responded, sinking into a chair and gesturing for us to do the same.

A flash of white-and-gray fur wobbled down Avani's back before sliding into her pocket. Albert clearly had feelings about being visible in this room, or by the imposing head of the MacBay family.

"I suppose my subtlety is stolen nearly as easily as my crown these days," my cousin responded.

"Is that what you think I want?" He met her gaze, his own hardening in response.

She raised her eyebrows in a challenge. "It's what your actions would imply."

He shook his head. "There may be an Assembly, but we all know the future of Lochlann lives and dies on your family."

Apparently not, if it was so precarious, but I didn't interject.

"And that's such a bad thing?" Avani asked.

He let out another long-suffering sigh. "It wasn't, when I thought you were all getting settled. But now..."

"Now my husband is dead," she said flatly. "And you, like the rest of our people, don't think I can rule without him."

"I think that your family has priorities that are not in order." His tone was gentler now. "Mac would have made a good king, but we both know that isn't why you chose him. You haven't left your castle in how long, but you came now, not to see your people, but because your cousin needed you? Rowan married only under threat of a war she nearly started, and the twins refuse to even consider arrangements that would benefit our people."

Avani clenched her teeth, looking away before she responded. "This isn't about all of us, though. It's supposed to be about Davin. Was his engagement not enough for you?"

Gracie shifted, and MacBay shot me a knowing look.

"You can lie to the people, and you can lie to the Assembly, but we both know that engagement was nothing but a ruse from the moment you stepped foot in this kingdom. The other lairds might pay arse-all attention to Socair, but I know damned good and well what a mess you left there."

"Which was taken care of," I told him. *Mostly.*

"Of course it was," he said with a trace of condescension. "Because you had your cousin to cover for you. Which is exactly my point." His tone turned more sincere, his fists clenching around the velvet armrests. "You keep playing games and you keep just barely winning, and one day, you won't. That is not a gamble I'm willing to take when our people's future is at stake."

Avani shook her head, a muscle working in her jaw. "Just because we act out of love doesn't mean we wouldn't do anything for our people."

"The problem, my dear, is when it becomes a choice between the two. That's not a choice I trust you to make." He pursed his lips regretfully. "Not then, and not now."

"So you'll let Davin pay for something you know he didn't do, just to prove a point to the monarchy?" She let out a disbelieving huff of air. "Do you honestly think a coup is better?"

MacBay ran a hand over his face, his calloused fingers smoothing out his short beard. "I don't know what he did, actually. What I know is that there are holes in his story and that once again, your family is bending over backward to protect their own rather than consider the bigger picture. Believe what you want, but I have no desire for the crown. I only want to see the family who wears it acknowledging the sacrifices required."

She held his gaze for a long moment, the air fraught with his disappointment and her betrayal.

"And what of your story, Laird MacBay?" Whatever familiarity had been in her tone was gone now, replaced with the unyielding timbre of the future queen MacBay didn't think her capable of becoming. "Where were you that night?"

He reared back like she had slapped him.

She only tilted her head. "If we would do anything for our family, and you would do anything for the people, then I'm not convinced that you wouldn't make a sacrifice for the greater good."

He swallowed hard, something indecipherable hiding in his narrowed gaze. "I have always been a man of honor."

"Then answer the question," I said, meeting his eyes.

MacBay glanced between the three of us before sighing.

"I was here, along with Gracie, in these suites until I went to sleep."

If I hadn't been paying such close attention, and if I hadn't become intimately familiar with the nuances of Gracie's expressions, perhaps I would have missed it – the minute, dissatisfied pursing of her lips, the blink that was just a fraction of a second too long – all things that told me MacBay was lying about where he was that night.

Which meant he was the only laird who didn't have an alibi.

Chapter Thirty-Three

GALINA

DAVIN WAS early to escort me to dinner tonight, but I didn't mind. I had sent Anna away as soon as I was freshened up, enjoying the small bit of independence I had back now, though I didn't quite know what to make of the dog just yet.

She seemed like she didn't know what to make of me, either, but neither did she stray far from my side except for when she dutifully checked the room upon entering. Even now, when Davin's familiar rap sounded at the door, she stood at attention just in front of me.

I placed a calming hand on her head, going to open the door.

Davin looked at me first, then my fierce companion, before his gaze fell to the enormous ring gracing my slim finger. For all his skill at hiding his expression, there was no concealing the confusion and subsequent revulsion that flashed across his features before he smoothed them out.

There went any doubt that he hadn't had a hand in picking the ring out.

Malishka stayed at my left side, gently pressing into my

thigh as I walked. It was a bit of an adjustment, getting used to her presence, but one I was already growing used to.

Once we got to the dining hall, I greeted first the king, then my uncle, as was appropriate. Just like Davin had, Uncle Mikhail looked first at me, then the dog that hadn't left my side all day, before finally landing on my ring. He arched an imperious eyebrow but said nothing about it.

Said nothing in general.

His silence wasn't quite ominous, but it was...concerning. He had agreed to let me stay until the investigation was over, but he certainly hadn't given his permission for another fake engagement. Yet he also hadn't sent for me since the first night we spoke, or delivered any threats.

For the second night in a row, he was seated next to the family heads, squarely between Logan and Jocelyn, who didn't appear to be outwardly perturbed at his presence.

Instead of leading us across from them like I expected him to, Davin made a beeline for the end of the table, near Camdyn MacBay. Or more precisely, near Gracie.

She let out a small sneeze, an apologetic look overtaking her features as she glanced between me and my dog.

He took the seat next to her, and Malishka dipped her massive head under the table, curling up right in front of the only available seat — right next to Fiona *storms-damned* Shaw. Before I could decide if that was better or worse than Davin being next to her, Gwyn and Gallagher came to sit across from us, and the soup was served.

King Logan announced the start of the meal in his booming, accented voice, and I dutifully dipped my spoon into what I realized a moment too late was crab bisque.

Lovely.

I looked to Davin, awaiting his commentary, but there was no sardonic look, no smirk, not even any judgment. He was busy, talking in low tones to the only girl he had been in something resembling an actual relationship with.

Something twisted in my gut that had nothing to do with the disgusting soup.

I had been at court long enough to know he would have married her if I hadn't come along. When he was backed against a wall, needing to settle down for the sake of the kingdom, it would have been tiny, gentle Gracie MacBay who he chose above the others.

And why not? She was kind, and open, Lochlannian, a favorite of the court, and apparently skilled enough in the bedroom to make him want to return to her when so few women held his attention.

The most obnoxious throat-clearing I had ever heard sounded next to me, pulling me from my thoughts with something far worse.

"Well, there's a solution no one has been bold enough to say out loud yet," Fiona said, a fake apologetic expression on her face. "If the MacBays were wed into the royal family and had a firmer hold on the politics there, everyone would get what they want."

I couldn't breathe. My lungs would physically not take in any air. A soft, wet nose nudged my hand beneath the table, Malishka apparently sensing my distress. I tried to take solace in it, but the truth of Fiona's words wouldn't quite leave my mind.

"Did you hear that, Twinsy?" Gwyn said in what could pass as a quiet voice for her. "If you would just propose to Gracie, we could all avoid the civil war her father's all but trying to start."

"I'll get right on that," Gal said easily, but his eyes flared with aggravation at Fiona, who arched a perfect onyx eyebrow right back.

I took a tiny breath in, then out, but the crushing feeling

on my chest didn't leave me throughout the entire meal. Not when I heard Gracie say *Dav* in a familiar way, or when Fiona shot me knowing looks over her wine glass, or when my uncle observed the entire scene with an expression I couldn't read.

It was all I could do to get through dinner. I barely remember Davin escorting me back, the concern that slipped into his gaze when he left me at my rooms.

"Are you—" He stopped, pursing his lips, and I remembered what he had said on the rooftop.

I would ask you how you're doing, but you would say you're fine.

"Are you having any trouble with Mikhail?" he said instead.

"No." I faked something closer to a normal expression. "Nothing I can't handle, and anyway, you have more than enough of your own problems to be concerned with."

Problems I'm actively contributing to. Was the Gracie solution something everyone else had seen? Was it something he was considering before I announced that we were betrothed? Should I ask him if he wanted to call it off now?

I couldn't get the words out, though, or any words out, with the way my throat suddenly felt like it was closing over. So I nodded my head and closed my door, all the while thinking how this was my fault.

All of it.

I WAS SPIRALING, drowning in an endless whirlpool of guilt and panic and panic and guilt, a perpetual cycle. My knees refused to hold me up any longer, so I slid my back down along the wall, crumpling to the floor beneath me.

I had lost Davin. And I had made Davin lose everything.

Everything seemed so clear now. Every road I could have walked down. The path I could have — should have — chosen.

Hadn't Jocelyn tried to tell me?

I understand, I had told her. But she had known it for the lie it was. Understanding came too late to help any of us.

It was clear to see now that if I had told Davin the truth from the very beginning, he would have taken care of it. If I had been able to bring myself to be honest with him, none of this would have happened.

Wouldn't his safety have been an easy price to pay for looking weak?

My breaths came too quickly, my pulse thundering in my ears while each of my missteps assaulted me. The quick rapping of Malishka's paws rang out as she paced between me and the door before coming to sit next to me. Her sleek head leaned against my shoulder as she let out a small whine.

"I'm all right, Malishka." I was even lying to the dog now, calling her by the name my father had used when he had tried to comfort me.

The herbs will grow back stronger, Malishka.

A rare stream of tears fell down my cheeks as I put my head against my knees, trying and failing to take a deep breath. I must have missed the sound of the door, because the next thing I knew there was a set of arms around me, and an unexpected voice in my ear, firm, but gentler than I had ever heard it.

"In and out," the low tone said. "Just like that."

From this distance, Gwyn smelled like wind and steel. It was comforting, reminding me of the days my father would take me to find plants growing in the mountains around our estate.

"I can't." It took everything I had to admit that, to her of all people.

"You can. It just feels that way now." She spoke with the same confidence she had wielding her sword, the confidence she seemed to have in every aspect of her life. Was that just her tone, or did she have experience with this same crushing feeling?

It was hard to imagine the fierce woman huddled on the ground falling apart the way I was now. Then again, she never would have wound up here. She would have fought to begin with, but I hadn't. I had tried to play a game, and I had lost.

Storms, but I had lost.

"Do you think he should marry Gracie?" I asked, throwing away what was left of my dignity.

Gwyn rocked back on her heels to look at me. This close, I noticed a pale sprinkling of freckles across the light-brown skin of her nose and cheeks, the pattern moving when her features flattened into exasperation.

"Davin was only talking to Gracie so much tonight because he needs to know something she knows." She said it in a voice that brooked no nonsense, like I was an idiot. "He doesn't want to marry her."

"He would have," I countered.

She gave a single, sharp shake of her head. "He would have done what he had to for his people, but he had plenty of chances to propose to her and instead, he proposed to you. She knows that, and so does stupid, meddling Fiona."

"I hate her," I muttered, talking about Fiona and also, unfairly, Gracie. Even tonight, Gracie had been perfect. She was kind to the servants, polite to the rest of the table, just like always. I knew it wasn't fair to group her in with Fiona's superiority and condescension. "Almost as much as you hate me."

"Don't get carried away," Gwyn said, raising an eyebrow, but the corner of her mouth twitched in amusement.

I took a breath, focusing my attention on Malishka while I wiped away the errant tears on my cheeks.

"How did you know to come in here?" I asked after a moment.

She looked at Malishka, then the door, then away. "You've been walking around like a lit powder keg for days. It was only a matter of time."

I nodded. That wasn't quite an answer, but I didn't press her further. I suspected Malishka had alerted Avani, and I didn't want to think about the entire stars-damned family knowing what a mess I was.

"But why would you bother?" I asked pointedly.

She sighed, settling next to me on the opposite side of Malishka. "You know, I genuinely like Gracie."

Of course she did.

"Even if her personality is a little more wet toast than I usually prefer in my friends," she added with a shrug.

I felt my lips turn up in the smallest hint of amusement.

Gwyn's tone turned more serious. "But there's no way she would have stared down the wrath of the lairds, her own uncle, and even Davin, then stood at his side while he was accused of murder. I'll confess, it took me a while to understand what he saw in you, but I think if you could ever pull your stubborn head out of your arse and learn to let some of this—" she gestured to all of me "—out before you combust, you might actually make it work."

I shook my head, the drowning feeling returning in spite of her words. "If he even wants that anymore."

She looked over at me in a challenge. "You won't know what he wants if you aren't willing to give him the options he deserves."

"What if I don't know how?" Another admission that nearly froze on my lips, but I forced the words out somehow.

"Then you learn."

It was so matter of fact, so very Gwyn. If you don't like something, change it. If you don't know something, learn it. Her black-and-white practicality was a welcome reprieve from the maelstrom of my own mind today. Though, I couldn't help but wonder if any of it mattered now.

"Will there even be time for any of this?" I asked in an undertone.

Time to make this right before the people punish Davin for something he didn't do, to focus on whatever we are before the kingdom goes to war.

Her features hardened. "Our family hasn't let the rebels win yet."

Maybe it was only her abundance of self-assurance speaking, but it still eased something inside of me. So I nodded, and she abruptly stood to go, getting to her feet with all the deadly grace of a predator.

"Well, that's all the togetherness I think either of us can stand." She strode over to the door, turning just before she opened it. "Just so we're clear, I still don't like you."

I smiled, hearing the almost-lie. "I'd be disappointed if you did."

Chapter Thirty-Four

DAVIN

EVERY DAY, it was getting harder to convince myself that we were going to find a way out of this. The investigation was going nowhere, and we were lacking solid leads, or any leads, really. Even Gracie had doubled down on her lie, insisting I was chasing shadows. She had made it clear she was done entertaining any further questions on the matter, and I couldn't very well force her to talk.

She was understandably loyal to him. MacBay as the Viper still felt wrong, in any event, so it wasn't worth alienating her by pushing the issue until I had more information. Something I was short of these days.

It seemed ridiculous that between Lochlann's entire royal family and its spymaster, we couldn't ferret out who was behind this, but as usual, none of the rebels were talking. There were still bodies cropping up in the villages, though, still whispers about the Viper who had to be connected to this somehow.

I went over the facts I had relentlessly in my mind.

At the festival, Tavish had looked terrified when I mentioned the Viper. He had glanced into the crowd, like someone there was watching him. Then he died, the same night Galina was taken by someone who was working with the rebels.

Did the Viper pave the way for Alexei to take Galina as some sort of distraction? Was Alexei involved to begin with? Tavish couldn't have been in the way of Alexei trying to break into Lithlinglau. My cousin was killed in his rooms, already incapacitated by a slow-acting poison.

A tapping sound interrupted my thoughts, and it took me entirely too long to realize it was coming, not from my quill or the front door, but from the balcony.

Where only Galina ever came.

I crossed the room in several quick strides, trying not to think about why she might be here and if I was ready for any conversations that might ensue. Bracing myself, I pulled back the curtains to find Galina standing on the other side of the glass, accompanied by the dog Avani and I had procured just that morning.

A gentle dusting of snow covered her hair and lashes, and her cheeks were already pink from the cold. The dog, too, had snowflakes rapidly settling in her fur. I worked quickly to unlock the door, stepping back for them to come in.

I couldn't help but give her a quick onceover, looking for any signs that something was wrong. Her eyes were red-rimmed, which could have been from the blustery temperatures, but given her presence here, likely wasn't. Otherwise, she appeared to be unharmed.

And gorgeous, an unhelpful voice in the back of my head reminded me.

Even in that thick, shapeless velvet dressing gown with her hair braided back, she was beautiful, but it was more than just her appearance. Her resting Socairan face was noticeably absent for the first time since I had found her in that inn, replaced by something...softer.

"Galina," I greeted, unsure what else to say. "Is everything all right?"

The sound of the door clicking shut echoed loudly through the room.

"As all right as it can be," she said, pushing an escaped strand of hair behind her ear in a rare display of uncertainty. The world's gaudiest ring glinted in the moonlight.

Had I known Blaine was still holding a grudge, I would have gone to fetch a ring myself. Clearly, he still hadn't forgiven her for leaving, since he ordinarily had excellent taste.

"What is it?" I asked, concern edging into my tone.

She spoke quickly. "Earlier, Gallagher mentioned something about a mountain of correspondence, and I know you must be at your limit, so I just thought, perhaps, since I wasn't sleeping anyway, I could help—"

Have I ever heard her ramble before?

"Help would be nice," I cut off her stream of words, moving further into the room.

She followed, gesturing to the dog. "Come, Malishka."

I turned back to look at her, curiosity and amusement getting the best of me.

"You named your ferocious guard dog *baby girl*?" I asked.

"Avani says she is still a puppy," she replied, somewhat defensively. "So it seemed fitting."

I hummed noncommittally, noting the light flush on her cheeks despite my very best efforts not to. It was harder when she was in my room, standing by my bed, looking so similar to how she had the night she had promised she would stay.

Then she had disappeared and returned as the earlier, guarded version of herself.

And now she was here.

Clearing my throat in an effort to rid myself of those thoughts, I pointed to a stack of letters, one of many teetering on the surfaces of my desk. My family had been helping me sort through them with varying degrees of success, but Galina had an organized mind and an eye for observation.

"If you want to start there, I'm trying to work out who might have actually seen something that night. Those are the contacts I've heard back from."

She nodded, and we set to work in silence, broken only by the crackling of the fire, the scratching of both of our quills, and Malishka's occasional yawn.

I tried to pretend the air between us wasn't charged with all the things we refused to say, tried to lose myself in the endless letters at my side. When I finally set my quill down to flex my hand, Galina's eyes tracked the motion before darting back to her letter.

Still, her own quill froze, and she delicately cleared her throat.

"I – I hated the soup tonight."

I looked at her askance. I had known that, of course, had teased her about it weeks ago, but she had never once admitted it.

"Did you?" I asked, raising my eyebrows slightly.

She nodded, slowly writing something on her parchment. "The flavors here can be overwhelming."

"As opposed to the light, inoffensive taste of borscht?" I couldn't help but tease her.

The corner of her mouth tugged up. "But borscht isn't so sweet and so rich."

"No," I agreed amicably. "Just revolting."

"You're revolting," she muttered, though her smile widened.

"Galina?"

"Yes?"

"Why are we talking about soup?" I had a guess, but I needed to know if she would confirm it. I was exhausted of the way we danced around everything.

She still didn't look up, though her quill paused again.

"You said I wouldn't answer, if you asked me things," she said, her brow furrowing slightly. "The implication being that I don't trust you."

Having thought about this extensively, to a frankly maddening degree, I couldn't find it in myself to argue. She *didn't* trust me. Hadn't, when it mattered, or even when it didn't.

When I said nothing, her shoulders tightened, but she went on.

"I'll never be like your family is, like Rowan is, or even Gracie, open and soft—" She took a moment to search for a word. "Expressive."

"I never wanted nor asked you to be that way," I said, steel in my tone.

She gave a sharp nod. "But I do trust you. The things that I kept from you were not about you...or at least, they did not feel that way to me at the time. It was just a part of my life I had hoped to leave behind."

I considered that from her perspective. Stars knew I could relate to wanting to outrun the past. How long had it taken me to talk about Mac? Longer than she had been away from Alexei, for sure.

"I can understand that," I said honestly.

"I should have seen how impossible that was," she said ruefully. "But I didn't want you to see me that way, when you were the only person who had ever thought that I was strong."

That pulled me up short.

"And you think what happened changed that?" My gaze bored into her, but she didn't turn.

She swallowed, sitting up straighter. "Obviously."

I thought back to the day she had come to my rooms in Socair, unyielding, even in the face of her injuries. How she didn't falter on the road back when we were threatened by rebels, when she was asked to sleep in a suffocating tunnel and ride astride for days on end.

She had stayed on the scene of an attack and treated injuries without hesitation, watched a hanging without looking away.

Then with Alexei... I may have been angry when I understood what she had done – and hell, I still was, but even then, she had remained steadfast and unflinching for days on end in the face of a man who she couldn't hope to physically overpower.

I could fault her decisions and her honesty, and yes, sometimes her pride, but I could never fault her strength.

"Galina." I said her name with a trace of exasperation. "I have thought you were many things over the course of the past few months, but weak was never one of them."

She met my eyes, a rare sheen of tears sparkling in her own.

"I was, though." Her voice was carefully controlled. "Not just with him, but with you. You were right. If you had asked me those questions, I would have lied. That is the life I was brought up in, the person I was expected to be. Alex–" She stopped before saying the bastard's name. "He would have wanted me to lie, to be whatever version of me fit into the idea he already had in his head. But that's not who I want to be with you."

I was frozen, torn between a rekindled fury at Alexei and another, more fragile emotion I couldn't quite name, something between sorrow for the place that she had been, and hope for the things she was saying now. Though both emotions were laced with caution because stars if we hadn't been close to here before.

"I never wanted you to be anything other than you are," I said after a moment. "I just wanted honesty."

She took a deep breath. "I know that. And I want to give it to you. I'm trying to figure that out."

It wasn't an answer to the questions that had been plaguing me every night, and it wasn't a solution to the distance that had crept between us, but it could be a start, if I let it be.

I held her gaze for several heartbeats. She was still poised, still Galina, but there were hints of vulnerability in her pale-blue eyes, in the defensive way she held herself and the hand that fiddled nervously with Malishka's fur.

"All right. Then I can be patient." For what, I wasn't sure, but it felt better than the alternative.

Better than losing her for good.

Relief flitted over her features before she turned back to her parchment. We didn't talk any more, but for the first time since before she left, the silence felt easy again.

And that scared me nearly as much as my impending murder charge.

Chapter Thirty-Five

GALINA

I AWOKE FEELING MORE hopeful than I had in a long time. Davin hadn't made any declarations last night, but he had said he would be patient. That was enough for me to decide what I was going to do next. No matter how long it took, I would stay in Lochlann until Davin understood that I wanted this. Wanted him.

I had been putting off this conversation for too long, sitting back and waiting for my uncle's reaction instead of being honest with him. Storms, I had been doing that with everything lately, so used to having my decisions made for me that I had stopped even trying to make them.

But it was time to move past that.

Still, my knees trembled as I walked the hallway to my uncle's rooms. Ewan escorted me to the door, but only Malishka and I went inside. I wasn't afraid of him. Not really. He had never hurt me.

Besides, something in his demeanor these past few days made me think he already knew what I was coming to say.

"Galina," he greeted, stepping back to allow me into the room.

"Uncle."

It wasn't until the door was closed and we were seated in the wingback chairs by the hearth that he spoke again.

"Have you come to tell me when you'll be finished with this charade so we can go home?" he asked in our dialect.

"You know that I haven't," I said in the same tongue.

Uncle Mikhail didn't argue, only looked me over shrewdly, then down at Malishka before nodding in confirmation. "And if he doesn't agree to marry you in earnest?"

He had never asked me if the engagement was a ruse, and I had never offered up that information, but he was a shrewd man. I swallowed, meeting his gaze fully before responding.

"This is still my home now," I said, folding my hands in my lap. "I can't go back."

Guilt churned in my stomach, though I was careful to keep my posture confident and my expression neutral. I was directly defying my duke — the leader of my clan and the head of my family.

And I wasn't going to take it back.

Several stilted seconds ticked by, the hands of the clock punctuating the sound of my thrumming pulse and the crackling of the fireplace.

Finally, Uncle Mikhail sighed, some of the stiffness in his shoulders giving way as he sat forward. "Was it so bad for you, in Ram?"

There was genuine curiosity in his gaze, along with something that looked a little like disbelief. I shook my head once.

"Not until Alexei."

His nostrils flared and his dark eyes narrowed. "Why did you not come to me?"

"Would it have changed anything?" I asked, keeping my tone even. "Would you have believed me?"

"It is a man's duty to protect his family." He clenched his fist, and I heard all of the things he wasn't saying.

He wouldn't have believed me because he wouldn't have believed that Alexei could have strayed from that same duty. But he was also apologizing, in his way, for not protecting me.

"I did not know," he murmured. "Not until you were taken. I tried to make you understand why you needed to come home, the position you put the clan in, and your family."

His expression flickered, and he swallowed down whatever emotion had threatened to expose itself, carefully securing his mask once more.

I thought back to the letters he had sent all those weeks ago. Were what I had seen as threats actually warnings? Or a mixture of the two? It was hard to say with my uncle, a man who had played both sides of a war. But I knew he wasn't without love, in his way.

Even with my marriage contracts, he had been kinder than he needed to be. When the notoriously brutal heir to Clan Bear was one of my best options, when there were lords twice my age vying for my hand, my uncle had only ever allowed negotiations with a lord known to be kind and upstanding.

Until Alexei.

"I was left with very little choice." It wasn't an apology so much as an explanation, but it was all I had to offer him.

"You have a choice now," he said stiffly.

I dipped my chin in agreement. "And I've already made it."

My words were like a sleigh teetering on the edge of an icy mountain, existing at the mercy of my uncle's weight. One shift, and I would go tumbling down.

"Even if it means you are removed from the clan?" His tone was quiet, almost careful, like he sensed the same precarious edge that I did and hadn't yet decided whether to let me fall.

I squeezed my eyes shut, that possibility feeling more substantial with my uncle in front of me declaring it so, but I had made my peace with my choice. If I fell over the edge, then my new family would be there to help me pick up the pieces. I understood that now.

"Even then," I told him.

Silence fell, and the sleigh in my head teetered precariously. Disappointment and fear and grief swirled like a blizzard around us, but for now it was only me and the man at whose whims I had existed for as long as I could remember.

Malishka moved closer, laying her giant head in my lap as her blue eyes searched for the source of my anxiety. I comforted myself by running my hands along her neck, using her to ground myself while I waited for my uncle to respond.

"I have already written to Nils," he eventually said.

I squeezed my eyes shut, resigned.

"I told him it was no fault of ours if his nephew decided to embark on an expedition, but we can hardly hold you to a betrothal with no groom."

My eyes flew open, my gaze snapping up to his. He looked away, letting out a slow breath while I tried to determine whether my mind was playing tricks on me.

"I have had more than my fill of the loch land, so I will take my leave within the week. Your parents will expect a visit soon," he added gruffly.

I could hardly speak, my lips numb with shock.

"Yes, Uncle."

He nodded in a clear dismissal, so I stood to leave, Malishka falling in step at my left. But as I reached for the door handle, I froze, knowing I would never get answers from him again.

"Why?" I spoke without turning around.

A deep sigh resounded from his spot near the fire. "You are still the pride of our clan, and I will not let Wolf take that from us."

I shook my head softly, hearing everything he was too

proud to say. That he wouldn't let Wolf take me, not again. That even though he had many weapons left in his arsenal, he was choosing to let me stay here.

I heard Jocelyn's words resounding in my head once more. You can't always choose who you love, but you get to choose who is deserving of your loyalty. My uncle was many things to many people, most of them negative, and his choices had lost him my loyalty.

But not my love.

TEA WAS EVEN LESS pleasant than usual. Fiona and Gracie were both at my table, along with Avani, who had bravely sat down beside me. Jocelyn and Gwyn were caught up at Fenella's table, which looked to be its own kind of fun.

For a solid hour, I had the privilege of enjoying Fiona's snide remarks and Avani's dry responses and Gracie's occasional amicable interventions.

It wasn't until Lady Andra was kind enough to join us for the last fifteen minutes that the tension eased at all. While Avani distracted Davin's former lovers, I fell into another easy conversation with Lady Jameson.

She didn't ask about my gaudy ring or point out that none of the other ladies brought their dogs to the table at court. Instead, we sipped on spiced apple tea and ate cinnamon rolls while she told me how beautiful Lithlinglau was in the spring.

It was nice, to finally feel like I was making a friend at court, one who wasn't related to Davin by blood or who hadn't desired to share his bed. At least, not according to Avani.

After the world's longest tea, there was more socializing before I went back to my rooms to freshen up for dinner.

By the time Davin came to escort me to dinner, I was almost reluctant to leave. I held my breath, curious if our tentative truce would hold. His eyes were guarded, but not as distant as they had been.

"Lady Galina," he greeted.

It was formal, polite, and I found myself unreasonably resentful of it.

"Lina," I corrected.

He raised an eyebrow, and I took a deep breath. *Small truths.*

"I like it better when you call me Lina." Actually, I preferred it when he called me *Love*, but I wasn't sure either of us was ready for me to admit that just yet.

His lips tilted up at the corner in a knowing smirk that made my entire body tingle in awareness. He looked perfect tonight in a deep emerald jacket that matched the embroidery on my paler green gown.

"Even though it's a heinous breach of Socairan propriety?" His teasing tone had some of the tension fleeing my shoulders.

Bantering with Davin was like breathing, and I was starved for oxygen.

I shrugged. "That's what makes it so suited to *you* saying it."

A low chuckle escaped him as he held out his arm for me. I wrapped my hand around his bicep, stepping just a bit closer than the stilted distance we had been keeping for the past week.

Our easier atmosphere continued through dinner, where I forced myself to admit that I preferred the leg of the hen even though it was messier to eat.

It wasn't anything important, not yet. My stomach still

churned when I admitted to disliking something I was supposed to like, and I couldn't look at him for ten solid minutes after acknowledging that I hadn't slept well the night before.

But true to his word, he was being patient, and I was trying. *Learning*, as Gwyn had said.

Once dinner was over, my uncle handed me a letter from my parents.

"It came this afternoon," he said gruffly.

I inclined my head. "Thank you, Uncle."

He only turned to go with a last disapproving look at Malishka, and I hurried to my rooms to open the first missive I had received from my parents in the months since I left Socair.

Malishka, it began.

It was from my father, then.

Your mother and I arrived home this morning. We are taking care of matters of the estate that were overlooked in our absence, and ensuring that all is well, should we need to travel going forward. In the unfortunate event that your betrothed cannot be located, I trust a trip to Lochlann will be necessary in the near future.

We, of course, will mourn him first.

SARCASM AND A WARNING. *Give it time to let things blow over before you have another wedding*. But they would come here, to Lochlann. I didn't know what would happen, if there would even be another wedding, but their open support was more than I could have hoped for.

And not just theirs. It didn't escape my notice that if the letter had come today, my uncle had written even before I came to see him.

The rosemary seems to have wilted in your absence, but I'm coaxing it back to life. It's resilient that way, useful not only for remembrance, but for weathering that which would destroy a more fragile plant.

With a pang, I thought of my rosemary charm on the bracelet I still couldn't bring myself to look at. I heard everything Papa didn't say. That he missed me. That he knew something had happened, but he trusted me to weather it.

All our love,
Papa and Mama

Then there was a postscript written in a different, equally familiar hand.

P.S. Gray was never your color, darling.

. . .

WARMTH SEEPED THROUGH ME, filling up the parts of me that had been cold and empty and damaged since I left them behind.

I rolled the letter back up, wondering at the speed of their journey, if Mama had traveled by horseback, if Davin's men had seen them home, or if it had been unnecessary. Somewhere in the furling of the letter, and the picturing of Socair, an idea formed in my mind, a small way to help.

Even if it meant asking Gwyn for a favor.

Chapter Thirty-Six

DAVIN

GWYN'S THUNDERING knock woke me before the sun even had a chance.

"They found him," she announced as she burst into my room.

I barely had time to wipe the sleep from my eyes before she was digging around in my trousseau, throwing a tunic and a fresh pair of trousers in my general direction.

"Come on," she complained when I wasn't dressing fast enough.

"Gwynnie, darling," I said while half-stepping into my left pant leg. "What in the hell are you talking about? Found who?"

"Edgar," she spat, and suddenly I was wide awake.

The guard who had helped Alexei sneak Galina out of the castle.

I quickly slid my other leg into my trousers and threw my tunic on over my head. Gwyn tossed my boots at me, and I threw them on without bothering to lace them. All I could think about was how close we were to answers, and how much I wanted to make that bastard pay.

I wasn't sure what state I had expected to find him in, but I wasn't sad when his eyes were blackened, his lip bloody, and his clothes torn.

He scowled at us as we approached his cell, his muscles clenching like he was bracing for a fight.

"Did we check for a false tooth?" I asked.

"Yes," Gal said from the corner of the room where he was examining a white molar under the low light of the lantern. "It was the first thing the soldiers did when they found him.

Edgar spat on the floor, showing us just how he felt about losing his only way out of this. His expression was set in determination, just like the others had been. He wasn't going to talk, not even with the threat of hanging.

That's what they had all wanted, a quick death rather than giving up an ounce of information on their cause. Even if it meant innocent men, women, and children would die for that cause.

I considered that and the fact that if we were in Alech right now, there would be other ways to exact information from him. Bloodier, but potentially more likely to provide results.

"And we're absolutely certain he was one of the men on duty that night?" I asked.

Gwyn stepped closer, crossing her arms over her chest. "Yep."

I nodded once, gesturing for the guards to let him out of his cell.

"I am going to be honest with you, Edgar," I said, rolling up the sleeves of my shirt. "I absolutely loathe traitors, especially when their actions cause harm to the people I have sworn to protect and the people I love."

My soldiers dragged him to a chair in the center of the room, and I waited for them to strap him in before continuing.

"So, let me go ahead and lay this out for you. You are going to suffer, oh, but you are going to suffer." I met his dark-brown eyes, fury and desperation mingling inside of me. "And afterward, when you're gasping for breath and bleeding out on my stone floors, I will ask you some questions. And you will give me the answers, because you know exactly what I am capable of."

Edgar swallowed, his gaze darting back and forth between me and my cousins, but they wouldn't help him. No one would. Not when lives were on the line and we were running out of time.

Leaning over him, I spoke in a lower tone than before.

"Let's begin."

HE BROKE before the skin on my knuckles did.

First with the location of his safe house. The soldiers had found him hiding in a tavern, but the barkeep said he hadn't been there for long. With a location, we could potentially find others, maybe even catch some correspondence with the Viper.

It felt like the first step forward we had taken since all of this began.

"So you never personally met the Viper?" Gallagher asked.

Edgar's eyes screwed shut, his jaw clenching tightly.

Finally, he shook his head. "No."

"No, you never met them, or no, you refuse to answer?" I pressed, and he grimaced.

"No," he said again, more firmly this time.

"Dammit." Gwyn hissed the word, throwing her hands

behind her head and resting them on her neck. "We are going to need you to give us something a little more substantial Edgar."

"I don't — I don't know anything else," he stammered, a far cry from the confident soldier he had been when we first walked into this room.

"You're lying." Gallagher's voice was like ice. "We will give you one more chance before we call the Captain of the Guard down to finish this interrogation."

He stepped forward, his voice far more deadly than I had ever heard it before.

"How can you live with yourself knowing that your people are responsible for the deaths of children? Of villagers who have done nothing to deserve it?" Gal took a breath, seething as he exhaled. He glanced down at his hands before meeting Edgar's eyes again. "I am tired of wearing the blood of the innocents that your Uprising has slaughtered. You claim you want change, but there will be no kingdom left to rule if you murder all of your people."

The man blinked, but there was a shadow of uncertainty behind his eyes, so I pressed the advantage.

"You think your family is safe just because you serve the Viper?" I prodded. "What happens when their village is next? When you aren't there to protect them and the Viper decides they're collateral damage, too?"

Edgar hung his head. He swallowed hard, defeat flashing across his features. Still, he stayed silent.

"Give us something," I said, running a hand through my hair. "One thing, and we'll give you a break. I'll even send down something for you to eat."

There was a long, stilted silence where I wasn't sure if he was going to speak, until finally, he shook his head, the words so quiet I could barely make them out.

"Riverwell," he said. "Last Tuesday, just after sunset."

I stared at him, every muscle still, trying to process what he was saying.

"That's the last place I met the Viper's contact," he added before hanging his head once again.

True to my word, I gave him a break, using the time to send word to every contact I had near there. I should have expected what came next, a crushing blow on the heels of our only real victory in weeks.

Instead, we walked out of his cell as promised. And even with Gwyn standing guard outside and Gallagher just down the hall, half an hour after we left, Edgar was dead.

After the entire day had gone to hell, I wasn't expecting to see Galina. We had spent the past few nights here together, pouring over notes and missives, trying to learn all we could about the Viper before she retired to her rooms for a few hours of sleep.

My cousins had been noticeably absent during that time, clearly aware of Galina's visits. At least they hadn't brought it up yet. Small mercies.

So I wasn't surprised when Gwyn and Gal headed to the room Avani was staying in instead of mine, but I was surprised to find my own suites occupied.

Galina was there, seated at my desk, leaning over what appeared to be a map. I had told her she was welcome in my rooms when I wasn't here if she needed to reference any of the notes, but this was the first time she had taken me up on it.

Malishka yawned and stretched from her spot near the

fire, her tail wagging as I walked into the room. Galina's reaction was more subdued, obviously, her gaze raking over my weary features and pausing on the darker spots that peppered my black coat.

"What's happened?" she breathed.

"The guard is dead," I said flatly, not bothering to explain further. I knew Avani had filled her in on where the twins and I had been for the entirety of the day.

Galina got to her feet, gesturing for me to sit down. I did, mostly because I was too tired to stand any longer. She poured me a glass of whiskey and pushed it into my hand, her fingers brushing against mine. I let my hand linger there for perhaps longer than I needed to before pulling it back.

Color flooded her cheeks, but she kept her features even until she raised her eyebrows in a question. "You think someone slipped him more poison?"

"We had already removed his false tooth. Maybe there was another we missed?" I theorized, running a hand over my face. "Unless it was just a coincidence with the timing of the break. Stars if I know."

"Did you inspect his clothes?" she asked, her brow furrowing in thought.

"Yes," I answered. "But not until after the fact. They had a normal amount of patchwork on them for a guard. Nothing overt, but easy enough to hide a capsule of poison in, I suppose."

She nodded thoughtfully. "Or it was in the food or drink."

"Which would be infinitely worse." That would mean someone here had poisoned him, that my staff was in on it, or the Viper had gone around them.

"So probably that one, then," she said drily, and I let out a humorless chuckle.

"The way our lives are going," I added, taking a sip from my glass.

My attention drifted to the parchment she had been focused on when I walked in. It was a map of Lochlann, and next to it was a row of tiny different-colored pots of ink. Upon closer inspection, there were symbols and words scrawled on the map, the colors correlating to the ink.

"What's all this?" I asked.

"Oh." Her cheeks flushed again. "I asked Gwyn to procure me a recent map."

That made sense, since Gwyn was probably the most familiar with our maps, given her extensive training from Uncle Finn. But that didn't explain why Galina needed one.

"What are the markings, though?" I gestured to where she had drawn small purple Xs, blue stars, red triangles, and other symbols, all with numbers to the side.

"I was wondering if it might help us, knowing where some of the attacks had been or where we have reports that allege the actual Viper was present. The Xs are the deaths by poison. The red triangles are where a potential meeting happened, and the blue stars are the outright attacks."

I studied the map with interest. Already, there was the barest hint of a pattern emerging.

"This is brilliant," I said.

"It's nothing." She shrugged. "I'm not even sure if it will have any results."

"No, it's perfect."

Her eyes flicked briefly to my lips, and I wondered if, like me, she was remembering the last time I said that word to her. The way I had whispered it over and over against the softest parts of her until we were both spent and out of breath.

She cleared her throat, looking away. "Well, I should leave you to get ready for bed. For sleeping, I mean."

"What else would you mean?" In spite of my truly terrible day, I couldn't help but tease her, just as I had the last time she slipped up while sitting in that very chair after one too many sips of whiskey.

Before she left.

A shadow passed over her face, like she heard the turn my thoughts had taken.

"Indeed," she said softly. "Goodnight, Davin."

She stood gracefully, walking toward the door with Malishka at her feet. Just before she closed the balcony door behind her, she stopped, her eyes fixated on the hazy night sky.

"I didn't give you a truth tonight." Her voice was low, but it carried in the still night air.

"No, you didn't," I prompted, sensing whatever she said next would have nothing at all to do with dinner preferences.

Her shoulders tightened, and she drew in a shaky breath.

"The truth is...writing that letter was the hardest thing I've ever done. Leaving Socair, being taken by Alexei — *storms*, even marrying him... Not one of those things compared to hurling lies your way designed to hurt you."

My breath seized in my lungs. She never spoke of her time with Alexei, had never brought up the letter, had never referenced the fact that she was kidnapped and forced to marry a man who abused her.

Now she was acknowledging all of those things, and she was saying that causing me hurt was worse than everything that happened to her. Before I could make sense of that or find my voice to respond, she was gone.

Her words hung in the air, playing over and over in my mind until they cemented themselves there. Swallowing hard, I reached into my desk drawer, pulling out a folded piece of parchment. I had memorized the words, folded and refolded the paper until it was nearly crumbling at each crease.

It had become like a talisman to me, a symbol of all the pain I couldn't let go of, where she was concerned. One more time, I opened it up, running my hands over the perfect script crafted by the steady hand of a woman trapped in a room with the embodiment of her nightmares.

Then I tossed it into the fireplace and watched it burn to ashes.

Chapter Thirty-Seven

GALINA

MY CONFESSION the night before was the first one that didn't fill me with panic. It was long past due, an admission he more than deserved.

And it wasn't a lie. Of everything that happened, hurting Davin had been what threatened to break me. He didn't mention it the next day, but things between us felt just a little easier.

Once again, long after the day was over and we had all retired for the evening, I found my way to his rooms. We spent some time updating the map with the information he had gotten from the prior day's interrogation. It painted an interesting picture of the Viper's movements and locations.

There were traces of the Uprising throughout Lochlann, but the attacks seemed centrally located in the south. We didn't have answers yet, but at least we knew where to focus our attention.

After that, I worked quietly at his desk while he wrote letters by the fire. Though the air between us was lighter tonight, filled with casual greetings and offers of whiskey and occasional polite conversation just as it had been at dinner, it felt more charged, too. Weighed down with tension.

Or perhaps it was only me who felt that way. I couldn't help but track the motion of his glass to his full lips, his deft fingers closing around his quill. Surely it was unreasonable to be jealous of glass and steel and everything that touched Davin when he still felt so far from me.

I was watching him more closely than I meant to, which is why I noticed the third time he stopped to massage his hand.

"I have a salve for that," I offered, belatedly remembering he had something far better at his disposal. "Unless you want to call for Gallagher..."

The corner of Davin's lip pulled up in a rueful smile. "Gal alleges he can't heal aches and pains, though I maintain that's just something he says to get out of curing our hangovers."

I considered what Gallagher had told me about his ability, wondering if Davin was right. I hadn't taken much time to reflect on our conversation since then, but in hindsight, I remembered what he had said, that his secret involved more than one person. I thought of Gwyn's unnatural speed and Avani's pet squirrel and the way Rowan always hid a smirk when my uncle coincidentally got rained on just as he was walking into her palace.

"Is it strange, being the only one without...whatever it is?" I asked, pulling the small tin of salve from my satchel.

Davin looked taken aback. He studied me for a moment, and I wondered if it was a topic I shouldn't have broached.

"I call it their *woo-woo* powers," he said after a beat. "Though they insist it isn't. He told you about the others?"

"No, I just put it together." I gently pried the lid off the salve, letting its pungent aroma out into the air around us.

"Of course you did." He smiled, but it died as quickly as it had come.

"I wasn't the only one," he said quietly, pain flaring in his sapphire eyes, "when Mac was around. By the time he was... gone, I was used to it, I suppose. It doesn't really come up."

"That makes sense," was all I could think to say.

I looked down at the tin in my hand. Expressing feelings wasn't something I felt would ever come naturally to me, but this was something I could help with.

Before I could give him the salve, Davin held his hand out to me instead. My heartbeat stuttered in my chest, even as I told myself how ridiculous I was being. I took his hand with my left one, reaching into the tin with my right.

Lightning crackled from every point our skin touched, but I ignored it. Or tried to, anyway, focusing on spreading the ointment evenly on the areas where the tension would settle in. The base of his thumb. His wrists. Then back again, massaging as I went.

"Do you always carry herbs on you?" His voice was low, and still, it startled me.

"I got into the habit, out of necessity," I answered too honestly.

Davin froze, his fingers going rigid in my hand. I looked up to gauge his expression, and his eyes locked on mine, brimming with concern and ire. He sucked in a breath to speak, but I cut him off.

"Don't," I said with a brief shake of my head.

Don't ruin this moment of normalcy. Don't make me talk about this right now.

He closed his mouth, his gaze softening. I started to pull my hand back, but he tightened his hold on it. Gentle, firm, *everything*. I couldn't let go – didn't want to.

"Your uncle is leaving in the morning," he murmured.

Of course he knew that.

"He is," I replied evenly, afraid to say too much when I wasn't sure where he was headed with his non sequitur observation.

"Alone?" he asked.

Oh.

"I told you I would stay." The words came out before I could consider them, and I braced myself for him to remind me that I had said that once before.

But he didn't.

"You don't want to go home?" His eyes bored into mine, belying the importance of this question. It mattered so much to him what I wanted, even now, even after everything.

His thumb rubbed small circles on my hand, tracing the outside of my fingers in a maddening pattern that stole my breath and my senses and made me want to throw caution to the wind and tell him all the things I had pushed back to the shadows for reasons that felt so, so stupid now.

So I did.

"I *am* home." I didn't even look away when I said it. "You're the only home I care about anymore."

He swallowed, then took a breath, letting it out slowly. I could swear I counted a hundred maddening heartbeats in the span of those seconds.

"Will you tell me why you left my rooms that morning?" His voice was a quiet rasp.

I let out a small laugh between a laugh and a sob. It was all so ridiculous now.

"Because I was a mess," I admitted. "And all my stuff was in my rooms."

He studied my features, searching for a truth, a lie, some form of confirmation. "That's it?"

"That's it." I willed him to believe me. More than anything, I needed him to hear the truth of those words.

"You weren't scared? Second-guessing yourself?" Disbelief edged his tone.

I shook my head. "No. I thought I would be back before you woke."

We both knew why I hadn't been. I saw the moment it dawned in his eyes, the shadow that passed over his features when the last shred of doubt left him. Saw when it was replaced by the realization that I would have been on my way back to his bed, ready for him to wake up with me in his arms, to spend the morning continuing the prior night's exploration of one another, if Alexei hadn't taken me instead.

It was a whole mountain of guilt I would just as soon leave behind, for both of our sakes. My remorse at lying, his at failing to keep me safe.

"You said you could be patient," I breathed.

Could he hear my heartbeat thundering as loudly as I could? Could he feel the tension flooding between us, stretching across the distance that I wanted so badly to erase?

"Yes," he said softly.

I caught his gaze, letting my guard down enough for my intention to blaze through. "But I don't want you to be anymore."

I wasn't sure who moved first. All I knew was that his lips were on mine, and it felt like the missing piece to every puzzle I had ever tried to solve. He pulled me into his lap in a move that was commanding and gentle and entirely Davin.

I opened my mouth to his, savoring the faint taste of whiskey and cigars on his tongue when he deepened the kiss. My hands found his perfect hair, disheveling it for him like I had wanted to do so many times in the past, before moving down the taut shoulders I had admired every day in that storms-blasted carriage ride from hell, and every day since.

Still, there was too much fabric between us. I deftly undid his buttons while he pulled the ribbon from my hair, sucking my bottom lip into his mouth. Finally, I felt his bare skin, the muscles taut and rigid under my fingers, under my lips.

He ran his hands through my hair reverently before standing to move us both to his bed. Then, inch by inch,

Davin reclaimed every bit of my skin, wresting it from the memories of Alexei's bruises with his overwhelming tenderness. Each kiss against my mouth, my jaw, my neck was an apology, a promise, an act of devotion and desperation in one. Like he was afraid I would disappear again the moment he woke up.

I'm not going anywhere ever again. I tried to will the sentiment into every press of my lips against his skin. There was no talking this time, no banter, just his hands on my skin, anchoring me to this moment.

Anchoring me to him, for good.

Chapter Thirty-Eight

DAVIN

I WAS HAVING the dream again, the one where nimble fingers lightly traced the intricate lines of the tattoos on my back. I wanted so badly to stay in that space, where I hadn't been accused of murder and Galina was still...

Galina was still here.

I turned, and she froze, her hand still suspended in the air. Her eyes searched mine as I roved over her perfect, nude form, taking in the fact that she was here and whole and alive and *here.*

She hadn't disappeared in the night. Hadn't left. Hadn't been taken.

I put my hand on her cheek, tracing the outline of her sharp cheekbones, down to her jaw, her collarbone, and lower while I tried not to imagine those same places covered in bruises, tried not to imagine how terrified she must have been when he was waiting in her rooms to kidnap her. When she stood across from him at an altar, and after...

"Davin." Her voice was gentle, but firm. "Don't."

She interrupted my thoughts the way she had last night. I slowly moved my eyes back up to her face, lingering on every graceful angle and curve along the way. Finally, I reached her eyes. They were steady and solid. Resolute.

Not delicate, and never weak.

"He doesn't get to exist in this space," she explained, taking a breath. "If there are…things you need to know, we can talk about them, but not here, and not now."

I considered her words.

"There's nothing I need to know unless you want to tell me," I told her honestly. "All I care about is that you're safe."

I hesitated before adding, "And mine, obviously."

She searched my expression, her lips parting like perhaps I wasn't the only one struggling to believe we had found our way back to one another.

"Obviously," she breathed. Then, she gave a small imitation of my smirk, her fingers tracing a tantalizing line along my chest, then lower, over the ridges of my abdomen. "But you forgot 'perfect'."

"Well, that was a given." I moved until she was underneath me, then leaned down to kiss her.

She made a contented noise against my lips, a sound I could drown in and still die happy. I twisted the silky strands of her hair around my fingers and gently tugged backward until I could drag my teeth along her neck, pausing along the way to press my mouth against her skin, to feel her pulse under my lips.

Slowly, I worked my way down her body, paying special attention to all my favorite parts.

"Davin?" She said my name somewhere between an exclamation and a question.

"Yes, Lina, Love?"

She let out a noise that was more needy than content this time, and I smirked against her hipbone.

"I meant what I said to the lairds," she said, the words coming out breathy.

"You want to talk about the interrogation right now?" I asked, shaking my head to skate my lips back and forth across her smooth abdomen.

"No, you *laskipaa*." Interestingly enough, the word was longer than it needed to be, the last syllable stretching on in a gasp. Then she murmured something entirely incoherent.

"What's that, Love?" I teased.

"I said, I do love you," she finally bit out.

I looked up, following the curves and arches of her torso until I found her perfect gaze on mine.

"I know," I told her.

And it was true. If I hadn't understood that before, I did now, in the light of everything I knew about the past few weeks.

She glared at me until I added, "And I love you. Obviously."

I spent the next hour showing her exactly how much while we shut away every demon from our past and ignored the hell raining down on us outside these doors.

But of course, it caught up with us eventually.

WHEN MALISHKA MADE her needs explicitly known, we finally forced ourselves out of bed to send her downstairs with Ewan. It was still early since sleep hadn't exactly been our priority.

I helped Galina back into her dress, though she alleged that my attentions were more distracting than helpful. She hesitated for a fraction of a second when she went to slip her hideous ring on, a grim sort of resignation passing over her features.

"Wait," I said, walking over to my desk. I removed her ring from the back of the smallest drawer. Crossing the room to her, I held out my hand for hers.

"Unless, of course, you'd rather wear your new one, if it's more to your taste."

Though I was teasing her, a voice in the back of my mind reminded me how fragile this all was, like we were standing on the brink, just one breath away from shattering into a million pieces.

A small smile tempted the corner of her mouth, her gaze locked onto the far more delicate engagement ring.

"I don't think that ring is to anyone's taste." She infused a lightness to her tone, choosing to exist in this bubble with me for a little longer.

"Tell that to Granny Siobhan," I countered. "It was her favorite."

She hummed noncommittally. "If she liked it so much, perhaps we should enshrine it with her in her tomb, forever."

I closed my hand around the offensive jewelry, setting it on the table behind us.

"And if things go badly with this evidence...will you still want to wear it?" I couldn't help but ask.

Her brow furrowed. "Why wouldn't I?"

"What if I'm exiled?" I clarified.

She raised her eyebrows. "Then we'll finally get away from court."

Something in my shoulders eased. We both knew she didn't mind court most of the time, but her meaning was clear. I slid the ring on her finger, determined that this time, it would stay there. She looked down at it, and I couldn't help but broach one more subject I had been curious about.

"Speaking of jewelry you won't take off... I notice that you don't wear your bracelet anymore."

Galina froze in the middle of lovingly tracing the designs of her ring, her eyes sliding up to meet mine.

"I don't like the reminders it brings." Her tone was final, but I couldn't help pressing a little further.

"The bracelet, or just one charm?" I prodded.

She swallowed, making a visible effort to force herself not to shut me down.

"Just one," she confirmed tightly.

I nodded, hesitating before offering, "You know, we do have a jeweler here."

She arched an eyebrow, though her eyes were still shadowed. "Of course you do. An entire jeweler devoted to Lithlinglau, and still, you stuck me with that ring."

"It would have crushed Blaine to tell him no after he chose it with such care." I moved closer to her, pulling her against me and pressing my lips against her temple. "But, if you were willing, we could remove that charm. Have it melted down. Perhaps replace it with something more to your liking."

Something like a dragon, for my house sigil, as was custom in Socair.

She peeked up at me through her lashes. "The ring isn't enough for you? You want me to wear a charm of yours, too."

"Oh, I won't stop there, Love. I plan on covering every inch of your body with the jewels of Lithlinglau. Tattooing my name on your skin." I moved my mouth along said skin while I spoke, and she gave a shiver that belied her feelings on the matter, even if she shook her head.

"In seriousness," I said, "we can get the charm removed so you can wear the bracelet again."

She let out a low breath, her fingers running over the skin on her wrist. Her lips parted, then closed before she finally nodded.

"I would like that. Taking the charm off. And replacing it," she admitted, her cheeks flushing.

"Don't worry," I told her in a soft growl. "I'll have you tattooed on my skin as well."

Galina's lips parted, her eyes blazing. "I'll hold you to that."

Consequently, we were late to breakfast.

Chapter Thirty-Nine

GALINA

BY THE TIME we left Davin's rooms, we had missed breakfast and made it to the dining hall with just enough time to endure an awkward court luncheon.

Laird Camdyn narrowed his eyes as we approached the seats that were reserved for us, something like confusion furrowing his brow as he studied us.

Fiona also watched us closely, our presence clearly more interesting than the conversation she had just been having with Gracie. Her hawk-like gaze homed in on every single detail between us — from the way Davin helped me into my chair to the casual way his hand brushed against my arm, and down to the delicate golden band with the ruby in the center that was finally back on my finger where it belonged.

"How interesting," Fiona said, arching a perfectly sculpted eyebrow. Her full lips pulled upward into what was a careful line between a smile and a sneer. "It would seem you finally found your ring."

Gracie looked sharply at her, features tight.

Fortunately, I was saved from having to respond when

Davin took my hand in his, making a show of examining both my finger and the jewelry.

"It would seem she has," he said before placing a kiss on my knuckles. "I think it suits her better than the other, though I know how much she loves my grandmother's ring."

It was an effort not to laugh outright as he met my eyes, adding, "We'll have to save that one for special occasions, I suppose."

"Like funerals," I replied under my breath so only Davin could hear.

"That is excellent news," MacBay's voice carried across the table, his tone carefully devoid of emotion. What little conversation had continued through the room was gone now, everyone's rapt attention on our table at the head of the room. "Wouldn't you agree, Lady Shaw?"

Something indecipherable passed between them before she returned her focus to her plate, a small smile playing at her lips.

Before I could read too much into the unusual exchange, a white-gloved hand placed a plate of dessert in front of me. An intricate blown-glass dish held a beautiful trifle. Layers of pumpkin and ginger cakes were topped with whipped cream and cinnamon.

The smell was...potent. Overwhelming.

I froze without entirely understanding my hesitation. I didn't love pumpkin, but I didn't hate it, either. Yet my entire body rebelled at the idea of the confection in front of me.

Which was ridiculous, obviously. Even as my mind raced back to the festival, which should have been a happy memory, I couldn't quite quell the nausea.

Malishka pressed her head against my leg from her spot under the table, and Davin eyed me with concern. I forced myself to pick up my spoon, to scoop up a small bite of the pale orange cream.

Slowly, I lifted the spoon to my lips, trying to keep my expression somewhere close to normal while I breathed through my mouth, but it was no use. Cinnamon and cloves, two of my favorite smells, mingled together with the overpowering, pungent odor of pumpkin.

My stomach churned, and suddenly, I was in a dark carriage. The curtains were drawn, the ride bumpy and uneven, and somewhere beneath the ubiquitous wintergreen scent of my captor, I could smell...pumpkin pastries.

Fingers pressed against my wrist, and I nearly yelped in surprise, but this touch was gentler, lighter, intended to guide rather than inflict pain.

I looked up to find Davin routing my spoon into his mouth, a playful expression masking the worry in his ocean eyes.

"You know this is my favorite," he said, giving the table his best smirk.

"I must have forgotten." I played along, though I suspected for a change, my show wasn't nearly as convincing as his.

"Well, that won't do for my future wife. I must insist you give the rest up in penance." He neatly plucked the plate away without giving me a chance to argue, making a display of eating it while his right hand brushed against mine under the table.

"I suppose I have no choice but to allow it, considering the gravity of my crime," I finally said, forcing a smirk to my own lips.

Then Gwyn and Gallagher chimed in with their twin banter, distracting the prying eyes from us. My heartbeat still pounded in my chest, and my stomach was still in knots, but with each soothing swipe of Davin's thumb, my panic ebbed away.

Safe. I was safe.

Even if I still struggled to feel that way sometimes.

After lunch, we went back to Jocelyn and Oliver's study. It was crowded with Davin's entire family, including the king, whose massive frame could crowd a room all on its own. I still didn't quite know what to make of the man who the whole world feared but Davin sometimes referred to as Uncle Logie-bear.

He loved his nephew, though, and that was enough for me.

"They found the other missing guard," Oliver announced once the door was shut. "Bennet."

It was clear from his tone just what state they had found the guard in, and even clearer from Davin's expression that he had already suspected as much. He nodded at me in confirmation.

"We received word just before dinner," Captain Finn added. "He died from the same poison as the others."

"No surprise there," Avani muttered. "We knew the Viper was behind this."

There was a long pause, tension filling the room as her words rang true.

"We didna fight a war just to let them exile our own because of a damned rebel," King Logan said, his brogue sounding thicker than it had been at dinner, something I was learning happened whenever he was angry or stressed.

"Better than a coup," Davin suggested in the patient tone of someone who was having the same argument for roughly the thousandth time.

The king glowered, his cheeks reddening with his ire. "I've no intention of letting either happen."

"Which brings us back to this," Jocelyn added. "The Uprising members we catch rarely talk, even if we can get their poison out before they use it. The poison itself is one of the few clues we have. There aren't many people who have access to the resources that would be needed to create and then hide something like that, not to mention the money and manpower that have come into play."

"Right," Oliver picked up, gesturing vaguely toward the hall. "At the very least, the Viper has to be working with someone who has those resources, so we've ruled out most of the less prominent families."

"And Galina and I have ruled out quite a few more between the letters and her map," Davin chimed in.

"Which primarily leaves the Jamesons, the MacBays, the Porters, the Grays, the Wilsons, and, of course, Fiona," Avani listed.

The room shifted uncomfortably while the family discussed how unlikely each of them were until Gallagher spoke up, his brow furrowing in thought.

"Aren't the Shaws known for their greenhouses?"

"Yes, but they certainly aren't the only ones," Oliver answered. "Besides, Lady Fiona doesn't strike me as someone who gets her hands dirty."

I arched an eyebrow at that, thinking we perhaps had different opinions on what Fiona was or was not willing to do with her hands.

"But she certainly has the resources to pay someone else to do that," Avani added. "And plenty of the Uprising to do her bidding based on their sheer blind hatred."

The Captain let out a bitter laugh. "By that logic, it could be any of them."

"But poison is traditionally a woman's weapon," Jocelyn said.

Gwyn's features flashed with indignation, but Davin nodded.

"Mamá would know," he countered.

Jocelyn neither confirmed nor denied his statement, and I gathered the fate of her late husband was one of the worst-kept secrets in the kingdom.

"So, you do think it's Fiona?" I spoke up for the first time since we entered the study.

Jocelyn grimaced. "Not necessarily. She doesn't have a clear motive that I can see, but I think we can't rule anyone out until we know what we're working with."

"If I could have one of those samples, I can look into it," I offered. I was by no means an expert, but we couldn't trust anyone outside of this room to look into it.

"I can help," Gallagher offered. "And catch you up on what I've discovered so far, which is very close to nothing."

With that settled, Davin and I headed back to our rooms. He dropped me off at my door for the sake of the guards, but it wasn't long before he made his way across the balcony, tapping lightly at my door.

I unlocked it to allow him entry, and he pulled me against him without preamble.

"Do you want to tell me what happened at dinner?" he asked, his voice soft against my hair.

"Not particularly," I said with a sigh.

He nodded, not pushing, and I reminded myself that I had resolved to give him more.

So I took a deep breath, adding, "But I will."

Then I made myself explain as much as I could while he listened without interruption. He didn't offer magic solutions or tell me things were fine. He just ran his fingers through my hair and put his lips on my skin and, little by little, helped lift some of the suffocating weight from me.

Now I just had to figure out how to do the same for him.

THE NEXT MORNING, once he had snuck back to his rooms, Malishka gave the quick yip that heralded Anna's arrival.

She loved my maid, who never failed to bring treats in her pockets. Today, she brought something for me, as well.

"The jeweler just finished with it, milady," she said, handing out an intricately engraved silver box.

I opened it to find my charm bracelet nestled in the velvet interior. Gently, I ran my fingers over the familiar charms. The rosemary from my father. The outline of the mountains from my mother, a reminder of the view we both loved from our sitting room. There was a tiny sparkling version of a jeweled egg from my uncle, as well, and a smattering of other charms that had been gifts throughout the years.

But it was pure, untainted by the wolf's head that had broken my skin and my spirit in the two years it marred my bracelet.

Of course, there was a charm in its place. It was a dragon, carved from silver with sapphire eyes, its wings spread out protectively.

I picked up the delicate chain, taking a deep breath as I clasped it around my wrist.

The familiar weight was comforting and...right, like a missing piece of myself finally snapping back into place after years of being fractured.

It was one step closer to putting this nightmare behind me for good.

Chapter Forty
DAVIN

If THE MOOD was tense the night before, I wasn't quite sure what to call it tonight.

Another man was dead. Another day had passed without finding the murderer. There was a restless and expectant energy in the air, the courtiers having once again made their side known based on where they sat at the massive dining table.

News had already spread about Edgar, and now Bennet, and the lairds and ladies alike were making their displeasure known about the fact that we hadn't yet apprehended the culprit. Which wasn't hypocritical at all, considering that just a week ago they had accused us of making up Galina's entire kidnapping.

Closest to my family were those who still supported us, while MacBay and the other leading members of the Assembly took their stand at the opposite end of the table, along with Lady Shaw, of course.

Her narrowed gaze followed us all the way to our seats — where I was more than a little surprised to find the youngest

MacBay. Gracie had taken the spot between Avani and Gallagher, and she appeared perfectly content to be there.

She smiled up at us, sniffling apologetically as Malishka drew closer. Still, despite her allergy and her father's clear disapproval of her association, she stayed seated, greeting both myself and Galina as we took our seats between the twins.

"Lady Gracie," I greeted back casually, lifting my wine glass toward her before taking a sip while she easily slipped back into her conversation with Avani.

Gwyn leaned over after a moment.

"Without Fiona's shadow looming over her, Gracie almost seems like herself again," she whispered so that only I could hear.

I couldn't disagree. She was more relaxed tonight than she had been in ages — more like she had been before everything between our families went to hell. I hoped this meant she was done avoiding me and finally willing to answer my questions.

It would be nice to know that we still had one ally among the MacBays. One friend.

When the meal was finished and servants ushered in dessert trays, the dining hall was once again filled with the smell of pumpkin. Galina stiffened at my side until the cloche was removed from her small plate, revealing a pear crisp instead of the maple pumpkin pies the rest of us were being served.

She glanced over at me, her expression softening into something like relief.

"You know, your story also led to a few other interesting developments," I added after a moment.

After speaking with Galina about the pumpkins, I hadn't been able to stop thinking about it. More specifically, about the fact that it could be the best lead we had found so far.

Already, my spies were gathering information on the vendors who had attended the festival, three of whom grew pumpkins. My men were ready and waiting for the signal to pull them in for questioning.

Galina watched me carefully, and I could tell that she was following that line of thought.

"You have a lead?" she asked quietly, and I nodded.

"Three."

Her expression mirrored my own, her relief just as palpable.

If we were right about this, it meant we were one step closer to finding the Viper and ending their reign of terror, once and for all.

After Gracie sat by us at dinner, I finally saw my chance to talk to her again. Knowing our history, though, I didn't want to just traipse to her rooms without explaining it to Galina first.

"Gwyn mentioned that she told you I think Gracie has some information that could help us," I began once we made it back to her room. "I want to try to talk to her tonight."

"All right," she said cautiously.

I took a breath. "And I should probably do it alone."

Galina did a valiant job of pretending to be unbothered by my announcement.

"All right," she said again, the words more constricted this time.

I met her gaze, my own narrowing in question. "You aren't going to ask me what it's about?"

"I trust you, and it's not my place to—"

"It is your place," I said, tilting her chin up and pressing a gentle kiss to her bottom lip. "And I want you to ask whatever you want to know."

She nodded, but still didn't say anything. I tucked a strand of hair behind her ear, leaning down to kiss along her jawline.

"Have I told you how sexy I find your jealousy?" I asked, only half teasing.

"I'm not jealous," she lied.

"Well, that makes one of us, then," I said, moving to her neck and pulling her against me. "Because I want to strangle everyone who even looks at you."

Her lips parted, a flush going into her cheeks like I knew it would.

"Fine. What are you going to talk to the girl — who the whole court thinks you should marry — about?"

I chuckled, moving my mouth back to her lips before I backed away to answer.

"I think that MacBay's lying about where he was the night Tavish was killed, and I think Gracie will tell me what it is, as a friend."

Galina raised a skeptical eyebrow. "Is that what you think she wants to be to you?"

"It's all I'm offering, Love. I would happily send literally anyone else, but Gwyn has no subtlety, and Avani has never been close to Gracie. She was home with her mother a lot when we were growing up, so she doesn't have many actual friends outside of Fiona and, well, me."

Galina met my eyes, studying them. "All right, then. As I said, I trust you."

She sounded surer of it this time around, and I gave her a genuine smile. All of our banter aside, I knew trust was difficult for her. For us both, if I was being honest. So I pressed another kiss against her lips, giving her the reassurance she would never ask for.

"And I will never do anything to break that trust."

Not again. Not when we had worked so hard to get here.

I FOUND Gracie in the courtyard.

She was almost unrecognizable, bundled up in her winter cloak, with fleece-lined gloves and a wool scarf wrapped around her neck. A dusting of snow covered the hedges, and frost made the walkways more slippery than not, but she didn't seem to mind.

"I was hoping I'd find you out here," I said, casually falling in step beside her.

Gracie turned to peer up at me with her wide brown eyes before darting a look behind me.

"Just you?" she asked lightly. "Does Lady Galina approve of you seeking me out privately like this?"

Though her words were playful, there was a hint of concern lining her tone.

"She knows we're friends," I said. "And she trusts me."

Gracie's brow rose in surprise, a half-smile tempting the corner of her mouth. We continued walking for a while, winding our way toward the back of the gardens before she finally spoke again.

"I'm happy for you, Davin," she said thoughtfully, but something in her tone said that she was dubious, too.

Which was fair, since I was sure it looked complicated from the outside. Stars, it had been complicated from the inside.

"I'm assuming that this isn't just a social call," she added as we made our way to the winter gardens. Gracie stooped down to pluck one of the delicate blue flowers that insisted on growing, despite the cold.

She met my eyes then. "Say what you came to say."

I sighed, running a hand through my hair as I braced myself to broach the subject that had made her shut down twice before.

"You said your father was with you the night Tavish died," I said.

"I did," she responded flatly, her gloved hand tightening around the small flower.

"But we both know that isn't true."

Whatever ease had existed between us a moment ago, and even at dinner was gone now. Tension filled the space between us for several long, stilted moments. She walked faster on the garden path, visibly agitated.

"I need to know where he was," I pressed, keeping in step with her pace.

She sighed, rubbing her temple with her free hand.

"Gracie, please," I said, stepping in front of her and forcing her to meet my eyes once again. "For the sake of whatever friendship we had, please, just tell me the truth."

I didn't miss her wince at the word *friendship* or the way her narrow shoulders deflated.

She tossed the flower to the ground, sighing. "He was where he is every night that my mother isn't with us," she said. "With Fiona."

My jaw dropped. The upstanding, noble, ever-righteous Laird MacBay was having an affair? With Fiona, of all people?

I reexamined the events of the past week under that lens, thinking of his narrowed eyes when she came onto me, his admonishment at her display of jealousy. Not because he was judging me for having a past entanglement with her, but because he was...possessive of her.

More than simple gossip, though, this gave her the motive we had been missing. If she was championing MacBay and our family fell, she could become the next queen of Lochlann. Of course, she had voted in my favor, and she was still angling for an attachment to me.

Then there was MacBay himself, who clearly wasn't the man he purported himself to be.

It was a hollow victory, knowing I might have just discovered the missing piece that tied one of our oldest friends to being the Viper.

Chapter Forty-One

GALINA

I SPENT the next day in the library trying to pretend there wasn't a ticking clock threatening the life I wanted so desperately and the family I had come to consider my own.

Endless walls of elegant white shelves with gilded accents took up the massive space, books on every subject filling them to the brim. Most of them were in the common tongue, but there were at least three massive shelves dedicated to the languages of Socair and Rionn, and some I didn't recognize.

Golden chandeliers reflected candlelight off the pristine white marble floors and there were small chairs, tables and sofas scattered for studying in any given corner.

It was an exquisite backdrop for such bleak work.

Gallagher and I set up near the herbology section, comparing the poisons from the false teeth to yet another endless textbook. We used most of the available space, with a separate table dedicated to the herbs and plants we were experimenting with to test the effects.

"How is Maisey?" I asked, refilling our water glasses from the pitcher on our table. "Have you asked her about any of these?

I gestured to the valley lily and bitterbloom we were dissecting. The lily caused abrupt heart failure but didn't cause inky veins. The bitterbloom had a fruity scent like the Viper's, but it was closer to citrus than apple, and not nearly potent enough to cause death in small quantities.

It didn't feel like we were getting any closer.

Gallagher's shoulders slumped as I set his cup in front of him.

"I have not," he said, his expression falling. "She has expressed her desire to be... further from all of this."

He returned to the textbook in front of him, but I still felt compelled to say something.

"I am sorry, Gal," I offered lamely. With everything going on, Gallagher had been a good friend to me. And I...had not returned that favor.

"It was probably for the best." He shrugged. "It's not like I can be with someone who's terrified of my sister, anyway."

As if his statement had summoned her, the door swung open and his sister stepped into the library on sure footsteps. Her red hair was braided into a crown on her head, and her sword belt matched the deep purple hues of her gown.

Even in a dress, she looked lethal. *Was* lethal. I wondered who Gallagher would find who wasn't terrified of her, at least on occasion.

"Dav needs you," she said to me by way of greeting.

My heart dropped into my stomach, my breath stalling in my lungs as I got to my feet.

"Is something wrong?" Gal voiced the question I couldn't seem to get out.

"No." She furrowed her brow, taking in my expression as realization dawned on her. "Nothing's wrong with Davin. He just needs your help with something."

Gal opened his mouth, then closed it, likely wondering the same thing I was. If Gwyn was being vague when she was usually so pointed, she probably had her reasons. So we wordlessly gathered up our notes, repacking the poisonous plants in their individual tins.

She led us through the castle to a back set of stairs I had never been down before. I could guess where they led, though.

There was only one thing below the bottom floor, and Gallagher's confused expression erased any doubt.

"He needs her in the dungeons?" he asked in an undertone.

"Either that, or Gwyn has decided to take care of this problem once and for all," I murmured, trying to calm my frazzled nerves.

"Like I'd be so sloppy," she said over her shoulder, but I didn't miss the note of amusement in her tone. "We caught the driver, but he's not talking."

My stomach lurched, surprise widening my eyes.

"In fairness, he's a bit short on teeth at the moment," Davin's voice sounded just as we rounded the dark corner. "But he's claiming he has no idea what we're talking about."

"How many did you take?" Gallagher asked.

"A few. We had to be sure we had the right one, obviously." He didn't even bother to make the lie sound credible. "Besides, after last time, I wasn't taking any chances."

And I couldn't blame him, not with everything at stake. The man had been happy to help kidnap an innocent woman and betray his own monarchy.

"So you need me to identify him?" I clarified.

Davin nodded, examining me in the flickering torchlight like he wasn't sure whether he should apologize for the necessity, or if I was all right with seeing the aftermath of torture he had helped inflict.

I dipped my chin, straightening my spine and deliberately ignoring the faint coppery scent in the air, the crimson drops of blood staining Davin's otherwise pristine waistcoat.

"Not delicate, remember?" I reminded him.

Something in his shoulders eased.

"Never delicate," he assured me.

He turned to lead us further into the maze of open cells. They weren't precisely dungeons. There were no dingy rooms with drains in the floor, no torture devices or the sound of screaming. Just a few spacious barred rooms that seemed to be more for temporary holding than anything.

We stopped at a corner cell, where a man sat slumped forward on the bench, a chain rooting him to each side. Davin's personal guards stood outside the cell, while MacBay's men had been ordered to stay at the top of the stairs.

Gwyn and Gallagher hung back, and I moved forward with Davin.

The man's hair was matted, but the same light-brown color I remembered. His clothes were crusted with blood, some dried, some fresh, and his hands trembled in the shackles.

I tried to dredge up some emotion. Sympathy. Vindication. But staring at the same body that had been the backdrop to some of the worst days of my life, I felt nothing.

When the cell door clanged shut, he slowly moved his head up.

"I already told ye, I dinna ken—" He cut off abruptly at the sight of me, his eyes widening.

Davin clucked his tongue. "I suppose news doesn't travel as fast wherever you were hiding out. Your all-knowing Viper didn't tell you that my fiancée was back, safe?"

"She—" He trailed off, looking between Davin and me with ever-growing horror, shaking his head.

"So, let's try again," Davin said casually. "We'll start simple this time since you are clearly of only middling intelligence. Did you drive the carriage that took my kidnapped betrothed out of Lithlinglau?"

He overly enunciated each word, digging at the man's pride.

"I didna ken she was kidnapped," he fired back, his dark eyes darting back and forth between us.

"Come, now. We both know that isn't true. Why else would you have been so secretive?" Davin asked, the muscles in his forearms flexing as he crossed the distance to jab a finger into the man's chest, right where his Uprising tattoo rested. "You weren't just the driver, were you, John?"

It was the first time I had heard his name. I wasn't sure why I noted it, or why it felt significant, but I filed the information away all the same.

"You were his contact for the Viper," Davin continued. "You got them all the way to Whitmire without being seen. You were there for that complete farce of a wedding. You knew she wasn't there by choice," Davin said, murder underlining his tone.

"The punishment for rebellion is a simple hanging," he continued after a moment. "But I think I'll come up with something special for the man who hurt my future wife."

John's face went even paler than his blood-loss accounted for. "I swear, she only said it was to get the Socairans out."

We both looked at him sharply. He clearly wasn't referring to me, when I was one of the Socairans in question.

"She?" Davin's word was loud in the silence that had fallen, the single syllable reverberating on the stone walls.

The driver shrank back, muttering the word *no* over and over again.

"You can't. You can't... My family."

"Perhaps you shouldn't have involved them with the rebellion if you were so worried about them," Davin said coldly.

"You dinna understand. You have to kill me. Please. You have to let me die now."

Davin said nothing for a long moment. Then, he reached

into his pocket and pulled out a small capsule of the poison. The man's eyes lit up with a macabre sort of hope.

"Tell me her name," Davin demanded.

John's face fell. "She never said it."

"Describe her, then," he ordered.

He shook his head. "It was dark, and she— she had a hood on."

Davin sighed, making a show of putting the poison back in his pocket.

"Wait!" John practically cried, the desperation in his voice palpable as he fixed his gaze on the pocket. "She...talked like you do."

"Like a man?" Gwyn asked from the corner of the room.

"No," he shook his head. "Like a highborn. Like— like a lady."

"And when did you first have contact with her?" Davin pressed, pulling the capsule back out and holding it up for John to see.

"Just before the festival, maybe a week or two before," he said quickly.

A muscle ticked in Davin's jaw. Wordlessly, he set the capsule on the bench. Then he placed his hand on my lower back and led me out of the dungeons.

We didn't look back, even as the screaming followed us all the way to the stairwell.

Chapter Forty-Two

DAVIN

WHILE GALINA RETURNED to the library with Gallagher, I went to do some research of my own.

The interrogation had taken up most of my day, so I hadn't yet gotten to talk to my new favorite suspect, something I planned to remedy now.

All the way down the hallway to the guest wing, I tried to make sense of what I knew. The Viper wanted my family off the throne. MacBay was trying to accomplish that same goal. He lacked the casual cruelty of the Viper, but Fiona had no known feelings or conscience to speak of.

And, of course, of-sodding-course, they were sleeping together.

Were they working together knowingly, or was she only using him to do her bidding? My fists clenched, and I took a calming breath. It was one thing knowing that the Viper was likely someone on the Assembly, another to have a name, to truly come to terms with just how close they were to everyone I loved.

I stopped outside Fiona's door, the first one in the long

hallway on the lower level of guest suites. She opened the door herself, raising a single dark eyebrow when she saw me.

"Expecting someone else?" I asked, keeping my expression carefully neutral.

"Jealous?" she purred.

I tilted my head. "Is that what you're after?"

"I wouldn't turn it down." Her tone left very little doubt as to what else she wouldn't turn down.

I grimaced at the necessity of being alone in a room with her, but I wasn't naïve enough to think she would talk with anyone else here. So I gestured for her to let me in her rooms, ignoring the horrified look my guards — and MacBay's — cast us.

They would report back to him, but at least they wouldn't gossip to the whole castle. And my men knew why we were here.

Fiona smiled like the cat that ate the canary, triumph shining from her bright blue eyes. At least, until the door shut and I turned on her.

"I think we both know that's not why I'm here, Fiona," I said flatly, refusing to turn my back on her.

She crossed the room to flounce on the small red sofa near the hearth, patting the cushion beside her in invitation. I stayed near the door, refusing to budge, and she rolled her eyes.

"Then why are you here, Davin?" She sounded bored now.

"Why are you with MacBay?" I countered.

Her obsidian brows rose in genuine surprise. The emotion was fleeting, though, and instead of trying to deny it, she raised a single slim shoulder. "I'm not sure you want me to answer that question."

There was something overly satisfied in her tone that told me I did not, in fact, want that answer.

"Is that all you get out of the arrangement?" I pressed,

trying to reconcile the Fiona in front of me with what I knew about the Viper. She had a loose moral code, one I used to share and appreciate, but standing before her now... It was impossible to reconcile her with someone who was capable of mass murder.

What could she possibly gain from being the Viper? And why throw her lot in with MacBay when she had very clearly tried to tie herself to me over and over again?

"Is that not enough?" she asked, genuinely curious. "It used to be for you."

I wanted to argue with her, but I couldn't when I had just been thinking about that very thing. How many times had I lost myself in someone else to ignore the things I couldn't cope with? Still, even then, I had my lines. And adultery wasn't something I ever knowingly engaged in.

"Surely there are other, less married options," I said after a moment.

She shook her head, the corner of her mouth quirking upward. "None with his power."

Was that really all there was? People dying and my family living in fear and my fiancée stolen, all so she could feel just a bit more in control? Or to become the queen of a kingdom she had stolen?

"Don't you have enough power?" I bit out. "An estate to yourself, a seat on the Assembly—"

"And a kingdom full of men to condescend me for both," she cut me off. "Don't play naïve, Davin. We both know the only real power any woman has is not found in an Assembly room unless you're one of the precious chosen royal few."

I bored my gaze into hers, trying to see past the flippant façade she put forth.

There were so many questions I had, but none that she would answer outright unless I was willing to drag her down to a holding cell. And if she was the Viper, accusing her now, like this, felt like a mistake.

"That's not a good enough reason to hurt people," I said quietly.

"I think it's time you leave," she said flatly. "If you're going to insist on being so...boring."

I shook my head, turning around to leave, headed to see someone I wanted to talk to even less.

I FOUND him sitting alone in the parlor, holding an untouched glass of whiskey in one hand and an unlit cigar in the other.

"Did you come to gloat about your visit?" MacBay asked when I sank into the chair next to him.

If I hadn't known his guards reported to him before, I certainly did now. They must have sent word when I was still in Fiona's room.

I reached into the snuff box and pulled out my own cigar, along with a small stick. I dipped it into a candle, then held it out to him. He nodded, so I lit his cigar and my own before blowing it out.

"Would it bother you if I did?" I asked, only somewhat sincere.

We both knew it would bother him. Whether or not it was because of his *attachment* to her, or because he was working with her, was something I hadn't figured out yet.

How he had fallen so low was another mystery. Camdyn wasn't a terrible person. Not a shining example of humanity, with his questionable loyalties to both his friends and his wife, but he had always been a good laird to his people, just like his father before him, just like he had raised his sons to be.

Just as I had with Fiona, I struggled to reconcile the man I had known all my life with someone capable of the Viper's sins. Did he know what Fiona was up to? Did he support her?

"She plays her games," he said a moment later, denial lining each of his words.

"Sometimes, they're more than games." I couldn't quite keep the anger from my tone.

His face reddened, his fingers clenching around his cigar just a little too tightly. "I know who Fiona is."

"Do you?" I asked. "And it doesn't bother you?"

His gaze narrowed, but he still didn't look up. "Don't pretend you don't understand the draw."

I scoffed. "I haven't understood the draw in some time. When I make promises to a woman, I keep them."

He ignored my jab. "Then why were you there?"

I took a puff of my cigar, giving myself a moment to debate how much of the truth to give him. We were running in circles, getting nowhere, so I took a gamble.

"Because a man in a cell told me something very interesting about the Viper. He said that *she* is a member of the nobility."

MacBay shot me an incredulous look. "You think Fiona is the Viper?"

I studied him carefully while I responded. "She certainly fits the bill, and it would explain your unlikely...attachment to her."

His dark-brown eyes flared with a rage I had never seen from him. Usually, he was more prone to even-keeled responses and the occasional bout of righteous indignation, but this was new.

"I want to help our people, not terrorize them," he growled. "You may be offended that I doubt Lochlann's prosperity under the guidance of a generation who hasn't been bothered to put the people first once in the entire time I have known them, but you can't possibly think that I would condone the murder of children. Try to recall that my village was one of the ones attacked by rebels before the war — a rebellion that was, by the way, led by a man your father later appointed to Council."

It was my turn to feel anger. I wouldn't allow him to attack the father of my best friend when I knew full well where his loyalties lie, and how his years leading a rebellion haunted him to this day.

"You know MacKinnon didn't condone those tactics," I said more calmly than I felt.

MacBay's expression was scathing. "I know he worked alongside a man who did, and now you've come to accuse me of doing the same without a shred of evidence."

"What a difficult position that must be for you," I said, wondering if he saw the irony as well as I did.

He narrowed his eyes at me. "There *is* evidence in your case. Quite a staggering amount of it, in fact. And all I asked is that your family be accountable for once in its *stars-damned* existence. That doesn't make me a traitor."

"Just an adulterer, then." If he was telling the truth.

He set his glass down on the table a little too firmly. "My private life is none of your concern."

I gave him a cold shrug. "It is if the woman you're sharing a bed with is systematically destroying innocent lives."

"She isn't," he spat. "And if I were you, I would be careful of the enemies you make when you're in such a precarious position yourself."

I got to my feet, snuffing out the end of my cigar. "You already made yourself an enemy without any help from me, and I will do what I have to in order to keep our people safe. Whether you believe me capable of it or not."

With that, I strode out of the parlor, having less than no desire to be in a room with him any longer. He had told me what I needed to know, anyway. Either he was a much better liar than I had ever given him credit for, or he genuinely believed Fiona wasn't the Viper.

That didn't mean she was innocent, though. Not when she was a good enough liar for them both.

Chapter Forty-Three

GALINA

Books were scattered all over the table. I had pulled tome after tome from the stacks, adding them to my pile to no avail. An ache formed behind my eyes that even a peppermint salve on my temples couldn't mitigate.

I scanned each text, jotting down notes on different plants and a few nuts and herbs that were recorded to have some of the same reactions as the poison, but none of them were extreme enough.

There was a mushroom called death-cap that could make you vomit blood, and an herb that, if eaten enough, could restrict oxygen and slowly suffocate the veins until your heart stopped beating. Then there was the nut that, if consumed raw, could dissolve the lining of your stomach.

Hell, there was even a tree with a fruit described as *tiny apples of death*. The milky white sap was enough to cause severe blistering and toxicity in the body, but the fruit was where the real poison lay. Their sweetness concealed the taste of poison, one that caused internal bleeding and suffocation.

The list went on and on, with each one offering more

gruesome side effects than the last. Yet none of them were what I needed.

Each failure to find an answer drove me closer to insanity.

Shaking my head, I rubbed my temples, wondering if it really could be Fiona. Had I sat across the table at tea from the person responsible for trying to murder me? The one who murdered countless villagers and was so terrifying, her followers chose to die horrible, painful deaths rather than be disloyal?

I thought of Davin, the look of defeat etched into even his sleeping face, the frustration that continued to build, threatening to tear down everything his family had worked for.

If I didn't find an answer soon, would the Viper win? Would she destroy everyone I had come to love so fiercely?

Slamming my book closed, I shoved it to the side before pushing my chair back to find another. There had to be an answer here, somewhere, and I wouldn't stop until I found it.

I was so engrossed in searching the shelves in the secluded back corner that I didn't notice the footsteps behind me until Malishka nudged my leg. I spun around to find Davin, his brilliant gaze sweeping over me like it always did when he first saw me. He never could seem to convince himself that I was safe these days.

It was a feeling I understood well.

"Have you taken a break at all today, Love?" he asked once he had assured himself of my wellbeing.

"Have you?" I countered, forgetting the books as I took a step closer.

Though he was as handsome as ever, there was fatigue etched across his features, and something else...an almost restless energy, closer to desperation. Like everything was slipping away from him and he wasn't sure who or what would be taken next.

Storms if I didn't feel that, too.

I placed a hand on his cheek, meeting his tumultuous gaze. There were no easy solutions I could offer. I was no closer than I had been before to figuring out this blasted poison, let alone who the Viper was.

But that didn't mean I had no comfort to give.

Driven by a pressing need to be closer to him, to combine my warmth with his until we both felt a little less lost, I lifted up on my toes. He leaned down to meet me without hesitation. His kiss was warm, sending tendrils of desire coursing through me, but he kept it chaste, no doubt being conscious of our surroundings.

I didn't want to be conscious of our surroundings, though. I didn't want to be conscious of anything but him. I wrapped a hand around his neck, gently scraping my nails against his head and deepening the kiss.

This time, he hesitated for a fraction of a second, long enough for me to second-guess myself before I felt his smirk against my lips.

Then he was backing me against the stacks with one firm hand on my shoulder and the other on my waist. He slid both hands down my body with tantalizing pressure until they covered my wrists. Then he gently brought my arms up until they were over my head, skating his mouth over to nip just below my ear.

"Is this what you want, Love?" His breath was scorching on my skin.

He pulled back just enough to read my face, and I nodded, peeking up at him through my lashes.

It was strangely empowering, the intoxicating waves of desire that crashed from his body to mine. The claiming of a space that had almost been taken from me, a home that someone was *still* trying to take from us both.

Davin's face went slack with need. He pressed against me, and I found that I liked the pressure, that I wanted more of it, needed to feel him. I wriggled a little until he tilted his head, rapid-fire gauging what it was I wanted in his endlessly sexy way.

He shifted his grip to hold both my wrists in one capable hand, gliding the other along the side of my body. He put the barest bit of force on his hold, examining me closely for my reaction – my consent.

My entire body flushed crimson-hot in reaction, and I cut my gaze to his. "Don't treat me like I'm–"

"You're *not* fragile," he cut me off with a growl, the words reverberating from his body to mine.

Then he was crushing me against the stacks with an intensity that was firm, but not quite bruising, lowering his mouth to my lips, my jaw, my neck, while his free hand inched toward my thigh.

Just like the night he had called me his, there was a marked difference in the feeling I got ceding control to someone I trusted absolutely with my safety – with myself.

"Not shy, either, apparently," he murmured.

"There's no one here." My protest was breathy.

"Yet. It isn't locked." Amusement glimmered in his tone and, once again, I felt his smile against my skin.

That gave me the smallest bit of pause. Then I remembered his haunted expression when he walked in, the way he had been unsettled and restless in the weeks since I left, and how at odds with that he was right now.

Besides, we were in the back of the stacks and Malishka was here to alert us. So I arched into him, a small smile playing on my own lips.

"Then we'll just have to be quick about it."

He slid his hand down to the hem of my skirts, slowly dragging his fingers up my calf, then my thigh. I gasped, and he covered my mouth with his, swallowing the sound.

"Shh, Lady Galina," he admonished me, dragging his

tongue against the seam of my lips. "This is a *library*. Can't you be quiet?"

He nipped playfully at my bottom lip.

"I can be quiet if you can," I murmured.

He let out a smug chuckle, inching his hand further up my thigh. "That's a bet I'm willing to take."

We both lost that bet.

AFTER OUR TIME in the library, Davin was no more inclined to leave my side than he had been when he came in. I couldn't blame him, not when I felt that same looming sense of urgency in every aspect of our lives.

If all of this was to destabilize the monarchy, would the Viper really be satisfied with an exiled Davin while the rest of the royal family was still in power? It felt like more than Davin's freedom was at stake here. All along, he had been safe, and I had been the target, but how long could that really last?

When he insisted on accompanying me to my rooms to fetch what I needed for the night, so I didn't have to come back the next morning, I didn't argue. I couldn't when that was how I had been taken the first time. Malishka was here now, giving me back pieces of my independence I desperately needed, but the threat still hung over us both.

I had no sooner walked through the door than I knew something was wrong.

Malishka growled, standing at attention, and I froze. Davin called for his guards and, together, they searched the room. I wanted to move, wanted to help, but all I could do was stare at the other side of the room.

The curtains fluttered around the shattered balcony door.

Jagged shards of glass caught the light, scattered amongst shredded remnants of the potted plants and herbs I had just coaxed back to life.

"Is anything missing?" Davin asked. His hands were on my shoulders, his fingers rubbing circles into my arms.

I forced myself to scan the rest of the room, looking once, then twice before I confirmed what some part of me already knew. Still, I crossed the room to my vanity, searching the open bottom drawer in vain. Even Anna knew not to open that drawer, not since I started keeping my notes in there.

And the poison. Anything I wasn't comfortable leaving overnight in the library.

"My research," I answered, giving him a pointed look that conveyed the rest.

"Gal has some as well," he said.

I nodded. I also had one vial left in my pocket that I had used to make comparisons today, but we both knew it was still a blow. If we needed to test any, to look closer or find other ways to compare it, we would run out quickly.

And we would lose our only solid evidence against the Viper.

Chapter Forty-Four

DAVIN

IT HADN'T TAKEN long to decide that Galina would move to my rooms permanently. There was no sense in moving her things even further away, and there was no way in hell she was staying there now.

As it was, I had Ewan and Hamish overseeing alternating shifts on our joint rooftop since the guard who had been stationed there had disappeared. Dead or a traitor, it was impossible to tell these days. But between Malishka in the room and my own guards outside the door, as well as my cousins just down the hall, we were as safe as we could be.

Which wasn't as comforting as I wanted it to be. Or Galina, if her faraway expression was anything to go by.

"You know I won't let anything happen to you," I spoke against her temple. "Not again."

"I do know," she said, turning so her light blue eyes met mine. "It's not me I'm worried about."

"Yes, yes." Gwyn's voice sounded behind us in the hall. "We're all in loads of danger of death and exile — and dethroning, in Avani's case — but I for one, think we should celebrate."

There was a beat of silence as my other two cousins joined her, Gallagher shaking his head in disbelief.

"Really, Gwynnie?" he asked.

But Avani shrugged like she agreed.

"Celebrate what?" I asked warily, casting Gwyn a sideways glance.

She strode closer, slinging an arm around my shoulder. "You two finally getting your heads out of your arses."

"Indeed, Gwyndolyn," Galina said drily, but she exchanged a look with Gwyn that held more than their usual mutual annoyance.

My oldest cousin clucked her tongue, her emerald gaze fixing on mine. "And you letting someone invade your precious high maintenance space," she added, pushing her way into my room and making a show of looking around. "Where will she put her things, Davin? We all know you've taken up the entire closet and then some. I swear, you have more clothes than I do."

She shoved past me into the aforementioned space. "Gallagher, go with Galina to fetch some of her dresses while I make space for them."

Galina looked at me, something between bafflement and amusement edging past the blank expression that had overtaken her features.

"You do need clothes," I said. Then, in a louder tone, I called to Avani. "Though, Blaine will never forgive you for taking this honor from him, nor for discarding his beloved clothes."

"Blame your manservant all you want, but you're a fashion hoarder."

Galina let out a small laugh, and it was worth all of the ribbing I knew was still coming. Gallagher tilted his head to her room, and she followed after one last lingering look in my direction.

Gwyn busied herself with removing all of my things from the table near the corner window, replacing it with Galina's few remaining plants.

"Why does anyone need three navy waistcoats?" Avani demanded from inside the closet.

"Don't be ridiculous," I shot back. "Only one of them is navy. The others are clearly midnight and cobalt."

"At least you're making this easy," she muttered, tossing said cobalt jacket onto the floor of my room.

"Just make sure you keep one in every color," I ordered, pouring several glasses of whiskey.

Gwyn poked her head into the closet to survey Avani's progress now that she was finished with her own task.

"Absolutely not," Gwyn told me. "You might be pretty, Dav, but even you can't wear whatever the hell this is."

She threw an admittedly hideous orange waistcoat into the growing pile just as Galina returned with Gal, who was laden down with an enormous pile of dresses. Two of the soldiers followed in a similar manner, looking distinctly uncomfortable with this assignment.

"In here," Gwyn directed them.

Several more trips went by that way until all of Galina's things were in my closet, my lavatory, my drawers. She stood in the center of the room, casting an uncertain look at her surroundings. I put my arms around her from behind, and she leaned into me.

"If it makes you uncomfortable, we can move it all into one of the guest rooms tomorrow," I murmured into her ear.

She slid her hands over mine, entwining our fingers.

"It doesn't make me uncomfortable," she said just as softly. "I'm just wondering how you feel about the changes to your space."

I looked around at the way her things were seamlessly integrated with mine, a small piece of our lives melding together. It felt like a living reminder that she was here to stay.

"Like I wish they'd happened months ago," I told her truthfully.

She relaxed somewhat in my arms, and I placed a quick kiss against her temple. Somehow, despite the chaos wreaking havoc on my home, the bloodstains on my floors, and the constant threat of exile and death looming over us, we had found a way to carve a space for ourselves here.

It was something my family had been doing for as long as I could remember with our late nights playing cards and drinking games, but it felt different with Galina here, even more special.

The sound of my cousins arguing grabbed my attention. Gal and Gwyn were bickering with Avani about the placement of furniture and how many times they had been forced to move the vanity already.

"But it looks stupid here," Avani said, looking to Galina for support.

When she didn't respond right away, Avani took it as silent support and snapped her fingers for me to come assist.

And so began the lengthy process of moving all of my furniture around. By which I meant that Gallagher and I moved the furniture while Gwyn graded us on our lifting stance and Avani directed with the help of her tiny fat squirrel.

Malishka, per usual, was fascinated by the rodent, circling Avani as she stared up at the creature. She let out several sounds that were somewhere between a bark and a snort. The squirrel squeaked indignantly in response while Avani did her best to keep the two separate.

"We could have called for the soldiers again," I grunted, pushing the bed into place.

"Then I would have missed out on the view," Galina said.

She hadn't said much throughout this process, but a small smile graced her lips now.

"Gross," Gwyn said.

"Seconded," Gal chimed in.

There was a small squeak from Avani's shoulder before she nodded. "Thirded and fourthed." Then she turned to Galina. "Are you sure there isn't anything specific you want? Do you have a preference how we arrange the sofa and chairs?"

Galina shook her head until I looked pointedly at her.

"Honestly?" I pushed.

She sighed. "Fine. I would like the mattress from my room."

I immediately wished I could take back my offer. That mattress was stars-damned heavy, even if we pulled the soldiers back in to help.

"Why do you like yours better than mine?" I asked.

She raised her eyebrows. "Because Fiona has never been naked in it..."

I wasn't sure if the ensuing silence was because what we knew about Fiona now was so much worse than when we thought she was just a seductress. Then I caught the questioning looks and realized it was because Galina was waiting for a response.

Shaking my head, I tilted her chin up until she looked me in the eye, then I assured her that Fiona had, in fact, never been naked in Galina's bed. That no one but Galina herself had ever stayed in that room.

Relief flashed in her eyes, and she nodded.

I couldn't blame her. I would have set the entire bed on fire if I had known another man had shared it with her.

All in all, it was a grueling few hours, but the exertion and the banter helped ease the weight that had settled on my shoulders. When my cousins left, Galina and I sank into the small sofa in front of the fire, Malishka curled up on the bearskin rug at our feet.

All the while, I tried not to think about how easily it could all be taken from me. How it almost had been.

WHATEVER FLEETING MOMENT of reprieve Galina and I had stolen for ourselves was ripped away before morning came.

News came in the form of a soldier banging on the door in the middle of the night. There had been another attack on another nearby village. This time, it was Riverwell, one of the villages just south of Alech.

The one Edgar had admitted to meeting at, not that long ago.

I ran a hand over my face. We had sent men to investigate, to search for safehouses, but it hadn't been enough to stop the attack. Instead, they died like so many others as the town was burned to the ground. Pyres of bodies were found on the other side of the river, near the border of Rionn.

Men. Women. Children. Plumes of black smoke and ashes from the bodies and the buildings hovered in the air like clouds of death and destruction, visible from the balcony Galina and I now shared.

There was some mild speculation about the attack being from our neighbors, the isolated kingdom of Rionn, but we knew better than that. Especially when this had been happening all around Lochlann, and some of the recovered bodies were littered with black veins and the Viper's symbol carved into their flesh.

"Does the king know?" I asked.

The soldier nodded. "They're meeting in your parent's study, mi'laird."

"I'll be there shortly. Bring me Lady Shaw as well," I ordered one of MacBay's men, closing the door so Galina and I could both dress.

While we had been laughing and rearranging furniture, someone had been ordering the slaughter of the people under our protection.

I kicked myself, nausea twisting my stomach. If I had only taken Fiona into custody before, would this have happened? Was I responsible for the bloodshed, just as much as she was, because I hadn't acted sooner?

Before, it hadn't seemed like the right time to confront her. We hadn't had all of the information we needed to make a formal accusation. The time for playing it safe was over. If I had to drag her to the dungeons to get answers from her, then I bloody well would.

But by the time I left my rooms, the soldier had returned, a frantic look on his face.

"Lady Shaw isn't in her room."

I let out a long breath, foreboding prickling over me. "Did you check MacBay's?"

Color flooded his cheeks. "We did, mi'laird. He hasn't seen her, either."

I exchanged a look with Galina, racing to the study to find my family already waiting. Along with Camdyn MacBay.

"Where is she?" he rounded on me as soon as I entered the room.

"Probably off murdering some more innocent children," I shot back.

"Don't play games with me," he spat. "Do you think I believe it's a coincidence that you came accusing her of being the Viper and then she was gone? Taking care of things the same way the rest of your family does, without regard to the law."

"No, I don't think any of us should believe it's a coincidence that right after she knew we were on to her, she disappeared." I shook my head in disgust. "I can't honestly tell if you're lying or just an idiot, but people are dying, MacBay. You pretend like that matters to you in one breath and then withhold information that might prevent their deaths in the next."

"Fiona didn't do that," he insisted.

"Then where is she?" I bit out.

"I don't know." His shoulders deflated the smallest amount. "Do you think I would be here if I did?"

"Yet you still believe she's innocent?" I challenged. "A whole village slaughtered and she's nowhere to be found, but surely she had nothing to do with it. If you're covering for her—"

"I'm not covering for anyone," he fired back.

His tone was defensive, but there was something else there too. Genuine concern. Because he was finally starting to believe us? Or because he was worried we would find her right when she'd escaped our grasp?

"I just refuse to help aid your witch hunt for an innocent woman while more people die because you haven't bothered to find the real person responsible," he added.

"That's enough," Uncle Logan cut in. "We willna be taking anyone without proof or cause. There's been plenty o' that to go around, and wasna from our family, as you'll damned well recall."

MacBay looked away, the irony of the situation settling over him. Of course, the difference was that I actually hadn't committed the crime I was accused of.

The king sent him a scathing look, unmoved by his belated remorse, but it was my father who spoke.

"For that matter, perhaps if you had helped us instead of turning on us, we could have worked together to face the threat to our kingdom. Those deaths do not fall on our heads alone, Camdyn."

For the first time since he had turned traitor in the Assembly room, the barest hint of shame flickered across MacBay's features.

A soft voice spoke from the doorway. "Just help them, Da'."

Gracie stood with a pained look on her face. "You just had the king's word that he won't hold her if she's innocent. Are you really willing to risk the lives of our people just to keep her from answering a few questions? Or to spite the people who were supposed to be our friends? For *her*?"

Before MacBay could respond, Uncle Finn strode in behind Gracie, taking in the room. "The men saw no one come in or out. There are no missing guards, and they're all checked daily for signs of the mark."

So no more dead men, then. Just traitors, hiding in plain sight.

Gracie shook her head, staring daggers at her father. "You have always been so blind where she is concerned. Hasn't she cost us enough?'

MacBay looked from his daughter to my uncle, a muscle clenching in his jaw. "Your word?"

"On my honor," the king responded.

MacBay took a deep breath, shaking his head back and forth like he couldn't believe what he was doing. "I don't know where she went, but I will tell you all I know to help find her."

Chapter Forty-Five

GALINA

The castle was in an uproar, rumors spreading like wildfire of Fiona being the Viper.

Davin still struggled to wrap his mind around it, and truthfully, so did I, but there wasn't much room for doubt when she had fled so soon after he made his suspicions known.

While Davin and Gwyn tried to hunt her down, I once again spent the day in the library with Gallagher, poring over as many books as I could find on poisons and taking careful notes to replace the ones I had lost.

Gal stayed with me for hours until a soldier delivered a message that his sister needed him.

While he was gone, Malishka and I paced the length of the library, searching shelf after shelf for several missing books. It was hard to believe their absence was a coincidence after the situation in my rooms.

Had Fiona broken in herself? Was she hiding in the castle now, waiting for her chance to… I didn't know how to finish that thought.

The soldiers had done a cursory check of all of the rooms, but storms knew she had plenty of resources to hide. A shiver ran up my spine, and Malishka let out a low whine in sympathy.

A delicate voice pulled me from my thoughts.

"Davin said I might find you here." Gracie's expression was casually exasperated as she scanned the table full of books and my ink-stained fingers.

"Lady Galina, when was the last time you took a break?"

I looked at the clock, realizing the time. We'd arrived shortly before dawn, and it was well past afternoon teatime. As if on cue, my stomach growled.

She smiled. "That's what I thought. I just had tea sent to my rooms. I thought you might join me?"

I glanced from her back to the table, very much not ready to walk away from my research so soon. I also had no burning desire to spend any time with Gracie, which wasn't fair, I knew. Especially when she was clearly trying.

I bit back a sigh.

She was always trying. Helping with this investigation even though it had to be an awkward position for her, standing at Davin's family's side even when it put her at odds with her own family.

I couldn't keep living in the past when she was trying to be a friend and an ally, not to mention a permanent fixture at the Lochlannian court. I'd have to get used to spending time with her someday. If Davin had told her where to find me, he must be thinking the same.

Storms, maybe the change of atmosphere would help me to think more clearly, and to remember some of the notes I'd made before.

"Tea sounds lovely," I finally said, making an effort to inject some warmth into my tone.

Something like relief shone in her brown eyes, and I felt guilty all over again for making her feel unwelcome, especially after Davin's remark that she didn't have many close friends.

"I thought it might," she said with a conspiratorial smile.

This time, I returned it.

After ripping a small bit of parchment from my notes, I scribbled a message for Davin, just in case he came looking for me, and placed it in the center of the table. Then, I pocketed my notes and the few scattered tins of poisonous plants Gal and I had been dissecting, leaving an instruction to the guard to let no one else in until I returned.

I followed Gracie out the door and down the hall toward the guest suites while she chatted about small things here and there. Ewan trailed behind us, since I still had a guard outside of my rooms, and Malisha walked at my side.

Once we made it to Gracie's door, she hesitated, her fingers hovering just over the handle. Her expression turned apologetic.

"Apologies, but could Malishka," she attempted the name, overly stressing the 'k' sound. "Stay in the hall? With my allergies, I'd rather not have her in my rooms."

I glanced between her and the dog, recalling the way my companion made her sneeze. Already, her eyes were watering like she was on the verge of an allergic reaction.

Gracie apologized again, but I assured her it was fine, even though a small part of me balked at the idea. Malishka had become as constant to me as my own shadow, my silent protector.

But she wouldn't be far, just on the other side of the door, and I couldn't stay this afraid forever.

Ewan, however, seemed far less confident in the arrangement. His gaze flitted toward the door and back to me. "Lady MacBay, it would make me feel more comfortable if I could do a quick sweep of the room, with everything—"

Gracie's eyes widened, and she swallowed hard before opening the door and cutting him off.

"Of course," she said, quickly. "Please."

She looked at me apologetically and there was a moment of stilted silence, both of us realizing that the Viper had been in these very rooms. That she had some association with Gracie, however unwilling on the latter's part.

And with Fiona still missing, we couldn't be too careful.

Ewan came back a few minutes later, offering me a quick, reassuring nod before taking up his position once again as guard, right outside the door.

"Enjoy your tea, milady," he said. "I'll take care of Malishka."

"*Sidet*," I ordered her, using one of the Socairan commands we had been working on before glancing up at Ewan.

She obediently sat just outside of the door next to Ewan, her large blue eyes widening like the separation made her just as sad as it did me. Giving Malishka one more scratch on the head, I followed Gracie into the room, forcing myself to breathe as she shut the door between us.

She led me through the suites she shared with her father, back to her private bedroom, closing the heavy door with a thud. The smell of black tea and pear scones washed over me, and my stomach growled again.

"I noticed you preferred pear desserts to pumpkin," she commented as she joined me at the table. "I hope this is all right?"

I took in her hopeful expression, combined with the presentation of the room. There was a small tea table near the foot of the bed, covered with plates and glasses and bouquets of winter flowers.

A kettle was hanging near a small hearth, near a cart that held tins of various teas and sugar cubes, along with a plate of honeycomb and the scones.

"It's more than all right," I said appreciatively, suddenly feeling horrible for not wanting to join her before.

She'd clearly put a lot of effort into this tea.

Gracie practically beamed as I took it in, clearly pleased with my reaction. I continued to scan the room, taking in the small details that made this space hers. I hadn't realized that she had established rooms at the castle, but with her history with the family, I supposed it made sense.

It was peaceful back here, tucked away from the sounds of the castle far more than the other guest suites. Feeling more at ease, I sat down while she served us tea and sandwiches.

The conversation came easy. Without Fiona's shadow constantly hovering over her, Gracie was pleasant and friendly, making the time pass more smoothly than I had expected.

When we were finished with our first pot of tea, I stood to make the second one, as was Socairan custom. Yet another way we preferred our debts to balance out, as Davin always teased me about.

"Oh, that's not necessary," she demurred, but I was already striding toward the kettle.

The hearth was situated next to a large window, the heat from the flames fluttering the pale-yellow curtains to reveal a stretch of balcony that was surprisingly similar to my own.

"Are you interested in gardening?" I asked, widening the gap in the curtains.

In addition to the decorative shrubbery were several smaller potted plants. Most of them were basic winter plants, easily recognizable, but there were a few more unusual ones.

Gracie stepped in front of me, her cheeks flushing.

"I am, but it's just a silly hobby, and it's a mess right now. Nothing like the way you've arranged yours."

She was short enough that I could still make out the admittedly chaotic array of plants before she hurriedly closed the thick curtains.

Tendrils of dread crept along my spine. There was nothing outwardly suspicious in a woman feeling insecure where her former lover's new fiancée was involved, and it made sense that any lady would endeavor to hide a messy space.

It shouldn't have been out of the ordinary, but my mind kept snagging on something important.

"I'm sure it's more than that," I said quietly, forcing an encouraging smile to my lips while I turned back to the kettle. "Hobbies always start out small, but if it brings you joy..."

In and out, I commanded my breaths, even as I pictured the patio in my mind's eye. The shrubs. The herbs.

The flower that was unlike anything I had ever seen.

Well, that wasn't quite true. It was like several things I had seen. Small white blooms of a valley lily, the smooth green stems and buds of oleander, leaves of nightshade, and there was a fruit, too... Small, pale green orbs like the ones that had been expertly sketched in the book I had lost.

Little apples of death.

A perfect, lethal, combination of the flowers I had been researching.

That's when I realized what my mind had been trying to tell me. *Nothing like the way you've arranged yours,* she had said. That didn't make sense, though, because my outdoor plants were on the floor of my balcony, not visible from the ground outside, and Gracie had never been in my room.

But the Viper had.

Chapter Forty-Six

DAVIN

SOMETHING FELT OFF.

The more I thought about it, the more confused I got, especially as my rage from the attack ebbed away.

MacBay might be blind, but we had questioned him extensively about Fiona once he was cooperative. He was in her bed nearly every night, which, if he was to be believed, would have included the night the Viper met with the carriage driver and the night that Tavish died.

If he was to be believed.

"What if we were wrong about Fiona?" I asked out loud, my fingers coming up to rub the tension from my temples.

A migraine was steadily forming there, intensifying every time I came back to this subject. There were too many things that still weren't adding up, things that were nearly impossible to parse through in my mind.

"Then why did she disappear?" Gwyn countered.

Avani shook her head. "I think you're letting MacBay get to you. Maybe he isn't lying, but Gracie said herself he was blinded by Fiona, and stars know he must have been to risk his family and his reputation just to have her in his bed."

I tapped my pen furiously against the table, going over the notes I had made from the various letters that had come in this morning. None of this conversation was new. We had been talking in circles for the better part of an hour.

Fiona was the likeliest person, given the facts we had. Besides, without her, the list of possibilities was too long to consider. Every wife, sister, daughter…

The door swung open to emit Gallagher, who was scowling openly at Gwyn.

"Next time you send for me, don't run all over the castle," he groused. "Stars, I thought something had happened when I couldn't find you."

She shot him a look between confusion and irritation. "I didn't send for you."

The feeling of wrongness intensified, spreading through my body like the Viper's favorite poison. Avani met my eyes, the same alarm flashing in hers.

"Who told you Gwyn sent for you?" she asked.

"Where's Galina?" I said at the same time.

Gallagher looked between us. "One of Uncle Logan's soldiers. And Galina's still in the library, or was, when I left half an hour—"

He didn't get to finish his sentence before I was out of my chair, already halfway to the door.

"Go track down the soldier," I called over my shoulder. "I'm going to check on the library, just to be sure." My attempt at casualness was fooling no one.

Gal nodded, taking Gwyn in the other direction, and Avani came after me.

"I'm sure she's fine, Dav. This is why she has Malishka," my cousin tried to reassure me.

But a thread of uncertainty tainted the edge of her words.

Logically, I knew the chances of something happening to Galina in the library were low. She had a dog trained both to protect her and to sound an alert for danger. She also had Ewan standing guard nearby.

I was probably worried over nothing, still on edge from the intruder in her rooms and the attack shortly after, from our main suspect as the Viper on the loose probably terrorizing people somewhere.

I had almost managed to convince myself of that when we emerged into the main hall just in time to hear a piercing, panicked scream.

My heart dropped into my stomach. I had never heard Galina scream before. Would I recognize it if I did?

If I had been all but running before, I was sprinting now. Down the hall that led to the guest wing, propriety be damned. The hallway was already crowded with courtiers trying to see what was going on and soldiers trying to block off the room in question. It was toward the end of the hall, in the few remaining empty guest suites where no one had any reason to be.

Please, don't be Galina. Don't be her. Don't let something have happened to her.

I chanted the words like a mantra, knowing they were selfish, that something terrible had happened to someone and I was effectively wishing it had happened to anyone else. I didn't care, though. I couldn't lose her now. Not when I had just gotten her back.

"Let me through," I demanded, hearing Avani make some similarly imperious remarks beside me. The crowd parted, and my heartbeat thundered in my chest so loud it drowned out the murmurs of the courtiers around me.

Finally, I was close enough to see legs. Still, unmoving legs in a deep purple skirt. The silk was intricately embroidered in a blend of Socairan and Lochlannian styles, just like the gowns Galina had commissioned. They were getting more popular now. That didn't mean it was her.

It can't be her.

My feet were like lead as I made my way to the doorway, questions whirring in my mind.

What color was her dress this morning? I had told her she looked beautiful, kissed her on her way out the door, but now I couldn't remember. Was it the purple one? Blue?

The seconds passed with agonizing slowness, the edges of my vision blurring as I finally pushed my way past the soldiers and into the room. All of the air left my lungs in a single breath, my chest deflating with something that didn't feel quite like relief.

It wasn't Galina.

It was Fiona.

Midnight waves framed a face that was no longer beautiful, marred as it was by dark spiderweb veins across her pale, pristine skin. That seemed like the largest indignity, that she had been stripped of the one thing she cared about the most.

The smell was enough to tell me that the body wasn't fresh, which meant she couldn't have been behind the attack.

She wasn't the Viper.

The Viper was still out there, and Fiona was dead, and someone had made sure Galina was alone.

Chapter Forty-Seven

GALINA

MY HANDS WERE FREEZING. Or perhaps that was all of me, paralyzed by the reality I found myself in, only seconds after giving in to my storms-blasted curiosity about the plants.

Was it insane to suspect Gracie of being the Viper? Or had we just all been blind?

The flower could have been a gift from Fiona or MacBay, but it was unlikely here in the space she had made her own. Despite the claims that the Shaws were known for their greenhouses, I doubted Fiona knew how to care for a plant, let alone cultivate one. That was undoubtedly all the work of her gardeners.

Besides, something about her as the Viper had been bothering Davin from the start.

Whereas Gracie... We hadn't even considered her. We hadn't bothered to look past her wide eyes and her blushing cheeks to notice how she casually pointed the finger at Fiona more than once or the unobtrusive way she was involved in everything at court without ever calling attention to herself.

That's what made her so terrifying to the people she commanded. This phantom villain that hid in the shadows with access to all of their secrets and loved ones. The person you would least expect, getting by with literal murder.

Spots appeared in my vision as I shot a surreptitious look at the door – the door that was on the other side of her — which she must have locked quietly while I was observing the room, if the shadow of the bolt was anything to go by. No doubt she had the key somewhere on her person.

I tried to remember every single thing Davin had ever said about her, whether she trained to fight like the rest of them. A memory hit me of Rowan casually commenting once over dinner that all Lochlannian women had trained since her mother made it popular during the war.

In, then out, I forced myself to breathe.

Gracie was the Viper.

I took another subtle breath, my lungs burning with the effort.

I was trapped in this soundproof room with the Viper standing less than three feet from me.

One more steadying breath, deeper and slower, but no less quiet. Finally, a modicum of calm washed over me.

Surely if she had wanted to kill me, she would have by now. Probably. I didn't feel any effects of poison, hadn't tasted any strange aftertaste in the mild black tea or the delicate sandwiches.

Besides, Ewan was just outside the door. He may not be able to hear us, but he certainly knew where I was. And if I was careful, I could use this as an opportunity to find out something, anything, that would help Davin.

At the very least, I needed to keep calm until I could reasonably leave.

Smile, I ordered myself. *Gently, genuinely.* I wasn't sure I managed, so I turned my face to ostensibly examine the tea options.

"Is it time for these delicious pear desserts yet?" I asked, gesturing to the tower of pastries on the cart near the tea in an effort to prompt her into taking them.

And sitting down, away from me.

"Of course." She grabbed the plate from right next to me, and I fought back a flinch as her arm grazed mine.

"I was wondering when you would ask," she said, setting the scones on the table and settling into her chair. "I've been looking forward to these all morning."

Her demeanor hadn't noticeably changed, but that meant nothing.

"Do we think the orange spice tea will be all right this time? It's my favorite," I lied.

It didn't complement the pear dessert at all, but Socairans were known here for our odd tastes, so I hoped she wouldn't question it.

"That sounds perfect, then," she said easily.

I almost, almost second-guessed myself. Then my eyes slid to the closed curtains that led to the balcony she hadn't wanted me to see. *No.* There was no doubt in my mind that Gracie was the Viper.

Now I just had to survive this tea long enough to tell Davin.

With numb fingers, I added the herbs to the basket in the teapot before pouring over the water. It would need at least five minutes to steep. Then we would drink it over dessert, which would take time. Davin would come looking for me before long, even if I didn't see an opportunity to leave.

I could do this.

I searched the small cart until I found an intricately woven tea cozy, slipping it over the pot.

"I don't see many of these here," I commented. "Did you make it yourself?"

"Stars, no," she said with a self-deprecating laugh. "I never had any talent for knitting. Do you?"

"It was expected, in Socair. I suppose you were busy training like the princesses and the duchess?" I said lightly, setting the pot down on the table.

"No one trains quite like the duchess," she said with another airy laugh.

So yes, then, but it wasn't something she wanted to admit to in this conversation. She played her games so, so carefully.

She nudged the tray of scones toward me, and I dutifully picked one up with the silver tongs and deposited it on my plate. The crystalized sugar on top fell from the pastry, clinking against the ceramic plate like tiny shards of glass.

Could she hear it as loudly as I did?

"Thank you," I said, glancing down at the pastry.

One of the poisons I studied had tasted like apple, not unlike the capsules from the viper had smelled. Would a pear dessert mask that taste? Would the poison even survive at baking temperature? The questions spun round my mind while I chose one for her next, depositing it onto her plate smoothly.

It was right on top, easily in a place where I could have plucked my own. She certainly hadn't baked the pastries herself, and there were no markings to distinguish between one that might have been tampered with and one that wasn't.

She cut into it with a blade that was sharper than the average butter knife, and serrated. Then she lifted a forkful to her mouth without hesitation. Short of assuming she had an immunity to the poison, something Gallagher theorized would be nearly impossible, it felt reasonable to assume the scones were safe.

Caught between fear of being poisoned and fear of giving myself away, I rapidly debated the likelihood of Gracie murdering me.

She had allowed me to choose my seat at the table. She'd given me the first choice of scones and hadn't hesitated to eat hers. She also had brought me to her rooms, knowing I had left a note for Davin telling him where to find me.

Hating the necessity of the gamble, I took a tiny, polite bite. It tasted exactly like the filling from the dessert Davin had ordered me. Still, I chewed slowly, on alert for any aftertaste or tingling sensations.

There were none that I could detect.

"So you knit, but what about your other hobbies?" she asked nonchalantly. "I heard you work with Gallagher sometimes. Do you want to be a healer, too?"

I certainly wasn't the only one fishing for information.

"Oh, no," I said, wiping my mouth with a cloth napkin and setting it back in my lap. "I do have an interest in herbs, though — making medicines."

Gracie nodded as if this was something she already knew. The clock ticked the fifth minute, and I reached out to pour us both a cup of tea.

"Is that what you're doing now? In the library?" Was there an edge to her tone, or was that only my imagination?

I picked up my teacup, willing her to do the same. She did, inhaling the spiced scent.

"Something like that," I offered.

"Anything in particular that you're researching?" she pressed, taking a sip of her tea. "I took a bit of an interest in that area when my mother got sick. Perhaps I could help."

I debated on how honest to be with her. If she was responsible for stealing my notes, and if she had paid any amount of attention to the books I had been reading in the library, then she already knew the answer.

"Lately, I've been looking into the poison the Viper has been using. Or trying to," I said evenly. "I keep coming to dead ends."

Gracie nodded and took another sip of tea while I pretended to do the same.

"Looking for a cure?" she asked.

I hesitated, my pulse throbbing in my temples as I tried to keep my breaths even.

How had we missed it before? The innocent act, the sweetness she always infused into her words... It was all a lie. This girl was nothing but pure calculation.

Again, I mentally reviewed what had been in my notes, trying to make sure my answer didn't give me away.

"Of a sort," I responded carefully. "Though more of a prevention, when you think about it. Narrowing down the source could help us stop the supply."

She arched an eyebrow, draining what was left of her tea. "Surely, that's not necessary when you already know who she is."

For the first time since my arrival, she let some of her intelligence burn through her guileless brown gaze. The hairs on my arm stood on end, each flutter of air from the drafty castle like a thousand knives drawing across my skin.

Wordlessly, I took a sip of the spiced brew, immediately bringing my napkin to my lips to capture the warm liquid. Placing it back in my lap with the damp side down, I finally responded.

"We still have to catch her," I said noncommittally.

I wanted desperately to lie outright, but every sense in my body was screaming that she would know if I did. Still, my misdirect wasn't enough. I saw the moment she dropped her shield.

Maybe she had realized that I knew from the moment I spotted that plant, or maybe I had given myself away in the meantime. Either way, she let her innocent guise fall away, affecting a calculating sort of pout instead.

"People really don't give you the credit you deserve, you know?" she said. "Something I understand all too well."

She sounded so sincere. Was this how she inspired loyalty from her sycophants? By finding ways to relate to them?

Fear made my mouth go dry, and I resisted the urge to swallow. "I'm sure you do."

"You know, I really did just want to talk to you today," she said, her tone almost disappointed. "I wasn't going to poison you."

She had noticed my failure to drink my tea. Of course she had.

Icy fingernails of dread scraped down my spine. My eyes darted to the door, even knowing it was locked. She followed my gaze and sighed, moving her knife closer to her plate in a clear threat.

With numb fingers, I reached for the teapot to refill our cups. First, I topped off mine, then I very carefully filled hers.

"We can still talk," I offered, my tone trembling on the last word.

She gave me a look that was more terrifying for the pity it held. Malice would have been better, easier to work with than the stone-cold resolution in her wide brown eyes.

"You know it's not that simple now."

For the first time, it felt like I was talking to the real Gracie. Not the simpering lady of the court, but the brilliant, deadly woman behind the mask of the Viper.

I risked a tiny sip of my tea, determined to keep her talking, to stall her any way I could. "So, I am a complication. Is that how you always justify your choices?"

She sighed, reaching for her cup, taking longer than usual to examine the light-brown hue of the tea. I held my breath, my heartbeat thundering in my ears until she finally took another delicate sip.

"Sacrifices have to be made," she said, pulling the cup away from her lips. "My father complains endlessly about the state of things, then he can't do what needs to be done."

"But you can," I said.

She nodded, somewhat placated. Still my lungs caught fire with every shallow breath I forced myself to take.

"And so can you," she said. "That's why I really did like you."

"That's why you were going to let me live." I slowly put together the pieces, the way the Viper had tried to kill me when I first arrived, then was willing to settle for my return to Socair.

"Among other reasons," she added. "I nearly realized too late that if you had died, Davin wouldn't have moved on."

All she had heard was that Davin had returned from Socair with a last-minute bride just in the nick of time. She hadn't known about our history, or that there was anything real between us. Storms, *I* had barely known back then.

I thought about all of the pain in Davin's eyes, the shattered expression he wore when he caught up to me and Alexei, and crimson spotted my vision.

"But if I left willingly, Davin would have turned to you." It took everything I had to keep the venom from my tone, and apparently, I didn't do a good enough job.

"You're the one who objected to bloodshed." She said it like she was explaining something to a child. "I would think you would approve of my plan."

Her plan of forcing Davin into a corner with the murder accusation, she meant. What was it Fiona had said? Everyone knew Davin marrying Gracie would be the easiest solution.

And without me, he would have done it for his family and for his people. I took another miniscule sip of my tea, hoping she would follow suit. She did.

"So all of this was just to marry Davin?" I asked.

Her gaze bored into mine. "You of all people should know what it's like to be without power. Without a voice. To be overlooked."

She trailed off, her brown eyes growing haunted. Then, a grim smile tilted the corners of her lips as she looked my way once more.

"You know, my brothers had it easy," she said. "They left home as soon as they could, and my father spent his time in Chridhe doting on the princesses, happy to leave me to take care of *her*."

Did she mean her mother? She went on before I could ask.

"And when I finally did come to court, well, we both know who he spent his time *doting* on then."

"But if you married into the royal family, you wouldn't have to worry about being on the outside," I guessed.

She scoffed, her fingers dancing along the handle of the knife.

"No. If I married into Davin's family, I could have become Queen."

I furrowed my brow, and she sighed. "Do you know how many people believe the throne rightfully belongs to Prince Oliver?"

And therefore, Davin. But if she had succeeded in destabilizing his family instead of pushing him to marry her, Laird MacBay would have become King. It wasn't hard to guess how long that would have lasted before she took care of him, and her brothers, too.

She won either way.

Gracie picked up the knife then, her expression hardening like she had read the horror playing out in my mind. My pulse picked up speed, galloping in my chest like a herd of wild horses.

"You have to know that Davin won't forgive you for this," I told her, still trying to stall for whatever hope there was of getting out of this.

She shrugged, as if this were an unexpected, unfortunate

situation we had found ourselves in, and there was nothing she could do about it now.

"He can hardly blame me if we're both attacked, like so many others have been, in his own castle. Obviously, I did everything I could..."

I blinked, stealing another glance at her nearly empty cup of tea.

"You really do think of everything," I said.

And I hoped like hell it was every bit the lie I meant it to be.

Chapter Forty-Eight

DAVIN

"We were wrong," I said out loud, the words sounding hollow to my ears.

Avani nodded, her eyes still fixed on Fiona's corpse.

One of the maids found her while cleaning the room, the smell of Fiona's body drawing her to a locked trunk in the closet. It was her scream we heard. Her trembling hands that had pulled the body out onto the floor while she waited for help.

Fiona's unblinking eyes stared up at the ceiling. She had been a lot of things: a liar, a seductress, an accomplished Lady and Assemblywoman. But now, she was dead.

Dread flooded my veins. "I have to find Galina."

"I'll stay here." She nodded back toward the hall. "Take the men with you."

I spun around, nearly colliding with a frozen MacBay. I half expected him to rage at me, to accuse me, to say he told me so. He did none of those things. He didn't even seem to see me as he took in the body of whoever the hell Fiona had been to him.

"Fi." He said her name in a single, ragged breath.

Shock and grief were etched plainly across his features. He hadn't done this, but someone was close enough to him, to us, to Fiona.

We had been so blind, and so very, very stupid.

I sprinted down the corridor with the soldiers behind me, not caring who saw anymore. None of it mattered if she was gone. I didn't bother with the library, not when the truth was raining down around me like shards of ice in a winter storm, piercing my skin and freezing me from the inside out.

Who else could it be, with the resources and clout and position to head up an entire rebellion? Who had access to family secrets and knew the ins and outs of the political arena like the back of their hand? I had asked that question a thousand times since I found out the Viper was a woman, ignoring the very obvious answer in front of me.

Who had come to my rooms fortuitously right after the Socairans arrived all those months ago, had asked questions in her gentle, open way? Who had tried to befriend Galina and warned me off of Fiona, the only person who might have been able to see the truth?

I wondered if that was why Fiona was dead now, because she had put the pieces together after finding out the Viper was a woman. Or had Gracie just needed a scapegoat?

We had made it so easy for her. Stars, when I asked about MacBay's alibi, I had been so focused on Fiona that I had missed Gracie all but admitting she had none.

Cursing the size of Lithlinglau with each endless second, I took the stairs two at a time, finally arriving at the second floor of the guest wing. Relief and horror mingled in my gut.

There, at the end of the hall, stood Ewan, along with Malishka. I had found her. But Galina was inside, without any protection, and the dog was nervously shifting on her feet.

"How long has she been upset?" I asked.

"Just for a minute or two, mi'laird," Ewan responded. "I'm not sure what's wrong with her."

"Did you try asking Lady Galina?" I asked, my hand going to the door handle.

It was locked.

"How long have they been in there?" I growled.

Ewan blanched, his eyes darting back and forth between me and the door. "Maybe an hour? I checked the room before she went in, mi'laird. It was safe—"

I turned away from him, panic flooding through my veins as my mind spun. Of *course* he thought it was safe. Of *course* he hadn't suspected Gracie. None of us had.

My hand froze in midair, unsure of how to proceed. If I banged on the door, I might alert them, might speed up whatever Gracie had planned. Finally, MacBay's guards would come in handy. His most trusted men. Surely, they had a key to these suites.

"Open the door," I ordered.

They exchanged a look, and I hardened my expression.

"The ladies are in danger." One of them, anyway.

The taller guard moved forward to open the door, and I held a finger to my lips. Malishka shot in like an arrow, looking frantically at Gracie's bedroom door in the back. She didn't bark, though, or scratch at it, like she understood the need for stealth.

On silent footfalls, I crept closer to the door, again gesturing for the guard to unlock it. He did, the metal scraping slowly in the lock with a noise I knew was far too loud. As soon as the bolt came free, I threw the door open as quickly as I could.

It wasn't quick enough.

Gracie stood behind Galina, holding a knife to my fiancée's throat. My stomach twisted as I met Galina's wide, remorseful eyes, only the smallest tremor in her hands revealing the terror she must be feeling.

Gracie's grip tightened, her expression cold and unwavering, and Galina sucked in a breath.

"My Lady?" the guard sputtered behind me while Ewan stepped closer, his hand on the hilt of his sword.

"I can slit her throat before any of you move," Gracie said with more ice in her tone than I had ever heard her use.

"Stay back." I held up my hands, both in a signal to make sure no one else moved and in an effort to placate Gracie.

"You don't want to do that," I said calmly. "If you let her go, I'll let you go."

"No—" Galina's protest was cut off by the knife digging into her skin.

"To do what, Davin?" Gracie mocked. "Live in exile, like you were so thrilled about doing?"

"What is it you want, Gracie?" I asked, not bothering to hide my desperation. "Name it, and it's yours."

She blinked slowly, as if taking a moment to consider. "Anything?"

I swallowed, looking at Galina's slim neck, her pulse beating visibly beneath the lethal edge of the blade. I tried to calculate how long it would take me to draw my dagger, to aim it, the likelihood that it would hit Galina.

"Yes," I breathed. "Anything."

Gracie raised an eyebrow. "Even if I want to be Lady of Lithlinglau?"

I didn't even have to consider it. I wouldn't marry her, but she could have my estate and my title if she wanted it so badly. I would give it to her just before I lit the match and made this place her tomb.

A small part of me acknowledged that even if I couldn't be sure of Gracie's impending demise, there was nothing I wouldn't do, nothing I wouldn't barter, to keep Galina safe. Alive.

There were wounds even Gal couldn't heal, and a slit throat was definitely one of them. I swallowed, forcing myself to speak past the blinding panic.

"Even then," I said, desperation bleeding into my tone. "You have to see there's no way out of this besides negotiation, Gracie. Just let Galina go, and I can make sure none of this ever gets out."

I wasn't sure if it was true, but it was the only chance I had. For a fraction of a second, I believed she had faltered, that she was going to let Galina go. Then her eyes bored into mine, something like pity filling them.

"You're a good liar, Davin. But you never could lie to me."

Then she pressed her blade into Galina's neck.

Chapter Forty-Nine

GALINA

THE CLOCK on the wall counted off each second like nails in the coffin we had built for ourselves.

Gracie's blade slowly bit into my skin. Warm droplets of blood spilled from the wound, down my chest and onto my gown, but I didn't move. Didn't breathe. Her hand twitched, driving the knife further in, and it took everything I had not to whimper, not to make this worse for Davin.

He lunged and Malishka followed, but I knew it wouldn't be soon enough. They were still on the other side of the vast room.

Everything had gone to hell so quickly.

I squeezed my eyes shut, thinking about all of the time we had wasted. How many nights we hadn't spent together, how many days I had wasted being angry about something that no longer mattered.

How many times we could have fixed things between us, but we had been too stubborn to take that first step.

I thought about the family I wanted to have with him. Did he want that, too? Would I ever get the chance to ask? Was it one more thing to add to the ever-growing list of regrets between us?

I had been so close. Close to having this life. Close to stopping Gracie before she could ruin it all.

For a single, heart-stopping moment, I had believed it was enough.

I had been so careful when I added the bitterbloom leaf to the tea, but maybe it hadn't been enough. Maybe Gracie had found a way to make herself immune to some poisons after all. I supposed it didn't matter now. Not with her knife at my throat and little left to lose.

She was smart, smarter than anyone had ever given her credit for. She had to know this was it for her, that she wasn't leaving this room alive.

So why would she let me?

Would this be her last act as the Viper? To kill me while Davin watched?

I took a stilted breath, waiting for the moment she would finally snap and dig the blade in deeper, knowing that there was nothing I could do to stop her.

Then, Gracie's hand twitched, the blade scraping the open skin and making the wound a little deeper.

My skin burned. The wound ignited every nerve ending in my neck like a raging inferno. But, if Alexei had taught me nothing else, it was the art of enduring pain. I could sit in perfect stillness, a façade of demure composure, while I bided my time for the pain to end.

That's what I would do now. I would wait for death to come, never giving her the satisfaction of hearing me scream. At least it was one nightmare I would save Davin from.

When the serrated edge of the knife dug further in, I saw nothing but blinding, white-hot stars. But I was still conscious.

The blade had stopped.

"Gracie?" The way Davin said her name was somewhere between a warning and a question.

She stumbled forward. This time, the knife slipped from her grasp, falling first to my lap before clanging against the floor.

The bitterbloom had worked. The herb was used to calm the nerves in small doses but acted as a paralytic when consumed in larger quantities. And more than that could lead to death. It wasn't the most efficient poison, but it was the only one that could be masked by the citrusy flavor of orange spiced tea.

And it had finally taken effect on Gracie.

Several things happened in the space between one heartbeat and the next.

I lunged for the knife while Davin stepped forward, neatly unleashing a dagger of his own. By the time I made it to my feet, Malishka's jaw was locked on to Gracie's arm. She growled and bit and dug her teeth into Gracie's skin until blood stained her white muzzle, but it didn't matter.

Davin's blade was in Gracie's chest.

Chapter Fifty

DAVIN

I STOOD in the Assembly room as the official proclamation was read, clearing me of all accusations. Then another one, listing out Gracie's charges in harrowing detail.

It hadn't been hard to unravel once we started following the thread. We found the maid who killed Tavish under Gracie's orders, once he was weakened by tea. That explained why he had been poisoned first, since the maid could just barely hold a sword.

The cufflinks, of course, had been taken after one of mine and Gracie's liaisons. One by one, the pieces had fallen into place. Everything except for why.

Had it really all just been so she could be Queen? Skeletons had come out of the MacBays' closets one by one, from Gracie's abusive mother to her absentee father and everything in between. Was it a reason? An excuse?

Worse, I wondered how we had made it so easy for her. The rebellion had only gained traction because of the people's lack of confidence in us. Perhaps Gracie had stirred that pot, added to it, but we had created it.

MacBay was in attendance as well. He had renounced his

title to his eldest son the day after Gracie had died. He looked more defeated than I had ever seen anyone look, his haunted, empty eyes tightening each time another atrocity was added to Gracie's list.

I took no pleasure in that. In any of it.

Over and over again, I saw the moment Gracie fell, contrasted the sweet girl who would giggle over pastries in my bed with the one who set fire to villages for the sake of a throne, and I couldn't seem to marry the two.

"You don't have to stay for this," Uncle Logan told him in an undertone, not for the first time.

My family surrounded me. There was, at least, relief in knowing that they were safer now.

"It's what's best for Lochlann," Camdyn replied, his tone as hollow as his features.

The worst part was, he wasn't wrong. The Assembly might not have believed us without MacBay's support. He hadn't struggled as much as I thought he would with the truth, not after Fiona was dead when Gracie was the last person to have seen her. Not after the recounting of events that his soldiers gave.

And not after the pages we found detailing the people she had worked with, lists to ensure no one could ever be free of her. There was also the matching cufflink to the one that was found on Tavish, pristine and tucked away in the bottom of her trunk.

It was harrowing, how close she had come to succeeding. Everything felt fragile in the aftermath – our lives, the throne, the kingdom.

Galina's hand covered mine, as if she sensed my distress. I couldn't help but glance at the unblemished skin of her neck, picturing it sliced open and dripping with blood. Gallagher had come in time to prevent a scar, but it lingered in my memory all the same, one more thing I hadn't been able to keep her safe from.

She squeezed my hand, shaking her head slightly.

Anchoring myself to her steady presence, I managed to get through the proceedings without going back down the list of everyone we had lost to these senseless games.

I left before anyone could apologize, or worse, mention Gracie's name. Galina wordlessly followed me through the halls and up to our room. She didn't stop there, tugging my arm gently to lead me out the door and up the stairs until we were standing on a frigid rooftop under the stars.

Malishka followed, happily curling up in a sheltered corner near the stairs.

The night was mostly clear, but small flakes of snow blew in from scattered, puffy clouds, settling on our hair and clothes. It was quiet and still, a much-needed reprieve from the insanity of the day. The month. The year.

I took a deep breath, inhaling the icy air and letting myself sink into the peace that only Galina could instill in me. She didn't try to speak or comfort me with empty words, but she did pull out a small flask, handing it over to me.

It was intricately carved and studded with tiny diamonds.

"Gwyn?" I asked.

"Your mother, actually," she corrected.

"Closet lush, that one," I said drily, taking a small sip of the aged, oaky whiskey.

It was delicious... To me, anyway. Entirely not to Galina's taste, though. She had brought it just for my sake. Several more minutes passed in silence before I finally took a breath to speak.

"I don't know where to go from here," I admitted quietly, staring out at the night sky.

She looked over at me, snow falling gently onto her lashes. "I don't, either."

A truth, one that would have been impossible for her to admit before.

Then she leaned closer to me, entwining her hand with mine. "But...I'm glad we don't have to figure it out alone."

She was right, and it wasn't something I would take for granted ever again. Not when it was so hard won. Looking at her now, I thought back to every version of her on every rooftop, each of them stubborn and proud and gorgeous and *her*.

I put an arm around her, spinning her gently toward me and leaning down to capture her lips with mine. They were cold, a contrast to her warm tongue when she opened her mouth to deepen the kiss.

I pulled away far too soon.

"Yes, if we're to be in a kingdom that may or may not hate us with soldiers who may or may not have been secretly working for the Viper, at least we have each other," I added in a lighter tone. "And Lithlinglau. And my occasionally dysfunctional family. All we need, really."

I felt rather than saw her tense for the smallest frozen moment before she forced herself to relax.

"*All* we need?" she clarified.

Her cheeks were pink from more than the snow, her ice-blue eyes wide with uncertainty. Perhaps if not for that, and the barest hesitation she had shown, I would have answered offhand. Instead, I tilted my head, running through the last thing I had said and trying to suss out her meaning.

Oh.

I cleared my throat against the sudden unrelated tightness, picturing a new generation full of hope and promise and love. Squeezing her a bit tighter, I spoke in her ear.

"I can think of a few more things. Or six or seven," I offered, mostly teasing her.

"Two," she corrected quickly.

I pressed another kiss against her forehead. "Well," I drew out the word, smirking down at her. "We don't have to decide right now."

"Well," she repeated in the same tone. "We can safely decide against seven."

I shrugged my shoulders. "You never know."

Did she hear the echo of the moment on the rooftop when she had insisted she would never need to call in her life debt? Did she feel, as I did, the momentary awe of realizing how close we had come to never having each other, to never having *this*?

One decision gone wrong, and we never would have wound up here. Or hell, one decision gone right, in our case.

Something in Galina's gaze told me she did understand.

"No," she agreed softly, peering up at me just as she had the first time we danced on a rooftop even colder than this one...with snow in her hair and stars in her eyes. "You never know."

Epilogue

GALINA

It was unseasonably cold tonight.

Lanterns were lit for warmth on either side of the two distinct masses of people. Richly dressed forms shivered in their black and white shawls, all but the King of Socair, and probably my parents, wherever they were seated.

It was hard to tell from where I stood at the back of the aisle, nestled amongst the trees. I wasn't cold, though. Excitement coursed through my body, warming me from the inside out. Besides, my dress had sleeves. They were thin red silk, but they covered me from my collarbone down, almost gracing the floor. Heavy brocaded crimson silk made up my skirts, trailing in soft folds behind me whenever I walked.

The music swelled, and I took another small step toward the aisle. Jocelyn and Oliver were with me now, but they would be walking down first to take their seats. In Socair, we met our groom alone. I hadn't wanted to ask my father to break tradition when he had broken so many already.

We both had.

As I drew nearer, I caught sight of Davin's family seated near the front, though he was still out of view, waiting for me at the end of the aisle, no doubt looking devastatingly perfect in his ceremonial kilt. It was still hard to believe that we were both here, safe. That no one would show up at the eleventh hour to take this hard-earned bit of peace from us.

I took a deep breath to steady my nerves, taking in what I could of the guests from my vantage point tucked behind the trees.

The king and queen of Lochlann sat in a sea of red-headed girls, next to the captain of the guard and his tiny wife. Behind them, Gwyn and Gallagher were on either side of Avani. Malishka sat at her feet, and her skirts trembled suspiciously like perhaps there was a rotund, furry animal in her pockets. She stared with haunted eyes at the floating candle in the lake. Mac's memorial.

Her smile was sad and wan, but it was resolute, nonetheless. She had worn the same smile as she helped me design my dress and every piece of my trousseau. Gwyn had helped also, even as she pretended she didn't want to be there while she doled out even more opinions than the designer had.

Rowan had arrived too late to partake in that, but not too late to partake in staying up all night with Davin and the case of vodka she brought. Here was hoping Gallagher had broken his rule about healing hangovers, since I was absolutely certain he could.

The music swelled, and Jocelyn turned to me.

"That's our cue." She held her hands out, ready to fix any stray hair or thread, but there were none. She smiled softly. "I never have to worry about you," she said with a small grin.

Then she nodded at Oliver, and together they helped bring my veil down over my face. The floor-length crimson fabric was artfully attached to a ruby-and-diamond headband, in the style of Socair. My mother had brought it, with a reserved comment about how she always thought red would be a better wedding color on me.

It was small, the way my parents showed their pride, but it was there all the same.

Jocelyn and Oliver took their leave, and a throat cleared behind me.

"Papa?" I asked in surprise.

"I am told that in Lochlann, the father escorts the bride down the aisle."

"You don't have to," I insisted. He had never liked to be in the center of things, and storms knew I had been the cause of plenty of trouble for him already.

"It's a tradition I am happy to follow, Malishka." Unlike the ones in Socair, he meant. Unlike the ones that had gotten me hurt.

I nodded, not trusting myself to speak, and he held out an arm. I was grateful for both his presence and his guidance as I made my way down a flickering aisle through the blurry red haze of my veil.

The walk was both too short and too long, like the months it had taken us to get here. Sometimes it felt like just last week I was marching out onto a rooftop to defy my uncle's soldiers for the first time in my life, all for the sake of a pair of ocean eyes that saw so much more than I wanted him to, even then.

But when I thought of all the things we had done and sacrificed and lost, it felt like a lifetime ago.

Now we were finally here. A day that had felt impossible. My father gently pressed on my arm for me to come to a halt, then he slowly lifted my veil. My heartbeat stuttered in my chest in anticipation.

And as usual, Davin did not disappoint.

He stood before me in a tartan kilt, black and white with the smallest hint of red stitching. A small, disbelieved gasp escaped me. They weren't his colors. They were mine. His shirt was black, and a deep red chrysanthemum graced the lapel. Of course, his hair was perfect, artfully falling across his brow and offsetting his cerulean gaze.

It was his expression that got me, though. He stared at me with pure, unadulterated awe, like I was his sun and moon and stars and oxygen. Like I was his *everything*, just as he was mine.

He swallowed, taking my hands in his. My father must have taken his seat, but I didn't turn to look, didn't notice anything else outside of Davin and his piercing gaze and the barest tilt of his gorgeous lips.

His hands were warm on mine, and I was so distracted thinking about it that I nearly missed the vows — nearly missed that Davin said his in my native tongue before using his own, and that he had taken out all forms of *obey* and *serve* from mine, replacing them only with promises of love and faithfulness.

Then he was leading me back down the aisle, to the clearing under the stars where we would share our first dance as husband and wife.

Husband. Wife.

Words that had meant so many things for so long to me, but they felt perfect now. Right.

Davin tugged me all the way against him, far closer than propriety, even for a newly married couple, considering the audience. I didn't care, though, especially not when he murmured in my ear, reminding me that I was Lady of Lithlinglau now.

His.

I never got tired of that. Because from his discerning eyes to his patient hands and his endless, ridiculous charm, Davin was perfect.

And more importantly, he was mine.

The End.

Want a super steamy bonus epilogue?? Click here to sign up for our newsletter!

Keep flipping the page for a sneak peek at Rowan's story, or click here to download your copy of the series!

And if you're all caught up on ElBin's books, you can click here preorder our next project; Of Elves and Embers!

PRONUNCIATION GUIDE

Davin	DAV-in (short a)
Galina	Gal-EE-nuh
Lochlann	LOCK-lan
Socair	so-CARE
Alech	ah-LEK
Chridhe	CREE-uh
Lithlinglau	LITH-lun-glow
Hagail	ha-GAYL
Masach	ma-SAUK
Mikhail	mi-KYLE
Alexei	a-LEX-ee
Isla	EYE-la
Aino	EYE-no
Avani	a-VAHN-ee

GLOSSARY

Laskipaa	Idiot
Svolach	Bastard
Svolochi	Bastards
Der'mo	Crap
Aalio	Arseling
Maliskha	Baby Girl
Radnaya	My Dear
Eejit	Idiot
Besklanovvy	Unclanned

A Message From Us

We need your help!

Did you know that authors, in particular indie authors like us, make their living on reviews? If you enjoyed this book, please take a moment to let people know on all of the major review platforms like; Amazon, Goodreads, and/or Bookbub!

(Social Media gushing is also highly encouraged!)

Remember, reviews don't have to be long. It can be as simple as whatever star rating you feel comfortable with and an: 'I loved it!' or: 'Not my cup of tea...'

Now that that's out of the way, if you want to come shenanigate with us, rant and rave about these books and others, get access to awesome giveaways, exclusive content and some pretty ridiculous live videos, come join us on Facebook at our group, Drifters and Wanderers

ElPin's Acknowledgments

You think this part would get easier, remembering who to thank and who to credit for the insane amount of support given to a project. But the problem is, we have been lucky enough to have the most supportive community of readers, authors, editors, artists and friends and the list only continues to grow with each project we finish.

We will try to name them all, but just know that there are already so many names missing from this list. <3

First of all, our Beta Babes. Ali, Michelle, Sarah J, Sarah M, and Andra - we love you so much!

You have loyally stuck with us for so many projects now and we are eternally grateful for your patience and rereading and honesty as we tried hard to whip these characters into shape.

DavLina would not have gotten where they are if not for each of you <3

Lissa, Kim & Katelin, thank you for being so willing to help us with this final draft! Your thoughts, comments, critique and swoons were VITAL to our sanity toward the end of this project!

Jesikah Potato Faerie Sundin... There are not enough words to express our gratitude and appreciation for you. We are truly not worthy of your constant support and friendship! *raises an entire bottle of Socairan vodka in your honor*

To our editor and one of our best bookish friends; Jamie,

Thank you for being constantly supportive and flexible. We don't deserve you, or your unending patience. Seriously, though... Thank you for always bending to our chaos and helping us polish our books to perfection. You deserve so much more Fireball whiskey than you're getting.

Samaiya!!! Babes, words cannot express how grateful we are for the moment you decided to enter our lives. You are so unbelievably talented and the art you have designed for our stories still just blows our minds! We have loved collaborating with you, and can't wait to see where the future takes us. Also, thank you for our gorgeous website and your constant insistence that we can look/be way more professional than we feel. We love you!!

To our author communities; our MoonTree Family, Forgotten Kingdoms babes, our Unprofessional Perverts, Jessica Fry, Heather Renee, Natalia Jaster, Olivia Wildenstein, and so many others... thank you, from the bottom of our hearts for your unending support and cheerleading as we dragged ourselves kicking and screaming to the end of this deadline.

A huge thank you to our Street Team and our reader group: Drifters and Wanderers. We seriously have the best readers out there. We are unbelievably lucky to have you. Thank you for sticking with us for the past five years! Here's to sooo many more!

Emily, what is there but to say thank you and we love you!? We're so grateful we can call you a part of our team. Thank you for putting up with us and helping us manage our lives, books, and sanity. <3

And finally, the biggest and most important thank you goes to our families. Specifically the men we force into kilts while we sign books, the ones who stay up to listen to us plot and whine and argue about our characters. The sexy beasts who still love us when we're a week into edits and can't remember the last time we showered.

You are the real heroes and we seriously couldn't do this without your love and support. Thank you for putting up with us and for believing us every time we say we're going to take a writing break. You know we're lying. We know we're lying. But it's that kind of support that has gotten us where we are today.

We love you both (in very different ways... This isn't a why choose scenario, people. Don't make it weird.)

About The Authors

Elle and Robin can usually be found on road trips around the US haunting taco-festivals and taking selfies with unsuspecting Spice Girls impersonators.

They have a combined PH.D in Faery Folklore and keep a romance advice column under a British pen-name for raccoons. They have a rare blood type made up solely of red wine and can only write books while under the influence of the full moon.

Between the two of them they've created a small army of insatiable humans and when not wrangling them into their cages, they can be seen dancing jigs and sacrificing brownie batter to the pits of their stomachs.

And somewhere between their busy schedules, they still find time to create words and put them into books.

www.mahleandmadison.com

Also By Elle & Robin

Coming Soon:

Of Elves and Embers

The Lochlann Treaty Series:

Winter's Captive

Spring's Rising

Summer's Rebellion

Autumn's Reign

The Lochlann Feuds Series:

Scarlet Princess

Tarnished Crown

Crimson Kingdom

Obsidian Throne

Twisted Pages Series:

Of Thorns and Beauty

Of Beasts and Vengeance

Of Glass and Ashes

Of Thieves and Shadows

Of Songs and Silence

The World Apart Series By Robin D. Mahle:

The Fractured Empire

The Tempest Sea

The Forgotten World

The Ever Falls

Unfabled Series:

Promises and Pixie Dust

Printed in Great Britain
by Amazon

33210999R00229